# MANNER
# OF
# DEATH

## ALSO BY STEPHEN WHITE

# STEPHEN WHITE

# MANNER OF DEATH

A DUTTON BOOK

DUTTON
Published by the Penguin Group
Penguin Putnam Inc., 375 Hudson Street, New York, New York 10014, U.S.A.
Penguin Books Ltd, 27 Wrights Lane, London W8 5TZ, England
Penguin Books Australia Ltd, Ringwood, Victoria, Australia
Penguin Books Canada Ltd, 10 Alcorn Avenue, Toronto, Ontario, Canada M4V 3B2
Penguin Books (N.Z.) Ltd, 182–190 Wairau Road, Auckland 10, New Zealand

Penguin Books Ltd, Registered Offices:
Harmondsworth, Middlesex, England

First published by Dutton, an imprint of Dutton NAL,
a member of Penguin Putnam Inc.

First Printing, January, 1999
10 9 8 7 6 5 4 3 2

Copyright © Stephen W. White, 1999
All rights reserved

 REGISTERED TRADEMARK—MARCA REGISTRADA

Library of Congress Cataloging-in-Publication Data

White, Stephen Walsh.
Manner of death / by Stephen White.
p.   cm.
ISBN 0-525-94440-0
I.  Title.
PS3573.H47477M36   1999
813' .54—dc21 98-26697
CIP
Printed in the United States of America
Set in Sabon
Designed by Julian Hamer

To Terry Lapid,
for three decades of friendship

. . . the best liar is he who makes
the smallest amount of lying
go the longest way.
                    —Samuel Butler

# ONE

Adrienne's tomatoes froze to death the same night that Arnie Dresser did.

September 27 is about a week early for a hard frost along Colorado's Front Range, but it's late for tomatoes. The only fruit left hanging on my friend's ragged vines the afternoon that initial winter cold front scooted south out of Wyoming were some hard green orbs that didn't appear likely to ripen before the millennium. Since I'd already made enough tomato sauce and salsa to fill half my freezer as well as a good chunk of Adrienne's, I didn't mourn the death of the tomatoes as much as I did the demise of the half-dozen fresh basil plants that had shriveled and blackened in response to the assault of the chill Canadian air.

Arnie Dresser's death was much more unexpected than was this first frost, but his passing caused me less initial reflection than did that of my neighbor's garden. The funeral was, thankfully, the first I would be attending in a long time, and I suspected that I would shed no tears at Arnie's services. I hadn't seen him in years, and we had never really been close friends. My presence at his funeral was indicated, I felt, so as not to show disrespect. If I had fallen down a steep cliff in the Maroon Bells wilderness and cracked my skull open on a rock before succumbing to exposure, I'd like to think that someone like Arnie would come and pay respects to me.

That's actually not true. Most days, I really wouldn't care. On insecure days, maybe. Most days, no.

Arnie—Arnold Dresser, M.D.—had stayed in touch. I had to give him credit for that.

Since our days training together in 1982 in the psychiatry department at the University of Colorado Health Sciences Center—he as a

second-year psychiatric resident, I as a clinical psychology intern—
Arnie always included me on his Christmas card list. Occasionally,
he would send a note to congratulate me on something he had heard
through the grapevine about my life, like my wedding, or to com-
miserate with me over some tragedy he thought we shared, like our
divorces.

Arnie's professional demeanor was a bit overbearing—okay, before he died, I considered him pompous and arrogant—but away
from work he was a nice enough guy who I never put much energy
into knowing well. After my training at the Health Sciences Center
was complete, I'd moved to Boulder to practice. Arnie stayed in Denver, enrolled in the Analytic Institute, and set up the de rigueur Cherry
Creek office-cum-couch. I had often considered Arnie's congeniality
toward me to be too much, even reaching the point of being gratuitous
at times, but had never given much thought to understanding it.

At his funeral, I expected to see a slew of other nice people and
some not-so-nice people whose faces I remembered from long ago in
my training but whom I never knew well, either. That's the nature of
internships and residencies. Short training rotations throw strangers
together for intense interludes of manic involvement and long hours.
It's no way to train quality health-care professionals, and certainly
no way to develop enduring social relationships.

If I were someone who was into class reunions, though, Arnie
would have been my pick for chairman. He seemed to have had a
need to stay in touch with a lot of us from his training years. In annual Christmas cards, he'd fill me in on news about many of the
other residents and interns from those days and tell me what had
happened to them. I recalled some of the names, but the faces that
went with them seemed to have composted in my memory. Other
names Arnie mentioned in his annual cards rang no bell at all. They
belonged, I suspected, to people he had included through some arbi-
trary misstep of his own recollection, as he confused me with someone else whose card he was writing while he took his annual long
Thanksgiving-weekend ski trip to Vail. Occasionally, reading the cards,
I'd get momentarily somber over the news of some tragedy, or feel
the reverberations of the stirring of ancient lust over the mention of
someone for whom I'd had romantic, or more likely purely lascivi-
ous, yearnings. But mostly, I didn't pay much attention. And since I
was not a Christmas card writer, I never wrote back.

My failure as a correspondent had never deterred Arnie, and I granted him points for persistence. So, despite the fact that a crisp September Saturday in Colorado offered an infinite variety of more enticing indulgences than attending a funeral, I decided that I would pay my final respects to Arnie Dresser.

Befitting Arnie's passion, which was climbing mountains, his services were going to be held in the high country at a gorgeous stone church outside Evergreen. The town of Evergreen meanders over picturesque peaks and valleys twenty miles west and a couple of thousand feet above Denver, just south of Interstate 70. If Denver at times seemed to yearn to be cast as a landlocked San Francisco, and Boulder auditioned for the role of Berkeley, Evergreen would line up to play a serviceable Sausalito or Tiburon. Evergreen was close enough to the metropolitan area to be a suburb, high enough to allow commuters to feel they truly lived in the mountains, and rural enough so that they could believe their domiciles were in the wild. But over the years this mountain oasis had started to attract cookie-cutter housing, which was soon followed by state-of-the-art supermarkets, and inevitably a Wal-Mart. The charm, sadly, has been tarnished.

The church was tucked away in the woods on the north side of the interstate. It was situated so that worshipers, or in this case mourners, could gaze out the big western windows behind the altar and see what God had wrought on one of His better days during that frantic week of creation. From the front row of the church's sanctuary, on a clear autumn day like this one, the Continental Divide stretched north and south farther than human vision permitted, the jutting peaks sided with glistening glaciers and framed by sky as pure as a mother's dreams.

Arnie Dresser's love had been climbing those mountains. But he hadn't been a rock climber or an ice climber. He wasn't one of those reckless types who conquered mountains while draped with enough ropes and hardware to stock a small-town True Value, inching upward toward the summit one handhold at a time. Arnie had been an avid recreational mountain climber. What he liked to do was walk up mountains, resorting to limited technical gear only when a particular rock face precluded a less determined stroll.

But on the other hand, it would be a slur to call Arnie Dresser a mere hiker. He was a proud member of the Fourteener Club, a loose assemblage of hiking-boot–clad outdoors people who had managed to ascend all fifty-four of Colorado's fourteen-thousand-foot peaks, from the diminutive Sunshine Peak at 14,001 feet to the majestic Mount Elbert at 14,433 feet. I'd trudged to the top of two of the fourteeners—Mount Princeton and Mount Sherman—so I considered myself officially one twenty-seventh of the way to membership. The fact that I'd been one twenty-seventh of the way to membership for the better part of seven years is an indication of the respect I could muster for those people, like Arnie, who had not only completed one circuit of Colorado's tallest peaks but had already completed two and eagerly gone back for more.

Arnie had come from a wealthy family, the Dressers at one time apparently controlling a sizable amount of the cable TV business in Wisconsin. I'd never before bothered to consider what lavish touches financial resources could bring to a funeral. I suppose I would have assumed that big bucks could provide the opportunity to occupy a fancier than necessary box in which to decompose, but Arnie's innovative send-off gave me a whole new appreciation of what family wealth could do to enhance a solemn good-bye.

The church service was brief, an inspiring mixture of nonoffensive liturgy from a tall laconic minister who I didn't think had ever met Arnie Dresser, and poignant Quaker-like testimony from the surprisingly large gathering of loved ones, friends, and acquaintances. Arnie's body wasn't actually present in the church; he had apparently already been reduced to ashes that were contained on the altar in a tasteful cherrywood box that looked as though it might have been designed to hold expensive cigars. The box was dwarfed by two huge sprays of freesia.

At the conclusion of the service a man younger than Arnie approached the pulpit and identified himself as the deceased's brother, Price. He invited the gathered mourners to leave the church with him and take a short hike down a dirt road through the nearby pine forest for a final good-bye. He didn't say why.

The trek through the woods ended in a clearing that was empty except for a helicopter, a gleaming black jet model that had seats for six, in addition to ample room for what little was left of Arnie.

I stood at the periphery, unsure what was going to happen next. I was secretly hoping for a lottery that would give me a chance to be one of five lucky mourners selected to accompany the pilot back up into the Colorado sky. But the passengers of the chopper had been pre-chosen. When Arnie's brother, Price, climbed in, I surmised that the fortunate few were family, with maybe a significant other or two thrown in.

I watched from across the clearing as the cherry chest was handed up into the cabin. The act was accomplished with so much reverence and ceremony that it looked overrehearsed, like a Super Bowl half-time show or the bridal stroll down the aisle at a wedding. Moments later, the helicopter lifted off with a pulsating roar and those of us left behind waved good-bye to Arnie Dresser for the last time.

Everyone on the ground was soon covered in a film of fine dust stirred up by the big blades. I wondered if the symbolism was intentional.

The person next to me yelled into my ear that the chopper was on its way to the Elk Range to return Arnie's ashes to the place where he died.

*The place where he died.*
The *how* of Arnie's dying was actually more interesting to me.

The story I had pieced together from news accounts and from mutual acquaintances who were busy either cataloguing rumors or spreading them was that Arnie had been alone, climbing a steep but nontechnical section of Maroon Peak in the Elk Range near Aspen. Climbing alone was apparently standard practice for Arnie since his divorce. When the accident occurred, he was well below timberline, late September being much too late in the season to be attempting to reach the peak of a fourteener without winter gear. Members of the mountain rescue team that had recovered his body and examined his clothing and provisions were certain that this had been a mere recreational jaunt. No witnesses saw the actual fall. The consensus, however, was that Arnie must have lost his footing on a notoriously tough section of trail and tumbled back down a rocky slope for almost one hundred and fifty feet before clearing a rock cornice and soaring through the air for another hundred feet or so.

That a climber of Arnie's experience and skill might die from a slip-and-fall seemed ironic. In the days before the funeral I'd heard speculation that he had been suffering from recurring bouts of vertigo, or that his heart rhythms had been irregular, or that maybe a TIA, a baby stroke, was to blame for the loss of balance that led to the fatal fall.

But no one knew.

What we did know was that when he came to rest for the last time, he was crumpled piteously on a flat rock high on the south side of Maroon Peak. The rock shelf where he died was the size of a racquetball court, and the left side of Arnie's skull was flattened like a carelessly dropped melon.

Over the course of that night the chill Canadian air blew down from the north and stole the remaining life from his weakened body.

It was the exact same cause of death as Adrienne's tomatoes.

# TWO

Lauren had decided against attending the funeral of a total stranger, arguing persuasively that life generally delivered enough grief and that she didn't see any reason to go inviting any extra. She'd never met Arnie Dresser and could barely recall the Christmas cards he'd sent that were always addressed to me, not us.

We had driven up to the mountains together. She had dropped me off at the church while she went across the valley to get pampered at the Tall Grass Spa on the other side of Evergreen near Bear Creek. By the time she came back to retrieve me at the church, the helicopter and all the cars but two had departed. The afternoon was warm, and I waited in the shade, sitting alone on a stone wall in front of the church.

September 27 was not only a little early for a first killing frost, but it was also a little late for that year's fall leaf season. Even at the lower elevations along the Front Range, the glory of the metamorphosis of the aspen leaves as they changed from sweet green to golden was already a few days past prime time. But Lauren and I hadn't been up to the mountains at all this month, and we thought we would take advantage of the location of Arnie's funeral to venture a little farther up I-70 in hope that some of the gilded splendor remained intact in the high country.

When she arrived back at the church driving my old Land Cruiser, Lauren had a warm glow about her that I associated with post-coital splendor. The spa treatments had left her sleepy and pink, and she asked me to drive as we left the church. As she got out of the car to move to the passenger side I found myself distracted by the sunshine that was sparkling off her raven hair. Lauren had recently cut her hair short for the first time since we'd met, and I was still getting used to the change. The novelty of seeing her long neck and sleek jaw exposed captivated me.

As she walked around the front of the car I checked her gait and was encouraged to see no evidence of a limp. My assessment of Lauren's health these days was an unconscious but constant concern, a kind of reflexive checking that reminded me of patting my pocket for my keys or touching my hip for my pager. I let myself feel encouraged by the evenness of the strides she was taking, though I knew damn well that the limp could be back the next time she got out of the car, whether that was ten minutes from now or five hours from now.

That's what her multiple sclerosis was like for us. I always kept an eye on it. It was a cantankerous dog that I always suspected could bite.

She asked about the funeral at the exact same moment that I wondered aloud about her massage.

She pulled a bare foot from her black clog and rested it on the dashboard. "I got a pedicure, too," she said. "That's why I was late."

I glanced over at her slender toes, with newly painted shiny violet nails. She has great feet. I said, "I like the color. It's cute. Sort of an *Addams Family* touch. Arnie's funeral was, well, different. Interesting. The service itself was unusual. Lots of people talked. It was nice."

"What was so different?"

"That came after. His body had already been cremated and once the services were over we all walked down this trail and there was this big black helicopter waiting to whisk his ashes back up to the Maroon Bells to the mountainside where he died. Somebody told me that his remains are going to be scattered from the chopper over the spot where he fell."

"Really?" She glanced over at me with a skeptical face. She wondered if I was making this up.

"Really. Big jet helicopter, six seats. Black, like a hearse. Took off from this little clearing down the road from the church. People waved good-bye as though Arnie was actually heading off to climb Everest or something."

"You wave, too?"

"No. Actually, I had been kind of hoping to be invited for a ride on the helicopter."

She said, "Oh, so you were being petulant. And what do you mean you wanted a ride? What about me? I was supposed to cool my heels while you flew up to the Maroon Bells to sprinkle ashes?"

"You were getting a pedicure, remember? You still want to go look-ing for leaves?"

"Absolutely. Central City?"

"No, I don't think so. I'm not up to fighting the gambling traffic."

"How about Georgetown, then? Guanella Pass?"

"Yeah, good. I'm hungry. You?"

"Famished. I didn't eat at the spa. I was in a Mexican mood. They were serving seaweed and some grain that I thought was bulgur but wasn't."

"Quinoa?"

"Maybe."

"Silver Plume for lunch, then?"

"Perfect."

I'd noticed that Lauren and I were having more and more conver-sations that felt like they had been scripted from a synopsis prepared by Cliffs Notes. For about a mile on I-70, I wondered what it meant.

Then I began to notice the golden leaves on the mountainsides and I didn't wonder anymore.

Our lunch destination was on the eastern slope of the Continental Divide, just downhill from the spot where I-70 burrows through the Divide at the Eisenhower Tunnel. The town of Silver Plume rests against the side of a mountain about two miles up the valley from its restored nineteenth-century mining sister, Georgetown. During the Colorado precious-mineral frenzy a hundred-plus years ago, George-town was gold and Silver Plume was silver. In the years since, George-town had been lovingly restored and painstakingly polished to a Victorian luster that probably surpasses its appearance during the 1880s. Silver Plume, in contrast, sits in rickety nineteenth-century de-caying wonder, with dirt streets, wooden sidewalks, and hitching posts that actually once had animals tethered to them.

Georgetown lives for tourists. Silver Plume somehow just man-ages to survive. In excess of ninety-nine point nine percent of the cars that exit I-70 at Silver Plume turn south to the parking lots for the Georgetown Loop Railway tourist attraction. To get to old Silver Plume you have to turn north of the highway and weave across a suspicious-looking wooden bridge and down a couple of narrow lanes that don't look like they're going anywhere you might deliberately want to be heading. One more bend and you're heading east on the main street in town. It doesn't take a western historian to know that

Silver Plume is nothing but a ghost town in training, one of the few remaining authentic vestiges of the Colorado mining west.

In the middle of Main Street, with big windows to catch the brilliance of the southern sun, was our destination, the KP Cafe.

The furniture in the cafe is as old as the building but not as well cared for. None of it matches. The attitude inside is friendly and warm. Folks who want to be left alone are left alone. Those who want to chat get chatted with. The food is just fine. When the coffee's fresh it's good, but sometimes it burns after it sits for a while on the big old Bunn machine behind the bar.

Lauren and I poked our heads in the door and said hello to the same waitress we'd had the last few times we were in. Her name was Megan. She suggested, and we gladly took, a sunny deuce by the front windows. We ate at the KP five or six times a year, always on our way somewhere else. It was sufficient frequency that we were treated like honorary regulars.

We both ordered Mexican and decided to split a beer.

Megan smiled at Lauren and ignored me. My memory was that she had done that the last time we were in, too.

Maybe thirty seconds after we ordered, another couple entered the café. I noticed their arrival because they were both in suits. Megan stopped wiping the counter because they were both in suits. His was a nondescript navy. Hers was a vibrant fuchsia trimmed with raspberry. I didn't recognize her but I knew that suit. These two had been at Arnie Dresser's funeral.

I whispered to Lauren, "They were at the funeral, too."

She glanced over. "In that suit?"

I shrugged. "I doubt if Arnie was offended."

"That's important, I suppose. But how does one offend ashes, anyway? Doesn't make it funeral garb in my book."

"I didn't know you had a book."

She punched me across the table as Megan directed the couple to a cramped table in back, near the door to the rest rooms. I assumed, with some confidence, that they weren't regulars. I watched with gossipy interest as the two of them immediately entered into a contentious discussion about something I couldn't quite overhear. Their upper bodies were leaning forward over the rickety table so far that their heads almost touched in the middle. Her voice was louder than his. I thought I heard the Deep South hibernating somewhere in it. I finally lost interest as Megan dropped a couple of menus on their table.

A minute or so later, Megan brought us our beer along with a basket of tortilla chips and some salsa that didn't come out of a bottle. As Lauren was taking her first sip of beer, her eyebrows arched. I turned toward her gaze and saw that fuchsia suit was approaching our table. I sat back on my chair.

She said, "Dr. Gregory? Dr. Alan Gregory?"

The woman wearing the fuchsia suit was apparently somebody I should have but didn't remember from long ago at the medical center in Denver. With more embarrassment in my voice than I felt, I said, "Yes, that's me. I'm Alan Gregory. I'm sorry, do I know you from the Health Sciences Center? I think I recall seeing you at the funeral."

She fingered the lapels of her suit jacket with both hands. "Yes, yes. I was at Dr. Dresser's services. But no, I didn't do my training here. I went to Georgetown. Not the little one we just passed down the hill, here. The big one in D.C." She laughed at her own wit and held out her hand to shake mine. "I hope you will please forgive my intrusion. My name is A. J. Simes. Dr. A. J. Simes."

I wasn't sure if I was ready to forgive her intrusion. I shook the hand she offered and said, "This is my wife, Lauren Crowder. Lauren, Dr. Simes."

"Pleased to meet you, Ms. Crowder."

I was afraid she was going to ask to pull up a chair. She didn't. I hoped her visit was over. It wasn't.

She said, "This may seem presumptuous—my walking up to you like this—and after you hear what we have to say, perhaps preposterous as well, but my associate and I feel that it's essential that we have a word or two with you, Dr. Gregory. I do hope you don't mind." She tilted her head toward her companion across the room, who appeared embarrassed and wasn't looking our way.

I sighed. "Actually, we're enjoying a rare afternoon out. Another time would be much better. I'll be happy to arrange some time to see you . . . both. Why don't I give you a card?"

She shook her head in a tight little arc, almost more of a shiver than a shake. "Please don't jump to conclusions, Doctor. I'm not usually an impolite woman. Not at all. Interrupting you like this makes me easily as uncomfortable as it is making you. What we want to discuss with you just shouldn't wait, I'm afraid."

Simes looked back over her shoulder at her companion. He was studiously avoiding her, his eyes raised toward heaven. It appeared that he was either in deep prayer or was into architectural relics and was doing a thorough examination of the pressed-tin ceiling.

Megan walked up behind A. J. Simes with two large platters of steaming Mexican food that she was gripping with potholders. She had a pained smile on her face and she was dancing back and forth from one foot to the other as though she had to pee. I was guessing that the aging potholders in her hands had lost some of their original insulating capacity.

Over Simes's shoulder, Megan said, "Careful, now, you guys, these platters are hot."

I cleared space in front of me for the food and asked, with minimal interest, "And why is that, Dr. Simes? I don't even know you. Why can't this wait?"

Simes moved her feet a little—though not quite enough for Megan to pass—and faced me directly. She turned her head toward Lauren until she was certain that she had her attention as well as mine. But she spoke to me.

"This can't wait because," she said, "after quite a bit of investigation, and a significant amount of contemplation, I'm relatively certain that someone is going to try to kill you, Dr. Gregory."

Behind her, the green chili burrito platters went down with a roar. Refried beans erupted into the room like lava from the Second Coming of Mount St. Helens.

# THREE

Megan said, "Oh shit. Frank, I need some help out here. Bring the mop. Bring the broom. Bring the damn trash can."

I stood to help. Megan almost shoved me back into my seat. "No, no. Sit. Sit. Your shoes are covered with green chile and crap. All of you, sit, damn it." She faced Simes, who didn't have a chair. "God, I'm sorry about my mouth. Oh, no. Look what happened to your pretty suit."

A. J. Simes didn't seem to know what to say. She turned to face her associate. His face was buried in his hands and he was shaking his head back and forth. With her back to us, I could clearly see the damage that the burritos had done to Dr. Simes's clothing. A pattern of splatters and chunks spread out like a fan from the top of her thighs to her shoulders. I thought that Henry Lee could probably do an entire lecture on the splatter pattern of green chili burrito platters off century-old pine flooring.

Lauren was dressed in black jeans and clogs. The damage to her wardrobe was, relatively, minor. She wiped her shoes clean with her napkin, stood, and slipped Dr. Simes's jacket from her shoulders. "I'll do your jacket. You'd better spin that skirt around and see what you can do with the back. I'm afraid it's not pretty."

*Somebody is trying to kill me? Why is everybody so damn concerned about the frijoles?* I actually looked out the window to see if there was someone coming my way with a weapon.

Dr. Simes said, "I'm so sorry. This is all my fault. I didn't handle this well." She headed to the rest room to salvage her fuchsia skirt and to try to escape her obvious humiliation.

Lauren went immediately to work on the back of the jacket with my napkin and a glass of water.

I said, "Did she say she thought someone was trying to kill me?"

Megan looked up from her catcher's crouch on the floor and said, "Damn straight that's what she said."

Lauren just nodded. I couldn't read her expression at all.

Frank and Megan made quick work of the burrito catastrophe. Lauren continued to dab at the jacket. A. J. Simes maintained her retreat to the bathroom. I'd been in that bathroom on a couple of occasions. Nineteenth-century charm ends at plumbing. Period, end of sentence. The bathroom of the KP Cafe was absolutely no place for a leisurely respite.

Without glancing up, Lauren said, "She has MS. Dr. Simes."

"She does? How can you tell?"

She shrugged. "Look at the muscles around her eyes. She forms her words a little too carefully. She's a little unsteady. I don't know. I can just tell."

I nodded. Lauren could tell. The mild form of the disease wasn't as invisible to people who lived with it as it was to the rest of us.

"What on earth do you think she was talking about? I mean, someone trying to kill me? Is she nuts?"

"I don't know. I got the impression that she was planning on telling us soon enough, though. Before the burrito thing, anyway."

Across the room, the man in the navy suit stood and approached our table. Lauren lowered the fuchsia jacket to her lap and smiled politely. I said, "Hello. I'm Alan Gregory. This is my wife, Lauren Crowder."

He held out his hand. "I know who you both are. I'm Milton Custer, by the way. Pleased to meet you."

Milton Custer was built like a redwood. Tall, thick trunk, thin limbs. His hair was salt-and-pepper, and his handshake was painful. "Call me Milt," he said. He tilted his head toward the back of the cafe and raised his left eyebrow. "But I think you should call her Dr. Simes."

Lauren asked, "What kind of doctor is she?"

"Same as your husband, ma'am. A psychologist."

Lauren seemed to be considering something, and said, "Won't you pull up a seat, Mr. Custer?"

Reluctantly, it seemed to me, Milt Custer sat, first twirling the chair around so he could straddle it. I sensed he liked the idea of having some kind of barrier between us. He removed his glasses and started to clean them. It turned out to be a complicated ritual that involved a tiny lavender cloth he pulled from inside a hard case that he retrieved from the pocket of his suit jacket.

As he polished the second lens, he said, "I didn't want to do it here. Tell you like that, you know, about what we think is going on and all. That was her idea. She was determined. First I told her I didn't think we should do it at the church—I mean, that's not right, at the church right after a funeral. I told her we should follow you home and tell you there. Where you feel more comfortable, safer, you know. But then you didn't go home, you came here, and then I didn't think we should do it here, either." He looked self-conscious. "For obvious reasons. But she was sure you guys were heading someplace overnight and insisted we better take care of things right now. Dr. Simes, she's single-minded sometimes. Maybe you might even say stubborn."

I asked, "You and she are . . . ?"

He considered the question. "Colleagues. Partners, I guess. For now, anyway."

*You guess?*

"And you both think someone is trying to . . . what? Hurt me?"

He reflected for a good ten seconds before answering. When he was ready to speak he stared right at me and nailed me with a glare that screamed *pay attention*. He said, "No. This guy is definitely planning to kill you. Merely hurting you would indicate failure on his part. And so far as we can tell, he hasn't failed at any of this, yet. He's batting a thousand."

*A thousand?* Instantly I wondered how many times the guy had been to the plate.

Lauren asked, "Who the hell are you people?"

I thought, *Yeah!*

Megan wanted to clean a little more thoroughly under our table and asked if she could move us all to a little alcove by the counter. A secondary benefit occurred to me: If someone took a shot at me over there, it wouldn't be as likely to endanger the other patrons.

A. J. Simes rejoined us a few minutes later. Lauren handed her the jacket and said, "I did the best I could."

She said, "Thanks. I'm so embarrassed."

I found myself examining A. J. Simes for indications of multiple sclerosis. Maybe there was something odd about the coordination of her eyes when she blinked. But so far she appeared to me to be just an attractive woman in her late forties who had an intriguing swirl of gray in a thick head of auburn hair.

Milt said, "They just asked who the hell we are."

Simes nodded. "Good question. May I sit?"

I said, "Please."

"I'm so sorry. That was infelicitous. Blurting that out the way I did. And I accept full responsibility. Including dry cleaning, of course."

Lauren said, "It's forgotten already."

"You are too kind. How to begin?"

I said, "I think you've already begun."

She widened her mouth into something that was either a sardonic smile or the beginnings of a snarl. "The easiest way to explain our interest in you, Dr. Gregory, is to tell you we're both ex-FBI." She lowered her chin at Milt. "My colleague is—was—Supervisory Special Agent Milton Custer, who concluded his career in Chicago. And I spent almost all my time with the Bureau in the Investigative Support Unit. Initially, at Quantico. That's in Virginia. As I said before, my name is Dr. A. J. Simes."

The "Doctor" stuff was beginning to sound pretentious. But I knew about the Investigative Support Unit.

I said, "That's Behavioral Sciences, right?"

"The name changed a few years back. A bureaucratic thing. But yes, a similar division. Most of the same responsibilities."

"Were you in VICAP?" I was asking if she had been involved with the Violent Criminal Apprehension Program, the team that profiled serial killers and sexual psychopaths, among others.

"Yes. You're familiar with our work?"

I said, "Unfortunately," but didn't elaborate about my friend Peter's murder a couple of years earlier by a suspected serial killer. I had a funny feeling that these two already knew about Peter's murder. "Were you a profiler, Dr. Simes?"

"Yes. It was one of my responsibilities. I have those skills and a significant amount of experience, and expertise, in the area."

Lauren had narrowed her focus. Her gaze was locked on Simes. Lauren, a deputy DA, was moving quickly into prosecutor mode. I was grateful. She was an astute observer and a more pointed interviewer than I was. She asked, "You said *ex*-FBI, Dr. Simes?"

Simes answered, "That's right. Ex. Mr. Custer and I are participants in a consortium of ex-agents and other ex-Bureau personnel who provide private consultation to law enforcement agencies, businesses, and, occasionally, individuals, on matters in which we might have particular expertise."

I remembered reading something about this group once. "Your organization was invited to participate in the JonBenet Ramsey investigation in Boulder, weren't you? A couple of years ago?"

"Some of our colleagues were asked to assist the family, yes. With one unfortunate exception, everyone who was contacted declined. We are quite selective about where we lend our resources and experience. That offer from that family was particularly easy to decline."

I said, "And now I assume you're on a different case? And you are lending your experience to . . . ?"

The two FBI types looked at each other. Simes nodded. Custer answered, "We've been given permission to inform you that we were retained by the mother of Dr. Arnold Dresser."

Given their presence at Arnie's funeral, I shouldn't have been surprised at the answer, but I was. Lauren pressed on with her earlier line of questioning. "Why did you leave the FBI, Dr. Simes?"

Simes raised her chin a little and said, "Medical disability." The way she formed her words communicated her desire that Lauren not inquire further seeking details.

Lauren said, "And you, Mr. Custer?"

"I did my twenty-five. I retired."

Lauren nodded as though their answers were somehow self-evident. "And Dr. Dresser's mother hired you to investigate something involving her son's death on that mountain, right?"

"Right," Custer said.

"Mrs. Dresser wishes for you to determine what, exactly?"

Simes replied, crisply, "She would like us to determine whether or not her son was murdered."

*Murdered?*

Lauren continued, "And by your earlier statement about the danger that my husband's in, I take it we can assume that you've determined that Dr. Dresser was murdered?"

Simes answered, " 'Determined'? Perhaps too strong a word for this stage of the investigation. But we've begun to assemble a body of evidence that indicates that it is possible, even likely, that Dr. Dresser's death was in fact a homicide and not an accident."

"And you are here with us, today, because you've made some connection that takes you from Dr. Dresser to my husband?"

Simes said, "We have reason to be . . . concerned. I felt—Mr. Custer and I each felt—that our concerns are strong enough and the evidence is substantial enough that it would be a dereliction of duty to fail to inform your husband that he, too, may be at some risk."

I protested, "I barely knew Arnie Dresser."

I felt Simes's gaze turn to me. It felt condescending, and I didn't like it. "If our theory is correct, the risk comes not from how well you knew Dr. Dresser, I'm afraid, Dr. Gregory, but rather from *when* you knew Dr. Dresser."

"I haven't spent any time with him for over fifteen years."

"Exactly."

Lauren looked at me and, I'm sure, saw the complete befuddlement in my face. She said, "What does that mean? 'Exactly.' What do you mean?"

Simes said, "That's the time period—the window, if you will—that appears to be important. Almost sixteen years ago. When Dr. Gregory and Dr. Dresser were in training together on an inpatient psychiatric unit at the Health Sciences Center of the University of Colorado in Denver. The unit was known as Eight East."

She had her facts right. I didn't find that reassuring, however. I asked, "Why is that important?"

A family with two small children was taking the table next to ours. Milt raised his voice above everyone's and said, "I'm not real comfortable with how all this is proceeding. Please, everyone, let's not do this here. Why don't we take a little walk, get ourselves some air?"

I hadn't eaten a bite. I wasn't at all hungry. I asked Lauren if walking was okay with her. She said it was. I threw forty dollars on the table to cover our beer, our burritos, and the havoc we'd precipitated and said, "Okay, let's walk."

The afternoon was radiant. The angle of the autumn sun and a light wind spiraling down from the Divide caused the aspen leaves on the mountain faces to twinkle like a million golden stars. Stark cumulus clouds were tugged and distorted by the winds as they floated against the blue sky. The steam whistle from the Georgetown Loop train pierced the quiet from across the narrow valley.

Milt said, "I love trains. I wish we had time."

Simes admonished him sharply, "We don't." If Dr. Simes had children, I was certain they never grabbed items off the shelf at the supermarket.

Lauren took my hand and we began walking toward the general store at the eastern end of the little town. She pointed toward the door. "Remember the bread? This place has great bread," she said to me. "We need to buy some before we leave today."

*Get bread?* I was beginning to go nuts inside. Two ex–FBI agents thought somebody was trying to kill me—yet everybody around me, with the exception of our waitress, seemed to be taking the news in stride.

Two more steps and I said, "Would somebody please tell me what the hell is going on?"

Milt looked deferentially at Dr. Simes. I couldn't tell whether his deference was the result of respect, or fear. She raised her chin to indicate it was all right with her that he proceed.

"Dr. Dresser had apparently been concerned for a while that something . . . odd . . . has been going on with the group of people he trained with during his residency in 1982. Specifically, he was worried about the group of interns, residents, and supervisors who were working on the . . . what? The Orange Team? Is that right? On that unit called Eight East in the hospital at the medical school. That includes you, Dr. Gregory. You did some training on the Orange Team on Eight East in the fall of 1982, didn't you? With Dr. Dresser?"

We were standing in front of a frame building that a hopelessly faded sign said had once been a livery. The structure looked as though it would fall over if I sneezed. I said, "Yes. I was one of the psychology interns on that unit then. That's when I met Arnie. He was one of the second-year psychiatric residents."

"Well, to get back to my story. Dr. Dresser was close to his mother. His father died quite a few years back and he and his mom have been real close ever since. He was kind of a compulsive letter writer and E-mailer and over the years he'd begun to express some continuing concern to her that the group of people he trained with on the Orange Team seemed jinxed in some way."

I asked, "Jinxed how?"

Lauren tugged on my hand. "I know it's hard, sweets. Be patient. Let him tell his story." My stomach growled. Lauren's tolerance for skipping meals was much lower than mine. If I was hungry, I guessed she must be famished.

Two young men in cowboy boots, Lee jeans, and worn Stetsons

paused next to us for a moment. I was feeling so paranoid that I checked their hips for holstered Colt .45s. No one spoke until they passed.

I broke the silence. "Okay, go on. I'm sorry."

"It's fine, I understand. This has to be totally strange for you. Us hijacking you like this. I'm just trying to present it to you in a way that doesn't sound more off-the-wall than it is."

Milt's manner wasn't coplike. I knew a lot of cops—was good friends with one—and Milt's manner reminded me more of bad news being delivered by a kind uncle than bad news being delivered by a cop. Still, I was impatient for him to get to the end of his story.

"Let's go back to the early eighties. You remember a supervising psychiatrist on the Orange Team named Susan Oliphant?"

"Yes. She was the ward chief." Next I expected to learn that she had become a full-time proprietor of the past tense.

"Do you know she died in 1989?"

"No," I said slowly, drawing out the long vowel, assuming what I was going to hear about the details of her death was not going to be good news. Had Arnie told me about Susan's death? I didn't think so. Maybe it was in one of the cards I never bothered to finish reading.

"She was a private pilot. Did you know that about her? She died in a plane crash. A little Cessna, a 172. The crash killed both her and her twelve-year-old niece. The plane crashed into a mountainside in the Adirondacks. Clear weather. Radio contacts with air traffic control just before the impact were particularly heartbreaking, made it clear to anybody who listens to them that the plane suffered some catastrophic mechanical problem."

"I'm so sorry." And I was. I had been fond of Susan. Some of the psychiatrists on the Orange Team treated the psychology interns as though we were younger siblings who had been tethered to them by parents who didn't have a clue how much of an annoyance we really were. Susan Oliphant hadn't been like that. I hadn't heard much of her over the years, only knew she wasn't in town. Once more, I tried to recall whether Arnie's Christmas cards had notified me of her death. I couldn't remember. Was I that callous? I hoped not.

Milt continued, "After a routine investigation, the NTSB ruled the plane crash to be an accident, caused by control-linkage failure. The impact was severe, though, and destroyed most of the evidence."

"She couldn't steer the plane?"

"Basically."

I touched Lauren's arm while I asked, "Manner of death?"

From the corner of my eye, I saw a tiny smile grace Simes's face. She was pleased at my question. With my words, she had realized with visible relief that she and Milt weren't going to have to connect the dots for me.

"Accident."

I don't know why, but I faced Simes. "But you don't necessarily concur with the coroner's findings on manner, do you?"

Milt answered as though he didn't even notice the slight. "We'll get to all that in a minute. May I continue?"

"Sure. Go on."

"Dr. Matthew Trimble?"

"Yes, I remember him. Matt was a psychiatric resident. He did medical backup for me on a few cases on the unit. He's dead as well?" I was playing stupid now. I knew about Matt's death. News of his senseless shooting had spilled through the mental health community in Colorado like a flash flood through a floodplain. It had touched us all, some more deeply than others. Matt was the only professional I knew who had actually gone ahead and arranged his career so that he could try to do as much good for people as the idealistic plans of his youth said he was going to do. I wasn't his friend, but I respected him immensely.

"Yes. He died in 1991. He was the victim of a drive-by in southeast Los Angeles as he was leaving a people's-clinic–type place where he was doing pro bono work with their drug program. He—"

"That's where he was from. Compton. That's where he grew up. He went back there to work."

"Right. No arrest was ever made in the case. It's still open. Local cops said it looked random to them. A Crip who was walking with him got hit, too. L.A. had a ton of drive-bys in those days. The Summer of Blood and all that." He paused. "Manner on that one was, of course, homicide. It's the only one I'm going to tell you about where the manner of death was homicide."

"How many more?" I said. I could barely form the words.

He didn't answer. He said, "Next one was 1994. A trickier one."

My heart crashed to my toes. *No, not Sawyer.*

"Dr. Wendy Asimoto."

I'd been holding my breath. I exhaled. I didn't know about Wendy's death. Though I hadn't thought about her in years, I had no trouble remembering her. I said, "Wendy was a psychiatric resident, too, second-year like the others. She was older than the rest of us, closer to thirty. She had already completed an internal medicine residency prior to coming to the medical center for psych training. I remember her as having a healthy dose of skepticism about psychiatry."

"Very good memory, Dr. Gregory." The compliment, and a surprised tone, came from Dr. Simes.

I had an impulse to tell them both to call me Alan, but I wasn't sure I wanted that level of intimacy yet. I said, "Is she the last one?" I wanted Wendy Asimoto to be the last dead shrink.

Milt looked up at the leaves and paused to let the cut of the steam whistle slice through the valley. He wasn't willing to give me a count, yet.

"Anyway, Dr. Asimoto dropped out of the psychiatric residency program after her second year. Decided she preferred internal medicine after all. By the time 1993 rolled around, she was working as a ship's doctor for the Cunard Line. Turns out she disappeared at sea off St. Petersburg in the Baltic on the fourth day of a twelve-day cruise in June of 1993. No one saw her go overboard. No body was ever recovered. She has since been declared dead. Manner of death on this one is still undetermined, but I think it's presumed accidental. We're not done looking into it, but there were rumors that she had begun to drink excessively."

"She was a cruise ship doc?"

"For a few years, yeah."

"And she was an alcoholic?"

"Perhaps. It happens."

"But you don't believe it? The accident part."

"May I continue?

"I'd rather that you be done."

Custer stared at me as though my impatience was concerning him. "No, I'm afraid I'm not done."

I was starting to get really nervous and I didn't want Lauren to know why. I said, "I think maybe we should go someplace and sit down."

Lauren examined my eyes, bit her bottom lip, slid her arm around my waist, and said, "In town, honey, the KP is about it, isn't it."

Simes looked weary. She said, "How about your car? It's big enough for all of us."

We started walking to the Land Cruiser. I desperately wanted a diversion. I didn't know what to do next. I didn't want to be with Simes or Custer when I heard that Sawyer Sackett was dead.

But the most troubling thing was that I didn't want to be with Lauren, either.

# FOUR

Milt Custer said, "This next one is the weirdest of them all. And it's the most recent. It happened in February, this year."

The blood seemed to vaporize from my limbs and I felt dizzy. *February? This year? That's after Arnie's last Christmas card. Maybe Sawyer is dead and I don't even know it.*

I was sitting on the driver's seat of my car and had enough of my wits still about me to recognize the irony of being in that position. Lauren had climbed into the backseat to allow one of the ex-agents to join me up front. For now, this was Milt Custer's show, and he claimed the shotgun position. Simes sat right behind me; I could see her impassive face in the mirror. Suddenly I wasn't sure whether her lock of white hair was an intense shade of blond or a prematurely advanced shade of gray.

The sun was heading down for the day, spending its last minutes perched along the peaks that framed the southern horizon, and the rays were beating down on the car. I turned on the power so we could lower the windows for some ventilation. Everyone but Simes did. When a breeze rushed through the car, she touched her hair twice with an open palm, side and back.

Lauren asked, "What do you mean? All the deaths seem strange to me."

Custer scooted sideways on his seat to face her. "You're right. But there's a lag here, timewise, I mean. We're talking over two years from the previous death. This one took our guy some time and careful planning. Method is creepier, too. This victim died in a home tanning bed."

I couldn't talk. Lauren said, "What? How?"

"She had a skin condition—what's that called, A.J.?" I noted that suddenly Custer sounded like a cop. I wondered whether it was an intentional change on his part or whether he was just returning to form.

Simes frowned and said, "I don't remember. Maybe it will come to me."

"Yeah, whatever. Anyway, she had to use a tanning bed for ultraviolet skin treatment. Did it at home, the treatment, a regular type of thing. Had this big fancy, bed—you know what I mean, you seen 'em? Like in those salons? One of those clamshell-type things where the top closes over you and you get zapped by lights top and bottom at the same time. Have to wear those little goggles to keep the fluid in your eyeballs from boiling. I'm a little claustrophobic myself. No way I climb into one of those things, let me tell you that."

*Please. Was it Sawyer? Please.*

"Anyway, she sets the timer, climbs in, pulls down the lid, puts on the goggles, and flips the switch. Immediately, two things go wrong. One, the timer malfunctions, never ticks down, so the lights just keep on cooking. Two, one of the hinges breaks so the bed won't open back up. When those two things go wrong at the same time in a home tanning bed, you have a recipe for roasting a human being to death."

Lauren asked, "Why didn't she just pull the plug?"

"Bad design. Cord comes out at the foot of the bed. No way to twist around to get down there with the top pressing down on you."

"And the hinge couldn't be forced back open?"

Custer shook his head and said, "It was badly jammed. No."

"No way to squirm out?"

"Not in this design."

"So she died?"

"Yeah, eventually. A relative found her after almost two days. But she didn't actually die for another thirty-six hours."

Lauren was appraising me with some mixture of pity and concern. Fortunately, she recognized my apoplexy. She asked Custer, "And, given the tenor of this discussion so far, you both suspect that the bed was tampered with?"

Custer said, "Timers fail sometimes, right? We're gonna take a look at that—the bed's still in evidence. But the hinge? Even the local cops thought that was odd. They tried to find the technician who last serviced the bed, which just happened to be the day before all this crap happened, and he was nowhere to be found. Had worked for the company for only six weeks. Disappeared right after that service call. Never picked up a paycheck. Never said good-bye."

"Did he service the hinges or the timer?"

"Wasn't supposed to. He was there to change the bulbs, that's all. The police looked hard at him. Had his photo taken for company ID, so there's that. Left a trail of paperwork, which looks to us like it's probably all false. He never lived at the address he gave to his employer. And after this lady gets toasted, he vanishes like a fart in a firestorm."

I thought Custer looked a little embarrassed about his choice of analogies. I knew Lauren was far from offended; her tongue was under her upper lip and I could tell she was busy piecing something together. Custer continued, "In case you're curious, manner on this one is undetermined, no surprise. Local cops don't like to hear about it from people like us, but the truth is that their experts can't be certain about any tampering, one way or another. Dr. Simes and I are encouraging them to pack up the whole damn bed and ship it to the FBI lab. My fear is that the guys who looked at it locally have managed to screw it up forever from a forensic point of view. For now, though, they don't have any hard evidence of foul play and they don't have the resources to track this guy down and question him."

Lauren asked, "He disappeared without a trace?"

"That's right," Milt replied. "That's not surprising, though. Our guy is good."

"But you have a photograph?"

"Yeah, but it's pretty worthless. Long hair and a big goatee. Tinted eyeglasses big enough for a clown to wear for an audition at Ringling's."

Lauren said, "So was she the last one? Before Dr. Dresser, I mean. Was it the last death?"

"Last one we know about. We found your husband easily enough, ma'am. We've identified one other staff member from the Orange Team who we feel might be at risk, as well. She's not been . . . available, so far. Out of town. One or both of us will go see her as soon as we leave Colorado."

"Who's that?" I asked, as nonchalantly as I could.

He tapped himself on the side of the head. "I'm sorry, I'm having a charley horse in my brain here. A.J., what's her name?"

"Sawyer Faire," she said without hesitation. "You remember Dr. Faire, Dr. Gregory?"

*Sawyer is still alive.*

I stammered, "Of course. She was, um, Sawyer Sackett then, another psychiatry resident. There were two interns and three residents on the team. My memory is that she quit. Left the program at Christmastime. Maybe this all has to do with something that happened after she left. If so, she wouldn't be in any danger at all."

With the news that Sawyer was alive, I felt like my lungs could process oxygen for the first time in ten minutes. I didn't want to talk anymore about Sawyer, so I asked Custer, "You didn't mention a name. Who was it who, uh, who died in the tanning bed?"

Simes answered from the backseat. I thought her tone was unnecessarily provocative when she said, "That was your clinical supervisor, Dr. Gregory. Dr. Amy Masters."

"Oh God." Amy Masters had been in her early fifties when she had been my clinical supervisor on the adult psychiatric inpatient service. She would have been nearly seventy when she was roasted alive in that tanning bed. "She was small, frail, she couldn't have . . ."

Milt finished my thought. "No, she didn't have a prayer of forcing those hinges open."

I stared out the windshield at this old western mining town, watching the shadows lengthening in the dust before they melded into the darkness. This late-day choreography of light hadn't changed in Silver Plume in a hundred years.

The inside of the car was quiet until I said, "I would like to go home."

Lauren objected. "Wait a second, sweets." She spoke again, directing her question to the two agents. "First, do either of you think Alan is in immediate jeopardy? Is this danger imminent?"

Simes answered after contemplating something long enough to aggravate my discomfort even more. "No, we don't. None of these deaths, if indeed they were murders, as we suspect, were impulsive. Quite the opposite. As you know, Dr. Dresser has been dead barely a week. As far as we can tell, no two deaths have taken place closer than eight months apart. If our suspicions are accurate, we feel that the man responsible is just now beginning to plan the death of his next victim. That could be Dr. Gregory. That could be Dr. Faire."

Lauren said, "Okay, then. Are you planning on telling us what you think we should do? Or are you just planning on terrifying us with innuendo?"

Before Simes could answer, I said, again, "You know, I really, really would like to go home."

Lauren ignored me again. "Are there any law-enforcement agencies that share your concern about this series of deaths?"

I was surprised to hear defensiveness in Custer's voice. "Remember, we've only been on this five days. It's preliminary. We've done good work. We have a lot more work to do, I'll grant you that. It's just us and some chits we called in. We don't have the resources of the Bureau here."

Simes's response was more to the point. She said, "The only formal investigation that's still at all active is the tanning-bed death. That would be Dr. Masters. There were no reasons to link the others together before Dr. Dresser's mother informed us of his suspicions about his colleagues' deaths. If you follow the trail as we've done, you will discover that we're discussing different jurisdictions in widely different geographic areas, hugely different MOs, and a long, long period of time."

Lauren began to employ her devil's-advocate voice. I knew she didn't believe the protest she was making. I doubted that Simes or Custer would be able to tell, though. She said, "And so far, if I follow that trail along with you, your formulation of this case, of the danger my husband is in, is based solely on coincidence and conjecture. You hear hoofbeats, and by my reckoning you're thinking zebras, not horses."

Custer said, "No, ma'am, no. That's not exactly right. Like you're suggesting, we started off following the hoofbeats, and we did it with a healthy degree of skepticism. But what we found, as we proceeded, is we found zebra shit. And that's why we're thinking zebras."

Suddenly, I recognized what I was watching. Lauren had managed to get these two cops to take on the role of having to convince a prosecutor about the quality of their evidence. The FBI types had done it a thousand times with federal prosecutors. Lauren had done it a thousand times with various local cops.

The mutual suspicion left everything slightly constipated.

Lauren said, "I assume you've taken your suppositions back to your old employer. A series of homicides that cross state lines certainly falls under the jurisdiction of the FBI. What do they say?"

Simes said, "We have discussed it informally with the Bureau. One of my old colleagues has expressed professional curiosity. He's asked us to develop this some more and get back to him. So that's what we're attempting to do. Proof in these cases is almost always elusive."

"Is there a specific reason why the FBI is reluctant?"

Simes cleared her throat. "Cases like these are the toughest serial crimes to recognize. And they are even harder to solve, Ms. Crowder. Identifying a link between two or more murders is usually accomplished through either physical evidence or eyewitness identification. In the absence of those things, we depend on pinpointing similarities in circumstances, similarities in victims, or similarity in MO. I'm sure you know all this."

Lauren countered, "And in these cases, you have none of those things. All you have is the fact that these victims—if indeed they are victims—worked together for a few months, what, fifteen years ago?"

"That's right. If Special Agent Custer and I are correct, we are looking at a murderer who has maintained a roster of intended victims for fifteen years. He carefully plots the murder of one victim at a time. He carries out those homicides in such a way as to make the deaths seem to fit in the context of the victim's life. He varies his method each time so that his hand is unrecognizable from case to case, and devises the murders so that the deaths appear accidental, or incidental. He leaves no calling card and takes no trophies. So far, he is demonstrating more patience than Job. And with the exception of the recent murder of Dr. Amy Masters in the tanning bed, from a law-enforcement point of view, he has operated almost invisibly." She paused. "He is going from doctor to doctor, one at a time. He is, in his own ironic way, making rounds."

Lauren softened her voice. I think she wanted Simes to admit how frail this construction was. She asked, "But despite all the hypothesizing in your scenario, you're confident enough of your appraisal that you've come to Colorado to warn Alan that he is a likely next target?"

Custer shrugged and said, " 'Likely' may be a bit strong, ma'am. Fifty-fifty's more accurate."

I wondered if Simes was going to correct him, adjust the odds a little. Eighty-twenty?

Simes caught my eye in the mirror and quickly added, "We *are* here to warn you, Dr. Gregory. That's true. And I hope you pay heed to how clever your adversary is. But we're also here to enlist your help. I've come to believe that to stop this man, to keep him from killing two more people, the first task is, obviously, to identify him and to find him so that we can bring him to the attention of federal and local law enforcement. And there are only two people who can help us identify possible candidates from the Orange Team on Eight East in the autumn of 1982. One is you. The other is Dr. Faire."

My breathing was shallow as I said, "Help you how?"

I turned on my seat to face her. Although I still couldn't feel any confidence that I was seeing the subtle problems with her eye musculature and couldn't discern any oddity in her speech construction, I could see something else. In Simes's face I saw the familiar visage of the visit of the afternoon ghost of fatigue. She looked just as tired as Lauren did.

*Maybe she does have multiple sclerosis.*

Stifling a yawn, Simes said, "We need to identify possible suspects."

"Who are you thinking?"

She turned her head and yawned into her fist. I saw frustration creep into her expression and wondered whether it was with me or with the appearance of the afternoon lethargy. She said, "Who would you guess might be responsible? Who might have the motivation and the patience to plan the murders of the entire professional staff of a specific psychiatric inpatient unit? A group of professionals who were working together for only six months?"

I knew, of course, where she was going. "You're thinking that an ex-patient is doing it."

Simes shrugged, and I detected a shadow of a smile in her thin face. She had managed to get me to say it. As though that could make it my idea. I reminded myself to be careful, that she was probably very good at what she did.

I said, "Why would a patient want us all dead? That doesn't make any sense. And anyway, no patient would have had contact with all of the doctors. Maybe two of us, maybe three. But no way all the docs. Each patient was treated by one resident or one intern. That's all."

"There was no group therapy for patients on the unit? That's hard to believe, Dr. Gregory."

"Okay, you're right. He could have had another contact in group."

"Just one other contact? Not co-therapists running the group?"

She already knew the structure of the team. "Okay, two. There were two group leaders."

"And—correct me if I'm wrong—if a patient was being seen by a psychology intern, that patient would also be seen by a psychiatric resident for medical backup and medication consultation?"

I nodded.

"And in group therapy, a patient could have had contact with the other intern and the other resident? That's possible?"

"Yes."

"And the residents sometimes ordered psychological testing of their own patients. A psychology intern would do that psychological testing, right? Face to face with the resident's patient. That's correct as well?"

The residents certainly did order psych tests. Too many, I thought. I often suspected that the orders were purely hostile, a way of increasing the psychology interns' workload. "Yes. The psychology interns occasionally did psych testing on the psychiatric residents' patients."

"So there are ways that all the residents and interns could be involved with a single patient."

"I suppose it's possible. But what about the two supervisors? What about Dr. Masters and Dr. Oliphant?"

Simes scratched her neck with the fingernails of her left hand and let me answer my own question.

Lauren had been busy doing math. "Wait," she said. "What about the other psychology intern? Nobody's talking about him."

"Her," I said. "Her name was Alix Noel. She died of leukemia a few years after the internship." I snapped my head to face Simes. "You don't suspect . . . ?"

"No, we don't. Not at this time."

I said, "I can't help you with this, Dr. Simes. I can't provide you with patients' names."

"Why is that?"

"You know why that is. It was a long time ago. And the identity of the patients who were on the unit then is protected by privilege."

She sighed through pursed lips to indicate her disappointment. "You and Dr. Faire are potential victims. Likely victims. And you are going to let protocol interfere with helping me identify a killer who may have already killed five of your colleagues."

"Protocol? Confidentiality isn't protocol. And you're talking a purported killer. I'll grant you this: you and Milt have spun a fascinating web here today. But that doesn't mean the spiders are all black widows." As the words exited my mouth I realized I had no idea what they meant. I tried to cover my inanity by making a follow-up statement that I didn't believe. "There's no evidence of a single killer that ties all of this together. Is there?"

She shrugged. "Want to bet your life on that?"

I shrugged.

"Want to bet Dr. Faire's life on that?"

*No, I don't, thank you.*

I asked, "Why don't you go directly to the hospital? Get the patient records from them?"

She raised her chin a smidgen and admitted, "The hospital has already refused to let us see them."

"What about the nursing staff?"

"They don't have the detailed patient knowledge that the interns and residents had. You know that."

"There was a social worker on the unit, too. To assist with the families. Her name was—"

"We're looking for Ms. Pope. We've been unable to locate her. She may be of some help. This could, of course, be a patient's family member we're looking for. You and Sawyer Faire are more likely sources of assistance. You would know the families as well as the patients themselves."

"I assume you're about to make a Tarasoff argument to me. Did you make one to the records people at the hospital?"

"Of course we tried. The director of medical records brought in the university attorney, who quickly pointed out the defects in my argument. As far as we know, no threat has been made to either you or Ms. Faire. Therefore, no potential victim has been identified. Tarasoff, therefore, doesn't apply."

*Tarasoff* v. *California* was a landmark California supreme court decision that mandated that mental health professionals have a "duty to warn" potential victims of violence after a patient has made an "overt threat" against an "identifiable individual."

For some reason I felt a need to win a pyrrhic victory. I pointed out, "Probably doesn't meet the 'overt threat' criterion either." Simes didn't respond, so I continued, "But you think that, unlike the administrators at the hospital, I'll ignore the fact that Tarasoff criteria haven't been reached?"

"To be frank, Dr. Gregory, we think you have a little more motivation to cooperate than they do."

"Staying alive?"

Her eyes were half closed when she said, "Mm-hmm. Staying

alive. Top-notch motivation. That's what my doctorate is in, by the way. Motivational psychology."

"Have you a motive in mind for the killer, Dr. Simes?"

"Sure. You guys ruined his life. So he's ruining yours. Or ending yours, to be more specific. I don't know how you screwed up his life. I don't know why he blames you. But when you're pondering possible motives for an ex-patient to commit these murders, please keep in mind that by definition, this group of possible suspects was not judged to be particularly well adjusted."

I swiveled on my seat and faced Lauren. I was trying to bind my terror but I was certain she could see it in my eyes. I said, "I'd like to go home. I'll think about all this a little better there."

"Hey," Milt said, trying to lighten the mood. "What more could we ask? Let's all sleep on it and talk some more tomorrow."

Simes glared at him. But she looked like she wanted a nap.

# FIVE

Lauren grazed my thigh with her fingers twice as we descended the steep hill out of Silver Plume. She used a comforting tone as she said, "You know, if I were dreaming this, or if this were a movie, Simes would look like Gwyneth Paltrow and Milt would be a hunk. You know, like Harrison Ford or Michael Douglas. And we wouldn't be scared to death." I glanced over and half smiled. It was the best I could do. For a mile or so we nestled our hands together on top of the gearshift lever and didn't talk. We were insulated in our own spaces as we contemplated the unsettling news we'd received from Custer and Simes. I pulled off the highway at Georgetown and stopped at the Total station, where we used the rest rooms and picked out some junk to eat in the car to try to compensate for the burritos we'd never had a chance to touch at lunch.

Lauren was asleep before we reached the cutoff to Winter Park, as I guessed she would be. It was a rare day for Lauren when MS didn't necessitate a nap, and an afternoon as stressful as this one had been was sure to aggravate her fatigue. I wondered if Dr. A. J. Simes was asleep next to Milton Custer in the front seat of their rented Ford Taurus.

I don't recall seeing any more golden leaves as the last of the day's light leaked away in the steep canyons west of Idaho Springs along I-70. At Golden I cut off the freeway and took Highway 93 north toward Boulder. The day was over and the night was moonless and dark as I pushed impatiently past the Rocky Flats Nuclear Weapons Facility, ignoring both the speed limit and the plutonium.

It was only a little more than an hour after leaving Georgetown when I turned onto the dirt lane that led to our Spanish Hills home on the eastern slopes of the Boulder Valley. Nothing had changed.

The city sparkled below and stars dotted the sky like glitter, faintly silhouetting the cutting peaks of the Front Range. The turn onto the lane where we lived felt ordinary. The view to the west was as spectacular as ever.

Our house was still too small and it still needed a coat of paint and a new roof. The windows still needed to be replaced or, at the very least, washed. Emily, our Bouvier, was bounding around in her dog run the way she always did after Lauren and I had been gone for more than an hour, especially when our sojourn took place over the dog's dinner hour.

As I parked the car, I focused all my attention on these constants, reassuring myself that the pattern of stars in the sky above still formed the same reliable constellations they always did. But a shining bright comet, as brilliant as Hale-Bopp, had entered my night sky, too.

It took all my effort not to stare and be blinded by its menace.

Emily had been alone since breakfast so I played with her and gave her some dinner and fresh ice water while Lauren went downstairs to take a bath. Once back inside the house, I flicked on the CD player and punched up some old Bonnie Raitt, raising the volume high enough so that Freebo's bass shook the loose pane of glass on the north side of the dining room. I turned the little black-and-white TV in the kitchen to mute so I could monitor the larger world for further intrusions into my peace at the same time I was caramelizing some onions for a frittata.

It appeared that Channel 4 was doing a piece about the autumn leaves. The story lost a lot of its luster in black-and-white.

Incongruously, I managed to get distracted. Things would feel fine for a few unfettered moments and then I would remember the events of the day and let myself consider the very strong possibility that someone with great cunning and patience wanted to kill me.

Across the small room, an architect's latest renderings for renovating our funky little house were spread out on the kitchen table. One side of the blueprints was held in place by a brass pepper mill, the other by an unopened jar of peanut butter.

The plans as drawn were much more extensive than Lauren and I had originally envisioned when we decided to embark on the often postponed remodeling. Our initial idea had been to enlarge the kitchen by adding a room to the north, and to tuck in a new study and master bath below it. But Lauren's recent history with MS reinforced the need to allow her full mobility on one level of the house, which meant, at the very least, adding a master bedroom and bath on the main, upper, floor. The current house was eight hundred square feet up and four hundred down. The architect's vision almost doubled the main level to accommodate the new spaces.

The whole prospect of turning my house over to a contractor had been overwhelming to me twelve hours earlier. Now, it felt unimaginable. I stepped over to the table, lifted the peanut butter jar and the pepper mill, and watched as the pages rolled together and tumbled to the floor.

It was a meaningless gesture but I derived some satisfaction from it.

I opened a bottle of Riesling and poured two glasses. The frittata was browning up nicely in the oven. I went downstairs to find Lauren. She was curled up on the bed, still in her cherry-red bathrobe, her black hair in short damp ropes, her breathing shallow and peaceful. I carefully laid a down comforter over her, kissed her wet hair, and turned off the light.

Her being asleep, it was okay.

I needed to think this through.

The German wine was crisp and I drank too much, or perhaps ate too little of the frittata, which wasn't anywhere near as good as it had looked while it was cooking. Regardless, I was a little buzzed by the time I carried the portable phone into the living room and punched in the speed dial number for my friend Diane.

I was busy convincing myself that Diane would understand. She'd been on the internship with me. She knew what it was like back then.

She knew Sawyer. She knew me. Diane and I had shared an office suite for years.

I listened to an annoying buzz in my ear for almost ten seconds before it dawned on me that her line was busy.

Years ago, I did a lot of court testimony as a forensic expert. Custody and abuse issues mostly, but I also evaluated accused criminals for some defense attorneys and for a few of the district attorney's offices in the counties surrounding Boulder. During depositions, or in the first few minutes of my cross-examination, I came to quick judgments about the nature of the adversarial attorneys. Occasionally I blew it, but more often than not I was able to make accurate determinations about the strengths that the opposition was bringing to the table.

Unconsciously, I had already gone through the same process with Custer and Simes. My appraisal was that Custer was the slipperier of the two. But Simes would, in the end, be a more difficult adversary.

Custer had spent a long time on the street without many scars from the road. That, in itself, was impressive. He was part good old boy, part small-town minister, and underneath, probably all cop. He deferred easily and naturally to Simes, but I sensed that it was a deference that was voluntary for him and was granted without granting any underlying status.

Simes was chippy. She knew that Custer was granting her latitude, and that irked her. She didn't want latitude; she wanted status. Maybe Lauren was right and Simes did have MS or a similar malady and that's why she'd been forced out of the Bureau on a medical disability. Maybe it had left her bitter. I wasn't sure. But I was leaning toward a conclusion that she had an overdetermined intellectual and professional arrogance that had been cemented by some monumental insecurity that she was struggling to tame as a lion tamer controls a big cat. Perhaps she could get her insecurity to sit down and stop growling, but she knew that at any time it might jump up off its perch and bite her head off.

I wondered, too, about their pairing. How had they ended up together?

Surprisingly, though, I wasn't wondering much about their conclusion regarding a serial killer at work. The pattern they had proposed seemed intuitive, easy to grasp. Once I crossed the bridge that led me from my skepticism, I also had to let go of traditional serial killer images. This wasn't Jeffrey Dahmer or Son of Sam or the Hillside Strangler we were talking about. This wasn't a sexual psychopath. If this guy was real, his closest malevolent relative was the Unabomber.

The person who was stalking me was obsessed. He was patient. He was meticulous. He was dedicated.

And he was a believer.

Add all those things up and what you have, I decided, is a psychological terrorist.

I hit the redial button.

Diane's husband, Raoul, answered the phone. He asked about my day and about the status of the leaves in the high country and we ended up chatting for a few minutes about the origins of the term "Indian summer." I tried to help him put things in a cultural context that would make sense back home in Barcelona. I'm pretty sure I failed. He also informed me that he and Diane were thinking of moving to a house in town. "Winters are too difficult up here. You know?"

A lot of snow fell sometimes in those steep canyons in the Front Range above Boulder, like Lee Hill, where Diane and Raoul had their spacious home. Winter started early and spring started late. And sometimes it seemed that spring was as much about mud as it was about flowers. Summertime could be a major burden, too. Well problems, deer problems, mountain lion worries, black bear worries, wildfire worries, flash flood worries.

I said, "Summers are hard on you guys, too. But the autumns are always special, Raoul."

"That's the truth, my friend. That's the truth. This time of year it's hard to think about leaving, but I think it's time to get urban. Maybe we'll move out east, by you. I like the views out there. But I'm monopolizing you. I assume you phoned to talk to the brilliant one?"

"Is that what she's calling herself now?"

"She guessed right about that thing that happened with Intel. We made a few dollars. Suddenly she's a wizard, you know?"

"I know. She's difficult when she's wrong, and she's impossible when she's right."

"That's my girl. I'll get her. At this moment, the brilliant one is in the kitchen, making a tart of kiwis and berries. I will be courteous until it comes from the oven. Wise, right?"

A minute later I heard a loud buzz in my ear, followed by "Hey, I'm rolling dough, so I have you on the speakerphone. You're going to have to speak as though you actually have a voice."

Diane teased me frequently about the fact that my everyday voice was soft enough to stuff a pillow.

I said, "I'll try." Then I thought better of it. "Listen, this isn't a speakerphone conversation. I'll call you back in a while."

"Oh no you don't. Hold on." The buzz disappeared and was replaced by one of Diane's admonishing tones. "You won't call back. You'll make me suffer wondering what it is I missed."

"What about the tart?"

"The dough's covered. Well?"

"I went to Arnie Dresser's memorial service today, and—"

"You were that close to Arnie?" When she wasn't in therapist mode, Diane's tone couldn't disguise a thing. This particular intonation said, "You shittin' me?"

"No. Not really, we weren't close. Just showing my respect, I guess." I didn't want to go into the whole Christmas card thing. Diane would have a field day with that information.

"You *respected* Arnie Dresser?"

"Diane, please."

"Sorry."

"The services were in Evergreen. Lauren came up with me, got a massage at Tall Grass while I was at the church. After—"

"Was it great? I heard that place is great. Tell her next time I want to go with her. We'll do a girl thing. Get a foot massage. Tea and tootsies for the ladies."

I smiled; I couldn't help it. "Yes, she said the spa was great. After the services, we drove up to the mountains to try to find some leaves. We stopped in Silver Plume for a late lunch."

"Silver Plume has a restaurant?"

"Diane, yes, Silver Plume has a restaurant. Do you really want me to digress again?"

"Sorry."

"And it turns out that two FBI agents followed us all the way from the church to the mountains."

*"What?"*

"Actually these two who walked up to our table in Silver Plume said that they're ex-FBI. They're consultants now. One was an agent in Chicago, the other one is a retired profiler, a Ph.D. in social psychology. Motivation. They said Arnie's mother hired them. Apparently she thinks Arnie's death might not be accidental."

"Wow! A profiler? Really? Like in *Silence of the Lambs*? What did they want from you?"

I wasn't fond of Diane's literary allusion. I asked, "Do you remember Susan Oliphant, from our internship year?"

No hesitation. "Sure. She was the ward chief on Orange. Never had her for supervision myself. But I liked her more than I liked any of her residents." Diane's inpatient rotation had been on the Blue Team.

"They told me she's dead. Did you know that she had died? I didn't know. She died in a private plane crash that they think is suspicious. In the Adirondacks. Quite a few years ago."

"No, I didn't know."

"What about Matt Trimble? Remember him?"

"Yeah, the black resident? I know he died. I liked him, too. He was cute. You ever see his legs? Michelangelo would have liked his legs."

I was tempted to digress myself. When had Diane had a chance to see Matt's legs? I controlled myself. "Wendy Asimoto?"

The air was still for a few seconds. "I don't remember her."

"She quit after her second year. But she was on the Orange Team, too, while I was there. She's another dead second-year resident. She disappeared while working on a cruise ship."

"Since when do cruise ships hire psychiatrists? What was she working on—the Divorce Boat?"

I could tell her mind remained more focused on her piecrust and her kiwis than on my litany of dead mental health professionals. "Diane, are you with me? Are you sensing a pattern here?"

"I'm reminded of that old joke about what do you call three lawyers at the bottom of a lake?"

I'd heard the joke, of course. But I didn't respond. I was speechless for other reasons.

She said, "A good start. Get it?"

"I've heard it."

"Okay, these FBI types think that there may be an evil force at work. Somebody killing psychiatrists."

Diane's reflexive sarcasm was set to "high." I needed to jolt her into focusing her considerable intellect onto what was going on. I said, "Not just psychiatrists, Diane. They told me that there is some doubt whether or not Amy Masters's death was by natural causes, either."

It worked. When Diane finally spoke again, her voice betrayed quivers of shock and hollow rings of sorrow. "Oh my God. Amy? No. Murdered?" Amy Masters had been Diane's outpatient psychotherapy supervisor during our internship year. Diane had thought that Amy walked on water.

"The story they tell certainly makes it sound suspicious. She may have been murdered. These two agents are looking into it."

"What do they mean? How did it happen?"

"You know Amy retired in San Diego? That's where she was from."

"I know. How? We heard she died after an illness. She hadn't been well for a long time. But that's not what happened?"

"She had a skin condition, nothing terminal, that required UV treatment. She used a home tanning bed for the treatments. These two FBI people think someone may have rigged the bed so that once she turned it on and closed it, it wouldn't go off, and she could never open it again."

Diane framed the picture in her mind. She asked, "And it was on the whole time? She was toasted?"

"Yes."

She was quiet. I thought I could hear her switching the phone from one ear to the other. "This is truly awful, truly gross. Has there been anybody else? What's that so far, four?"

"Arnie is number five. What ties everyone together is the Orange Team on Eight East, fall rotation, the year we were there."

I heard her inhale deeply. "Sawyer was there, then, too."

"Yes, she was. They—the agents—haven't talked to her yet. They're on their way to see her."

"But they're worried? About her? Aren't they? And about you? They're worried about both of you."

"Yes. That's why they followed Lauren and me. To tell us that I may be in danger."

"Alan, we're talking Sawyer, here. Right? Brings back a shitload of memories, doesn't it? It's because this involves Sawyer Sackett, that's why you called me tonight, isn't it? Otherwise—I know you— you would have casually mentioned something to me at the office to-morrow. 'Oh, by the way, Diane, the FBI thinks somebody's trying to kill me.' Like that, right?"

"I guess."

"Does Lauren know about you and Sawyer?"

"No. We've never been a couple that does the ex-lover, romantic time travel thing."

"Me and Raoul neither, thank God. I'm not sure I want to know every pillow that pretty head of his has ever been on. I wonder if that's denial. Hell's bells, of course it is. Have you talked with her since, well, you know?"

"You mean Sawyer?"

"Of course I mean Sawyer. Jesus."

"No. I don't even know where she went after she pulled out of the residency. She got married, I guess; one of the agents said her name is now Faire. You haven't talked with her, have you?"

She made a dismissive noise but didn't even bother to answer my question. "So you don't know why she . . . ? You still don't know why . . . ?" Her voice trailed away. Diane was rarely at a loss for words.

"No."

"What's their point? These two agents. Are they going to do anything to protect you?"

"No, that's not it. I think they want to frighten me enough that I'll want to help them put together a patient roster from that fall on the inpatient unit. For possible suspects."

She scoffed, "You can't do that."

"I've been thinking about it, Diane. Ethically, I couldn't do it even if I wanted to. But the reality is that I can't remember the names of patients from that long ago. Maybe two or three have come to mind. That's it. Could you name your patients from your inpatient rotation?"

"Of course, most of them. My own patients, anyway. But then, I'm smarter than you are. Hey, why ex-FBI? Why not the real thing?"

"These two haven't convinced anybody but me that all these deaths are either, A, homicides, or B, connected to one another. The deaths share no similarities. On only one of them has the manner of death been determined to be—"

"Wait, what's 'manner of death'?"

"Determination of agency. You know, like who or what's responsible for someone dying. Suicide, homicide, accident, natural causes. It's a coroner's thing."

"I thought that was cause of death."

"No, cause of death is whatever results in the termination of life: the immediate *how*. Cancer, gunshot wound, asphyxiation, whatever. For example, if cause of death is 'gunshot wound of head,' the manner of death would depend on who pulled the trigger and why. Get it?"

"And what about the brains that get scrambled by the bullet? What's that?"

"The scrambled brains would be the mechanism of death. Okay?" Diane grunted. I decided it meant she got it. "Anyway, on none of the deaths but Matthew's is the manner of death even considered a homicide by the local police agencies. The five people who have died have died in five different locations. And the various things they died of—those are the causes of death—couldn't be more different."

"Other than that all the dead people are professional staff from the Orange Team in the fall of 1982?"

"Right."

"But you believe what they're telling you?"

"I guess I do. The consequences of not believing them are a little intolerable. I realize, though, that I'm looking at these two as adversaries. I'm not sure why that is. It doesn't feel exactly right. I mean, they've gone out of their way to warn me about this guy. Why would I look at them as though they're the enemy?"

Diane was silent. I knew, for her, the act required monumental effort. She wanted me to answer my own question.

"I suppose because they want me to walk them through the psychiatric records of a bunch of innocent people in hopes of finding one guy who's decided to spend his entire life killing off a bunch of doctors."

She said, "When you put it that way, it makes me think that maybe you should narrow your search and start looking only at managed care administrators. They certainly have impeccable motives for wanting to kill off a gaggle of doctors."

I smiled.

She continued, "What does Lauren think?"

"I'm not sure. She was with me the whole time these two FBI types were talking. From her questions, I think she feels this has more merit than she's comfortable with. She fell asleep as soon as we got home."

"Is she okay?"

"Yeah. She's fine. You know how tired she gets. This is routine stuff."

Diane must have heard some defensiveness in my tone. She said, "I have to ask, you know."

"I know."

"How quickly does this guy work? I mean, how imminent is the danger to you and Sawyer?"

"Apparently, he works slowly, methodically. The two deaths that are closest together in time are the most recent ones. Amy Masters and Arnie Dresser."

"And that is what, eight months or so, between those?"

"More or less."

"Do you have a gut feeling about this? Who it might be?"

"No, I'm drawing a blank on that."

"Nobody you guys put on a hold tried to fight you on it?"

"No."

"Did you do any commitments?"

"Personally? Not that I recall. I remember a couple of memorable psychotics from the unit. But no, no big hassles over anything. But then we may not be looking for one of my patients."

"You saw almost everyone in group, though? You heard about everybody in rounds, and met everyone in Community Meetings?"

"Yeah. I'm sure I crossed paths with almost everybody who was admitted for more than a day or two. Over the course of a six-month rotation, that's a lot of patients, though."

"In the morning when you wake up, if you still believe what these FBI agents are telling you, you're going to have to find Sawyer, Alan."

"I know."

"How do you feel about that?" She even used her best shrink-voice to ask the question.

"I'd rather not."

"See her? Or feel?"

"Diane, please."

"Did you ever stop loving her?"

"It was a long time ago."

"Don't distract. It won't work with me."

"She was your friend, too."

"Whatever. It wasn't the same."

"She crushed me, Diane."

"That's not what I asked."

# SIX

Once, from a helicopter that was hovering inside an extinct volcano in Hawaii, I saw a circular rainbow. A full three-hundred-and-sixty-degree orb of color. It was miraculous.

Once, in the desert outside Taos, I saw a boomerang of lights dot a parcel of sky the size of an aircraft carrier and speed away with the velocity of elsewhere. It made no sense.

And once, after a single glance of blond hair and a fleeting look at the barest of profiles, I fell in love with a strange woman from across a crowded room.

I can't explain any of it.

I'd arrived in Denver on July first, 1982, to look for a place to live. Although the psychiatric residents began their rotation at the beginning of July, the psychology interns began a month later, on August first. I landed in town early because I wanted to get settled and to get familiar enough with my new surroundings to try to make some of my anxiety evaporate.

The housing office of the University of Colorado Medical Center was located on the south side of the campus on the first floor of an old brick building. My experience with university housing offices told me that they were of relatively little utility, but two days of classified ad hunting had left me without an apartment, so I stopped by on Friday morning to check the listings of available flats and rooms.

I wasn't feeling hopeful.

Four of five seats were taken at a long table on one side of the housing office. I settled onto the last seat on the right end and reached for the closest card file. I was flipping through it—"apartments to share"—without much interest because I'd already decided I didn't want to deal with a roommate. I clearly recall the instant I felt her presence across the room from me; I was reading a listing that was so full of acronyms I couldn't decipher what any of it was supposed to mean.

I felt her presence physically, as though a cool breeze were brushing over my bare skin. As I looked up to find the source of the sensation, I laid eyes on her. A clerk on the other side of the counter was smiling right at her, saying, "Thank you, Doctor." The woman's blond head was turned away from me, her chin tilted up and slightly thrust forward. She had a small daypack slung casually over her right shoulder. Her shoulders were bare, her skin the color of freshly oiled pine. Her sunny hair was haphazard and short, her neck tan and long. The ring finger of her left hand was naked.

I never saw her eyes that day.

I returned my attention to the index cards long enough to exhale and process my reaction. I felt a smile creep onto my face and thought, *Why not?* I dropped the card file, picked up my appointment book, and faced the room.

She was gone.

The hallway outside the office was empty. At the adjacent staircase, I listened but I couldn't hear a flutter of steps retreating either up or down. Stepping outside, I scanned for her blond head in the distance, and thought for a second that maybe I saw her crossing Eighth Avenue, but then I wasn't sure. I rushed back inside the building and parked myself outside the entrance to the women's rest room for almost five minutes.

She never came out.

The blond woman had disappeared. My feelings about her vaporizing ambushed me. I should have felt, maybe, a sense of lost opportunity, or perhaps a touch of disappointment. But I ended up feeling terribly disconsolate, as though a lover had just told me she really just wanted to be friends.

I assured myself that my overreaction was a sign of my temporary insecurity. I was in a new town, I had an internship coming, and with it new responsibilities, and new opportunities to screw up. I had no apartment and a budget that was about as flexible as my fifth-grade English teacher.

That's all this overreaction was about. That's all it was.

Twice more that day I stood still as a statue, thinking that once again I could feel her nearby. Both times I waited for the invisible breeze to pass again over my exposed flesh.

It never did.

Late that afternoon I chanced onto a small duplex that I liked on Clermont Street only a couple of blocks from where I would be working. The apartment was a one-bedroom that cost fifty dollars more a month than I could afford, but it was available immediately and I wouldn't have to drive to work or extend my motel stay, so I rationalized away the extra expense.

I made a final trip to the housing office to remove my name from the "needs apartment or flat" roster. Of course I checked the room for her. Of course she wasn't there. The only person in the room at the end of the day was a clerk, a rotund man with the blackest hair and darkest eyes I'd ever seen in my life. I offered him a smile and told him he was losing a customer.

"Found a place?"

"Yeah, a duplex on Clermont."

"Congratulations. Name?"

"Gregory, Alan."

He looked up from his pencil. "Which one's first? Gregory, or Alan?"

"Alan. Gregory is my last name."

"Just a second," he said, while he wheezed through his mouth and flipped through his card file. "Here you are. Okay, you're history. Got an address for me? For the university directory?"

I gave him my new address. In my mind, as I did, I saw her daypack hanging from her shoulder. In my mind I remembered that it had an embroidered monogram on it.

SAS.

Once again, I thought, *Why not?*

"I'm looking for someone who was here earlier in the day. A girl, a, a woman. I don't know her name. Her initials are S—A—S. The directory you mentioned? May I take a look at it, see if I can find a match?"

"You know her initials but not her name?" His face turned suspicious. "You're what? A resident?"

"Clinical psychology intern."

"And what? You want to ask her out or something?"

"Exactly. Something."

He shivered a little, as though he couldn't imagine doing what I was doing, looked at me askance, and asked, "Got ID?"

"From the medical school? No, not yet. Psychology interns don't start until August one."

He shrugged as though he had no interest in my romantic explorations. He said, "Don't have the new directory printed yet, but you can see the typewritten list they've sent me so far." He flipped through a thick file. "Here's the S's. Maybe she's in here." He pushed the stapled pages across the counter at me and turned his attention to a big bottle of diet Dr Pepper.

I carried the directory over to the long table against the wall. The dozen or so pages had thirteen entries with the initials S.S. I was a little discouraged. Why couldn't her monogram have read KTZ?

Five of the names belonged to obvious males. I ruled them out. Of the remaining eight names, three were M.D.s and one was a Ph.D. Earlier that day the clerk in the housing office had called the woman "Doctor." I ruled out the names of the four without doctoral degrees.

Three of the remaining names had obviously female first names. The other one's first name was Sawyer.

Sawyer Sackett. Androgynous. Couldn't exclude it.

I turned and asked the clerk if I could use the phone.

He said, "Think I care?" I was pretty sure he would be listening to every word I said.

I called the work number of the first of the Dr. S.S.s, Susan Sipple, Ph.D.

I was connected to a secretary at the School of Pharmacy.

"Hello, I'm trying to reach an old friend who lives in Denver. Her name is Susan Sipple. Is—?"

"Dr. Sipple? Just a moment, please."

"No, no, no. Excuse me. I want to make sure I have the right Susan Sipple. Could you describe her for me?"

"Sure. She has brown hair and beautiful green eyes and—"

"About how old would you say she is?"

"I don't know, maybe forty, forty-five."

"I'm sorry to trouble you, but that's not my friend. Thanks."

I hung up and had roughly the same conversation with a more suspicious someone named Tammy in the School of Nursing regarding a professor named Sandra Sorenson.

My next call let me know that Sylvia Spencer, M.D., of the Department of Pediatrics was now working at St. Jude's in Memphis.

I was left with Sawyer Sackett's name. The directory listing had her living in the six hundred block of Cherry Street. Which happened to be in the general direction that I thought I might have seen the blond head disappear across Eighth Avenue. I called the listed work number for Dr. Sackett.

A voice answered, "Clinic."

Big help there. "Hello, I'm trying to reach a Dr. Sawyer Sackett. The one I'm looking for has a middle initial of A. Is this the right number for her?"

The woman responded sarcastically, "You think we have two Dr. Sawyer Sacketts on staff?"

"I just want to be certain."

"I don't know any doctor's middle initials. I barely remember my brother's middle initial. Do you want an appointment?" Her tone told me she thought I could use one.

"Is Dr. Sackett blond?"

"You want to know Dr. Sackett's hair color?"

"Please. I don't want to bother the doctor if it's not the right one."

Exasperated, the woman said, "Dr. Sackett has blond hair. May I ask what this is about?"

"I'm another trainee."

"Is this about a patient?"

I lied, "Yes."

"Well, she's with a patient. I'll tell her you called. Your name, Doctor?"

The gender finally registered. *She said "her." She said, "She's with a patient."*

Pleased, I said, "No. I'll call her back."

"Suit yourself." She hung up.

I handed the directory back to the clerk in the housing office. He asked, "You find her?"

I nodded. "Think so."

"Good luck," he said.

"Thanks," I said. "My luck wasn't too good this morning, but it's improving, I think."

The next day I moved my few belongings into my new furnished apartment. I was pleased with how bright the apartment was and delighted I could walk to work in two minutes. Twice I took breaks from my chores and made the two-block stroll to Cherry Street where

Dr. Sawyer A. Sackett lived in a prim little Tudor that was camouflaged by junipers.

I didn't see her and didn't know what I would have done if I had.

I spent half of Saturday night drafting a note to her. I spent the other half convincing myself that any self-respecting woman would view my efforts as moronic or dangerous, not romantic.

The next morning I woke up at five, got up at six, gave myself a pep talk, and walked by her house. Instead of using the mail slot, I slipped the note into the Sunday *New York Times* that had been dropped onto her front walk. I hesitated about the placement of the note, finally deciding that the missive should be placed, appropriately, in front of *Week in Review*.

Most of the next week passed and she didn't call. I convinced myself she was involved with someone. Denver was hot and dry, my apartment wasn't air-conditioned, and I was regretting moving to town so long before my internship was set to begin.

I thought about Sawyer Sackett a lot. Way too much. With monumental effort, I forced myself to stop strolling past her house twice daily. I didn't really want to be spotted by her boyfriend or husband.

On Friday afternoon, my phone rang for only the second time since it had been installed. It startled me.

After I said hello, an unfamiliar, sweet female voice asked, "Is this Alan Gregory?"

My mouth turned dry. I managed to say, "Yes."

"Hi." She laughed. "It's not who you're hoping for. My name is Mona. Mona Terwilliger. You don't know me, but I'm a friend of Sawyer Sackett's."

"Oh," I said as casually as I could. "The note."

She laughed again. "Yes, the note."

"When I didn't hear from her I figured she was offended. Or at the very least, uninterested."

"Actually, she thought it was sweet. I think she did, anyway. She showed the note to all her friends. Listen, I'm having a party at my apartment tomorrow night. Just a casual thing, a couple of dozen people. Sawyer thought it might be fun if you came. You interested?"

"Yes. I am. I am interested. She'll be there?"

"She says she will. But you never quite know what Sawyer is going to do. Don't worry, the rest of us are a lot of fun. Especially me."

She gave me directions to a condo near Cheesman Park and said the party started at sunset. "You can come early if you want. The view is special."

Later, after a lot of years on the Front Range in Colorado, the Terwilliger name would feel familiar to me. Mona's family owned a fence company that dominated the industry from Fort Collins to Colorado Springs. On every installation the company placed a burgundy tin plaque that read "A Terwilliger Fence." Some of the considerable family income had been used to buy the tenth-floor condo on Race Street where Mona lived with her younger sister on the east side of Cheesman Park, just a half mile west of the medical center campus.

I had been buzzed into the lobby and took the elevator to the tenth floor. The door to the condo was open, so I walked in. The place was a sea of green. Pine green carpets. Sea green wallpaper. Lime green Formica on the kitchen counters. Appliance green appliances. No one greeted me. Everyone who had arrived before me had assembled on the balcony to watch the blue sky melt into the oranges, reds, and purples of sunset.

Cheesman is one of Denver's three jewel parks. Built on the site of a nineteenth-century cemetery, it is a large urban oasis of grand design that is blessed with stunning views of the mountains. The park was beautiful, but not as beautiful as the sun setting over the distant mountains.

And certainly not as beautiful as Sawyer Sackett.

I was confident I would have radar for Sawyer, and I spotted her immediately. She was leaning back against the railing on the left side of the balcony, her hands behind her, the contours of her chest accentuated by her posture. She was smiling, slyly I thought, talking to two men who looked a little older than me. I hesitated in the dining room while I poured myself a glass of wine. I concluded that the two men with her were physicians, real doctors, and I didn't have a chance with her.

For a few more moments I enjoyed my anonymity, realizing that no one knew who I was. And no one knew what I looked like.

Another minute or so passed before a tall woman with a recent perm and a big smile walked up to me and said, "Hi, I'm Mona."

"Alan Gregory," I said. "Thanks for the invitation."

We shook hands.

She took a half step back and eyed me. Then she moved forward, standing no more than ten inches away, and said, "You're cute. She's gonna like that. I didn't peg you as the shy type, though. Why are you hanging out in here?"

I shrugged. "This is all pretty odd for me, Mona. What I did, I mean, with the note and everything. It's not something I've ever done before. I don't know exactly what to do next."

Mona touched a small pendant that hung at the top of her breasts, exactly where her ample cleavage was exposed. Her fingers lingered on the jewelry until she saw my eyes drop.

Point, Mona.

"You shouldn't be self-conscious about what you did," she said. "I'm sure by now everybody here has heard your story."

I laughed. "And that's supposed to be reassuring?"

"Sure. It was romantic, what you did." She appraised me carefully. "Once they lay their eyes on you and see how cute you are, all the women in the room will wish you had sent them the note. And once they see you with Sawyer, all the men will wish they had written it."

"You're quite sure of yourself aren't you?"

"I have ulterior motives, Alan Gregory. I don't know her well. Sawyer. But what I think is this: She's intrigued by you, by what you did, what you said in your note. And my guess is that she's going to think you're gorgeous. But I think—no, I'm sure—Sawyer ultimately is going to blow you off. And I know that besides her, I'm going to be the sweetest thing you meet at this party."

She touched the pendant again. I tried not to look.

I failed.

Sawyer walked up behind her.

"So are you the one?" she asked, laughing.

"I am."

"You've got balls," she said, "I'll give you that. I'm Sawyer." She stared at me, her eyes never leaving my face.

We shook hands.

I said, "Thanks for taking the chance."

"What chance is that?" she asked.

I started to reply, but she walked past me, poured two inches of Maker's Mark into a wineglass, speared a big shrimp wrapped in prosciutto, and took long strides back out to the balcony.

I didn't say another word to Sawyer that night but watched her from a distance as I made small talk with Mona and a few of the other guests. Darkness descended and smothered the park. Sawyer was never by herself for more than a few seconds. She attracted men the way a salt lick attracts deer. The dance she did as men approached her was unsettling to watch. She flirted, yes, but without any joy. Her eyes were daring but not inviting. Not once did I catch her stealing a surreptitious glimpse my way.

I made a quick judgment that she was wounded and that I was the perfect one to comfort her. I also decided that the other men couldn't see it—her distress. This intuition about her pain was not a benevolent assessment on my part. I met Sawyer at a time in my life when I couldn't imagine someone wanting me for who I was. I entered virtually every relationship endeavoring to decipher what I could provide to cement someone's interest in me.

That evening, it turned out, my radar about Sawyer Sackett was accurate. My assessment, unfortunately, was flawed.

# SEVEN

Sawyer had left the party at Mona's condo early, arm in arm with the pair of men she had been talking with on the balcony. I tried not to let my imagination run away with me and ended up leaving shortly thereafter, first promising to meet Mona for racquetball the following week at someplace she called the DAC.

Mona was a philosophy student at Denver University who had met Sawyer at a lecture they were both attending at the Natural History Museum. Mona turned out to be as bright as she was flirtatious and as much fun as she had advertised. She was also one terrific racquetball player. She took me two out of three games on the air-conditioned courts at the Downtown Athletic Club on the edge of Denver's business district. Mona was an attractive woman and a bold, amusing companion, but nothing was clicking romantically for me with her. I thought she might be disappointed. She said she wasn't. We made plans to have lunch and to play again the following week.

But she refused to let me fish around for information about Sawyer. "I'm not telling you a thing, not that I have much to tell," she said.

"She's hurting about something, isn't she?" I asked.

Mona seemed surprised by my query. "Sawyer?" She narrowed her eyes.

"Yes."

"I don't know about anything."

"But you see it too, don't you?"

She shook her head in a way that suggested that I drop it. "You're on your own with Sawyer, just like me, just like everybody else."

"That means what?"

"She's not an easy woman to be friends with. It means what it means," she said.

In my original note to Sawyer, I'd promised not to call her unless she called me. Technically, she hadn't called me, so I kept my promise and didn't phone her. I'd been tempted, but I hadn't succumbed. I was so asinine with infatuation that I had myself convinced that this was actually my game and that I had written the rules.

The party invitation had raised my hopes that I might hear from her, but by midweek I'd decided that I'd failed the audition that Sawyer had arranged at Mona's soiree. So I was surprised on Thursday morning when I found a note in a pink envelope in the copy of the *Rocky Mountain News* I collected from my front porch. The note summoned me to a restaurant called the Firefly Cafe at four-thirty that afternoon. It was signed with a flourishing S.

I checked for perfume. None.

I arrived at the restaurant right on time.

She seemed relaxed. And happy to see me.

"I got off lucky. My brother's name is Clemens. It's my daddy's thing. He read *Tom Sawyer* to me for the first time when I was only four."

We were sitting on the little patio on the west side of the Firefly, on East Colfax, not too far from the medical center. I was trying to convince myself that this plate of soggy nachos and these cold beers on a muggy July afternoon constituted our first date. But verbalizing that to Sawyer—seeking consensus, as it were—felt both immature and foolish. From the moment I saw the back of her blond head that first time, Sawyer wasn't a "let's be friends" candidate for me.

She had to know that. I hadn't felt so erotically charged since high school.

Other than that half minute in Mona's dining room, I hadn't really been able to look at Sawyer up close When I finally had the chance, I noticed right away that her eyes danced constantly. Save for an occasional blink, they never seemed to narrow at all, instead were always open wide to everything in a way that was not incredulous, not naive, but daring and daunting. And sad, too. Heavy. I continued to feel some assurance that her sadness was going to be my entrée. The temptation I felt was to lock on to her eyes, to submerge myself in them, to count the golden specks that dotted the blue like a design for a flag for some country where I wanted to live forever. But her irises danced so incessantly that I hesitated, perhaps knowing that I was doomed to follow, never to capture them, certainly never to lead.

I know that now. That day, though, I was captivated by the chase. I was inspired by the challenge to find a way to comfort her.

I was stupid.

I said, "Besides Clemens, do you have any other brothers or sisters?"

"You mean Huckleberry and Pudd'n head?"

My face obviously conveyed the fact that I believed her. I didn't consider that she'd probably used this line fifty times previously.

She said, "I'm kidding. It's just me and Clemens."

It would have been a perfect time for her to ask me about my family, or my siblings. Or where I was from. Or what I was doing at the medical school. But she didn't ask. If I had been paying attention, it would have taught me something important about Sawyer. But I wasn't and it didn't.

The ominous gray form of an approaching thunderstorm had been looming to the west from the moment we sat down on the restaurant patio. Presaging its arrival, wind began to gust through the nearby elms and one prodigious blow actually sent a limb flying from a big cottonwood across the street. The wind died after two or three minutes. Seconds later, the first sharp crack of lightning made it difficult for me to think. A second brilliant flash preceded a roaring clap of thunder by only seconds. Hail the size of baby peas began to pelt the canvas awning above our heads.

I stood to move inside.

Sawyer didn't.

"It's just a little thunder," she said as a loud snap that sounded like a tree trunk breaking swallowed her words. I was torn between staying alive and staying in the presence of a captivating woman.

I sat back down.

The rest of the patio patrons had already scurried inside. The hail that was falling now was the size of acorns. I said, "Are you sure you don't want to go inside? We can watch the storm from there."

"People say these things pass in minutes most of the time in Colorado. It's not like back home. This is kind of fun. Let's wait it out. How many people actually get struck by lightning, anyway?"

I was thinking, very few. But I was also assuming that the statistics were heavily skewed by the fact that most people had the good sense to go indoors when lightning was illuminating their faces as brightly as a portrait photographer's flash. I figured that of the remaining few—

those who insisted on remaining outside during thunderstorms—a reasonably high percentage was actually struck by lightning.

I also figured that, by and large, this natural selection tended to improve the gene pool.

I said, "You're sure?"

She parted her lips slightly and smiled a shy smile. Right then, for the first time, I began to believe my premonition that Sawyer had secrets. Immediately, I filed the thought away in a place that would make the insight difficult to retrieve.

Behind her in the parking lot, the hail was soon deep enough to shovel.

The thunderstorm was being pushed east by powerful winds aloft and it passed, thankfully, in minutes. The sky cleared first to the west. The hail turned quickly to rain and moments after that the brash sun was beating down on the ice balls that had accumulated in the parking lot. Sawyer had finished her beer. Our waitress finally decided it was safe to venture back out to the patio, and Sawyer called her over and ordered a Maker's Mark neat.

She said, "I've been curious about something. What made you think I wasn't going to read your note and decide you were some psycho?"

"I thought about it. I figured that I didn't have much to lose. Anyway, most psychos, especially your successful ones, don't leave their names and phone numbers with their intended victims."

"You think you know a lot about psychos?"

"Yeah. I think I do. Enough anyway. I'm starting my internship in clinical psychology at the hospital in a couple of weeks. I'll probably learn a little more about psychos there."

I thought I saw her jaw muscles tense. She didn't say anything.

"After I decided to write the note, I assumed you would be either offended or intrigued by it. That you would decide that my gesture had been either terribly romantic or appallingly desperate."

"Which was it?"

I decided to be honest. "A little of both, probably."

She seemed to take a moment to process that. "Why? Why was it so important that you meet me?"

"I wasn't sure at first. I felt kind of crazy when you seemed to disappear from that office before I had a chance to, to . . ."

"Try to pick me up?"

"Introduce myself. I still don't know what it was. You ever see somebody across a room and feel that your life is never going to be the same again? You ever have a day when gravity seemed to totally disappear?"

Sawyer didn't answer. Her eyes skipped away. For ten seconds or so she wasn't even in my vicinity.

The waitress delivered Sawyer's whiskey. She took a long pull, downing half of it, and said, "And?"

With that solitary word, her voice was suddenly devoid of melody. I was surprised to feel a hard surface in there, somewhere. It was as though I'd bitten into the seed of a fresh cherry that I thought had already been pitted. What did I do? I spit it out and moved on.

"Well, that was what it was like when I saw you in the housing office that first time. And, believe me, I barely saw you. I didn't see your eyes that day. I didn't see you smile." I leaned across the table in my best imitation of a flirtatious pose. "I saw your neck and your hair and the tip of your nose and your lips, maybe your lips. I saw the skin on your shoulders. I didn't even know then that you're as"—I swallowed—"as lovely as you are. I just knew that I had to try and find out exactly what had happened between us in that room."

"And what might happen later? Right? You wanted to know that, too?"

"Yes. I wanted to know that, too."

She brought her hands together as though entering into a prayer. She raised them in front of her mouth. "Nothing happened between us that day, you know. I didn't even know you were there."

"When a radio station sends out a signal, it doesn't know who's listening. Far as I can tell, that doesn't detract from the message."

She ignored my analogy and said, "So what happens now, Alan Gregory, note writer?"

"This." I waved my hand over the table as though I were a magician who could make cocktails and tortilla chips and frijoles disappear. "I get to begin the wonderful process of getting to know you."

"Do you?"

I sat back confidently. "Sure. I'll show you. Watch. What kind of doctor are you, Sawyer?"

She shook her head and pushed her chair back from the table. "No. That's not the way to know me. You'll have to find another way. You showed me you have some imagination. Really, that's why I'm here right now. You're going to have to use that imagination if you want to know me." I remember thinking that she looked playful. Though, in retrospect, I'm more certain she was looking smug.

"I can find out. I could call your work number again and ask what kind of clinic it is you work at. That's pretty easy."

"Knowing that won't tell you much."

"If I press Mona enough, she'll talk."

"Mona doesn't know."

"Doesn't know where you work?"

"Don't be silly."

"Doesn't know what, then?"

She nodded approvingly at my question. She said, "There you go." Abruptly, she leaned forward, her breasts crushed against the edge of the table, her eyes doing a private waltz just for me. "Do you want to sleep with me?"

I thought about it for the time that it took my eyes to blink. I said, "Yes, Sawyer, I do."

"Good," she said. "Now I know more than you do."

If I were truly insightful I would have recognized that Sawyer had just used sex to create a dangerous fjord between us.

I wasn't. I didn't.

# EIGHT

Three relatively rare events occurred the morning after Arnie Dresser's funeral.

Lauren woke before I did.

I was hungover on good Riesling.

And I learned that the FBI was coming over for dinner.

I couldn't do anything about the first two. The last one, though, I thought I could at least influence. I could call the motel where Simes and Custer were staying and cancel the repast that Lauren had arranged while I slept in. Canceling, however, felt more petulant than prudent. My other option, I decided, was to go along for the ride and bring an objective observer to the table.

Lauren was rushing out the door for an early appointment at the courthouse but said she had no objection to the second option, so I phoned Sam Purdy before I left for my office. Sam, a detective with the Boulder Police Department, had been my friend for a long time. If you asked, he would be happy to assert that he had been on a Christmas visit to his family in Minnesota the night JonBenet Ramsey was killed, was never assigned to the case, and insisted he was "untainted" by the resulting fallout.

I explained to Sam about Arnie Dresser's funeral, the weird lunch in Silver Plume, and the two ex–FBI agents. He said it sounded like so much bullshit to him and asked me for the ex-agents' names. I told him. Then, with increased interest evident in his voice, he asked what we were planning on having for dinner. I told him I didn't know for sure but it would probably be Thai something.

"Tie something what?"

"Thai, as in Thailand. Asian food."

"Is it like Chinese?"

"No, different. Thailand, Sam. Curries, coconut milk, basil and cilantro, fish sauce. There are other Asian cuisines besides Chinese."

"Doesn't mean I want to know about them. Boulder has restaurants from countries that aren't even recognized by the UN, that serve food that isn't sold in any grocery store I've ever been in. I can't keep up, so I don't even try. I like Italian and Mexican. That's adventurous enough for me."

"I think you'll like dinner. Almost for sure, we'll have salad and chicken and noodles and rice."

His voice took on a skeptical shadow. "But it's not going to be anything like my mom's chicken and rice. Right?"

"Maybe a little spicier. Your mom's not Thai, is she?" I knew well that Sam's parents and their parents and probably *their* parents were from Minnesota's Iron Range.

"My mom thinks people from Milwaukee are foreigners."

"Don't worry, Sam, you'll like dinner. Can you do seven o'clock?"

"Yeah. Can I bring anything?"

"Just your skepticism."

"I never leave home without it. So, tell me, worldly one, do people from Thailand drink beer?"

"Absolutely. I'll get some Singha. Thai beer. Has jasmine in it."

He made some noise I interpreted as relating mild disgust. "Listen, one more thing."

"Yes?"

"Actually, two more things. Buy some Bud on your way home. And do I have to use chopsticks? I hate chopsticks."

"They're optional."

He said, *"Bueno."*


I was glad that my Monday schedule was busy. I had eight patients to see between nine-thirty and six. I didn't want a lot of free time to think about Custer and Simes, methodical murderers, and Sawyer Sackett. A full day of other people's problems was a perfect prescription for distraction from my own paranoia.

Diane's day was as frantic as my own, but she found a few minutes to come down the hall into my office for a brief visit after lunch.

"Well?"

Once Diane was in the loop, she acted as though she were the proprietress of the loop. No one else in the loop was permitted to be reticent. I knew all those rules, so I filled her in on the latest developments.

"Lauren and I are having the FBI over for dinner tonight. I've invited Sam to sit in."

"Really—a local cop and the feds at the same table. You're trying to see if oil and water really do mix?"

"I just want his take on things. He's smart. I'm kind of hoping he'll convince me that they're blowing smoke."

She seemed amused at my capacity for denial. "You thought any more about Sawyer since last night?"

I lied. I said, "No. Diane, that was a long time ago."

"So was the Holocaust. But for some reason I just can't understand, the Jews are still suspicious. Come on, certain things are hard to forget, Alan. And most of the time, they really shouldn't be forgotten."

I didn't respond immediately.

"Do I need to expound on my analogy? How about black America, lynching, and the KKK? Does that ring a bell?"

"You're being a little over-the-top, Diane. I haven't forgotten about Sawyer, but I'm not terribly eager to revisit all that, either."

"You know, until lately with Lauren, I've never considered your relationships with women to be the most mature corner of your personality, but whatever it was that went on between you and Sawyer was an absolute nadir, and certainly not a paradigm of mental health. Yours or anyone else's."

"Including hers?"

"Including hers. Maybe especially hers. You two were a pair back then. Oh my. Jesus."

"Thanks for your confidence. But I'd be lying if I told you I wasn't at least a little bit afraid it would happen all over again. That I'll see her once, and . . ."

"And, let me make a guess. Your testicles will once again swell until they're bigger than your brain?"

"Something like that."

She smiled at some idea she was having before she said, "You know, Alan, maybe . . . maybe Sawyer's gotten fat and ugly. Maybe there really is a god or a god-ette whose sole role in heaven is to exact retribution from beautiful blondes with great bodies."

"She was your friend, Diane."

"And what? I can't be jealous of my friends? What planet do you live on?"

"When I find her—*if* I decide I need to find her—how about this? I'll bring her over to your house to meet Raoul. He'll—"

"No. No, no, no. You keep Sawyer away from Raoul, Alan. The man is *weak*, I tell you, he's weak. Sawyer's a natural blonde and Raoul's currently on this Marilyn Monroe nostalgia kick that worries me no end. You haven't been over to the house for a while, but we now have Marilyn coasters in our living room and there are old *Life* magazines everywhere."

I tried to picture it. "Marilyn Monroe tchotchkes along with that big Neiman of the World Cup over the sofa? Oooh, that must be a good look. Now there's a decorator's dream."

She laughed. "I'm embarrassed to admit that Raoul bought yet another masterpiece by the God, LeRoy. This one's bullfighting, for heaven's sake. The World Cup is now in our bedroom." She glanced at her watch and warned, "Don't say what you're thinking. Listen, I have a patient to see, one whose denial, by the way, doesn't even begin to approach yours. We'll continue this later."

I checked the little light on the wall of my office that indicated that my next patient had arrived as well. "My next patient's here, too. See you."

Lauren made it home from the DA's office before I made it home from my practice. She'd been busy; she had a green papaya salad chilling in the refrigerator along with a huge platter of chicken breasts marinating in something that was redolent of fish sauce and hot chili oil and cilantro. I was left with the easy work: getting the jasmine rice started in the rice cooker and throwing together some sesame noodles with green onions.

The day had been warm, almost hot, and I suspected we would be eating out on the deck to take advantage of the evening breezes. But Lauren had stacked plates and napkins and glassware and chopsticks and silverware on top of the pool table that consumed the center of the dining room, which indicated to me that we were going to be unfolding our dining room table from its home against the east wall and dining inside.

As we struggled to move the heavy fruitwood table out into the room, I asked her why we were eating in instead of out.

"I told you. Dr. Simes has MS. She'll be more comfortable in here with the air conditioning."

"You're that sure she has MS?"

"Yes." With that she started downstairs to rest before everyone arrived. She was gripping the handrail tightly as she descended the stairs. I pulled the rice cooker from the pantry and started water boiling for the noodles.

As I hoped he would, Sam arrived before Simes and Custer. He'd driven his own car, an old fire-red Jeep Cherokee, but he was still in his work clothes, which always seemed to include a plaid shirt and pastel tie. This sport coat was green corduroy. I wasn't sure I'd seen it before and wondered if he'd actually bought new clothing.

Under his right arm, he was carrying his very own six-pack of Bud.

Emily, our Bouvier, greeted him like an old friend. Few visitors were spared Emily's usually ferocious welcome, but she'd liked Sam right from the first time they'd met.

I thanked him for coming over and took his six-pack to the refrigerator. Since one of my responsibilities in life is expanding Sam Purdy's narrow cultural horizons, I poured him a Singha instead of a Budweiser and carried it to him in the living room, where he was sitting on the sofa, talking on the telephone. He pointed at his pager and I handed him the beer.

I prayed he wasn't going to get called away before he had a chance to size up Simes and Custer for me.

After a minute or so he hung up and took a long draw on the beer. His mustache was dotted with foam. "My page? Lucy's warning me about a call. There's a house with a suspicious smell in North Boulder. She's getting a warrant so she can go in. She'll call if it turns out to be what it smells like."

"You'll have to go?"

"Yeah, I'll have to go." He held up the beer glass and smiled at me warmly. "Now, why don't you stop messing with me and go get me a Budweiser. This tastes like somebody dropped a gardenia in it." Sam's wife, Sherry, was a florist. Generally, he knew his flowers. Not this time.

"Jasmine," I corrected.

He laughed. "You're confusing me with someone who gives a shit."

Lauren came upstairs and embraced Sam, who pecked a kiss to

her cheek. She looked lovely in a long rayon skirt and a small black knit shell that was supported by straps thinner than the tender noodles I was cooking in the kitchen. But Lauren also looked tired.

"You nap?" I asked.

She shook her head. "I'm way too nervous about all this."

I was surprised. "You haven't seemed nervous."

Sam interrupted, "Hey, you guys? By the way, I checked these two out. The ex-agents? They're legit, apparently. He's a—"

Emily's feet scraped the wood floor like a dog in a Disney cartoon and she mouthed two crisp barks. Her pads finally found purchase on the oak and she ran at warp speed to the front door. I told her, "Quiet," and she barked louder.

I repeated myself. So did she.

Lauren watched my charade with the dog and then, in a firm voice, said, "Emily, sit." Emily did.

"Down." Emily lowered herself to her haunches.

Reluctantly, I thought.

"Stay." Emily stayed.

Lauren looked at me and admonished, "You have to work with her if you want her to listen to you."

Sam found Lauren's comment particularly amusing.

Outside, two car doors slammed. A moment later the doorbell rang and Emily whimpered and stared plaintively at Lauren. But she stayed down.

The ex-agents stood at the front door looking like a couple that had been married a long time. Milt towered over A.J. but he seemed to soften his contours so as not to overwhelm her petite form. She was dressed in a yellow pantsuit. Actually, it could better be described as a YELLOW pantsuit. It would have had to pale considerably to approach the brilliance of a ripe banana. The woman liked color.

The two ex-FBI agents were, appropriately, more interested in Sam Purdy and Emily than they were in Lauren and me. I wondered if Simes and Custer accurately assessed that the one who wasn't growling at them was actually the more dangerous of the two strangers.

Lauren said, "Hello. Please come in. Please. That's Emily—she's more harmless than she looks. And this is Sam Purdy. Sam, Dr. A. J. Simes and Milt Custer. Formerly of the FBI."

Sam said, "Hello, Doctor. Mr. Custer." Everyone shook hands with exaggerated civility.

Simes looked at me and asked, "Is Mr. Purdy your attorney?"

I was about to ask if I needed one but was distracted by Milt. He was shaking his head as though he'd already discerned Sam's role.

Sam laughed out loud and said, "Hardly. It's 'Detective' Purdy. I'm a friend of these two. They asked me to listen in, if you don't mind. I'm just here to provide another point of view."

"You are a detective with . . . ?" The question came from Simes. She didn't say whether or not she minded that Sam was present. I guessed that she did.

"Boulder Police Department."

She nodded to herself and responded crisply, "I'm not sure I understand. None of what we are discussing with Dr. Gregory and Ms. Crowder has taken place in Boulder, Detective."

Sam shrugged, said, "Yet," and he let the word hang like a belch at the dinner table. "Regardless, I'm not here in a capacity that's any more official than yours, Dr. Simes."

With that little volley complete, Lauren suggested we all move into the living room.

Milt was wearing a sport coat, which he shed as we moved to the other side of the house. Beneath the jacket was a polo shirt that had a little logo on it and the word "Augusta." I guessed golf. Milt helped Simes onto a chair before filling one end of the sofa. Sam took the other end. Other than the size of their heads—Sam's was too big, Milt's too small—the two men were about the same size and shape.

Lauren offered wine and everyone declined. Beer? No. Anything? No.

Lauren asked Simes whether the temperature in the house was okay, whether she was comfortable.

Simes eyed her curiously, took a deep breath, and said, "Fine. Thank you for so much for asking. And it's so kind of you to offer to feed us after the bad news we've brought your way."

Milt said, "Yes. Kind."

"If what you suspect turns out to be true," Lauren replied, "you're the ones doing us a kindness. Anyway, our brief history together in restaurants has not been particularly auspicious."

Milt laughed generously and said, "I'm glad you see it that way. It's been my experience that in these circumstances, people often prefer just to shoot the messenger and be done with it."

Sam reached forward and scooped up a handful of cashews. He

began popping the nuts into his mouth one at a time. I found the activity distracting and assumed that was his intent.

I faced Simes and said, "On the phone this morning, you suggested to Lauren that you would have some new information for us tonight. Maybe we should get right to it, clear the air before we eat. This, I don't know—whole situation—is leaving us a little on the anxious side."

Sam smacked his lips loudly and sucked some nut fragments from a crevice near his upper molars. Everyone looked his way. "Hey, before we move on to new information, let's review what we know already. I'm in a secondhand position here, and I don't like being in a secondhand position." He faced Milt. "You ever like getting briefed by the briefees and not the briefers? Me neither. I prefer to hear it from the guy who develops it. The source."

Milt seemed to be taking Sam's measure but didn't hesitate long before he launched into a synopsized rendition of the tale of the dead doctors. I didn't like hearing the parable the second time any more than I had liked hearing it the first. When Custer finally finished, I expected some questions for him from Sam. Instead, Sam leaned forward and grabbed some more cashews.

Simes raised her chin toward the western sky, smiled at Lauren, and said, "This view up here is lovely. Just lovely. I don't know how you ever manage to leave to go to work."

The sun had disappeared behind the Flatirons and the splintered high clouds above the mountains were lighting up in pastels. The dark canyons—Boulder and Sunshine—knifed back into the Front Range like jutting black holes. It was lovely. I have never grown tired of it.

Sam said, "Yeah, it's gorgeous. But that's not all you got, right?" His tone was matter-of-fact, not at all confrontational.

Simes spun on him. Her eyes blinked a split second apart. She parted her lips slightly but thought better of speaking.

Sam continued, "If that's all you have, you would have spent some more time developing things before scaring the shit out of my friends. If this guy strikes the way you say he does, he strikes slowly. Time isn't the issue. Still, you follow Alan and Lauren from a funeral and spring this on them in a cafe over brunch? And you don't breathe a word to the local law enforcement authorities who might have an interest in protecting them?"

A. J. Simes seemed more irritated than defensive as she said, "We've discussed these deaths with each of the local jurisdictions where they have occurred, Detective. We've—"

"Call me Sam."

"Sam. We've met with varying degrees of, shall I say, skepticism, about our suggestion that each of the deaths may have been a homicide. We've met with even greater skepticism about our hypothesis that a single offender may be responsible for the entire series of murders. It's my opinion that the evidence becomes compelling only when it is viewed in its entirety."

Sam popped another nut. "But, by now, I'm sure you've run your suspicions by your colleagues in Virginia. My guess is that they've had the opportunity to view this in its entirety, right? Why didn't they bite?"

"Perhaps," Simes said, "they have had the benefit of sufficient experience . . ." She paused and seemed to be choosing her words with increased care. ". . . with similar crimes to recognize the inherent difficulty in connecting evidence from disparate homicides with varying MOs over extended time periods."

Sam ignored the professional dig, sat all the way back against the cushions of the sofa, shook his head, and turned to face me. "They've decided there is something you don't need to know, Alan. I'll be damned if I know why that is. Hey, is anybody hungry here but me?"

I was growing more anxious rather than less. Sam's presence was supposed to make me feel better, not worse. I reminded myself that I trusted his instincts. I said, "Chicken will take about five minutes on the grill, Sam."

"Why don't you go out there and get it started? I'm starving. Sherry says I shouldn't eat too many nuts."

I waited a moment to see if either Simes or Custer was more easily provoked than I expected—they weren't—so I stood and walked to the kitchen. Lauren and I exchanged puzzled glances. I grabbed the marinated chicken from the refrigerator and carried it outside to the grill, while she began to arrange the rice and the cold food on the table. In the middle, she placed a big galvanized bucket full of beer bottles and ice. Loudly, Sam reminded her not to forget to include Budweiser. I heard him belatedly call out, "Please."

Inside, the three cops started talking. From my vantage on the deck, I couldn't hear them. Simes had moved from her chair to a perch on the edge of the coffee table. Each was leaning forward into their tight huddle. I guessed they were engaging in conspiratorial whispers abut what it was safe to reveal to me and Lauren regarding the man who might be plotting to kill me.

The fact that I wasn't included pissed me off.

# NINE

The chicken charred up beautifully, and as I carried the platter inside the aromas of jasmine and fish sauce and sesame mingled together in a wonderful Southeast Asian symphony.

I said, "Dinner is served."

Small plates of green papaya salad graced each place setting. Beers were passed around.

I drank. I picked at the papaya salad, one of my absolutely favorite foods in the world. I drank some more beer. Other than the sounds of mastication, the table was silent. I couldn't stand it.

"Okay, tell me," I said. "What the hell's going on?"

Sam smiled at the other guests and asked, "May I?"

Simes nodded.

Sam wolfed down the rest of his salad and placed his fork on the plate. I was glad he liked the salad. I had no plans to tell him that the main ingredient was under-ripe papaya.

"They didn't want to tell you yet, Alan. They would have preferred to wait, develop things a little more. Problem is that without help from one of the doctors who was there in 1982, this investigation could stall out like Sherry's minivan trying to climb up to the Eisenhower Tunnel."

"Go on."

"The social worker you used to work with—" He stopped himself and looked across the table at Simes and Custer. "Here I am doing it. One of you should tell this story."

Milt checked with Simes. She closed her eyes regally.

"The social worker on Eight East was a woman named Lorna Pope. You remember her?"

I nodded. I remembered Lorna well. The social worker was responsible for the initial family evaluations for patients admitted to the unit. All the interns and residents worked closely with her. I said, "Lorna was an interesting woman. She was dating a Denver Bronco at the time I was on the unit. A placekicker, I think. She was a sports nut; a great skier. Had a healthy disdain for the residents and interns. Refused to date them. If I remember correctly, her father was a doctor. She used to say that although they might need one in an operating room, she couldn't imagine needing one in a bedroom. Something like that. That was Lorna."

Milt said, "Once again, I'm impressed. I hope you remember as much about all the patients as you do about the staff."

"Please don't tell me that Lorna is dead, too."

Simes spoke. "We don't know. Her family doesn't know. She . . . um, she disappeared."

"Disappeared?"

"She went on holiday to New Zealand with her new husband. Her third. They vanished."

*Third?* "Vanished?"

"Went out one day sightseeing, never came back to their hotel. Their car was discovered in a church parking lot on the other side of the island a week later. Nobody remembers seeing them."

I swallowed some beer. "Passports?"

"In the safe in their hotel room."

"Are they presumed dead?"

"No. It hasn't been long enough yet. They're listed by the U.S. embassy as missing."

I was almost numb. I was actually thinking, *So what? What's one more?* It was easier to think of her as number six, not as Lorna. I'd liked her a lot. Lusted after her a little. To myself, as much as anyone, I said, "I'm so sorry." Like Simes and Custer, I was assuming she was dead.

Sam said, "Tell them when, Milt. They need to hear when."

Milt said, "Yeah. That's what's important. When. See, she disappeared in July. July of this year."

The meaning of those words didn't immediately register. Then I heard Lauren gasp.

I asked, "July? Two months ago? This July?"

Simes replied. "Yes, this July. Please keep in mind that we haven't been able to pin this one down at all. We're discussing events in New

Zealand, not New Jersey. It could all be coincidence. We don't know."

I stated the obvious. "But if it was him, things are compressing. Timewise. Things are compressing, aren't they? That's the concern?"

Simes answered. "If it was him. Yes. If it was him in New Zealand, we're looking at a rapid, rapid acceleration in his activities. If it was him, it means that he has committed three murders in a little over seven months."

Milt said, "Four. Don't forget Lorna's husband."

"That's right. Four."

"So he could be stalking me right now. Or Sawyer. He could be planning to kill one of us tomorrow?"

Simes said, "He could. I don't think so. But, yes. He could."

I disagreed with her earlier contention. "You do want to alarm me. You don't only want to warn me, you also want to scare me into helping you."

Incongruously, Simes said, "This is fabulous chicken, isn't it, Milt? But the answer to your question is yes. The danger to you may be more acute than we revealed yesterday. We wanted to develop the New Zealand situation a little better before we discussed it with you. And the need for your assistance is, well, crucial. But I think we made that clear yesterday."

I touched my lips with my tongue. Gazed over at Lauren. I could see the fear in her eyes. It was the same wariness I saw in her violet eyes when she had the first inkling of a fresh exacerbation of multiple sclerosis, during those hours when she didn't know if she was going to be merely annoyed by the progression of her disease, or debilitated by it.

I said, "If you're looking for the names of patients, you'll need to look elsewhere. As you well know, Dr. Simes, ethically I can't start giving you the names of patients from back then. Nearly all of them are absolutely innocent. At this point in time, none of us can predict the impact on their lives of revealing their identities and their histories."

Milt said, "But we may be able to predict the impact of not revealing their identities."

Simes said, "I promise we will be discreet."

"That doesn't cut it. You know that."

She closed her eyes for twice the length of a blink. Opening them, she said, "Dr. Faire said you would say that."

With the mention of Sawyer's name, I suddenly felt a tightness in my chest and abdomen. I was afraid I was going to burp.

She said, "Dr. Faire, that's right."

"I thought you said you hadn't found her." I told myself I hadn't stammered, but I had.

"That's not quite correct. We haven't seen her. But we spoke with her this morning by telephone and will meet with her soon. She's implied that she wouldn't cooperate unless you did."

The jasmine rice in my mouth seemed to congeal into a plug of gelatin the size of a golf ball.

I couldn't swallow. Lauren asked me if I was all right. Her tone told me she already knew the answer to her own question.

No more than a minute later, Sam's partner, Lucy, paged him to let him know that the search warrant had arrived and that the smell coming from the old house on North Broadway was, indeed, exactly what everyone's nose suspected it was. He excused himself to investigate the suspicious death.

But before Sam could throw his napkin onto the table, Simes announced that they, too, should be going.

Within ninety seconds, the table was empty of guests, the lane was empty of cars, and Lauren and I were alone.

I told her I would clean up the kitchen.

She told me she would take Emily out for a few minutes and then get ready for bed.

Twenty minutes later I walked downstairs, quietly peed and brushed my teeth, took off all my clothes, and climbed into bed. The west windows were cracked open and the dry, cool autumn air left the room perfect for sleeping. I curled onto my side and scrunched the pillow under my ear. I was trying hard not to think about Lorna, and was failing.

I was trying hard not to think about Sawyer. I was failing at that, too.

I was trying hard not to think about someone trying to kill me.

I was failing at that, too.

I just wanted to sleep.

Beside me, Lauren's breathing was slow and sang the soothing rhythm of slumber. I tried to match the cadence, to be captured by whatever peacefulness she'd found. But my mind quickly crossed the Pacific, and I was wondering what part of New Zealand Lorna had been visiting when Lauren's voice startled me. She said, "You awake, babe?"

"Yeah," I said, trying to sound sleepy.

"This is really scary, Alan."

"Yeah, it sure is. I don't know what to do next. My first impulse is to call the cops, but the cops and FBI are the ones who called me."

"You have to consider helping them, Custer and Simes. You know that. This guy, he could try to kill you tomorrow."

"I know. I checked all the doors twice before I came down here. I think we'd better get an alarm installed."

"This killer, this guy, he doesn't seem like the kind of guy who is stopped by alarms."

"Still. Can't hurt."

"I have a better idea. Let's move back to my place on the Hill. I'm between tenants. There are more neighbors in town than here. That house already has an alarm installed."

"And do what here?"

"Cancel our weekend in Taos. Use the time to move out. Turn this place over to the contractor. Get the remodeling over with. This isn't the time to go away. Not with all this hanging over our heads."

"I thought going away seemed like a great idea."

"Not under the circumstances, sweets. It didn't work for your friend Lorna. It didn't work for Arnie Dresser. We have a few little problems to solve first."

I rolled toward her. Her body was cool and soft. We struggled for a moment to find a position that was right.

"You're probably right. I'm not sure how relaxing it would be to get away, given everything that's going on."

"I wouldn't relax."

"You're really ready to do the remodeling?"

"Yes. I'm tired of talking about it. We can put this off forever arguing about where to put the recessed lighting and what kind of trim to put around the windows. It's time to just do it. And I know I'll feel safer living in town until all this . . . other stuff settles. Out here it's just Adrienne and us."

She kissed me on the top of my chest, just below my collarbone. She said, "Alan?"

"Yes."

"I think maybe you should tell me about Sawyer."

"About Sawyer?" I said, startled.

"Well, yes," she said. "About you and Sawyer. What went on. Whatever went on?"

"You're sure?"

"No. I'm not at all sure. Asking makes me terribly anxious. But I think I need to know."

"Yes. I suppose I should tell you."

# TEN

**B**y the time August first finally arrived and my inpatient rotation on Eight East was due to start, I'd managed to learn a few facts about Sawyer. I had called back the clinic where she worked and discovered that it was an outpatient psychiatry clinic, the exact same clinic where I, too, would soon begin seeing outpatients.

I wasn't too surprised to discover that Sawyer Sackett, M.D., was a psychiatric resident. And since she'd been on campus longer than I had, I guessed that she was a second-year psychiatric resident. Mona Terwilliger had reluctantly confided that Sawyer had attended medical schools in Florida, and that her family still lived in Virginia, where she grew up.

I have to admit that I was disappointed to learn that Sawyer was doing her training in psychiatry. I'd pinned my hopes on pediatrics. Or family practice. Or maybe one of the surgical sub-specialties, like OB-GYN. Although I had not actually spent any time praying that she wasn't training to be a psychiatrist, I wasn't looking forward to sharing turf with her.

What else did I know about Sawyer by the time my internship started?

Not much.

I wondered about that a lot. Worried about it some. But soon the pressures of my training took almost all of my attention.

The day my initial rotations were assigned and I knew that my first inpatient rotation was going to be adult Orange Team, I phoned Sawyer at home and asked her nonchalantly—I thought—what inpatient unit she worked on.

"Eight East," she'd said. That meant the adult unit. The adolescent unit was on the seventh floor.

"Blue Team or Orange Team?" I asked.

"Orange," she said.

"Me, too," I said. "I just received my assignments. This should be weird. You'll probably be doing my medical backups."

"Probably," she said. I was trying hard to appear nonchalant. Sawyer was clearly succeeding.

The first meeting I attended on Eight East was rounds. The meeting was held in a conference area adjacent to Dr. Susan Oliphant's office. Susan was the ward chief for the Orange Team.

In addition to the ward chief, daily rounds were attended by all the residents and interns, by the chief psychologist—my supervisor, Dr. Amy Masters—by the team social worker, Lorna Pope, by the head nurse, Kheri Link, and by any of her staff who were free to attend.

Unlike the residents who are making rounds on some of the medical floors of the hospital, the trainees in inpatient psychiatry don't traipse from room to room carrying charts and asking patients questions about their condition before being grilled by their attending. Instead, we sat in an oblong circle and reviewed history and therapeutic progress, medication status, community and group process, and family meeting information on all the current patients. I also quickly perceived that we were to try to act as though we were brilliant and compassionate enough to have a prayer of helping the troubled people down the hall.

The ward chief and the chief psychologist had roles different from those of the trainees. Their job was to let us know when we were being brilliant and compassionate, and, conversely, when we were being ignorant and condescending. Occasionally they managed to accomplish this with an amount of humor and kindness that left our swollen egos unlanced. Usually they didn't bother being so delicate.

That first day in rounds, I found myself sitting in an uncomfortable sled chair between Arnold Dresser, M.D., and Wendy Asimoto, M.D., two of the three residents on the team. Amy Masters was across the room whispering something to Lorna Pope, the unit social worker.

Wendy and Arnie were leaning together in front of me, comparing notes about a seminar they had to attend that afternoon on the new

CPT-IV codes. I didn't have a clue what a CPT-IV code was, but didn't want to embarrass myself by inquiring. I was sure it was something I should have already learned in graduate school and that my ignorance about it would soon cause me great humiliation.

A minute or so later, Sawyer entered the room along with a tall, thin woman with a narrow face, sandy hair, and brilliant green eyes. I tried to act unconcerned at Sawyer's arrival; I even pretended to be part of the tête-à-tête about CPT-IV codes that was occurring over my knees.

While Sawyer took a chair almost directly across from me, the woman who was with her walked across the room, fumbled with some mail that had been piled on the desk, and dropped her briefcase unceremoniously in the middle of the blotter. Her back turned to the room, she asked, "Who are we missing?"

Dr. Masters said, "It appears we're dragging one of my interns, Susan."

Arnie smirked. "He's probably lost."

Lorna added, "Susan, nursing is just finishing up a restraint. I don't think they'll be on time either."

"Who's being restrained?" Arnie asked, nervously, I thought. I didn't know him at all then, but later I would realize that Arnie's question was precipitated not by curiosity but by worry that one of his own patients was misbehaving, which Arnie would definitely consider a black mark on his record.

Lorna said, "Sorry, Arnie, I'm afraid it's Travis again. He was threatening one of the nurses this time, had her cornered in the corridor by his room. Thought she was that Frieda person he's always talking about. He was using his toothbrush, you know, holding it like a knife in front of him. He doesn't go down easily—it was a tough restraint. He's really strong."

Before Arnie could say anything Susan Oliphant asked, "How much Navane is he on, Arnie?"

Arnie said, "I upped it to forty."

"Is it enough?"

Arnie opened his mouth. For a second, nothing came out. He said, "Given the recent history, I think—"

Susan pressed him. "Is it the right drug?"

Wendy Asimoto said, "What about Thorazine or Haldol?"

I looked around the room at the psychiatric residents. At Sawyer. At the other two. They had started on July first, so they had been on the unit a month already. A month was a lifetime in a training rotation.

They were experts.

The lexicon of medical school training said that students first see a procedure, then they do the procedure, and then they teach the procedure. Well, Sawyer and her two comrades, Arnie and Wendy, had already seen one. They had already done one. And now, with fresh blood on board—the other intern and me—they were going to be eager to teach one.

Susan Oliphant looked over her shoulder and scanned the room. "We'll deal with Travis in a few minutes. Let's get started somewhere while we're waiting for the other intern." She looked at me with mock seriousness before saying, "I don't like waiting for people, do I, Wendy?"

Wendy smiled her reply with her dark eyes. She said, "No, waiting is not your best thing, Dr. Oliphant."

Susan continued to fumble with her mail while she looked over her left shoulder at me.

"You must be Dr. Gregory. Right?"

I hesitated. I thought this might be a trick question. Technically, I wasn't a doctor, yet. I wouldn't receive my Ph.D. until after I completed my internship. "I'm Alan Gregory," I said, sidestepping the question.

The obfuscation didn't work with Susan Oliphant. She said, "Here, on Orange Team, you're 'Dr.' Gregory. You get a temporary promotion, get to wear the figurative white lab coat. Patients in the hospital don't want to think students are providing their care. They want to believe that we're the best, most experienced damn healers who have ever set foot on this planet. They want to be treated by doctors. So for a few special months, you get a dispensation. You're Dr. Alan Gregory. Everyone, meet Dr. Gregory and introduce yourselves."

Arnie Dresser made a noise I couldn't quite interpret, but I would have guessed it had some familial resemblance to contempt.

Susan didn't turn around. She'd heard the noise too, apparently. She said, "Arnie, the best therapists are those who don't believe they are God's gift. Dr. Gregory, introduce yourself to the team."

The room took on the silence of a chapel.

I wasn't ready.

I had prepared myself for this day for four years of graduate school. Classes, seminars, patients, supervision. Reading. God, so much reading.

I had prepared myself for this moment since four-thirty that morning. I was wearing my best gabardine trousers and a wool sport coat I considered stylish but not too trendy. My shirt was white, my tie brand-new, my shoes shined. My socks were interesting.

The reality was, though, that despite all my preparation, I felt like a kid. An impostor. I was still occasionally carded in bars. If I didn't look old enough to drink, how could I possibly be old enough to provide adequate treatment to a schizophrenic?

I felt confident enough with outpatients in clinic settings. I felt that my training had left me with many of the skills necessary to help the ambulatory distressed. Psychologists are trained to use the power of the therapeutic relationship to effect change in their patients. Often, in outpatient settings, those skills sufficed.

Psychiatrists, too, were trained in the art of psychotherapy. But, in addition, psychiatrists possess medical degrees and, thus, the knowledge and authority to assess medical problems and the privilege to prescribe drugs.

Clinical psychologists have a powerful arsenal that consists of one weapon: psychotherapy. The temptation, of course, when one is carrying nothing but a hammer is to treat everything as though it is a nail.

And I feared that my hammer, no matter how skillfully I wielded it, wouldn't work here. Not with this unit full of crazies.

Amy Masters caught my eye, and with an expectant smile, nodded at me to proceed. Her face was as nonjudgmental as my grandmother's had always been. Dr. Masters had been here a long time, had seen a lot of interns come and go. She had seen the self-doubt, maybe felt some of it herself at one time. She had supervised the doubters.

And she was telling me to go on.

"Good morning," I said. "My name is Alan Gregory. I'm a new clinical psychology intern and I'm delighted to be here." Right then, having spoken my first untruth, I made the mistake of looking toward Sawyer.

She was smiling into her lap.

I was rescued by the rushed entrance of the head nurse and two members of her staff along with the other psychology intern, a young woman I'd met briefly at orientation earlier that week. Her name escaped me.

She said, "Sorry I'm late. I couldn't get my key to work."

A trace of annoyance in her tone, Susan Oliphant asked, "Why didn't you just get buzzed in?"

The intern said, "I did. Problem was I was trying to open the wrong door. I got myself buzzed into the adolescent unit. All the patients there were *younger* than me. And I thought I had been assigned to a unit where the patients were supposed to be older than the doctors. Hi, everybody, I'm Alix Noel." She smiled a brilliant smile.

Amy Masters said, "Well, Alix, you're Dr. Noel now."

Alix looked at me, then at Amy Masters. She said, "Cool. I'm a doctor now? Does that mean I skip the rest of my internship? Even better, can I, like, totally forget my dissertation?"

Everyone laughed.

Of course, none of us knew then that that day was the first time that all of the dead doctors would be together in one room.

The introductions lasted about five minutes. I was looking forward to Sawyer's, hoping I might learn something. I didn't. She stated her name, said that she was a second-year resident and had a particular interest in forensic psychiatry. She smiled at Alix, didn't once look at me.

Since neither Alix nor I had yet picked up any patients, the residents took turns reviewing their current cases. They did the reviews from scratch for our benefit. History, medical history, reasons for admission, precipitating events, treatment course, meds. Everything.

Sawyer went first.

She was dressed in a tartan skirt that reached the middle of her calves and a long-sleeved white blouse that an hour earlier I would have bet good money wasn't even part of her wardrobe. The social bluster and gaminess that was so much of what I had seen on our quasi-date during the hailstorm was absent. She was precise, professional, perhaps even a little shy. She presented her four cases with confidence and a trace of humor. She accepted compliments and criticism from Dr. Oliphant and from her peers with the same grace. Perhaps my judgments were colored by my lust, but I thought she showed surprising sensitivity in presenting her two active cases, a young first-break schizophrenic and a severely depressed woman in her forties. Dr. Oliphant was pressing for electroshock; Sawyer wanted more time to work with her patient in psychotherapy.

I realized for the first time that the Sawyer I'd met at Mona's party, the Sawyer I'd risked life and limb to have cocktails with in a thunderstorm, had either been putting on an act for me or was putting one on right then. I also realized that I didn't know which was true.

That should have warned me off.

It didn't.

It intrigued me.

# ELEVEN

**A**fter rounds, Alix and I were introduced to the rest of the Orange Team staff and to the other therapists who worked on the unit. Alix rushed off to an outpatient clinic appointment. I had a few minutes to kill before I was due to meet my new supervisor in the psych ER, so I loitered outside the nursing station hoping to learn when I would be assigned my first patient.

Sawyer walked up to me and introduced herself as though we had never met. She called herself "Dr. Sackett."

I got the message.

She suggested that since we would be working together, we get to know each other better, and wondered if I was free for a late lunch at the Campus Lounge on Eighth Avenue. I said I thought I could do that.

At one-thirty she was waiting on the sidewalk across the street from the campus. In my brief stay in Denver, I'd already learned that the tacky restaurant and adjoining bar were a hangout for the medical school staff and students. I waved and she smiled in a way that made her mouth widen without the corners rising at all and said, "Hi. I forgot my appointment book. I'm lost without it. Totally lost. Why don't you come to my house instead? I'll fix a sandwich or something. Do you mind? Please."

"Not at all," I said. The levity in her mood surprised me. We hadn't been together since that night at the Firefly during the thunderstorm. I expected more of the same gaminess.

But it was absent. I considered it propitious.

\*   \*   \*

We walked in silence for the block and a half to her home. With her arms crossed she held a small satchel against her chest like a schoolgirl. At her house, I followed her down a narrow brick walkway to the backyard. We climbed three rickety stairs and entered a tiny kitchen through a battered screened-in porch.

"Why don't you check the fridge, see if there's anything you want. I'm going to get out of this skirt. It's way too hot for today." She disappeared into another part of the house.

I hung my jacket over a kitchen chair and ignored the refrigerator, which was humming loudly. I used a glass from the dish drain to get myself a drink of water from a big glass bottle that was resting on a ceramic crock across the small room. The water tasted great, so I got another, and sat on one of the kitchen chairs.

Sawyer walked back in after two or three minutes. She had changed her outfit and was wearing a short-sleeved floral blouse, a light-weight khaki skirt, modest pumps, and panty hose.

She looked preppy.

I was surprised.

In her hands she held the day's mail. She smiled at me before starting to flip through it, quickly setting aside everything but an envelope constructed of good blue paper. "Excuse me," she said, slitting the letter open.

She turned her back to me, crossed the room to the sink, and started to read. I couldn't be sure, but I thought I heard a whimper or moan escape her lips. She flipped the single page over and began to read the back. Her posture weakened and she rested her elbows on the sink. Her left hand sifted through her hair.

After a minute or so she stuffed the letter back in the envelope and hiked out of the room as though I weren't there.

I was alone for a good five minutes before she returned. She stood in the doorway.

"Bad news?" I asked. "The letter."

She lowered her eyes and moved her head in a way that wasn't yes, wasn't no.

"Want to talk about it?"

She swallowed. "It's nothing. The past."

"Didn't look like it was nothing." Impulsively, I grabbed her hand as she walked by me.

When she didn't pull away from me, I reeled her closer. She hesitated slightly, but not enough to warn me off. I continued to pull until she was facing me, not more than a foot from the chair. "What is it? What upset you?" I said.

I reached for her other hand. She tensed. I could feel her weight pull against me. For a second I thought she intended to move away, but she relaxed, stepped forward, raised her left leg, and straddled me on the chair, lowering herself gingerly to my lap.

She said, "It's nothing, really. Forget it. You're feeling a little more bold today than you were the last time around, aren't you?"

"This particular situation doesn't feel as dangerous as thunder and lightning and hailstones."

Her voice was heavy. She said, "You never know."

"Maybe you haven't heard? I'm a doctor now. Like you. So I get to be righteous. Cocky."

Sawyer said, "Cocky?" and laughed softly.

The sound was pleasant and lifted my spirits. I tried to recall whether or not I had ever heard her laugh before.

She said, "You think I'm arrogant, huh?" Her tone wasn't defensive. Maybe a little mocking, I thought, as though I had badly misjudged her character with an ill-chosen adjective.

"You're something, Sawyer. I'm not sure what."

With her left hand she reached forward and grabbed the knot on my tie. With her right, she gripped the fabric below. I thought she was going to choke me. Playfully, of course. But instead she began to release the pressure, loosen the knot, and fumble with the button beneath.

I also felt her weight shift on my lap as the soft mass of her spread legs seemed to find cushion against my groin. Her breasts were only inches away from my mouth.

"Don't let the residents on the unit fool you. We were all terrified a month ago, too. A month from now you'll begin to feel invincible, too. The terror was unwarranted then, the invincibility isn't warranted now."

"I figured all that. But the bravado is . . . is so refined, it's scary."

"We have seminars on conceit in medical school. It's a required course." With these few words, I thought she wiggled just the slightest bit. But it could have been my imagination.

My tie was loose, open all the way to the first button on my shirt.

She had been looking past me while we talked. I captured her hands and slowly released them before I reached up and touched the sides of her face with my fingers. I was particularly gentle as I touched her, as though I were lifting the petal of a rose. Her cheeks were soft to my touch, all powder and tender flesh. I traced an invisible line to her jawbones and lifted her face until I captured her gaze in mine.

She permitted me to examine her eyes for only a moment and then she looked away. I moved my face and met her eyes again, maneuvering as delicately as I could, the same way I might try to corral a ladybug.

For an instant, Sawyer tried to fly away from me again, but then, to my surprise, she let me lock onto her dancing eyes for two or three seconds. The light sparkled off her speckled irises like confetti falling to the ground.

Then she was gone.

I felt even more pressure in my groin. This time, I was rather certain it had nothing to do with Sawyer shifting her weight.

She flitted a glance my way and said, "You know, you're making me uncomfortable."

"Ditto." I squirmed on the chair.

She laughed again. "That's not what I mean."

I leaned forward and kissed her on the chin. Held the position long enough to begin to memorize the sensation of her skin on my lips.

Abruptly, she turned her face away from mine, but I persisted and I moved my mouth lower and kissed her on the side of the neck below her ear. My lips were parted and as I touched her with my tongue I tasted salt and inhaled the perfumes of flowers and spice.

In the midst of a protracted exhale, she said, "I have a two-thirty patient in the clinic."

I slid my fingers up and into her hair. It was as soft as down.

I said, "I guess that means we had better hurry."

With my hands on the back of her head, I pulled her face to mine and moved my lips to her mouth. For the first time, we kissed. I tasted her breath and our tongues jousted in the neutral territory between our teeth. After three tantalizing parries, our tongues finally touched and I felt a jolt shoot down my limbs that was pure electricity.

My hands tugged at the back of her blouse and her hands were on my belt and seconds later, it seemed, her weight was off my lap and she was sliding my trousers to my knees. I slid my hand up her thigh and discovered the panty hose were only thigh-high stockings.

This outfit wasn't as preppy as it had looked. Briefly I was aware that this seduction wasn't really mine. The thought vaporized.

She reached between her legs, took me in her right hand, and lowered herself back onto me in one uninterrupted thrust. I felt the moisture and the warmth and the tightness and for an instant felt nothing else in the world. I couldn't smell, I couldn't taste, I didn't know if I was breathing. The rest of the world was gone.

She pressed down harder, until I could feel the flesh outside of her as well as in. I pulled her body to me with both my hands and tried to raise myself off the chair to meet her.

She whispered, "Don't move." Although the words were hushed, the message was not.

For a moment we were still.

Then I moved.

Her voice sad and desperate, her lips behind my ear, she said, "Please. Please. Don't move. Please. Oh, don't move."

She gasped.

I wondered if she was about to cry.

Into her hair, I asked, "What would you like, Sawyer?"

I felt her fingernails hard and sharp in the flesh of my shoulder. She answered, "Just fill me, okay? Just . . . fill me."

The next morning, Sawyer wasn't at rounds. I wondered about her absence until I was distracted by the news that I would be getting my first inpatient that afternoon, a transfer from the crisis unit at the mental health center in Jefferson County.

An hour later, I attended my first Orange Team Community Meeting—Sawyer was there this time—and for the first time I met Arnie Dresser's already legendary patient, Travis, who was fresh out of eight hours in restraints and sixteen more in an isolation room.

Travis was an incredibly skinny man. I guessed he stood around six-two yet weighed no more than one-forty. His blond hair was almost white. He was balding on the crown and his hair had receded so dramatically on his temples that what remained resembled a platinum horseshoe that someone had hammered into place high on his pale forehead. While the other patients and the staff members were finding seats, Travis began to slowly shake his head back and forth while his mouth continuously formed the word "no." The elderly woman next to him stared at him with a dull expression on her face, the whole time making the hand and face motions necessary to apply and reapply lipstick.

Of course, her hand was empty.

A quick assessment of the room found no one else who looked more disturbed than anyone I'd seen on my last crosstown trip on a city bus.

Dr. Oliphant said, "Travis?" in a soft voice. "Would you prefer to be excused from this meeting today?"

He didn't hear her, or he ignored her. I couldn't tell.

More sharply, she repeated his name. "Travis."

He looked up at her, still mouthing the word "no."

"Would you prefer to be excused from this meeting today? Perhaps try again next time when you're feeling a little more in control?"

Travis raised his chin and tightened the tendons in his neck. He said, "I'm sitting here. I'm sitting. I'm minding my own business. My business." He stared at the ceiling tiles for a moment before lowering his chin to his chest.

Dr. Oliphant said, "The Community Meeting isn't about your own business, Travis. Are you prepared to pay attention to what's going on and to participate with the community this morning? Or would you prefer some more time alone? It's just fine if that's what you need." Her words were soft, an invitation to withdraw, not a threat of exclusion.

I was impressed at her manner.

Travis looked up once again, this time appearing startled that the room was full of people. He said, "I . . . I . . . I'll do whatever it takes, I says. I'll do whatever it takes to makes . . . takes to makes . . . the nurses think me of a gentleman. Kind man." The form of his words was as mangled as their meaning, as though he were trying to enunciate through a mouthful of yogurt. I remembered all the Navane he was on and assumed the pharmaceuticals were the culprit. Travis was taking enough antipsychotics to stop a marauding bull elephant. Certainly enough to slur his speech.

Dr. Oliphant said, "That's fine. You're welcome to be with us, then." With Susan's approval, Travis was going to be permitted to participate in the Community Meeting.

Attention turned next to Olivia, the woman with the imaginary lipstick. A nurse asked her to finish her makeup after the meeting. With an audible huff, Olivia dropped her hands to her lap.

I spent most of the rest of that first Community Meeting wondering whether my first admissions would have any familial resemblance to Travis or Olivia, or whether they would resemble one of the other members of the community. The other patients who lined the dayroom that morning appeared sadder than most, angrier than most, or more medicated than most. But I could see myself sitting down with any of them for psychotherapy.

But if my first patient was as psychotic as Travis or Olivia, I figured I might just as well pack up my briefcase and go home.

I had my pants around my ankles and a length of toilet paper in my hand when I heard the commotion that started on the unit around ten-thirty that morning. The staff rest room was at the end of a narrow hall near the occupational therapy room. I finished up on the toilet, washed my hands, and gingerly made my way back down the hall toward the unit to see what the heck was going on.

Halfway back to the unit corridor, I stopped in my tracks as I heard Arnie Dresser insist loudly that Travis put down the knife.

"Now, Travis. Now. Put down the knife. Put it down." I thought Arnie sounded much more frightened than authoritative.

And what the hell was Travis doing with a knife? I figured it must be one of the little flimsy plastic jobs that dietary served with patients' meals.

I continued down the hall to the spot where it intersected with the corridor, poked my head around the corner, and tried to see what Travis was doing. Twenty feet away, his back to me, Travis was holding someone hostage in front of him. Ten or twelve feet beyond Travis, a few doctors and nurses were grouped together trying to coax Travis to release the knife. Behind them, even farther down the corridor, the rest of the staff were busy hustling patients out of their rooms toward the dayroom, away from danger.

From where I was standing, I could only see the back of Travis's head. The skin on his neck was bright red, so brilliantly red it looked sunburned.

Travis cried out, "Frieda. Frieda. Frieda."

With the plaintive voice of a street beggar, Arnie said, "That's not Frieda with you, Travis. That's Dr. Sackett. You don't want to hurt her. And you don't want to hurt Frieda. Put down the knife."

*Sawyer?*

I looked again and saw some wisps of blond hair protruding above Travis's right shoulder.

He had Sawyer. And he had a knife.

All of Travis's attention was directed at the posse in front of him. Either he had already decided that no one was behind him or in his current mental condition he was incapable of considering the possibility that danger might come from some other direction.

I backed into the hallway and considered my options. A fire exit behind me would sound an immediate alarm if I used it to go for help. But Travis's reaction to an alarm was unpredictable, and that unpredictability would present an unacceptable risk to Sawyer's well-being.

I assumed someone had already alerted hospital security anyway.

Okay, I said to myself, what do you know about Travis that might help?

What I knew was that Travis was psychotic. His diagnosis: paranoid schizophrenia. DSM III 295.33. Which meant Travis had a thought disorder, which meant I didn't have a clue about the current reality he might be inhabiting. I could safely assume that it wasn't the same one where I was hanging out.

That Travis had confused Sawyer with Frieda told me he was delusional. At rounds that morning, Arnie had reported that in addition to his ongoing delusions about Frieda, Travis had reported hearing auditory command hallucinations—voices telling him that he should accomplish various acts, usually not things like jogging or playing Scrabble. Travis had assured Arnie that he was ignoring the voices.

I also knew that Travis was taking forty of Navane.

All in all, this wasn't a pretty picture.

One of the hallmarks of severe psychosis is thought disorder. One of the trademark symptoms of thought disorder is ambivalence, the inability to choose between alternative actions. I wondered if I could use that to my advantage, to briefly paralyze Travis with ambivalence by giving him an alternative to ponder, anything other than slicing Sawyer with the knife he was holding to her body.

That might give us enough time to disarm him and restrain him.

Or I could do nothing. Allow the people with experience to handle this.

The doing-nothing alternative was winning my favor when Wendy Asimoto screamed, "He cut her! Oh, no, Travis. She's bleeding. Don't do that, don't do that. Oh, God."

Arnie's voice shook. "Travis, please put down the knife."

Travis said, "Blood."

I waited to hear Sawyer cry out.

But the next voice I heard was Wendy's. She screamed, "No, Travis, no, not again! NO! WHERE IS SECURITY?"

Then I heard Sawyer whimper and Travis say, "Frieda, Frieda."

Without further contemplation, I left the sanctuary of the hallway and walked briskly down the corridor as silently as I could and tapped Travis on the shoulder. I adopted a tone that was as close as I could manage to the one I had heard Susan Oliphant use that morning in Community Meeting.

I said, "Excuse me. Travis?"

He turned his head just a little.

"Travis? It's Dr. Gregory."

He turned a little more. I could see the knife now. It was a little red Swiss Army pocketknife, the kind so small you can hang it from a key chain. The shiny steel blade was stained with Sawyer's blood.

I said, "Would you like to go back to your room now? It's a little safer in there, don't you think? I think that might be a good idea."

He seemed to be considering my presence, or my words. Or something. He dropped his hand—the one that was holding the knife—until it came to rest at least six inches away from Sawyer's flesh. Doing so exposed his chest and upper body to me for an instant.

I didn't hesitate. I drove my shoulder into the small opening as hard as I could, lifting his thin frame away from Sawyer and off the floor. He came down hard against the wall, looking stunned.

Seconds later, he was being restrained by the staff.

Immediately after tackling Travis, I had grabbed Sawyer. She felt heavy in my arms as I eased her down to the floor. Her blood was running down my fingers, down my arms, and she felt to me as though she were melting into a puddle on the floor.

When I looked up again, the staff had Travis in restraint, preparing to move him toward the isolation room.

He was moaning, yelling about his shoulder hurting, asking about Frieda.


Wendy Asimoto was a board-certified internist who was retraining in psychiatry. She took over Sawyer's care.

Sawyer's two wounds were to the side of her neck, and in the seconds that it took Wendy to get pressure bandages over the lacerations, they appeared, to my untrained eye, to be superficial.

But nobody wanted to take any chances, and the moment a gurney arrived on the scene Sawyer was helped onto it and transported with haste toward the elevators and the emergency room.

Wendy Asimoto went with her.

Arnie Dresser wanted to talk to me in the nursing station.

With a somber look on his face, he said, "Thank you so much. I can't believe what you did out there. I'm so grateful. I don't know what I would have done if Travis had, you know—"

I stopped him and tried to be reassuring. "Arnie, Travis is your patient, not your kid. You're not responsible for what he was doing out there." The reality was that if one of my first patients had attacked another doctor, I would have been so humiliated I would probably have resigned my internship.

Arnie wasn't listening. "Maybe Travis needs different meds. Maybe more isolation. I don't know. I don't know."

"Susan approved his being back on the ward. We can all learn something from this, right?"

"Whatever I can do to repay you. Anything. You let me know. You'll let me know, right?"

I didn't have the courage to tell him that I hadn't been brave for him. Or for Travis. I'd done it for Sawyer.

I had my back slapped by a lot of people in the next few minutes. I was told I was a hero. I was hoping my accidental gallantry would earn me some credits I could cash in when I screwed up, which I knew was inevitable. The whole time I was fighting the urge to run downstairs to the ER to check on Sawyer.

# TWELVE

Lauren was cool to me the morning after our Thai dinner party.

The night before, after I'd begun to tell her about Sawyer, we'd lain in bed and she'd posed a few questions that I knew she didn't really want to ask and that she knew I didn't really want to answer.

The first came after a pregnant moment when she kissed me on one of my nipples. She asked, "Did you love her? Sawyer?"

Of course, I'd considered the question many times on my own over the years. Had I loved Sawyer? The answer was that I adored Sawyer Sackett so long before I discovered whether or not she was deserving of my adoration that I probably never got enough emotional distance to love her in any manner that approached what I'd developed with Lauren.

I didn't want to admit to my wife that my adoration of another woman had been so blinding, though, so I said, "I wasn't real mature back then. I thought I loved her. Knowing what I know now, I know I didn't really. It's not anything like what we have."

I had only the dimmest hopes that those words would be palliative. So I wasn't surprised that they weren't.

She was slowly tracing her index finger up and around one of my breasts and then under and around the other. And then again. I realized she was forming the mathematical symbol for infinity.

She asked, "Do you still have feelings for her?"

"Feelings? No. I don't even know her now. I probably didn't even really know her then."

Lauren shifted her weight, and I could smell the conditioner she used in her hair. I inhaled more deeply, hoping for perfume. No.

"But there's something there, isn't there? She could still push your buttons, couldn't she? If you saw her tomorrow, it would still stir something up?"

With my fingernails, I began scratching long gentle lines from the crack in her ass to her shoulder blades. This particular caress usually made her purr.

Not this time.

I said, "You want me to be honest?"

She laughed and the ironic timbre of her chuckle chilled us both.

"No," she said, slapping me semi-seriously on my hip. "I want you to be reassuring. What do I want? I want to hear that I'm your one and only. I want to know that you haven't decided you made a mistake by marrying a woman with multiple sclerosis. That's what I want to hear. But . . . if this woman, this Sawyer, could still get you going, even after all these years, I should probably know that before we start looking for her."

"You are my one and only. And, no, I don't want to see her, Lauren. I've never been tempted to find her."

"You're not curious?"

"Let's just say that a long time ago, I came to the conclusion that she's not good for me."

She didn't miss a beat before she said, "Or for us, right?"

Which, of course, was where the money was.

"You're good for me, Lauren. I love you. Deeply. I'd marry you again tomorrow."

"You're sweet, and you always know the right things to say," she said, but she didn't sound reassured. She grew quiet for a moment, and her breathing changed. When she spoke again, her tone had taken on a rougher burr. "You know, it's a nightmare that this guy is out there, somewhere, threatening your life. It's a double nightmare that indirectly he's also threatening ours, our life together. I'm not sure we have any true choices in this. We either wait for him to try to kill you and hope he fails for the first time in his illustrious career as a serial killer. Or you have to go see your old lover Sawyer in order to try to save your life."

She paused and added, "Even if it kills us."

At breakfast she said she had decided that she wanted to build the garage we'd been so ambivalent about adding to the remodeling project. She was tired of climbing into a hot car in the summer and didn't want to face another winter of frosted windshields. She asked me if I'd think about it.

I had to admit her timing was pretty good. If she had asked me to add an Olympic swimming pool and an indoor tennis court to the remodeling project, I probably would have assented.

Right after I rinsed our breakfast dishes, I phoned the architect and ordered working drawings of the garage.

We signed an AIA agreement with our eager contractor over the lunch hour. He had informed us that he was primed to get going, and apparently he wasn't kidding. The ink on the contract wasn't yet dry when he said he wanted to begin demolition on Thursday morning.

We said we'd be out of the house by Friday afternoon. Disappointed, he asked if he could demo over the weekend.

Lauren looked at me and shrugged her shoulders. I raised my eyebrows in a "why not" gesture.

The contractor's name was Dresden Lamb. We'd heard from friends who used him that he always scheduled scuba diving holidays at the end of his big construction projects. It gave him a selfish reason to meet deadlines, a fact I appreciated.

I said, "After we're out, Dresden, you can tear it apart whenever you're ready."

He said, "Good. First, I have to get the new windows ordered. That's always a problem, getting the windows delivered on time. Then I'll get the demo boys in here. This project's gonna cook. You watch. We'll have your home torn apart in no time at all."

The metaphor wasn't lost on either of us. But neither of us mentioned that he might have plenty of help with that endeavor.

I finally reached Sam Purdy later that afternoon. He was still wrapped up in the investigation of the unexplained death on North Broadway, but he didn't think it was going anywhere important.

He said, "Sorry I had to rush away last night. Everyone's noses told them this might be a homicide."

"It isn't?"

"No. Looks more like the guy who lived in the house had a heart attack and fell down some stairs. Broke his neck. He probably just died and then stewed for a few days until he smelled bad enough to bother the neighbors. Happens sometimes."

I needed to get him talking about Custer and Simes. "Sam, what's your impression about last night? How nervous should I be?"

"About all those dead doctors you worked with? Very nervous. I think this is serious stuff. They've been thoughtful, those two ex-agents. This isn't some bullshit story they're cooking up."

It was exactly what I expected to hear from him. But by nature I'm such an optimistic guy that I was holding out hope that I'd be surprised.

In my best sardonic voice, I said, "Great. That's not what I wanted you to say, you know. I don't have a clue what to do next."

Sam laughed and said, "You know what her name is? Simes, I mean? Do you know what A.J. stands for?"

*What?*

"No, Sam. What does A.J. stand for?"

"Ambrosia June. Her name is Ambrosia June Simes. How's that for a moniker? I'd call myself A.J., too, if my parents planted that one on me."

I didn't want to talk about Simes's unfortunate name. "Sam, what am I going to do?"

He sighed. "I don't know, Alan. I'm thinking on it. And I'll talk to some people I know. The whole thing is too goofy for words. With the way this guy works, I mean, I've been thinking that staying out of his way is like trying to protect yourself from mosquitoes in Minnesota in July. No matter how many precautions you take, one of them always seems to get your blood."

*Huh?* "This guy's a little more dangerous than a mosquito, Sam."

"True, but what do you do? Get a bodyguard? Start living on the run like a Colombian drug lord? Change your identity? How do you defend yourself against someone who is so clever at finding ways to kill people?"

"Sam, you're my expert here. You're the one who's supposed to be supplying the answers, not the questions."

"Sorry. Listen, I'm working on it, okay? For now, I'm going to ask the sheriff to spend a little more time patrolling Spanish Hills. You guys have an alarm system, don't you?"

I thought, *As though that's going to be much of a deterrent.*

"We're moving into town this week, Sam. To Lauren's old house on the Hill—you were there a long time ago; I don't know if you remember. We've been planning to do some remodeling for a while and we decided to go ahead and get it done. Lauren says she'll feel safer in town. But yes, her house has an alarm."

"Is it monitored?"

"Yes."

"Remind me, what's the address?"

I told him.

"When are you moving?"

"This week. Should be in there by Friday."

"Well, don't be surprised if you see a lot of patrol cars in your neighborhood. By the way, does Lauren still carry?"

"What?"

"That little Glock? Have you forgotten about the Glock?"

How could I forget about the damn Glock? "As far as I know, she still has it, Sam. But I don't think she actually carries it with her any longer. I haven't asked."

"Well, ask. And if she doesn't have it with her, ask her to think about it. You know how to use it?"

"No."

"It's time you learned. I'll set it up. And I'll talk to the sheriff about a carry permit for you, too."

"I don't want to carry a gun, Sam."

He snorted, not even attempting to hide his derision. "Get over it. This isn't about liberal angst, Alan. This is about self-protection. Got it? What I'm telling you is that you need to learn how to use a handgun. I'm not trying to recruit you to become a lobbyist for the NRA."

"Yeah, well, I'll think about it. That's a big step for me to take, Sam. You know how I feel about guns. Listen, while you're pondering all this, would you focus on something specific for me, please?"

"Sure. Like what?"

"Give some thought to how you would do it. If you were this guy, this killer, how would you kill me so that it looked like an accident?"

"I don't need to think about it too much. I know what I'd do."

"Go ahead."

"You're not going to like this, but after studying your lifestyle for a good, say, forty-eight hours, I'd decide to kill you on your bicycle. Run you off the road on one of those streets that go nowhere east of Boulder. Sabotage your equipment so your bike does something it's not supposed to do while you're coming down one of the canyons. I'd do something like that."

"That's what I thought you'd say."

"Don't you agree?"

"Yeah. That's what I'd do, too. You think I should stop riding?"

"For you, that's like you telling me not to follow hockey any more. I'm not sure you can do it. Could you?"

"If it means staying alive, I suppose I could."

"That gives us two things that you can do. Learning how to use a weapon. Giving up your favorite sport."

"If I stop riding, he'll just find another way, though, won't he?"

"Yeah. He will. And Alan?"

"Yes."

"You have any clues who this might be? Those two, Simes and Custer, are right, you know. It's probably a patient from that unit you all worked on. When you think back on those days, any of your patients seem capable of this? Do any of them seem homicidal?"

"I've been trying to remember them all. I've thought of a few patients who were angry enough to do it, plenty who might be crazy enough to do it, but no one who was actually resourceful enough to do it. This guy is so resourceful. We have to remember that. He's a meticulous planner. That really limits the diagnostic categories for someone in an inpatient psychiatric unit."

"Go on."

"The vengeance, too. To hold on to this sense of injustice—fury—for so long requires an immense reservoir of vengeance."

"So he's bright, resourceful, and vengeful. Work with that. Expand your list of adjectives. Every adjective you're able to add shortens your list of potential suspects."

"You're right. I hadn't thought about that."

"He's in your memory somewhere. You know that, don't you? You're going to have to dig him up. He left a scrap there, somewhere. It's like physical evidence. You know Locard's principle, don't you?"

"No."

"When a criminal comes in contact with a surface, he always leaves a trace of evidence behind and he always takes a little something with him. This is the same. He left something there for you to find. But it's psychological trace evidence. You're going to have to find it."

"I know I will, Sam. Trouble is that it was a long time ago. Memory fades."

"His hasn't. The murderer's. That's what sucks."

Simes and Custer had checked out of their motel in Boulder. I left a message at their voice-mail number, asking them to call. I didn't tell them that what I wanted was information on how to get in touch with Sawyer.

I didn't want to give them the satisfaction.

I knew that these two were actually trying to save my life, but for now they felt like adversaries. I was desperate to know who from my past might be targeting me. Whether they liked it or not, my partner on the search was going to be Sawyer, not them.

I arrived home from work on Wednesday afternoon to find two new additions to the gravel lane in front of the house. The first was a blue rollaway trash bin that looked larger than our house.

The second was an outhouse crafted of molded plastic.

It was really going to happen. Dresden and his demo boys were going to tear our home apart.

I played with Emily for a while and then busied myself packing. Lauren and I had decided to box the place up ourselves and pay someone to move the things we couldn't use into storage.

While I was tackling the clutter of the hall closet, the phone rang. I checked my watch, hoping it would be Lauren. It was five forty-five; she was due home soon.

"Dr. Gregory? Milt Custer here, returning your call. I'm kind of hoping you're about to tell me you've had a change of heart. We sure could use your assistance with this."

"Actually, no, Milt, no change of heart. But I have decided that it makes sense—that it's prudent—that I do want to compare notes with Sawyer about some things. Could you please tell me how I can reach her?"

"What do you hope to accomplish?"

"I'd like to talk about this with somebody who was there. Someone who's in the same shoes I'm in. That list has grown uncomfortably short. Right now, it begins and ends with Sawyer Sackett."

"Her name's Faire. Sackett was her married name. She's using her maiden name once again. We just did a brief interview with her."

*Married? Sawyer was married when she was at the medical school? No, Custer's information must be incorrect.*

I wondered what else he was wrong about. Hoped it was everything.

"I need to consult with A.J. before we send you off to see your old friend. Make sure she's okay with it. For right now, that's her piece of all this."

"Sawyer's her piece? And what, I'm yours?"

"Hardly. A.J. is coordinating all the psychological aspects of the case. The profiles, the professionals, the scenarios. I'm taking care of the investigatory aspects. The nuts and bolts of the crimes themselves. So discretion says I should ask her about you and Dr. Faire having a rendezvous. My guess is you'll hear back from her shortly. Me, I'm on my way to New Zealand in a couple of hours."

*Oh God.* "Lorna?"

"Yes. Ms. Pope. A couple of bodies have been found. The local authorities have been kind enough to offer to let me observe their work."

"Is there evidence that they were, you know, um—"

"Murdered? Can't say at this point. Nothing obvious like bullet holes, but we're apparently talking some serious decomposition. The autopsies are scheduled for tomorrow in Auckland. I think I'll be there in time, but I've never really understood this international date line thing. I don't know whether the plane I'm on will be arriving in New Zealand yesterday or tomorrow. And I can't believe I'm going to be sitting in one of those crappy little airplane seats for the next fourteen hours."

# THIRTEEN

She lives in Santa Barbara. You know, California? But she's not there now. At least I don't think she is."

Simes had phoned me no more than fifteen minutes after I hung up with Custer.

"You really don't know where she is?" I asked, more than a bit disbelieving. I suspected that if they really wanted to, Simes and Custer could find J. D. Salinger before breakfast, Amelia Earhart before afternoon tea.

"No. She told us she's on the road a lot for her work, but she wasn't especially eager to hand us an itinerary after we laid out our concerns."

"What's her work?"

"She's a consultant for some organization that provides psychiatric evals for prisoners in the California penal system. A legal aid type thing."

I could tell that Simes was not enamored of Sawyer's choice of vocation. I said, "Really?"

She didn't respond. Perhaps she couldn't believe I would question her truthfulness.

"Do you have her number in Santa Barbara? I guess I'll just leave her a message and wait to hear back from her."

I could almost feel Simes's reluctance to part with the information. She hugged it as closely as a mother does her baby before handing it over to a stranger. "I'm concerned that you and Dr. Faire may try to lock me out of this, Dr. Gregory. You wouldn't be planning on doing that, would you?"

"If I said no, would you believe me?"

"No, I wouldn't."

"Good, I'm glad we understand each other. So, are you going to give me the number or not? You know I'll get it from someone else if you don't."

"You may get her number but . . . you can't get there from here without us. Without Milt and me. It's crucial that you recognize that now, early. Before you make mistakes. This man is targeting one of you this very minute. He's examining your lives, assessing your vulnerabilities, planning his . . . activities."

"I'm not going to do anything with you and Milt, or without you and Milt, before I speak with Sawyer. It's that simple. We're wasting time."

Simes gave me the number and added, "I'm expecting to hear from you quite soon. As soon as you speak with her, as a matter of fact. You and I need to be on the same page about this offender. Why? Because I'm beginning to know him already. What he's doing. Why he's doing it. How he's doing it. Even what he's likely to do next. It's crucial that you do whatever is necessary to get yourself to a place where you can take the profile I'm developing and attach a name to it for me."

My reluctance to personalize this murderer was overwhelming. I didn't want to know him. I didn't want to let him be real.

I said, "Please, A.J., let's not go there right now. I need to speak with Sawyer first."

She ignored my plea. "Remember Andrew Cunanan? The man who killed Gianni Versace, among others?"

"Yes."

"He's your model, Dr. Gregory. If you want to identify this offender, start with Cunanan's profile. Anger. Vengeance. Power. *Power.* Don't forget power. Then anonymize him—take him off the cover of *Newsweek.* Increase his IQ by fifty points, maybe more. Decrease his impulsivity by a factor of a hundred. Exaggerate his feelings of being a victim tenfold. And then, then give him the luxury of time. All the time in the world. Do that and you'll have our guy. He's Andrew Cunanan and he's Theodore Kaczynski, all rolled into one lethal package."

Her tone grew excited as she fleshed out this demon that was targeting Sawyer and me.

Right then, I realized something important about Simes. Talking with reluctant civilians—like me—wasn't her bread and butter. Anthropomorphizing monsters was. Her specialty, her love, involved doing psychological evaluations on people whom she'd never met.

"Cunanan killed himself when he was cornered."

Without the slightest hesitation, A. J. Simes said, "This guy won't. That's the difference."

"Why not?"

"Cunanan was on a spree. Compared to this man, Cunanan was an amateur on a lark. This guy is a professional. He's dedicated. This is his life's work. Remember the Unabomber, too. He didn't give up. He didn't stop."

Something else Simes said resonated long after we hung up.

*Anonymize him.* Comparing this man to Gianni Versace's murderer, Andrew Cunanan, she'd said I had to anonymize him.

This murderer—if he was a murderer—was not currently a fugitive from the law. He wasn't on any Most Wanted list. As a matter of fact, until Arnie Dresser's mother grew suspicious and called for assistance from Simes and Custer, no one in law enforcement had been looking for him at all. No one had even suspected him of a crime— let alone a string of murders. With the exception of the relatively sloppy murder of Amy Masters in the home tanning bed, no police agency had even bothered to look for suspects in any of the deaths.

The man who wanted to kill Sawyer and me had been enjoying the luxury of total anonymity.

The reality of serial killing is that most serial killers aren't identified until they're apprehended. But the crimes of serial killers are rarely misinterpreted as accidents or deaths from natural causes. From the discovery of the first brutalized body, the cops are usually out looking for a psychopathic killer.

And the killer, nameless or not, therefore, has to do his gruesome work while he's looking over his shoulder.

But not this guy who was after me.

He wasn't a typical serial killer. There were no sexualized or ritualized components to his atrocities.

His victims weren't strangers.

He wasn't a typical spree killer, either. There was no particular rapidity or impulsiveness to the murders. The victims weren't chosen based on serendipity or circumstance.

His victims weren't celebrities. He didn't appear to be concerned with infamy or notoriety. Quite the opposite.

*And what's more, right now, today, he's not even the least bit worried about being caught.*

This man thought he was so good at causing people to die that nobody was even looking for him.

As I moved to the kitchen and began to wrap dishes and glasses from the cupboards in old pages from the *Daily Camera* before packing them away in wine boxes I'd picked up at Liquor Mart, I began to puzzle about ways to use that fact to my advantage.

Lauren came home with take-out Chinese. We sat in the living room to eat. Things were still tense.

I said, "Help me figure something out, okay?"

"Okay."

"Prosecutor and wife?"

She smiled. "Sure."

"This guy"—I didn't know what else to call him—"thinks he's so smart and so good that nobody knows what he's up to, right?"

She thought for a moment, then said, "I'd say that's true. He's been at this project of his for years, with impunity so far. I'd be surprised if he thought anyone was wise to him. Yes, I'd say he's feeling pretty smug."

"So, is that good or bad? I mean, from our point of view. In terms of finding him, do we want him complacent, or do want him nervous?"

She narrowed her eyes. "From an investigatory point of view, I think you could make an argument either way. What are you suggesting?"

"Let's say, for instance, I get a bodyguard and we build a ten-foot fence around the house. If he's watching me, he's immediately going to know something's up, right? He'll know I'm protecting myself."

"Right. If you put up a billboard like that, he'll know that you've put two and two together and deduce that we have the pattern figured out—that somebody's killing people. But that doesn't mean he's going to assume that we're on to *him*. He's a very cocky guy, remember."

"Right, I agree. Now—today—he's working under the assumption that he has at least two levels of insulation from all these murders. One is that no one in authority has concluded that any of these people was murdered. The other, of course, is that no one is looking at him as a suspect in any particular crime. If I start surrounding myself with self-protection, he'll know for certain that his first level of insulation is gone and that the second one is, at the very least, in some jeopardy."

Lauren seemed to agree. "Makes sense. The question is, How will he respond? Will he back off? Or will he accelerate his plans?"

"Yes," I said, "that is the question. Simes doesn't think he'll give up if he's cornered." I shared Simes's impression that we were looking for a morph of Andrew Cunanan and the Unabomber. "So what do you think?"

She put down her chopsticks and kissed me with moo goo gai pan breath. "If we had a clue to who he is, Alan, we might be able to make an educated guess about the answer to that question." She kissed me again, chewing lightly on my bottom lip. "So who is he?"

"I've been over it ten times, sweetie, and I don't have a clue. Nobody from back then seems to be right."

"But you don't remember them all, do you?"

"Not even close."

"It's probably someone who didn't make much of an impression, you know? Not too crazy. Not overtly threatening. Just somebody who felt that what you all did to him ruined his life."

"That makes it even harder. I've been thinking, what about going to the press? Get everybody looking for him?"

"I thought about that, too. But looking for whom? And is the evidence so compelling that the media will think that something is actually going on? I mean, there hasn't even been enough evidence to convince a single jurisdiction that something is amiss. Simes and Custer can't even convince their old colleagues at the FBI that some criminal genius is at work. If one of your mildly paranoid patients brought this story to you, what would you think? Would you believe him?"

"I don't know. Maybe not."

"If a stranger walked into the DA's office and laid this out to us, we'd probably snicker at him after we sent him packing."

"It's funny. I hadn't thought about people not believing us. I was more worried about the consequences of the witch-hunt they would start on all those patients if they did believe us."

She reached down and scratched behind Emily's ears. "This guy, Alan, if he's killed all these people the way we think he has, don't you think he'd just view the scrutiny as another challenge? He'd still find a way to finish what he started."

"That's my take, too. He likes being the smartest. He likes the fact he's the most clever." I paused. "You're at risk, too, sweets. It's not just me."

"I know. Innocent bystanders die too."

"We can't just sit and wait for him to try to kill us."

She sat back against the seat cushions of the sofa and sighed deeply. She said, "I can't believe I'm saying this, but . . . I think the only answer is for you to go see Sawyer, damn it."

I held her gaze and dribbled rice grains from my chopsticks onto my lap. "You're sure that's best?"

"No." She shook her head with vehemence.

"You want to come with me?"

"No. I've decided to trust you with her."

I threw away the white take-out boxes and the disposable chopsticks and finished my beer before I picked up the phone and dialed the number in Santa Barbara that Simes had given me. The mailbox greeting at the other end was institutional, not personal. I was grateful not to have to listen to Sawyer's voice, yet.

At the tone I said, "Sawyer? This is Alan Gregory. Please give me a call." I left my pager number.

Lauren had been across the kitchen, filling Emily's bowl with fresh water. She said, "That's it? That's your whole message after all these years? 'Please give me a call'?"

"That's it." I touched her below the ear and leaned in and kissed her cheek. "We should have working drawings on the garage by the time the demo is over. Dresden doesn't think adding it to the project will slow him down much, if at all. He has a lot of confidence."

With her left hand she traced the line of my jawbone. "You need a shave," she said.

"Probably."

"This garage is the same one we talked about a few months ago, right? It will hold two cars?"

Puzzled, I said, "Of course. That's what we decided."

Then I understood her meaning. She was making sure I was still planning on being around to take up one of the two slots.

My beeper vibrated at eight-thirty. I touched the tiny button to still the signal and left it anchored to my hip until Lauren moved to another room.

The number on the screen was local.

I called my voice mail. A patient had forgotten the new time of her appointment and wanted to know if it was eleven or one.

I called her back, told her the appointment time, and said that I would see her the following week.

She said, "We'll talk about this, won't we? Me begging you for a new appointment time and then immediately forgetting when it is?"

My silence allowed her to answer her own question.

Sawyer's call came in at eleven. Lauren was asleep beside me. My beeper was still set to vibrate, not chirp, and it almost wandered off the nightstand before I was able to corral it.

The area code on the screen was 805. I didn't know where that was. But I knew in my bowels that 805 was where Sawyer was.

I pulled on some sweats and a T-shirt and climbed upstairs. Emily followed me. I had the sudden awareness that this night would be the last time I would be sleeping in my old bedroom, ever. Tomorrow night we'd sleep at Lauren's old house on the Hill. When we came back to this house we'd be sleeping in the new bedroom we were building upstairs.

I carried the portable phone to the sofa and sat, scratching Emily under her chin and rubbing her ears before I punched in the number from my pager screen.

Maybe half a ring later, I heard, "Alan?"

My pulse was up, my breathing shallow. Her voice sang for me the way it always had.

"Yes," I said. "Hi, Sawyer. Long time."

"I never thought I'd talk to you again as long as I lived. Didn't think I had the right."

Was I hearing remorse from Sawyer Sackett? I reminded myself how badly I'd always read her. "I never expected to talk to you, either. Figured that things had changed so much that it would just never happen. But here we are, right? And the circumstances couldn't be more strange."

When she responded to my words I didn't notice any of the pressure in her voice that I felt in my own. She asked, "You've talked to those two, I take it? The FBI odd couple?"

"Custer and Simes. Yes. They're the ones who gave me your number in Santa Barbara. Where are you now?"

"Central Coast. In San Luis Obispo. In a hotel, a quintessentially weird place called the Madonna Inn. My bedroom looks like a stall in a medieval barn. Last time I was here I stayed in the flying saucer room. I think I prefer that one. This one's harder on my allergies."

I didn't know what to say. San Luis Obispo is a couple of hours north of Santa Barbara on the coast. Simes said that Sawyer traveled for her business. "You up there on work?"

"Yes, work. One of the facilities I visit is near here. So . . . do you want to catch up a little bit or do you want to talk about all our dead friends?"

"Both, I think. How are you, Sawyer?"

"I'm . . . peaceful, Alan. Not joyful. Peaceful. Life has taken a lot of turns I never would have chosen. And I've managed to embrace this place where I've ended up. I feel good about that. You?"

*What the hell did that mean? Me?* "I was better a week ago, Sawyer. But things have been good for me. I'm married and . . . I have a good life."

"Kids?"

"Not yet. You?"

I thought I heard her swallow. Her next words were "Do you believe them? Custer and Simes?"

Okay, we weren't going to talk about kids.

"Yes, I believe them. Not a hundred percent, but enough to make me crazy. You don't?"

"Actually—no—I believe them as well. As you can probably guess, over the years I'd lost touch with everyone except for Susan. After she died in—when was that plane crash?—I really never knew what happened with everyone's lives. I never heard about any of the deaths."

"Did, uh, those two agents tell you about . . . Lorna?"

"No. God. Don't tell me."

I didn't.

She said, "Tell me."

I did, concluding, "Custer is on his way to New Zealand tonight to check it out. I talked with him a few hours ago. He's hoping to be able to confirm the identification and the circumstances."

Sawyer's tone became wispy, lacy. "I really liked Lorna. She knew about us. I think she was the only one on the unit who knew what we were up to. Did you know that she knew?"

"No, I didn't. But I liked her, too. Her death hurts a lot. There are times when I don't know whether I'm more sad or more scared about all this."

She said, "Yes, I know. Lorna, God. It's just you and me now, isn't it?"

"Of the professional staff, yes. Unless you include Kheri."

"Oh no. Do you think we need to worry about her? Oh my."

"I don't know. I haven't thought about her until right now. But if he targeted the social worker, maybe he'd go after the head nurse, too."

"Do you know where she is?"

"No, do you?"

"No."

"I can check with some people at the school. See if anyone has kept in touch."

Sawyer's tone lightened. Almost playfully, she asked, "So are you going to save my life again, Alan?"

"I didn't save your life. That man wasn't going to kill you, Sawyer."

"I wasn't talking about that crazy patient with the knife, Alan."

"What do you mean?" I said, and I tried to picture her right then, in her funky theme hotel room. How long was her hair? How had she aged?

"You saving my life—it had nothing to do with Arnie's patient and the pocketknife. It was something else that you don't understand. You couldn't understand. Because I never told you."

"What—?"

"We have a decision to make, right now. You and me."

"You mean about whether to cooperate with Simes and Custer?"

"That, too. I meant about where to meet. Do you want to come here, to California? Or should I come to where you are? Or do you want to surprise me and leave me a note in my morning newspaper and let me know exactly where it is we'll rendezvous?"

I couldn't tell whether her tone was mocking or inviting. Jesus.

# FOURTEEN

Friday evening, we finished moving out of Spanish Hills and moving into Lauren's old place on the Hill.

Saturday morning, Dresden's crew began to demolish the interior of our little house.

Saturday afternoon, at 3:46, I was sitting in the exit aisle of a United 737 shuttle that was lifting off on its way from Denver to Las Vegas.

Sawyer had said she'd be waiting for me at the gate.

In my mind, of course, she hadn't aged. Her hair hadn't grown. Her body had lost none of the elasticity or allure of its youth.

In my mind, of course, she was still an enigma. She was still someone who could bring out every juvenile sexual urge I'd ever felt. She was the embodiment of every embarrassing immaturity it had taken me two marriages to outgrow.

As I waited for the jumble of passengers in front of me to clear the aisle, I reminded myself that I didn't blame Sawyer for what had happened that autumn.

I blamed myself for succumbing to her. Actually, I hadn't succumbed; I'd thrown myself at her feet.

I reassured myself that I'd grown since then. A lot. I was stronger now. I'd learned to love and not merely fall to infatuation. I'd learned to insist that I be loved in return.

I was confident that I could handle Sawyer. This time I would be impervious to her charms.

Then I saw her standing there, and for a dangerous moment, I was an intern again. Breathless.

And stupid.

She was waiting across the concourse, and she didn't rush to greet me.

Though it penetrated, I didn't avoid her gaze. Her hair wasn't as blond as I remembered and was much longer, almost to her shoulders, with a little outward curl at the ends. She stood proudly, her shoulders back, her hands loosely clasped together in front of her. She was wearing white jeans and sandals and a tight vest made of medium-weight denim. The denim was faded.

The most striking thing about her, though, was the change in her face. She'd aged, yes. But it was the difference in her smile that struck me. When Sawyer used to smile, her mouth and face had opened gloriously. When she smiled my way—and it wasn't a frequent enough occurrence—I remembered the brilliance of her front teeth and the radiance that seemed to glow from her parted lips.

Now, though, as she smiled a greeting across the expanse of terrazzo, it was a smile borne only by her eyes, which were framed by pale sunglasses of a tortoiseshell almost as blond as her hair. Her mouth didn't open at all. The smile seemed less joyful than I recalled, but somehow more sincere and serene.

I was still five feet from her when she said, "I've gotten fat and old. And look at you—there's not an ounce of fat on your body."

I shifted my carry-on bag from my left shoulder to my right and moved forward to embrace her. She hesitated.

I hesitated, too. The resulting hug was polite.

I said, "I've taken up cycling. It keeps me in shape. I don't know about you getting fat, though. I think you look great, Sawyer." I stepped back and took her in. "I only wish the circumstances were different."

Wistfully, I thought, she stared into my eyes. "That's what I was wishing all those years ago. About us. I just wanted the circumstances to be different. It's funny how things come around, isn't it?"

"What do you mean?"

"Later. Come on—I'm not sure we should linger here. We don't really know what this man who's killing our colleagues is up to."

I had promised myself that I wouldn't say anything inane. My next line, therefore, constituted a broken promise. "Your hair has gotten longer."

Her eyes widened into another smile, and she lifted her hair from her neck with the back of her hand. If Lauren had been beside me she would have been able to tell me whether or not the gesture was intended to be flirtatious. On my own, my wife maintained, I was clueless. Most of the time she was right.

"You like the flip? Or is it too retro? Makes me look a little like Doris Day, don't you think? Which is exactly why I used to keep it so short. And now the Doris Day look is back. Maybe my time has come. One of the cons I work with told me that I look like Carmen Diaz's older sister. That's not bad, right? Better than looking like her mother."

"I think you look great." I hoped she heard in my voice that I meant it but meant nothing by it. "Where are we going? Should we get a car?" I asked.

"I don't think so. Do you gamble?"

"Gamble? Like slot machines? Not usually."

"Doesn't matter. I do. It helps me relax. We just need to find a public place to talk, and the casinos are as good a place as any. Come on."

We grabbed a cab outside the terminal and she said, "The Mirage, please," to the driver.

"How was your flight?" I asked.

"My flights are always good," she said, as she swiveled on the seat to face me. "This guy? Who may have killed Arnie? I don't know about you, but I'm working under the assumption that from now on, he's following one of us. It's probably not literally true, but still, better safe than sorry, right? I'm hoping it's me he's following today, not you. There's no way he could have stayed with me today. You bought your ticket at the gate, right? No reservation?"

"That's right."

"Good."

I was occasionally looking past Sawyer out the window of the cab. I hadn't been to Las Vegas since I was a teenager, and I found myself as distracted by the glitz as I was by Sawyer and her paranoia about being followed. Las Vegas seemed to be an odd mixture of age and youth, and so was Sawyer. Yes, she had put on a few pounds, but mostly the years had made her appear less brazen.

Not Las Vegas, though. This new Las Vegas was as brazen a place as I'd ever seen.

\* \* \*

I think she felt me hesitate at the edge of the casino. She reached back and took my hand, leading me far into the interior of the huge space. She looked around for a moment, finally selecting two stools at a five-dollar blackjack table. She directed me to the end seat on the right of the crescent-shaped table.

She laid a hundred-dollar bill in front of her. I pulled out my wallet and decided to limit my contribution to the Las Vegas economy to twenty dollars.

"The whole casino is under surveillance all the time. I have a friend who works here, at the Mirage, in security. I don't think he's here—our adversary—but if he is, we may get a record of it."

"What kind of record?"

While the dealer exchanged our bills for chips, Sawyer raised her chin toward the ceiling. "Video. Every square inch of this floor is monitored every second of every day. My friend is watching us right this minute. He's going to keep an eye on the rest of the floor, see if anyone else is watching us too."

She placed a chip on the line. I did the same.

"You know how to play?"

"I know the general idea."

"Good. The rest is easy. I'll teach you."

For the next twenty minutes, she did. I lost a few hands, won a few hands, hit a couple of blackjacks, and mindlessly cashed in another twenty. She nursed her stack of chips into almost two hundred dollars. I was impressed.

I was also perplexed. I didn't know why I was sitting in the casino at the Mirage on a Saturday afternoon playing blackjack with an ex-lover.

"Sawyer?"

"Mmm."

"What are we doing here? More to the point, what are we going to do about this maniac and these two ex–FBI agents?"

Sawyer seemed to be ignoring me as she focused on her hand. I wondered if she was counting cards. Finally, she decided to split a pair of tens. Without looking over at me, she said, "You know who it is?"

"No," I said, "I don't. You do?" I was relieved that she might have figured out the puzzle.

"I've been thinking that it might be one of two guys. Wendy had a patient, an angry, angry young man. Remember him? I think he was in oil and gas. What did they use to call themselves back then? Land man, is that it? Yeah, I think he was a land man. Kept announcing at Community Meeting how much our 'imprisonment' was costing him. Does he ring a bell?"

The dealer graciously added an ace to the first of Sawyer's two tens and a jack to the second. Sawyer cleaned up twice as the dealer busted. I'd been sitting conservatively on an eight and a six and won my hand and a tip bet I'd left for the dealer. I now had eight five-dollar chips in my pile, which meant I was even. Cool.

I didn't recall the patient of Wendy's that Sawyer was talking about. I said, "The man you're describing doesn't sound familiar. Sounds like it could have been ten different guys. Twenty."

"Okay. Let me describe him a little bit more. He was young then. Mid-twenties, and little, smaller than me, about five-five, five-six, and—oh, oh—his hair was as red as these chips. And he kept a pocket comb with him all the time, was always combing his hair."

I nodded. The comb did it. "I remember him now. He wore madras, right, had nothing but madras shirts? Wasn't he picked up by the police on I-70? If I'm remembering the incident correctly, he was on the elevated portion, wasn't he? Near the Stock Show, wandering around? Claimed he was looking for oil? Had some ritual about kneeling in front of the mileage markers?"

"That's the guy. When they found him he was barefoot, otherwise totally dressed in Bronco orange. First-break schizophrenic. Wendy got him stabilized on Thorazine right away. The good news was that the Bronco garb disappeared and we got treated to the madras. The bad news was that we all had the misfortune of viewing his underlying personality disorder. Not a pretty sight."

It didn't feel right. I shook my head. "I don't see it, Sawyer. Let's say it's him and he's psychotic again. If that's the case, he's not stable enough to pull this kind of thing off. Let's say his psychosis is under control. Even after his thought disorder disappeared, he was impulsive, just a little firecracker, right? I've been thinking that we should be looking more for a depressed guy. Or a paranoid character disorder. Maybe even a high-functioning obsessive-compulsive. Something like that."

"Maybe you're right about the little oil and gas guy, Alan. But I'm not sure I agree with you diagnostically. I don't think we should rule out psychotics. It could be somebody with a severe thought disorder or even a severe mood disorder, for that matter. What about a bipolar who's well controlled on lithium? Or just a manic who cycles slowly? You know, someone who only kills his doctors during the manic phase?"

She was making an interesting argument about patients with mood disorders. "You're making a good point," I acknowledged. "I hadn't thought about a slow-cycling manic. But I'm not convinced the oil and gas guy is the type we should be looking for. You don't think we should consider Travis, do you?" Travis was the patient of Arnie's who had attacked Sawyer with the pocketknife.

She shook her head. "No. He's too crazy and too impulsive."

I pushed my chips forward and stood up. "Would you mind cashing out. Please? This is too distracting for me. Let's get a beer or something. Your friend can follow us with his cameras, right?"

Her eyes lit. "Almost anywhere," she said.

At her suggestion, we settled into a booth in the coffee shop. She ordered a Cobb salad and a Diet Pepsi. I ordered a turkey sandwich on wheat bread and a beer. She hadn't even glanced at the menu. I said, "You come here a lot?"

She shrugged. I wondered if she was appraising my words for the weight of judgment. I, too, wondered if there were any stray ounces there.

"What's a lot? I gamble to relax, get away. I come here sometimes—to Vegas. I go to Reno and Tahoe, too. I'm pretty good at blackjack, not quite so good at poker. Good enough that it's cheap entertainment for me."

All these years had passed and there were a thousand things I wanted to know. Our food arrived in minutes; the casino kitchen didn't want its customers spending any unnecessary time away from the gaming floor. I swallowed a bite of my sandwich and asked, "Are you married? Involved with someone?"

The tiny lines around her eyes and mouth softened and smoothed out. "There's a guy I see in L.A. And a judge in San Francisco. But not seriously, no. I did marriage. I did it twice."

"And twice is enough?"

She didn't respond. She cut a big piece of romaine into tiny little pieces and went to work on a sliver of hard-boiled egg.

"You know, I didn't know you were married when I met you. You never said anything."

She placed her silverware down and lifted her napkin to her lips. "Technically, I wasn't."

"Okay. I'll try to be more precise. I didn't know you had been married when I met you."

She lifted her fork and speared a cherry tomato. She swallowed once even though there was no food in her mouth. She raised her chin, stretched her neck back, and closed her eyes.

I couldn't fail to be assaulted by memories. Moments before orgasm Sawyer did this same thing. A throaty groan would complete the picture.

When she looked back down at me, tears were in her eyes. "I can't do this now. Not with you. Not yet. I'm not ready to go back there. Let's just deal with murderers, okay? I do that every day."

"I'm sorry if I intruded on something, Sawyer. I didn't mean to upset you."

"It's okay. You don't know about any of that. I never . . . anyway. I don't know, I'm sorry, too."

I changed the subject. "Why don't you tell me who your other candidate is? You said you had two people in mind."

She had turned her attention to a pair of televisions above the bar. One was tuned to CNN. The other was a college football game. I couldn't tell who was playing. Without looking over at me, she said, "You remember a patient of mine named Elly? You saw her for me, on a consult."

I smiled. "Of course I remember Elly. You don't suspect her, do you?" Elly had been an eighteen-year-old girl when she was admitted to the unit for depression, anorexia, and suicidal ideation. She'd been Sawyer's patient, but I'd done a psychological testing battery on her.

"God, no."

Sawyer remained focused on the TV. I tried to remember whether she was a football fan.

She said, "But Elly's the reason we can't cooperate with Simes and Custer on a patient roster."

I tried to make sense of the connection, but couldn't. "I don't get it."

"Elly's full name, if you recall, was Eleanor Trammell. Since then, she's married. Her name, now, is Eleanor Ward."

I followed Sawyer's gaze up to the television screen. The CNN logo flashed across the screen. I wasn't getting it.

"Eleanor Ward," she said. "CNN? Ring any bells?"

"Oh," I said. "*That* Eleanor Ward." Immediately I saw the face in my mind. Eleanor Ward was one of the regular anchors on *Headline News.* "You know, I always thought that woman looked familiar, but I'd never made the connection."

"No reason you should have. Her hair color is different. And she's gained twenty pounds."

The mention of weight helped me recall the details of why Elly Trammell had been hospitalized. "Your point is that if her history— I mean her psychiatric history—was made public, it could really screw up her life, couldn't it? Professionally?"

Sawyer moved her attention from the television back to her salad. She said, "Professionally. Personally. You bet it would. There are probably a dozen more people like her, too. Patients who were on the unit back then whose lives would be turned upside down if we revealed their names and what they'd been through. So we're on our own. We can't sacrifice all those people to help those two feds."

"Ex-feds."

"Oxymoron. It's like ex-Catholic. Or ex-shrink."

"What are you implying? That some learning can't be overcome?"

"Yes, I am saying that I believe there are some things in life that change people forever. Some things you can't get over. That's exactly what I'm saying."

"I don't know about that. But I'm not going to argue with your conclusion. We can't give them a patient roster. No. There're too many unknowns."

She glanced back up at the televisions. "Good. I'm glad we're not going to fight about that."

"I do have a cop friend in Boulder whom I trust a lot. He'll do what he can to help us out. I've explained everything to him already."

"We can't give him names either, Alan."

"I know that. He knows that. Don't worry about him. So who's your other candidate?"

"Actually, I was thinking of one of my own patients, a young, angry borderline guy who I didn't like very much. He spent half his time on the unit in isolation, screaming at somebody or another. I think his name was Romewicz or something like that. But in coming up with him, I've been focusing more on the anger than the capacity for planning. I think you may be right. It may be better to look for who would be capable of it first, and look for motive second."

I said, "Wait a second. . . ."

"What?"

I touched my index finer to my temple. "Do you remember the guy—what was his name—everyone on the unit called him D.B. He was Arnie's patient, I think. It was a relatively brief admission, he was—"

She smiled and her eyes sparkled with confetti. "I remember him. He was the guy who said he would tell us the identity of D. B. Cooper if we let him off his seventy-two-hour hold so he could go back to work. He even announced the deal during Community Meeting. Asked for takers."

"Yeah."

"He was admitted that weekend we were . . ." Her voice faded away, cushioned by memory.

I finished her sentence. "In Grand Lake."

"Yes. We were in Grand Lake."

I smiled at the memory. "I'm trying to remember whether I met him or not. Did you meet him?"

"We met him. We were back in time for Community Meeting the day he was discharged. We both met him."

I couldn't get a mental picture of him. "Has that guy ever been found? The hijacker, I mean? D. B. Cooper?"

Sawyer shook her head. "You know, I don't think so."

Like most Americans, I'd been fascinated by what D. B. Cooper had managed to do in 1971.

On Thanksgiving eve of that year, a man using the name Dan Cooper purchased a ticket with cash and boarded Northwest Airlines Flight 305, bound from Portland to Seattle. The man who called himself Dan Cooper was later described by flight attendants as a polite, shy, middle-aged guy who was dressed in a dark suit and a tie. He sat in his assigned aisle seat in the middle of the plane and generally attracted no attention to himself until he handed a note to one of the young flight attendants, informing her that he was hijacking the airplane.

His demands included a highly detailed request for ransom and, curiously, four parachutes.

The plane landed in Seattle, where it was delayed for refueling, for delivery of the $200,000 in twenties that Cooper had demanded, and for delivery of the four parachutes. Cooper permitted the paying passengers to deplane and chose two flight attendants who would stay aboard as hostages.

After once again taking off, the plane flew south under flight conditions dictated by the hijacker. The route Cooper specified was an indirect, slightly westward, slightly looping path toward a refueling stop in Reno, Nevada, with an ultimate destination of Mexico City.

Cooper ordered the pilot to fly the Boeing 727 unpressurized at an altitude of ten thousand feet or less, with the landing gear in the down position. He specified that the flaps should be at fifteen percent, and that the airspeed should not exceed one hundred and fifty knots.

Cabin records indicated that fourteen minutes into the flight, Dan Cooper hit the lever that lowered the airstairs at the rear of the 727, the only commercial aircraft in use in the United States with stairs that extended from the stern of the plane. Approximately ten minutes after lowering the stairs, somewhere over the wilderness drainage of the Columbia River just north of Portland, Oregon, Cooper slipped into one of the four parachutes, climbed down the lowered airstairs, and jumped into the rainy night with his ransom strapped to his chest.

He would never be seen again.

D. B. Cooper became a certified folk hero.

Dan Cooper—whose name was later mistakenly reported by the press to be D. B. Cooper—had accomplished the first criminal hijacking ever to take place in U.S. airspace. To this day, he remains the perpetrator of the only successful hijacking ever to take place above U.S. soil.

Almost ten years later, in 1980, two kids playing on the northern shore of the Columbia River recovered $5,800 of Cooper's marked booty. Despite extensive efforts, searchers found no more of the loot and no trace of the parachute. Cooper's body was never discovered.

I asked, "What was his real name? The patient who said he could finger D. B. Cooper?"

Sawyer said, "You know, I don't remember. I'm trying to remember the stories. I think he said that he worked at—what's that place called west of Denver, where they make nuclear weapons?"

"Rocky Flats. That's right, he said he worked at Rocky Flats. His thing was that he was complaining that he was going to lose his security clearance because he'd been hospitalized in a psychiatric unit. What did he do there? Do you remember? Was he a scientist of some kind?"

"No. I don't— Wait. He was in security, wasn't he? Didn't he tell everyone he carried a gun at work?"

"Yes. And he told us that D. B. Cooper was someone he worked with at Rocky Flats. And he insisted that he had proof."

We puzzled about other ex-patients for most of an hour. The fishing felt futile. None of the candidates felt right. Sawyer and I agreed that it was possible that the patient we were trying to identify might be someone neither of us knew well. Like the man unit staff had nicknamed D.B.

After a poignant silence grew into more than a minute, she said she had to get back to the airport.

We grabbed a cab outside the casino and she directed the driver to someplace called Desert Aviation.

At the unfamiliar destination, I felt a familiar feeling. With Sawyer, I was, and always had been, just along for the ride. "Where are we going now?"

"That's where my plane is. After you drop me off, the cab can take you back over to United."

"You have a plane? You flew here yourself?"

"I do. I did. I travel all over the state every week to prisons and courts. The plane helps keep me sane. My schedule would be psychotic without it."

"Something else I guess I didn't know about you."

"I didn't fly back then, during the residency. It's something I learned about ten years ago from my father. The plane was his. When he began to develop glaucoma, he gave it to me. Flying has turned out to be another one of my relaxing things."

"Your job must be stressful. All these relaxing things you do."

She glanced at me sideways before resuming a tense stare out the side window. "Stressful enough, I guess." She paused. When she resumed, the volume was barely above a whisper. "But in my life, Alan, it's not the hurricanes or the tornadoes I worry about anymore. It's the volcanoes."

"What—?"

She managed a small smile. "Think about it."

The taxi pulled up outside a modern one-story structure that was attached to a long rectangular hangar. She grabbed her bag and began to pull herself out of the car without even a simple touch for me. I wasn't ready to let her go.

I said, "He killed Susan in a plane, you know."

"I know. I'm taking precautions." Her tone amused me. The same voice a young woman might employ when assuring her parents that she is always—always—careful when she's with a boy.

I wouldn't be easily dissuaded. "He may be an airplane mechanic. He may have access."

"I have a locked hangar for my plane. And I've used the same mechanic for years. I've asked him to do all the work himself for a while. He's agreed to that. My preflight checks are . . . exhaustive. A real pain in the butt." She pulled her hair off her neck, then released it. "I'm worried, too," she said.

"Maybe you shouldn't fly again until we understand better what happened to Susan. Simes and Custer are collecting all the details. They'll be back to us soon enough."

Her tone changed. She admonished, "Maybe you should get out of the advice business."

"I'm sorry," I said, although I didn't think that my caution was anything but prudent.

"It's okay." She grabbed her bag again and raised herself from the car. She leaned down before she closed the door and said, "Alan, what about Chester?"

I said, "Jesus, Sawyer. I never thought about Chester."

"Maybe we should."

"God, yes."

She took a step away without saying good-bye. Then she turned back to the car and said, "Alan?"

The desert wind was blowing in short intense gusts, and she was holding her hair from her face with one hand to keep it from her eyes. I had to lean sideways across the seat to assess her expression. It was, I thought, somber.

"Yeah?"

"Did you love me? Back then. Did you really love me?"

I got out of the car, walked around the trunk, took the bag from her shoulder, and lowered it to the macadam. I embraced her the way I had wanted to in the airport terminal. She was stiff at first and didn't return the hug. Finally she softened. I could feel the tips of her fingers begin to probe the muscles on my back. I could feel the pressure of her breasts against my abdomen. I could feel her cool breath caress the skin on the side of my neck.

Into her hair, I said, "The very best I knew how."

# FIFTEEN

Lauren was asleep when I got back to Boulder near midnight.

I felt odd sliding the unfamiliar key into the unfamiliar lock in this house in town where I hadn't slept since Lauren and I were dating. Those recollections of that earlier autumn when I'd been falling in love with her were decidedly mixed memories. There had been the exhilaration of romantic discovery, but those faltering first days in our relationship had also been marked by a gnawing tension. I feared the return of that tension now that Sawyer had reappeared in my life.

Some of the tension back then had been Lauren's distrust of me. We blamed her mistrust, with facile ease, on her illness. Was it true then? Partially.

What about now?

Partially.

My take? She didn't feel consistently lovable. So she had trouble believing I really loved her. And she insisted on believing that her illness was the solitary barrier to her sense of security. Without it, she wanted to believe, she would be secure as a woman and we, as a couple, would be fine.

The couple part was true. We would be. I believed that.

But, deep in my heart, I also felt that even with multiple sclerosis in the equation, we, as a couple, would be okay. Not ideal. But MS wasn't the only flaw in the silk cloth that we'd woven into our marriage coverlet. In falling in love with Lauren, in committing to her, in marrying her, I took the last steps of a journey that was freeing me of my juvenile quest to find an ideal mate. In fact, when I met Lauren I was separated from a gorgeous, witty, brilliant woman I'd married after convincing myself that she was perfect.

I assumed, always, that in her life, somewhere along the way, Lauren had made the same judgments about me and my imperfections. She had determined that I had plenty of flaws and that she loved me anyway.

I fell in love with her despite her insecurities, despite her inconsistencies, despite her illness.

I fell in love with her because of her usual joy and her surprising nurturing, because of her remarkable reservoir of courage, and because of her wisdom, and her beauty.

In doing so, I thought I had found the right woman for me. Not the perfect woman, though. I no longer had that illusion.

I felt that way before I went to Las Vegas to see Sawyer. Seeing Sawyer, touching her, had unsettled me. Still, as I crawled into bed next to Lauren in her old house on the Hill, I felt assurance that I had married the right woman.

The unfamiliar city noises distracted me as I tried to find sleep. I heard cars downshifting in the distance, and closer listened as two dogs barked up some competitive tree. I listened to the wind whistle down canyons. From my other bed in my distant bedroom across the Boulder Valley I could barely even discern those canyons as charcoal slashes in the landscape. Even Emily's big dog sighs sounded different as she fought to find a corner that provided comfort and security.

Twice I thought I knew what Sawyer had meant by professing her fear of volcanoes, not hurricanes. Twice I knew that I was guessing.

I sat up in bed and looked at Lauren's bedside table for the Glock. It wasn't there. Would she keep it under the pillow? I didn't know. I hoped not.

I thought about Chester some more and knew he was now on my list for keeps.

I tossed. I turned. I didn't believe that Lauren was actually asleep beside me.

Out loud, I said, "We're fine. Don't worry. I love you."

She didn't stir.

She greeted me warily at breakfast. I embraced her longer than I normally would have.

I told her I was grateful for the bagels and coffee and fresh-squeezed juice.

"How did it go?" she asked.

Was she asking whether I'd learned something useful or how things had gone with Sawyer? I chose the more benign fork in the road. "Okay. Good. Sawyer and I are on the same page about not divulging the patient list to Custer and Simes. We came up with some possible suspects to look at. I want to talk with you and Sam about how to check them out. I don't even know how law enforcement goes about locating people, sweets. I'm sure there are ways, though. Right?"

She smiled and said, "Yes, there are ways." She found something interesting in the bottom of her coffee mug. "So how is your friend? After all these years? Did you enjoy seeing her?"

*My friend?* "Sawyer was a lot of things to me back then, Lauren. But she was never my friend."

"That's funny."

Her voice told me she found the revelation soothing. I was tempted to elaborate, but didn't. Instead, I said, "But to answer your question better, I, um, I think, I don't know . . . she's . . . it's like she has a limp."

"She . . . limps?"

"Figuratively. Psychologically. Being with her, it's like an old, serious injury has healed. But one leg is shorter than the other one or something. Or the scar tissue won't really allow her to move gracefully. It's like that. Being with her, she's restricted. Tight. Jerky, awkward."

"What injury?"

"She didn't say. I didn't ask."

Her eyes scorned me. "I can't believe you didn't ask. Are you attracted to her still?"

I didn't want to follow Lauren wherever she was heading. Was there a reasonable way to answer?

"If I am—so what? She's attractive, but it doesn't mean anything. I mean, I think the new receptionist in your office is pretty hot. And didn't you recently admit that you thought that attorney you creamed last week on the drunk and disorderly is a pleasant addition to the local bar?"

The scorn in her eyes flashed a frosting of contempt. "What's different is that I didn't used to date him."

"You're right."

"And you really think Trisha is hot? She has no boobs at all. I didn't think she was your type."

"The older I get the more I don't think I have a type. I'm actually becoming a more equal-opportunity lech." I didn't confess that I was constantly amazed at how many different ways women can find to be lovely.

"So she's still pretty, too? Sawyer?"

I touched my wife across the table. "Like you, Lauren, she'll be beautiful until she dies."

With a suspicious tone, she said, "You're getting smoother as you age, you know that?"

I shrugged. Saying thank you felt risky.

Lauren and I had promised each other we were going to check on Dresden's progress in Spanish Hills every day, either before we went to work or after. While she showered and dressed to get ready for this Sunday morning visit I cleaned up the breakfast things, but couldn't seem to master the controls on Lauren's antique KitchenAid dishwasher.

She jiggled the handle on the door and the machine started. "It's cranky sometimes," she said. "Like me."

Across town in Spanish Hills, we passed Adrienne and her son, Jonas, as they were heading out the lane. Adrienne honked and waved at us but didn't slow her new Suburban. Adrienne is petite. Behind the wheel of the massive Chevy, she looked like a ten-year-old driving a school bus. I felt a pang of guilt about what our construction project must be doing to her peace and quiet.

I made a mental note to send her some flowers.

Approaching our house from the lane—from the north—nothing much looked different about it. Momentarily, I wondered if Dresden's demo crew had actually started work as promised. Then I noticed the debris that was already protruding from the top of the huge blue rollaway. It was over half full. It was definitely not half empty.

Lauren and I were relentless recyclers. Every couple of weeks we left our papers and cans and bottles out for Eco-Cycle. Our efforts seemed ironic, and futile, as I realized we were rather cavalierly throwing away most of our house.

It would take a lot of plastic bins full of aluminum cans and glass bottles to make up for this.

At the meeting where we had signed the contract with Dresden, he had warned us what to expect in terms of progress. "Things fly at first," he said. "The simple fact of this business is that *de*-struction is much, much faster than *con*-struction. So don't be surprised at how fast we can bust up your house at the front end of the job, and don't be too frustrated at how long it takes to put it back together and paint it at the other end."

I tried to steel myself for what we would find inside.

Lauren opened the front door and said, "Oh my God."

I peeked over her shoulder. The experience reminded me of seeing my leg for the first time after it had been secreted away in a plaster cast for fifteen weeks when I was a kid. I knew the leg was mine—it was protruding from my hip, after all—but I didn't recognize it as the appendage I knew so well.

And this house was no longer the domicile that had been my home of over ten years.

Most of the interior walls of the upper level of the house were gone. Four-by-eight beams held the joists aloft, the beams supported, it appeared, by four-by-fours and prayer. Only small sections of the ceiling remained intact. Where we had once had a small dark kitchen we now had a small dark cavern with exposed stud walls, naked drain-pipes and supply lines, and silver snakes of electrical conduit. The dismal space brought back memories of torture chambers I'd seen in B movies from the sixties.

Two-thirds of the south wall of the house had been demolished. The empty space that had been created was interspersed with support columns constructed of rough studs. Sheets of even rougher plywood covered the opening. Vertical slivers of light leaked in through the cracks.

Lauren said, "It's so clean in here. I expected, you know, Los Angeles after the big one."

The orderliness of the space was not exactly my first impression. But I had to admit it was true. I said, "It is pretty neat. Dresden and his demo boys have certainly tidied up after themselves." Other than the hanging conduits and the exposed plumbing stubs, the place appeared ready for the next phase of construction, whatever that might be.

She gazed around the room in a way that worried me. When she finally spoke, she affirmed my intuition. She said, "You're not going to like this. Don't get upset, okay? But I think we should go ahead and replace those windows. Don't you think that makes sense after all?"

To save money, we had decided to preserve as much of the existing glass as we could. I sighed. "Which windows?"

She pointed toward the dining room, where we kept her pool table. But she said, "All of them, I guess. Consistency of fenestration is important."

*Consistency of fenestration?* Resigned to the fact that we would be placing a new window order, I said, "Everything? All of them? Even the picture windows in the living room? That's a lot of glass, sweets. It will cost thousands."

"Don't you want them to match?"

We still hadn't ventured farther into the house than the entryway. She knew, with the chaos I had just invited into our lives, that I wasn't about to argue with her about a few windows. I started walking toward what had been the living room. "Do you want to call Dresden about the change? Or should I?"

"I will," she said.

I contemplated the fact that twenty-four hours after the start of construction, we had already managed a probable fifteen thousand dollars in change orders. I was wondering if that level of impulsive largesse might get us into Guinness when Lauren said she wanted to see what they had done downstairs.

She shoved aside a sawhorse in order to descend the stairs to the lower level of the house.

What happened next took three seconds. Five tops.

I thought—I was certain—that the world was ending. At least the portion that I occupied.

A two-by-four had been jammed into the supports of the sawhorse. As Lauren shoved the sawhorse aside, the stud was pulled along with it. The other end of the stud was simultaneously yanked out from beneath a temporary support column that stood tall in the middle of the room. As all this occurred, a squeal reminiscent of a large animal dying a torturous death filled the cavern of joists and trusses above my head.

The support column fell to the wood deck with a concussion that was way out of proportion to its size.

Lauren screamed, "Alan!"

I looked up to see one end of a long ceiling joist slipping from the spot where it should have been secured to its intersecting beam by a joist hanger. The joist began to fall in a short arc toward my head. I barely had time to move before the two-by-eight grazed my arm and crashed to the floor at my feet.

I waited for more lumber to fall.

None did. Another joist sank a few inches and squeaked. Another one shuddered and groaned. But the single ceiling joist was all that came down.

Lauren rushed to my side, skipping over the fallen joist. She said, "You're bleeding. Are you okay? I'm so sorry. Did I do that? Did I make that come down? Come on, let's get out of here, it's not safe."

I figured standing still was the most prudent thing I could do. For half a minute I stared at the joists and trusses, trying to determine if anything else was about to tumble down.

I examined my biceps. I was bleeding. One of the nails that should have been holding that joist in place had slit my skin. I said, "I think I'm okay. Just a scratch. I'll probably need a tetanus shot. God, I hate tetanus shots."

"Why did that happen? Should that have happened?"

"No, that shouldn't have happened. Do you have your phone with you? Let me call Dresden."

Dresden lived in the town of Louisville, which was actually closer to our house than was most of the city of Boulder. Less than ten minutes later, he was parking his big Ford pickup on the lane.

He wanted the story again. He said, "A joist fell? You're sure?"

"Two others came loose. Go check for yourself, Dresden. Do you have a hard hat?"

I might as well have been warning one of the Joint Chiefs about the dangers of UFOs. He said, "Joists don't fall from ceilings on my jobs, Alan. I don't need a damn hard hat."

Dresden spent about five minutes inside while Lauren finished dressing my arm with first-aid supplies from the car.

Our contractor spoke even more slowly than usual when he rejoined us. "This is crazy. So tell me what happened again."

Lauren was eager to repeat her tale. "I wanted to go downstairs to see what you guys had done down there, but there was one of those things in the way at the top of the stairs. What are they called?" She turned to face me.

"A sawhorse."

"Yeah. There was a sawhorse in the way. So I slid it back a couple of feet. When I did—"

"Don't forget the stud. Somebody had jammed a stud into the brace of the sawhorse."

"Yes. And when I moved the sawhorse, that board—it's a stud, is that what you called it?"

"Yes, a stud."

"That stud moved. And then those two sticks that were holding up the ceiling fell and then that big board came down from the attic and almost hit Alan in the head. It could have killed him."

Dresden turned his head to me for help in the same polite way a politician consults a translator on a foreign junket.

I said, "The stud that was caught in the sawhorse had also been stuck under the temporary support column that was holding up the joists. When Lauren moved the sawhorse, the stud moved and came out from underneath the column, the column fell, then the joist squealed, and then it just came crashing down right next to me. Two others came loose."

Lauren clarified, "Right on top of you, you mean."

Dresden had been standing. He sat beside us on our little front stoop and removed his baseball cap. This one read "Belize." I think he had a cap from every place he had ever scuba dived. I was beginning to believe it was a large collection. He smoothed down his dusty brown hair and replaced the cap on his head. "Alan, somebody wanted to bring the whole center section of the roof down. It wasn't just one joist that was sabotaged."

"You're sure?"

"I'm sure. Listen, we didn't leave it like this. I was the last one here at the end of the day. I'm the one who put the sawhorse in place at the top of the stairs. Just as a precaution, since we'd already removed the stair rail. There was no stud anywhere near it when I left last night. No way. It was around seven, maybe six-thirty, when I left. And there was no stud shimming up that support column. No way in the world I'd use the end of a long stud to shim a column. That column was cut to length and nailed in place. Nailed to the floor, and to the beam in the ceiling." He paused. "Lauren, Alan, I don't work this way. I'm careful. I'm neat. I'm methodical.

"I would never leave a site that sloppy. No way. This was malicious."

Lauren looked at me with tears in her eyes and said, "Oh my God, Alan. Oh my God."

Dresden's face turned ashen. He thought she was upset about him.

Dresden offered to call the Boulder County sheriff to report the incident as vandalism, and he said he would wait for the deputy to arrive. I pulled Lauren off to the side, huddled with her for a moment, and then accepted Dresden's offer. We didn't tell him we didn't think he was dealing with a simple vandal.

On the way back across town, I wondered what I could conclude. I couldn't be sure that he hadn't been planning to kill me under a collapsed roof, but also had to entertain the possibility that he merely wanted to warn us. Maybe he wanted us to be looking over our shoulders, listening for the other shoe to drop. I didn't know why, though, because it didn't seem to make sense. His job—killing me—would certainly be easier if we weren't wary of his approach. I considered the possibility that he was just letting me know that he knew we were on to him, and that it didn't matter to him.

He was smarter than we were. He was more clever. He was more resourceful.

After she calmed enough to recover her usual astuteness of problem-solving, Lauren agreed with my conclusions about the incident, but she was intent that practicality, and not hypothesizing, rule the short term. She wanted to call her friend John at Alarms Incorporated and have him hang motion detectors inside the house to keep intruders out during the remainder of the construction.

Although I felt this particular adversary would be amused by that particular impediment, I didn't say so. To me, such a deterrent was akin to using a kiddie gate to hold back an angry Doberman. But she said having the alarm in place would make her feel better, so I demurred. The calculator in my head clicked our change orders up to a new total, this one a few hundred dollars higher.

I, too, had some concrete matters to attend to. Custer was in New Zealand. Which meant I had to phone Simes and tell her about the sabotage. I was aware that I would have preferred to report this news to Custer, not Simes. But before I talked to either of them, I wanted to consult with Sam Purdy and get his advice.

Sam didn't respond to his beeper, so I tried him at home. His wife, Sherry, answered.

"Hi, Sherry, it's Alan. Is Sam around?"

"Alan, hi. No. He's, um, he's in the hospital." She started to cry.

"God, Sherry, what's wrong?"

She swallowed away some sniffles before she continued. "He had some, uh, terrible pain in his back yesterday morning when he was out front playing roller hockey with Simon, and he, uh, well, I . . . I made him call the department doctor. The doctor didn't like what Sam was describing and made him come in for some tests, and they took him right to the emergency room and—"

"Sherry, is it his heart?"

"Well, they thought so at first, but they did a, a—what do you call it?—with the heart?"

"An EKG?"

"Yes, and that went okay, I think, but then he got a high fever and the pain got worse and they did another test, an IVP I think they called it, and now they say he has a kidney stone. And he's still there, at Community Hospital, getting antibiotics. I just came home to be with Simon for a while."

My own heart was pounding at the news. "So he didn't have a heart attack?"

"No, they said he didn't. The pain was from the stone."

"Did he pass it? The stone?"

"No. The doctor's going to go get it tomorrow or the next day, after they bring his fever down."

"Do you know his doctor's name?"

"I'm sorry, Alan. I'm so upset, I don't remember."

"Is it a woman? A small woman?"

"Yes," she said hopefully.

"Dr. Arvin. Dr. Adrienne Arvin."

"Yes, that's her."

"I know her, Sherry. She's great. Sam's in good hands. And she knows him from some police work."

"That's nice." I thought she sounded relieved.

"How are you doing with all this, Sherry?"

She said, "I was so scared," and again she started to cry.

# SIXTEEN

I didn't bother calling Sam first. He would have told me not to come.

Lauren was ambivalent about visiting the hospital with me. Ultimately, she decided to remain at home with the alarm on, with Emily at her side and with her Glock close by. For the first time since I knew she owned it I liked the fact that she had a handgun.

At the door to Sam's hospital room I didn't knock for the same reason I hadn't called. Although the bed was situated so that he couldn't see the door, Sam apparently heard it squeal open as I entered his room. He said, "Jesus, you want more blood? Do you people drink it or something?"

I felt great sympathy for his nurse, for his urologist, Adrienne, and for the laboratory technicians.

I walked into his line of sight before I said, "No. I don't really want your blood, Sam. How you doing?"

"Alan," he said, looking away from me. "You talked to Sherry?" The unsaid part was "Damn it."

He knew I'd talked to Sherry. I nodded. "This must have been pretty scary," I said, taking in the IV and the tubing that disappeared below the sheets.

"They won't let me do much. My back is killing me. What time is it?"

"It's almost one."

"No. What time is it exactly?"

I looked at my watch. "Twelve fifty-one."

He had been watching the television with the sound turned off.

"So," I said. "Adrienne's your doctor?"

He shrugged as though the question didn't interest him much. "She said she'll get it out of there. She talks about it like it's a cavity she has to drill away, you know? Suggested I not worry about it."

"And?"

"And what?"

"Are you managing not to worry about it?"

"You ever had one? A kidney stone? She told me—your friend Adrienne—that she has women patients who have had stones and who have gone through childbirth. They prefer childbirth. I can only tell you that when the damn thing starts moving around it feels like my worst fear of being shot. Man, does it hurt."

"Where is it? Your kidney or your ureter?"

"Tube. It's in the tube." He stared at me and licked at his lips, which looked parched. He said, "I'm forty-three next week, Alan. I've got a little kid. I can't have health problems. I just can't. I've got to get back to work. Yeah, I'll manage not to worry about it."

"Apparently you do, though, Sam. Have health problems. Otherwise this is a pretty elaborate charade that Adrienne's pulling on you."

I could see his mandibular muscles constrict into tight balls the size of walnuts. "Look behind me. What's my blood pressure?"

I checked the monitor. "One-fifteen over seventy-eight."

"Pulse?"

"Eighty-three."

"And I have those numbers even with you sitting here making me anxious. My cholesterol is one fifty-eight. Not two fifty-eight. One fifty-eight. Maybe I'm a little overweight, I'll grant you that. I could lose ten pounds, twenty even. And, sure, the job is a little stressful sometimes. But how bad could this really be? I think it's a fluke. That's what I think."

He wanted a co-conspirator. Although I wanted to be comforting, I couldn't bring myself to help him affix this psychological Band-Aid.

As casually as I could, I asked, "What's the prognosis?"

"I think I'm fine." His words were clipped and dismissive. It was as though he were describing twisting his ankle and was maintaining some fragile confidence that he'd be able to walk it off.

"When do you get out of here?"

"My fever goes down, then she goes in and gets the stone. During that part I sleep, thank God. Then I go home."

"Goes in how?"

He shivered. "Right through my dick."

I decided that confronting Sam's denial was neither in his best interest nor mine. Instead of pressing him, I asked, "What about changes? What's Adrienne recommending?"

"What changes?"

"Lifestyle changes. Exercise. Diet. Stress." Sam's appetite was prodigious. His choice of foods had always been dictated by his belief that his low cholesterol was God's way of telling him he had a license to eat plenty of saturated fat. My guess was that Adrienne was going to caution him away from calcium and tell him to exercise, reduce his stress, and drink more water.

I didn't think he exercised regularly, but when we'd bicycled together I'd always been amazed by his endurance.

"The little doctor said we'd have a chat about those things before I leave the hospital. She also said she's going to be putting something up in there for a while. A stent, I think she called it. She said I couldn't run around chasing bad guys until she took it back out."

"Adrienne actually said 'chasing bad guys'?"

"Yep." He shook his head. "So I'm going to be on leave for a week, ten days. It's going to drive me nuts."

"You know," I said, "I think I may have an idea to help you pass the time."

After I left the hospital I stopped by my office and used the phone there to call Simes's beeper/voice-mail setup and to leave a message for Sawyer. I told each of them that I would be at my office number for thirty minutes and then I would be going home.

Simes's call came first, five minutes later. "Dr. Gregory? Dr. Simes."

"Please call me Alan."

"Okay, Alan. I assume this must be important."

"It is." In as much detail as I could muster, I related the story of the construction sabotage.

She was silent for a good ten seconds after I finished the tale. She asked, "What does your detective friend think?"

I found the question interesting. It informed me that Simes respected Sam Purdy. That was good.

"Lauren and I live in the county, not the city. So it's the sheriff, not the police. Sam doesn't know what happened, yet."

"You're calling me before you call him? That's interesting."

I didn't want to talk about Sam's health, although I wasn't sure why. "What do you think? Is this sabotage related to, you know?"

"Is it sabotage?"

"The contractor feels certain that it is. I have no reason to mistrust him."

I could almost hear her shrug over the phone line. "There are some problems developing with our theory. You should know."

"Such as?"

"Your old supervisor? Dr. Masters? The local police finally tracked down the tanning bed repairman. The one who looked so dirty? Well, now he looks clean. He's been hopscotching around trying to hide from an ex-wife, heard she was getting close, asking around about him in town, so he split. As best we can tell he's never lived in Colorado."

"Amy's death may have been an accident?"

I felt the distant shrug again. "Possibly. Or it could mean that this offender we're pursuing is as smooth now as he was six years ago and that he killed her without raising any more suspicion than he did in any of the other murders. For now, let's just say it makes it more difficult for Milt and me to interest the various jurisdictions in collaborating on this investigation."

"And your colleagues at Quantico? What do they think?"

"This, unfortunately, fuels their skepticism. The repairman was our only solid lead."

Simes's affect remained an enigma to me. I went fishing. "Are you questioning your assumptions about all these deaths?"

"No."

"It's not a possibility?"

"You want to take this risk?"

I didn't hear the slightest waver in her tone. Was it confidence or bravado? I didn't know. "Have you heard from Milt?"

"Only that he's arrived safely in New Zealand. I expect some news later today. Milt loves E-mail almost as much as he loves golf and trains."

"Will you keep me informed, please?"

"As warranted. Have you seen Dr. Faire?"

The question came out of nowhere and caught me upside the head. I couldn't muster a lie. I said, "Yes," but wished I had just a smidgen more sociopathic blood running through my veins.

"And?"

"She and I are in agreement that we don't have any right to help compile a patient list for you. We spent some time puzzling together about some old patients who might be harboring a grudge."

"A grudge?" She laughed. "Are you kidding? This guy has a grudge like Arizona has a canyon. And who did you come up with?"

I didn't respond. It seemed less confrontational than saying I wasn't going to tell her.

"Don't make this more tedious than it needs to be, Alan. In case you've taken your eye off the ball, Milt and I are trying to save your lives."

"You know I can't tell you the identities of the patients who were on the unit back then."

"Then don't. Although I would love some names from one of you, I'm more interested right now in profile, not identity. You can give me details about potential suspects that I can compare with my working profile."

I sighed. "I'm not sure . . . I don't know."

"You're not sure what? That you trust me?"

"Actually, I'm pretty sure that I don't trust you. I'm sorry."

"Don't be sorry. I'm hoping it's a character trait of yours. Let's say your suspicions are confirmed about the sabotage on your remodeling project. What would that tell you about this man we're seeking?"

Her tone reminded me of a professor's questions during a graduate seminar. Reflexively, I tried to be appropriately thoughtful. "It raises the question of whether he's done this before. Been provocative before he actually kills someone. Do you have any evidence of that?"

"Later. It's a good question, though. Stay on that road. Let's say he hasn't. That this is new behavior, something we haven't discovered about the prior murders. What does it tell you?"

"Well, I've been puzzled by the acceleration in the time frame that it takes him to accomplish each murder. Amy Masters, Arnie Dresser, and now Lorna Pope close together. Things are speeding up. He's using less time to plan each attack. That's a significant change. Maybe this sabotage is evidence of yet another change. Maybe if this was just taunting it's indicative of a new phase."

"Maybe. Go on."

"Well, okay, say it's true. Perhaps it's a sign he's getting more and more reckless. Maybe—"

"Why? Why would he suddenly get more reckless?"

"Maybe his need to isolate his affect is becoming more determined—is, I don't know, requiring more frequency. Or . . . ?"

"Or what?"

"Maybe his underlying mental disorder is fluctuating. Maybe getting worse. Or maybe getting better. Sawyer raised the possibility that he has a slowly cycling mood disorder. Maybe there's been a change in the cycling. Maybe he's bipolar and the manic phases are more frequent."

"Don't stop."

"Or maybe it's not too complicated psychologically at all. Maybe he's running out of time."

Over the phone line, I heard a dog bark. A little yap dog. An appetizer dog. Simes said, "Perhaps you've been wasting your skill in a small-town practice, Dr. Gregory. You may have a calling here."

"Boulder isn't a small town."

"Not my point."

"I'm not at my best right now. What is your point?"

"The rules are changing. Our killer is evolving, as consecutive killers always do. He's feeling pressures we haven't yet identified. The result of those pressures is that he's changing his pattern. That may make him easier for us to catch. Then again, it may make it more difficult."

"Why more difficult?"

"Predictability works in our favor."

"So does recklessness, though, right?"

"Yes and no. Think about it."

"Don't we have to assume that the faster he kills the more mistakes he's likely to make? His obsessiveness is his salvation. His patience and planning have provided him great cover so far."

"An interesting assumption. And probably an accurate one. However, if your argument turns out to be true in the current circumstances, it only benefits the one of you who is killed second."

"I don't understand. What do you mean?"

"If he gets sloppy or careless while killing you, for example, we may well be able to use his mistakes to identify him before he kills Sawyer. Or vice versa. But one of you will die to protect the other. Although it's usually the case that subsequent murders provide new pieces to the puzzle, it's not a price I'm terribly eager to pay to flesh out my profiles."

Lauren met me at the door with a catbird-seat grin on her face. "Sawyer called. You just missed her."

*Oops.* "Did you get a number? I phoned her from my office to fill her in about the sabotage in Spanish Hills."

"She knows. I told her all about it." Lauren pirouetted away from me as she said those words. I couldn't see the expression on her face. I followed her back toward the kitchen.

"You told her?"

"Want some tea? I'm going to make some. She doesn't like what happened any more than we do. How's Sam?"

I wanted to hear about Sawyer but didn't want to appear insensitive to Sam's plight, so I related my impressions about him while she fixed the tea.

She handed me a mug and we moved into the little living room.

"That's too bad. I'm glad Adrienne's taking care of him, though." She ran her fingers through her short hair and said, "Sawyer seemed nice."

*Nice?* "You talked for a while?"

She nodded. "She was curious about me, I think. And I was curious about her. But I liked her."

"I'm glad, I guess."

She found that amusing.

"I spoke with Simes. Told her about the house."

"Is she worried about what happened?"

"It's not her house."

Lauren laughed.

"But there's some problems with the working hypothesis about Amy Masters's death. You know, the tanning bed?" I filled her in.

"That's really disappointing. I was hoping we could get some official help with all this."

"It doesn't appear to be on the horizon. I'm afraid we're stuck with Custer and Simes now that Sam's on the disabled list."

"Don't worry," she said. "Sam Purdy plays hurt. And we have Sawyer. Don't forget Sawyer. I think she's resourceful. Oh, I almost forgot. She said she remembered the name of the guy who used to play chess all the time. And she thinks she may know how to find him."

"Chester," I said. "We used to call him Chester."

# SEVENTEEN

**S**awyer may have remembered Chester's name. What I recalled most clearly about him was that he needed a shower and a CARE package that included a gift set of Right Guard and a tube of Crest.

Chester arrived on the unit during the last few days of a glorious October. Although the weather was cool and clear, his reality was suffering a sleet storm of manic delusions. The primary delusion that was driving Chester had to do with God's impending visit to a cemetery east of Denver. The cemetery, out near what once was Lowry Air Force Base, is an immense forested place called Fairmount. Chester was determined that it was his duty to free God from a terrestrial prison where He was confined inside one of the graves in the cemetery. Toward that end, Chester had spent the last few days prior to admission wandering the graveyard, examining headstones, looking for signs that would tell him in which particular grave God was trapped. Somehow, Chester came to the conclusion that God would be lurking beneath the headstone of a dead person whose surname contained the name of a chess piece.

At night, Chester intended to dig up the graves of the prime candidates whom he'd identified during his daily strolls. He would do this systematically until he managed to free God from his earthly confinement. Over the course of his two-night quest Chester uncovered the mortal remains of one Samantha King, one Beverly Knight, and one man named Theodore Rook who had died in 1937 and whose loved ones had thought it fit to grace his headstone with a limerick of dubious taste.

Chester dug up no pawns.

The cops corralled Chester near dawn on the second night of his odyssey as he was meticulously clearing the sod from above Sylvester

Bishop's boxed remains. The authorities brought him—Chester, not Sylvester—to the psych ER at the medical school. The admitting doc downstairs in the ER was a psychiatry resident named Sheldon Salgado. After a brief workup, Dr. Salgado assigned Chester a tentative bipolar diagnosis and told the charge nurse on Eight East that he suspected that her new admission had slept for no more than a few hours over the course of the entire last week.

The doc taking admissions on the Orange Team that night was Dr. Sawyer Sackett. After doing her own intake workup, and consulting with Susan Oliphant in rounds the next day, Sawyer introduced Chester to lithium carbonate and Haldol. After his psychosis began to abate in response to the medications, she introduced him to me.

Sawyer and I were well into our strange little romance by the time Chester was admitted to Eight East on Halloween weekend in 1982. In the months since I'd met her, I'd expected our relationship to evolve along some predictable line into a semblance of a boyfriend-girlfriend thing or to disintegrate along some equally predictable path into oblivion.

It had done neither.

What it had done was prove the law of physics about every action causing an equal and opposite reaction. Each time I edged closer to Sawyer—asking her for one too many dates, encouraging her to choose me over work, wanting to spend a night together and actually seeing what she looked like in the morning—her work became more pressing, or her fears about our relationship being discovered suffered some acute swelling. And she would quickly move beyond arm's length until I took the requisite step back.

One night she kissed me good night and shooed me out the back door of her little Tudor to send me on my way home after an evening of sex that I thought had been particularly inspirational. Together we had spent two long hours discovering some sensual oasis that I was certain no human had ever visited before.

That's how naïve I was.

To my back, as I retreated down the concrete steps into her yard, she murmured, "Don't become another of my obligations, Alan. Please."

Her tone had been soft and still freckled with the hoarseness of sex, but when I turned to see what expression was on her face, all I saw was the transient glint of kitchen light off her golden hair as the door met the jamb and the lock clicked shut. Through the gauze curtains I watched her turn away, enjoying one last glimpse of the curve of her breasts and the elegant profile of her neck.

I walked home slowly, trying to savor the afterglow of our lovemaking, trying to make it last. Along the way, I decided that Sawyer's parting words to me had been plea, not warning.

In those days I was much more adept at fathoming the depths of other's psyches than I was at plumbing the reaches of my own. By the time I had stripped off my clothes and settled naked into my double bed, I had succeeded in reassuring myself that Sawyer had been pleading with me. She had not been pushing me away.

She was asking for my patience.

Before I slept, I didn't get very far in beginning to understand the genesis of her concerns.

And I didn't spend anywhere near enough time trying to read the tea leaves of their consequences.

And by ten o'clock the next morning, the psychology I was most fascinated by wasn't Sawyer's. Or my own.

It was that of this new patient of hers, whom we'd nicknamed Chester. She'd asked me to do a psychological testing battery on him.

Psychological testing has never been one of my clinical passions. In skilled, inspired hands, the results of the process can be a fascinating glimpse into shadowed recesses of the psyche. Properly interpreted, the insight gained about the patient can be both practical and clinically useful. But the administration, the process of testing, is always—always—tedious. Over the course of my graduate school years, at least three professors had spent hours of class time trying to convince me otherwise, but the reality is that formal psychological testing is a time-consuming, mind-numbing task that I would gladly leave to my colleagues.

That Monday near noon, Chester and I sat across from each other, a laminated table between us, in a small room in the occupational therapy center on one end of the inpatient unit. I tried to engage him in an initial interview. How had he ended up here? What was he feeling? What did he think about being on the unit? What were his goals during his stay? What about family? Friends?

Chester wasn't biting.

His answers demonstrated a limited repertoire that consisted primarily of wrinkled brows, shrugs, and an occasional "I'm afraid that I'm not interested in that particular subject." Already, I was getting the impression that the projective parts of this test battery, which require active participation from the patient, were going to be accomplished with record brevity. I took solace in that.

Earlier that morning at rounds, the staff had reported that Chester had spent most of his weekend huddled over a chessboard in the dayroom. So I asked, "I understand you enjoy chess?"

His eyes widened and he opened his mouth and exhaled. His breath wafted my way. It was so fetid I had to compose myself not to react. He said, "I do," with exaggerated gravity, as though he were stating a marital vow.

"Are you good?"

"Nineteen eighty-seven," he said.

His response constituted either a loose association, a bad answer on a mental status exam question about what year it was, or some numerical fact about his chess skill that I was too ignorant to interpret.

Since his mental status had shown him oriented by three during a morning nursing assessment, I guessed either B or C.

To camouflage my ignorance, almost always a mistake with patients, and to keep him talking, I said, "Nineteen eighty-seven. Huh."

He shook his head and snorted through his nose. He scratched his scalp with his left hand and examined his fingernails to see what interesting residue had accumulated beneath them. He flicked a couple of specimens onto the tabletop before saying, "You don't know what that means, do you, asshole?"

I sat back on my chair. I'd been on the inpatient unit for—what?— almost three months. In internship weeks, which accumulate like dog years, that made me a veteran. Actually, it left me only a couple of months shy of being an expert. I didn't have to put up with this grief from a patient. I said, "I'm getting the impression that you might be having some difficulty with our roles."

"Which means what?"

"That your hostility might reflect the reality that you don't like the fact that you're the patient and I'm the doctor."

"Or perhaps my hostility reflects the fact that I'm being asked to genuflect before a knave."

"We have a lot of work to accomplish together. Do you think we can accomplish this task with some degree of civility? I'm doing my best not to insult you. I expect the same from you."

"Is it so hard? Not insulting me?"

"That's not what I meant."

"Oh. I see. It's only what you said."

I took a deep breath. "I didn't schedule this time to argue with you. If we're unable to proceed now, we'll reschedule and do this another time. Is that what you prefer?"

"That seems to increase the probability of my spending additional time in this no-star hotel. If you simply admit you don't have a fucking clue about the game of kings, I'll be civil."

"Okay. I don't know what nineteen eighty-seven means. Does it refer to chess, or your chess skill?"

"Let's not talk about chess. The subject interests me only when the person I'm conversing with is fluent in the language."

By then, I was set up to administer the WAIS-R, the Revised version of Wechsler Adult Intelligence Scale, the most widely used IQ test of the time. I said, "As you wish. Why don't we talk about something more neutral, then? For instance," I said, and proceeded to dictate the precise wording of the first question of the Information subtest of the WAIS-R.

He replied with an equally precise answer that earned him a full score. I was surprised that he deigned to answer at all.

I tried the next question on my list. Again, he answered. Again, he answered correctly with a brevity and clarity that hinted at genius.

He stayed with me through that subtest and on to the next. I didn't know much about Chester, but I learned quickly that he thoroughly enjoyed the challenge of outwitting not only me but also the constructors of the test.

Forty-five minutes later, I knew Chester's intelligence quotient. Chester was the smartest person I had ever tested.

The projective tests that I would administer after the WAIS-R, the Rorschach and the TAT or Thematic Apperception Test, require a test subject who is willing to be verbally engaged, even effusive. At the very minimum, responsive. That did not describe Chester's demeanor that morning. We breezed through both tests in less than an hour. He was so guarded that I believed the results would be next to useless, but he did seem to take some pleasure frustrating me. That, too, was, of course, grist for the mill. I had higher hopes for the MMPI, which he would self-administer under nursing supervision over the course of the next day or two.

After the testing session was complete, I ran into Sawyer in the nursing station. I said, "Your patient is kind of bright."

"Really? I suspected that. How bright is he?"

"Sawyer, the man's IQ is one seventy-seven. I've never tested anyone whose IQ came close to that."

I let the number hang in the air between us. An IQ of one hundred was "average." One-fifty was usually considered "genius." One seventy-seven was stratospheric.

"Wow," she said, smiling. "This will be odd. Treating someone who's almost as smart as me."

I wished I knew if she was kidding.

As the Halloween holiday gave way to the beginning of November I saw little of Chester. With an on-board blood level of lithium growing sufficient to provide a buffer against the tides of his mania, he became a quiet man who kept to himself in the unit dayroom. Each day, he would choose a chair and table by the window, set up a chessboard, and work out solutions to chess problems that he created for his own amusement. Usually he refused offers to play a game. Occasionally, though, a sadistic streak would surface and he would accept a challenge from another patient or a staff member. He would beat them in no time at all, and would be certain to demoralize them in the process and taunt them at the conclusion of the game.

In therapy groups he remained sullen and condescending. His edgy demeanor was directed not only at the professional staff, but also at any other patients who stepped in his path.

Chester stayed cool with Sawyer, his psychiatrist. She told me once that their therapy sessions felt more like fencing, however, than chess. Chester didn't attach himself to anyone else on the staff, either. Even difficult patients often identify one ally among the staff. Usually they choose a nurse or a mental health assistant. Not Chester. He never chose a confidant.

On day six of his admission, the second of his two permitted seventy-two-hour mental health holds expired, and Sawyer, in consultation with the ward chief, Susan Oliphant, decided that Chester's current mental condition, although certainly not stellar, didn't warrant certification. After the second hold expires, certification is the required next legal step to hold someone against his or her will for continued treatment. Since certification involves a longer period of loss of freedom—ninety days—it is more cumbersome legally than a seventy-two-hour hold. Certifications, therefore, are used infrequently, and one would not be applied to Chester.

Chester decided to check himself off the unit and out of the hospital as soon as Sawyer notified him that his hold had expired. Although Sawyer made a valiant attempt to persuade Chester to stay in the hospital voluntarily, he wouldn't budge. He seemed to soften a little as she spoke with him and actually went through the motions of accepting a referral for outpatient follow-up with his local mental health center. Ultimately, though, his discharge was AMA—against medical advice.

We talked about him briefly at rounds the next day. None of the professional staff expected that he would take any of his prescribed lithium post-discharge. We all thought that someone on our unit or at the inpatient unit at Denver General across town would see his face again soon. How soon would he be back? There was no telling. The next time his bipolar disease cycled into mania could be next week, or next year.

I don't imagine I'd thought about Chester more than once or twice since that day after he was discharged.

# EIGHTEEN

Lauren asked, "Is he a good candidate? The chess player?"

I wondered about her choice of words. "Candidate," not "suspect." I said I wasn't sure about how good a candidate he really was, but I told her what I could remember about him.

"There's not much there," she acknowledged, "other than the fact that he's smart enough and methodical enough to pull it off."

I didn't disagree with her assessment. Smart enough and methodical enough carried a lot of weight, though. "He was a bitter, resentful man. But there were quite a few of them on the unit back then. I just don't remember any of us pissing him off enough that he'd want to kill all of us."

She pulled a pillow from the other end of the sofa and hugged it to her abdomen. "From a psychological point of view, if he was doing it, killing everybody, when would he be committing the murders? Would he do it when he was sane, or when he was crazy?"

"You know, it's a good question. Given the nature of these crimes, I would say it would have to be when he's sane. The delusions he was suffering during his manic phase are too unpredictable for the kind of long-term planning necessary to carry out these murders. And violence of this kind—actually of any kind—is certainly not typical of bipolar disease. For all we know, his illness may be well controlled on lithium and he may cycle into mania infrequently, giving him plenty of time to develop his strategy and plan his next murder."

"And you don't recall anyone humiliating him, or embarrassing him? Nothing like that?"

I shook my head and simultaneously shrugged my shoulders. "Sawyer probably remembers more than I do. She spent a lot of time with him during that week. When you talked with her on the phone, did she say what his name was?"

"No," Lauren said, "she didn't." She stood and stretched and kissed me on top of the head before she added, "This doctor in the ER, the one who admitted Chester that first night, what was his name? Maybe he knows something. Have you thought of talking with him?"

I hadn't. "His name is Sheldon Salgado. He's still in town—actually he's on the faculty at the medical school. He's a pretty big deal these days in biological psychiatry. It's a good idea, sweetie. I'll call him."

But at first I couldn't bring myself to call him. Now that Lauren's suggestion had placed Sheldon Salgado on my radar, I was afraid I would learn that he, too, was already dead. That Chester or D.B., or somebody else, had covered all the bases ahead of me and knocked him off.

Sheldon Salgado was a *mensch*. A star at Harvard Medical School, he could've gone anywhere he wanted for his residency in psychiatry. But his wife, a pediatrician in training, matched at Colorado. Never considering the prestige factor, he followed her here.

I hadn't known him well during our training. Our paths had crossed on a few rotations, that was it. What did I remember about him? Sheldon was thin as a whisper, stood an inch or so under six feet tall, and had great taste in ties. Long before the rest of the psychiatric community converted, he was preaching the doctrine that psychobiology was the key to the etiology of mental illness and pharmacology was the key to treatment. Although the residency rumor mill pegged him as an average or below-average psychotherapist, even as a resident he was renowned as an astonishing interviewer. His diagnostic skills shined particularly brightly in the ER. When I was an intern, he was in the third year of his residency, and he had been appointed chief resident on the Emergency Psychiatric Service.

At the end of the year, after his training was complete, he took a teaching and research position at the school. His diagnostic acumen kept his referral practice booming with requests for second opinions and medication consultations. Over the years I'd sent at least a half-dozen of my own patients his way seeking advice on whether they might be responsive to pharmacological intervention.

Although I didn't agree with all of his prescriptions, I always learned something from his opinions.

*    *    *

During the course of one of the patient consultations he had done for me, Sheldon had offered me his home phone number after a frustrating week of phone tag. I jotted that number onto a scrap of paper, hoping he hadn't changed it, and called him from a pay phone at Delilah's Pretty Good Grocery on the corner of College and Ninth. I cursed my own paranoia the whole time I was walking the few blocks from our temporary house to the store.

What was I worried about? I was worried that our telephone at home was tapped. I was worried that I would be followed if I drove to Denver to meet with Sheldon. I was worried that if the killer had not already considered killing Sheldon Salgado, by getting in touch with him I would give my homicidal adversary a damn good reason to remember who it was who admitted him from the psych ER to the psychiatric inpatient unit.

Sheldon answered the phone himself. I was greatly relieved that he was alive. Weird.

"Sheldon," I said, "it's Alan Gregory."

"Hi. Hello," he replied in a way that made it perfectly clear he didn't remember who I was and was pretty certain he didn't want to be talking with me.

"We've talked before about some patients I've sent your way. I'm a psychologist in Boulder? And believe me, I'm terribly sorry to bother you at home. Especially on a weekend."

"It's all right. This is where I try to be on the weekends. What can I do for you?" His tone was contained. He was being polite, but not gracious. People always wanted things from him. He was not always thrilled about it.

I had given some thought to what might be the most productive way to engage Sheldon's interest in my dilemma. I said, "I've recently been contacted by two ex–FBI agents who are concerned that Arnie Dresser's recent death might actually have been murder. You heard about Arnie's death?"

"Yes. Tragic."

Terse.

"Well, these two ex-agents believe that there is some reason to be concerned that a patient Arnie was seeing during his residency may somehow be responsible for his death. I'm hoping that you might have some memories of that patient, and that you might remember something, some details, that would assist us in making some sense of all this."

" 'Us'?" He paused. "Why are you calling me about this, Alan? What's your connection to Arnie Dresser?"

I was hoping he would ask that question. I used it as an entrée to walk him through the entire progression of this dark absurdity, beginning with Dr. Susan Oliphant's plane crash in 1989 and ending with Lorna Pope's recent disappearance in New Zealand.

Lorna's death seemed to have a special meaning for him. He interrupted my story and asked, "Lorna is dead?"

"Missing. Some bodies have been found. One of the FBI agents is in Auckland, now, trying to see—what? I don't know . . . to see if the body is Lorna's. To try to determine if she was murdered too."

"Lorna and I stayed in touch for a while after my training. She and my wife used to play tennis. I don't think I've talked with her in a couple of years, though. She's real sweet." The phone line crackled in my ear. Neither of us spoke for fifteen, twenty seconds. Finally, he said, "This sounds quite far-fetched, you know. This story. If what you're suggesting is true, this would be a highly atypical series of crimes for a psychiatric patient."

"Yes. I know."

"How is Sawyer? What became of her?"

His question was small talk. I didn't recall Sawyer ever mentioning a relationship or friendship with Sheldon. I guessed he was buying some time while he tried to make sense of the jigsaw I'd thrown at him. "I saw her yesterday, actually. She seems fine. She consults in the prison system in California. Competency and sanity and death-penalty issues mostly."

"Really? And she shares your concern about . . . all this?"

"Yes."

I heard a string instrument, I thought a cello, playing in the background. The same few bars, over and over. Workmanlike, and monotonous. He said, "You're calling me for more than information, aren't you?"

"I guess so. Quite simply, I'm concerned—I'm actually more than concerned—that you might be on this man's list, too, Sheldon. You, or someone else from the psych ER. If it turns out that this story has merit and it's an ex-patient from Eight East, you know as well as I do that the admission may well have come through the psych ER. I'm even frightened of leading this guy to you by making this call. I mean, if he hasn't thought of it on his own already. To be extra safe, I'm making this call from a pay phone."

"I guess I should offer my gratitude." He didn't. A long silence told me he was trying to digest my paranoia and other aspects of my mental health. "But me particularly? Why?"

"Well, yes, you particularly. One of the patients whom Sawyer and I are concerned about is someone we're relatively certain that you saw in the psych ER. Sawyer followed him on the Orange Team. I did psychological testing on him. He was a bipolar guy, a chess player, had been picked up by the police out at Fairmount Cemetery digging up graves, and—"

He chuckled. "Yes. He was trying to release Jesus from a casket or something. I remember him. I did see him before he was admitted. I'll check my consultation logs, see if I have anything useful on him."

"You'll what?"

"I keep a record of everyone I've ever seen. I've done it since medical school. Like a diagnostic diary. Just some brief notes about everybody. Mental status, impressions, diagnosis, referrals."

"Do you keep names?"

"Just initials. You don't remember this patient's name?"

"Sawyer thinks she does. But I don't know it." Consultation logs? I'd never heard of such a thing. "You wouldn't by any chance have seen another patient we're concerned about? We don't have a name on this one. A male, late twenties, worked at Rocky Flats. He may have stuck in your memory because he offered to trade the identity of D. B. Cooper—you remember the hijacker?—in exchange for immediate discharge from the unit."

"I remember him, too. Absolutely. I must have seen him myself or heard about him at rounds or something. Wait, no, I saw him, I saw him. In fact, he made me the same offer about divulging D. B. Cooper's identity when I saw him down in the ER. I have to admit I was tempted. The whole D. B. Cooper thing has always captured my attention."

"You were tempted?"

"Kidding. Let me check my logs. When were you on inpatient rotation? When were these two admitted?"

"Fall rotation, 1982. The chess player was admitted just before Halloween. A day or two before, maybe. D.B. was Thanksgiving weekend."

He chuckled. "That's ironic, don't you think?"

"Why?" I failed to see the irony.

"That's when the original hijacking occurred. Thanksgiving weekend. Portland to Seattle on Northwest."

"I'd forgotten."

"I haven't. You remember a movie called *Brian's Song*? About Brian Piccolo, the football player with cancer? It was on TV the first time that same Thanksgiving weekend. The two things have always been linked together in my memory. D. B. Cooper and *Brian's Song*."

"I loved that movie."

"Me too. Give me an hour to dig out the right logs. I'll call you back. What's your number?"

"How about if I call you back, Sheldon?"

"You're quite serious about all this, aren't you?"

"I'm afraid so."

I didn't want to go home, so I walked down College Avenue toward the little commercial district where the eastern boundary of the Hill butts hard against the rest of Boulder. The retail establishments on the Hill exist primarily to serve students from the adjacent university. Bars, coffeehouses, music stores, and bicycle shops are overrepresented. I didn't want a drink, so I stopped into Buchanan's Coffee Pub for something warm. I was the oldest person in the place and, from what I could see, one of the few whose sole source of extraneous metal in my body was my dental fillings.

The coffee was good. The music playing in the room was not too different from what I remembered from my own college days. I couldn't understand any of the lyrics, though. I rationalized that it wasn't because I was getting old, but rather because I was out of practice.

After coffee I window-shopped and browsed for CDs. Time dragged. I people-watched from a bench on Thirteenth Street for a while, grew bored with that, and finally found another pay phone and dialed Sheldon's number again. He answered on the first ring.

"I have them both," he said.

"Great. This is great."

"You have the dates correct. The man you call D.B. is in my records under the initials C.R. I have him down as agitated, oriented, with pressured speech, and some curious obsessive/compulsive features. You know, as I read my notes, I realize he's one of those patients who I wouldn't even consider for admission these days. Not given the current managed-care environment and the advances we've made with medicine. And it says clearly in my log that he would gladly trade D. B. Cooper's identity for a quick discharge."

"Do you have a precipitant?"

"Yes. Apparently, he lost it at work. Was threatening someone, wouldn't calm down. They said he was talking crazy about a conspiracy."

"Work was at Rocky Flats?"

"Yes, that's correct. Security department."

"That's it?"

"Let's see. Well-groomed twenty-nine-year-old white married male, one child, with no previous psychiatric history. Da da da da da. No family history. Denied suicidal ideation. Denied hallucinations and delusions. Da da da. That's it."

"Diagnosis?"

"Rule out 301.40. Rule out 312.34 and 297.90."

"I'm sorry, Sheldon, I don't have the DSM codes memorized."

"Compulsive personality disorder. Rule out intermittent explosive disorder and atypical paranoid disorder. It says here that I made a call to Wendy Asimoto about him; she was up next. That's it—that's all I have on him. The other one—"

"Just a second. You sent him to Wendy? Sawyer and I recalled that Arnie Dresser treated him upstairs."

"Maybe. Happened all the time. According to my notes, Wendy was next up for an admission, but if she had already picked up a new patient—one who hadn't come through the ER—then by the time D.B. made it upstairs he would belong to the next doc on the list. In this case, Arnie."

"Oh."

"The other one? The chess player? His initials are V.G."

"How did he present?"

"Classic acute mania. Delusional. Agitated. Irritable. Grandiose. He was demonstrating flight of ideas, pressured speech, lots of clever chess associations. Cops said he was more euphoric than irritable when they first picked him up, was certain that they were there to help him dig up the graves."

"History?"

"Didn't get any. His interview wasn't coherent from the point of view of collecting reliable facts. Lorna would have followed up with his family upstairs, wouldn't she?"

I reflected that it was probably what got her killed. I said simply, "Yes. She would have contacted his family."

"I hope this helps."

"It does, Sheldon. A lot. Thank you. Listen, I don't know how to ask this next question without sounding totally paranoid. But would you like me to give your name to these two ex–FBI agents?"

"You really think I'm at risk?"

"I don't know. I don't have any way to know."

"Even if this vessel holds water, there's currently no evidence that the man you're looking for is seeking targets who never worked on the Orange Team. That's correct, isn't it?"

"For now, yes. But—"

"But it only takes one to destroy the pattern?"

"Yes, it only takes one."

"I'll be careful. For now, I think I'd prefer to stay out of it, please. And say hello to Sawyer for me. She was a special lady."

"I will. Thanks for your help. Please take care of yourself."

# NINETEEN

Lauren met me at the door, one hand on her hip, the other against the wall for balance.

"Hi. I've been worried about you. You're going to need to do a better job of letting me know how long you'll be gone, okay? I was about to use your pager to check on you."

I was sensitive to the possibility that her concern might be bound tightly with criticism, but all I heard was the gentle caution of someone who cared about me. The remanding she sent my way felt sweet, and generous, like an unexpected back rub.

"I'm sorry. You're right. I'll do better about staying in touch. I walked down to the Hill for coffee, and I reached that ER doc, the one who may have admitted that patient, Chester, to the unit. To be on the safe side, I thought I should use a pay phone to call him."

She puffed her cheeks out a little and stared at the cordless phone on the hallway table as though she had just realized it could be a dangerous instrument. "I hadn't thought about that . . . that he might have the ability to do that, you know, to tap our phone. I have to remind myself how sophisticated this guy is. He's not just a schoolyard bully, is he?" She shook her head. "So you think this other doctor you talked with, he could be at risk, too?" She answered her own question. "Of course he could."

I nodded. "If I'm being watched, there's no sense marking a trail that leads to him. The good news is that he was able to remember some things that may help Sawyer and me identify this guy."

"Anything you can tell me?"

"I can tell you anything but names, hon. He just provided some information about the nature of this man's initial presentation that first night in the psych ER. Sheldon's a great diagnostician, so I put a lot of weight on his impressions. But there's nothing earth-shattering in what he remembers. At this point, though, anything at all feels like a gift. I need to let Sawyer know about it as soon as I can. Did you get a sense of whether or not she'll be home tonight?"

"She faxed this to you," Lauren said, as she grabbed a sheet of paper that was beside the phone on the hallway table. Lauren's new plain-paper fax machine occupied the lower shelf of the same table. "It's her travel plans for the next few days." She read a few lines silently and shook her head side to side. "San Diego, San Quentin, Sacramento. This woman sure gets around."

"She has her own plane. Flies from one prison and court to the next, all over California."

Lauren furrowed her brow. "That's worrisome. That she flies her own plane. Considering what happened to that other pilot doctor. Her plane was sabotaged. That's the theory, right?"

"Right. I think it's worrisome that Sawyer is a pilot, too. But Sawyer's pretty cavalier about it. Feels she's taking adequate precautions." I explained about the locked hangar and the trusted airplane mechanic.

Lauren touched me on the shoulder and said, "As far as precautions are concerned, that sounds to me, unfortunately, like the functional equivalent of the rhythm method. I think I need to have another talk with that girl."

"Speaking of that. One of us needs to clue Adrienne in on what's going on up at the Spanish Hills house. The vandalism, especially. I don't want her or Jonas walking into any booby traps."

Lauren said, "I spoke with her while you were gone. You know Ren. It didn't faze her at all. She feels pretty bulletproof in life. She'll keep her eye on things and she'll do her best to keep Jonas away from the construction equipment, which isn't too easy for a boy his age. She's pretty sure there's some link between testosterone and power tools."

"She say anything about Sam and his kidney stone?"

"Not a word. And I didn't ask."

I had to smile. Adrienne was a good friend and a wonderful neighbor, but she didn't talk out of school about her patients. "Any other calls?"

"Yes, I spoke with Sam. He's really somber, Alan. I don't think I've ever heard him this . . . I don't know, scared, maybe."

"Is he home?"

"No. The stone came out this morning. He hopes to go home later today. And he said to tell you that he likes your idea. Wonders if you'll come by around seven tomorrow morning. But he warned you the first few days, she told him he has to take it pretty easy." She paused. "It's nice of you to offer to exercise with him. He could use someone to be with now. A friend."

"It's not all magnanimous. He can use an exercise partner. I can use a bodyguard. And I may take him out to breakfast, too. Show him what saturated fat actually looks like."

"I think," she said, "you're pushing your luck. Exercise is one thing, changing Sam's diet . . . that's something else entirely." She walked up behind me and embraced me, forcing her pelvis against my butt in a pleasing rotation. "You don't have much of an ass, you know?"

"I make up for it by occasionally being an ass, though."

She bit my upper arm near my shoulder seconds before I felt her lips on my neck. "You know, the kids are asleep—"

"We don't have any kids."

"Shhh. We're not expecting any visitors."

"Almost no one knows that we live here. And certainly none that we'd welcome, anyway."

She couldn't reach my ear with her tongue, but I could tell she was trying.

Sam met me at the door to his house the next morning. He and Sherry lived in a small ranch house in North Boulder, west of Broadway, not far from Community Hospital. As he stepped out onto the compact wooden porch, I thought he looked like an old boxer who was facing the prospect of roadwork after ten years away from the ring. I couldn't tell whether his sweatshirt was older than his sweatpants, but they were both older than his only child.

"You look all right, Sam, given what you've been through. What are you supposed to be doing this morning?"

"Walk twenty, twenty-five minutes. Easy, no hills."

"You're ready?"

"No. But if I say screw it and get in the car and go get a doughnut or two, Sherry promises she'll divorce me."

"I don't have a patient until nine. Let's get some breakfast, too, afterward. I'll begin to teach you how to eat."

"I know how to eat."

"Okay, I'll teach you how to eat healthy."

"God, I'm going to hate this."

"Probably," I admitted. "North Boulder Park?"

"Sure. Me and the rest of Boulder's health nuts."

I wasn't surprised by his sarcasm, or his cynicism. I wasn't taken aback by the barely subdued anger. I was surprised, however, by the depth of his depression. He'd lost something over the weekend. Some invulnerability. He'd lost it, and at this moment he didn't expect to ever, ever get it back.

As we walked he scratched at his side frequently, just below his ribs. Nonchalantly, I thought, I asked about pain. He said he just had an itch. I didn't know whether to believe him or not. On the west side of the park, about halfway into our walk, he asked me, incongruously, about Elton John. Usually, Sam and I talked about work, or hockey, not bisexual rock-and-roll stars.

He said, "You like his stuff?"

"Yes, I do. The early stuff mostly. I haven't paid much attention since he insisted I know his sexual preferences better than I had any interest in knowing them."

Sam shuddered. Elton John's lifestyle was way out of his comfort range. "Me, too. I like the early stuff best, too. Remember that song that has the line in it, something like 'I thought the sun was going down on me'? Remember that?" Sam actually tried to attach a melody to the lyric. I forced myself to swallow a snicker.

He scratched at his side again. I said I remembered the song.

"That's what I thought when the pain hit. I figured I must be dying. I heard that song playing in my head and I felt, holy shit, the sun is going down on me. It's, like, high noon in my life—okay, maybe it's mid-afternoon—whatever, you know. But it's early. And the damn sun's going down on me."

I said nothing but looked over so that he would know I was listening to every word.

"But then I decided that maybe what it was is that, you know, it all got dark because of an eclipse. Just some celestial event. That this wasn't really a sign it was over for me. That I didn't need to act like some ancient wiseass who didn't know why it was so dark in the middle of the day. I mean, I didn't have to rush out and start killing virgins. I could wait it out, learn from it. Be enlightened, you know."

"That's an impressive insight, Sam."

"Yeah, well, I'm an impressive guy, Alan." He looked over at me with soft eyes that I couldn't recall seeing before. "Is this kind of what it was like for you when Custer and Simes showed up and told you this guy, this old patient, wanted to kill you? Was it the sun-going-down thing? I mean, is that how you felt, too?"

We paced out another ten steps before I answered. "You know, Sam, it is how I feel, still. I feel, like, here I am, I'm trying to live a decent life, and now, at any moment, this thing, this guy—this asshole—thinks he can jump up and bite me in the jugular anytime he chooses. And when he chooses—bingo, it's over."

Sam said, "That's how I feel about my body right now. It's king. It's the one running the mortality show. Maybe it'll make another stone. Maybe it'll leave me alone. I don't know how it'll happen. I don't know when. I don't really know why. And I don't feel that there's a hell of a lot I can do about it."

"There's always eating well and stress reduction. I can help you with that."

"I think I'll let you. Within limits. And I can teach you some things that will help you with your maniac."

"Like?"

He unzipped the ass-pack that was tethered around his ample waist and pulled it open far enough that I could see the glint of light off his pistol. He said, "I need to teach you how to use one of these. For you, it will have the same prophylactic value as me reducing my calcium intake and lowering my body fat percentage."

"I don't know, Sam."

"It's a package deal, buddy. You teach me about soluble fiber and yoga. I teach you about semiautomatic handguns. I guarantee you that you're getting the better part of this bargain."

Over breakfast at Marie's I introduced Sam to fresh fruit and the glories of toast without butter. He tasted oatmeal for the first time since he'd moved out of his mother's house.

It was a start.

I also caught him up on the sabotage to our renovation project, my trip to see Sawyer in Las Vegas, and my conversation with Sheldon Salgado.

His first comment almost caused me to choke on a crust of bagel I'd smuggled in from Moe's.

He said, "You and Lauren doing okay?"

Sam had never asked before.

"I think so," I said. "We have stresses, you know. This thing with me. Her illness. It can be hard."

He looked over at me, his spoon halfway to his mouth, and nodded. He said, "I like eggs better."

I waited for him to go on more about my marriage. And I considered asking him how he and Sherry were dealing with his illness. Instead I said, "There are some things you can do to help. Other things I think I'm going to have to do on my own."

"Confidentiality shit?"

"Yeah. Confidentiality shit."

"I understand." The growl in his voice said he didn't really. "What do you need?"

"You have any contacts in security at Rocky Flats?"

"You planning an assault?"

I told him I had a lead and that I needed to talk with the man who was head of security at Rocky Flats during the time I was an intern in Denver.

"You're piquing my curiosity."

"I bet. Can you get me the name?"

"Easier than you can get me a fat-free doughnut."

# TWENTY

If I didn't have a great little shack of my own that was undergoing renovation across town in Spanish Hills, I decided that I wanted to live where Reginald Loomis lived. He had a little place that backed up to city greenbelt on the west side of Fourth Street between Iris and Juniper. His wide, unfenced backyard segued, unobstructed, into the foothills of the Rocky Mountains. His closest neighbors to the west were the wild animals that combed the ridges of the jutting hogback a few hundred feet away. In that short distance the elevation rose at least a thousand feet.

Mr. Loomis's shack did not appear to have ever been renovated. Actually, I wondered whether the siding had ever been painted. I guessed that the frame house had been built in the thirties and that Reggie Loomis had bought it for a song in the mid-sixties, before Boulder became cool and northwest Boulder became chic. The shake roof was older than I was. The windows were single-pane and probably leaked like a special prosecutor's office. The concrete walkway had more fissures than the tax code. The front lawn wasn't really a lawn at all, but rather a collection of grass and weed clumps that dotted the dusty expanse between house and street like an archipelago.

But, despite its many shortcomings, I could only dream of owning Reggie Loomis's home. I would have to win a damn good lottery jackpot to afford the half acre of ground this little shack was occupying. I suspected that at least one salivating Realtor knocked on his door each week praying he'd decided to sell.

I'd pondered my approach to Mr. Loomis from the moment that Sam had called me with the name and address of the man who had been chief of security at Rocky Flats during the early eighties. Sam had called himself and Mr. Loomis neighbors. "Only difference between us is eight blocks and about a half a million bucks." I decided right away not to approach Mr. Loomis via telephone, and I resolved to be relatively straightforward about my problems when I spoke with him. I hoped he would do the same for me in return.

The early eighties were a difficult time for anyone working at Rocky Flats Nuclear Weapons Facility. The plant, now in perennial shutdown mode, hugs a huge piece of prime, though partially radioactive, real estate not too many miles south of Boulder along the Front Range. The facility has been a source of controversy since its inception. Protests against the plant, which made plutonium triggers for nuclear warheads, were constant, and must have put particular pressure on anyone who was involved in plant security. The majority of the protesters wanted the plant shut down out of support for nuclear disarmament. A minority just wanted the damn thing closed because it had no business existing upwind and upstream from a major metropolitan area.

Reginald Loomis was retired from a tough job that had probably made him popular with very few of his neighbors.

He answered his door in a fashion I would call leisurely. I saw the light change behind the peephole in his front door from shadow to bright and back a good thirty seconds before I heard the rasp of the dead bolt being thrown. The door opened without a squeak. Given the state of the rest of the house, I was surprised at the lack of audio accompaniment to the operation of the hinges.

"Mr. Loomis? Reginald Loomis?"

He clenched his jaw. "No one calls me Reginald but strangers and my mother. And you, sir, are not my mother. Whatever you're selling, young man, I'm not buying. Unless it's youth. I'm always interested in buying a little youth."

"I'm not selling anything, Mr. Loomis. I'm hoping you will be kind enough to help me track someone down. Someone who worked for you about fifteen years ago at Rocky Flats."

Reginald Loomis was a gaunt man with white hair. Other than eyes the color of blue bank checks, his face was not blessed with much color. But at that moment, I thought he paled even further.

"You said fifteen years, right?"

"Right, actually a little longer. Nineteen eighty-two."

He seemed to get his color back. "That was a long time ago. And I had a lot of people working for me back then. In plant security, the

early eighties, that was prime time. I didn't know all the staff. I'm
not so sure I'd remember much that would be of help to you."

"I'd be grateful if you would try. I don't know where else to go."

"Who are you?"

"My name is Alan Gregory. Dr. Alan Gregory. I live and work
here in Boulder. I'm trying to find someone I was involved with years
ago. Someone whom I need to re-contact. One of the only ways I
have of finding him is to use the fragments of information I recall
from my brief contact with him in the early eighties. One of those
fragments is that he worked in security at Rocky Flats. And that you
were his boss."

He shifted his weight and his face moved farther into the shadows. "What's his name? This man you're after."

I didn't want to admit I didn't know. I said, "May I come in?
Would that be all right?"

His voice took on urgency as he said, "I asked you a question.
What's the man's name?"

"I wish I knew. But I don't remember his name. The best I can do
is initials."

"Well, then, what are those?"

"His initials are C.R."

His lips silently formed the two letters and he looked past me, out
across Boulder toward the dry prairies that began the sweep of the
seemingly infinite midwestern plains. His shoulders dropped an inch
or two. As much to himself as to me, he mumbled, "Why don't you
come on in then?"

Maybe walking into the tent of a Bedouin ruler would leave the
same impression on me as walking into this little North Boulder
bungalow. I don't really know. But the disrepair of the outside of
Reggie Loomis's house could not have left me any less prepared for
what I found inside.

The modest house was probably only nine hundred to a thousand
square feet, but a good half of it had been converted into a kitchen. I
was speechless at how it had been renovated.

He noticed my reaction—had, apparently, been waiting for it. And
he was proud that his house had caused it. "Don't worry," he said.
"Everybody reacts that same way the first time. I kept a little bedroom and the original bathroom pretty much the way they were. The
rest of the house I modified to fit my needs. Have a seat. Please. Over
at the counter."

I followed him toward the back of the house, which was all kitchen.
He sat on a stool next to a huge worktable and I sat beside him. Almost immediately, he popped back up and said, "Some coffee?"

"Sure."

"Espresso okay?"

"Absolutely."

He nodded his approval and moved across the room to a piston-
driven espresso machine and began to grind beans to make us coffee.

I tried to digest the rest of the room. It was dominated by a lapis
blue enamel La Cornue six-burner range. A few months back, Lauren had sent for a catalog from the company and had not so dis-
creetly let me know that she coveted one for our remodeled kitchen.
I had choked, literally, at discovering that the range cost more than
every car I'd ever owned but the most recent one.

Across the room from the La Cornue range, a big stainless steel
and glass two-door commercial reach-in refrigerator/freezer dominated the opposing wall. The kitchen countertops were all made of
either polished granite or stainless steel, except for one large alcove
that was fitted exclusively for baking. That countertop was a gorgeous bronze marble. The pot rack suspended from the ceiling above
the worktable in the center of the room was adorned with a dizzy-
ing selection of cookware, some of it oversized, most of it gleaming
copper.

Reggie Loomis's voice knocked me out of my reverie of astonish-
ment. "Can I offer you a scone? I made them this morning. They're
currant and buttermilk. Perfect with coffee."

"Sounds great. Thank you."

He placed a demitasse of espresso and a dessert plate with a scone
in front of me and then retrieved the same for himself.

I tasted the scone and chased it with a sip of coffee that was
coated with a perfect layer of *crema*. "This is delicious. Do you,
um—I don't know how to ask this—do you run a catering business
or something from here?"

He laughed. The sound was contained, even self-conscious.
"Hardly. How do I explain all this? Some people rot in front of the
TV when they retire. I call it tube rot. Some play golf. Some people
fix up old cars. I have a friend who drives around the west in an old
RV. Me? I decided that I'd indulge myself during my retirement by
doing what I've always loved best. And I love to cook. My momma

taught me to cook. It's always been my vice. I'm never going to have a kitchen with a better view, I thought, so why not just do it here?"

I allowed myself a moment to savor the view that dominated to the west. The grasses on the hogback sparkled like a field of gilded wheat. I noted that the sky was the same color as my host's eyes. "Yes," I said. "Why not?"

"I outfitted this place for less than it would cost to buy my friend's Winnebago. Did most of the work myself. Even had to cut a hole in the wall to get the La Cornue in here. Do you know it's seven years old? Looks brand-new, doesn't it? It's the one thing I own in this world where I can honestly say there is nothing better. That, sir, is the finest cooking appliance on the planet. Probably in the whole solar system, but of course that's just speculation."

"It's . . . truly impressive. My wife and I have just started to renovate our kitchen. I wish I'd seen what you did here first. The range is something."

"Yes, the best. There's no better," he said.

"Are you married, Mr. Loomis?"

"Oh, was. Yep. But that ended."

"Children?"

"They moved to Texas with their mother. I was never partial to Texas. Or to Texans, for that matter. She was. Is. Good kids, though. Boy and a girl. Good." He had a wry smile on his face as he spoke of his distant family. I couldn't imagine why.

"So you just cook for yourself?"

"Lord, no," he exclaimed, patting himself on the abdomen. "I do love to eat, but I try to be cautious as well. Moderation, you know? Discipline. It makes everything possible. Everything."

"So what do you do with all the food you make?"

He appeared quite embarrassed by my question. I wasn't sure he was planning to answer.

Finally, he said, "I feed shut-ins. Sick people. Disabled people. Word gets around at church, so I find out who could use a little hand. Who needs it. Some folks donate ingredients for me. The pastor keeps a pretty fair garden behind the church in the summer, and when the Lord steers the hailstorms elsewhere, the bounty from that garden of his is impressive. I fix what I can. People seem to appreciate well-prepared food. I learned that a long time ago.

"I do breakfast on Monday, Wednesday, and Friday. Supper on Thursday and Sunday. Sunday's a tough one for the shut-ins. They appreciate the food on Sunday most, I think. So breakfast and supper is what I do. I like the mornings best. Folks aren't so tired. Each morning, I choose a different one of my guests to go to last so I get a chance to chat with everybody once in a while. I don't drive anymore, so I get some help dropping the trays by. A church lady usually. She and her son, with one of those big Chevys. What are they called? They look like troop transports? Evening meals, the pastor sends somebody over from the church. Sometimes he and I, we do it together."

I was touched by the generosity of his spirit. "Suburbans. Those big Chevys, they're called Suburbans. It's wonderful, what you're doing here."

"Wonderful? I don't know. Sometimes it feels generous. Sometimes it feels selfish. Who's to say?" He drained his coffee. "Who's to say what's good and bad in this life? Things I was once so proud of . . . well, now." He lifted his cup, using it as a prop. "I mean, other than a fine cup of coffee and an almost perfect scone, who is to say what's good and bad in this life?"

I shrugged. "You're right, of course. Who's to say?" I paused, then added, "It sounds like you're a religious man."

"Me? Religious? Hardly. But the beauty is . . . the beauty of it is that to God, it doesn't seem to really matter. The Lord has been gracious always. Generous often. And forgiving when I've needed it. What more can one ask?"

He stood and fussed with the dishes, moving them from the work-table over to a stainless-steel dishwasher built by the same German company that manufactured my spark plugs. His back turned to me, he asked, "C.R., right? You're looking for an ex-employee of mine with initials C.R. That's a tough puzzle. Inadequate data to work with, I'm afraid. That'd be like trying to concoct a decent little couli-biac when all you've been told is that the dish contains a portion or two of wild rice."

"And that would be hard?"

"Yes, it would." He smiled warmly. "But, believe me, it would be worth it. You ever had coulibiac?"

"I don't believe I have."

"Then you haven't. You wouldn't forget that. No . . . be like forgetting your first girl."

"Maybe I'll have a chance someday."

He didn't offer to whip one up for me. Instead, he returned his attention to my request. "But I don't recall any C.R.s in my employ. May have been a few. Odds are that there were. What did he look like?"

"He was a white male, late twenties. Normal to stocky build. Light complexion." I tried to manufacture a snapshot in my head. I couldn't. "I'd say average height, five-ten, six feet. Maybe one-eighty. Crew cut, I think."

"That sounds like a hundred guys. Half the security officers at the plant looked like that."

"No one specific?"

"Sorry. If anything jogs my memory and makes this guy pop up, I'll be sure to let you know. You have a card? A business card you can leave with me?"

I pulled one from my wallet and held it in my hand. He was still across the room. I wasn't ready to be dismissed. I wanted him to keep talking. "It must have been tough at Rocky Flats then. In the early eighties, especially in security. So much was going on, so much, I don't know, negativity. In the country, in the community. It must have been a tough time."

"Oh, it was negative, all right. The pressure was enormous. Not only from the plant management. But from the Energy Department, the FBI, even some spooks who came around who I was sure were CIA. There were the damn protesters at the fence, the terrorist threat was constant, industrial espionage was always a concern, and there was always the problem of keeping tabs on the damn plutonium a damn microgram at a time. Not to mention keeping track of all the damn dirty waste. Well, well. Employees, too. Had to keep an eye on all of them. I swear half of them couldn't be trusted to check a fence for shorts. It was a hard time. But we had no incursions. I'm still proud of that. In my eight years as chief, we had no incursions."

"Incursions?"

"Penetrations of the internal security perimeter. None of the bad guys got in to sabotage us. I considered that was my primary responsibility. Counter-terrorism. Protecting the plant from subversives."

I didn't even want to consider the consequences of the havoc a bad guy could cause inside a place as toxic as Rocky Flats. A little plutonium here, a little plutonium there . . . I was tempted to ask Loomis if any of his predecessors or successors had been less successful at protecting the internal security perimeter than he was. But

I feared he would begin to realize that he was talking out of school, and shut up.

"You were chief for what years?"

"1979 to 1987. Retired in '87."

"How many years did you have in?"

"Started in '63 as a guard. Twenty-four years in all. Some of those years were better than others. I used to be a hothead, see. Thought I knew everything. Made myself miserable for a stretch there at the beginning."

"Youth," I said.

He seemed to contemplate something. "I stayed young and foolish longer than most, I'm afraid. Never too late to grow up, though. That's what I finally decided. Confucius said that the best time to plant a tree is ten years ago. The second-best time is now. That says it all, I decided. That says it all."

I said, "In 1982, this employee I'm trying to find, this C.R., apparently caused a disturbance of some kind at work. The incident at the plant, whatever it was, was serious enough that someone in authority felt the employee needed to be evaluated by a psychiatrist. He was taken directly from work to the emergency room at the medical school hospital in Denver."

As casually as I could, as I was playing my second-best card, I examined the profile of Reggie's face. He remained, I thought, impassive. Perhaps his eyebrows elevated a millimeter or two, but that was all.

"You that psychiatrist?"

"No, I'm a psychologist."

"I recall that happening a couple of times. Disturbances. Employees who couldn't cut the mustard, handle the pressure. Sometimes I think just being around the juice made some of them crazy."

"The juice?"

"Plutonium. That's what I called it sometimes. Don't recall who might have been involved in those incidents, though. Like I said, long time ago. Wouldn't have taken much to get us to ferry someone away from the site back then. We required discipline at Rocky Flats in those days. Military-style discipline. Didn't tolerate much lip."

He still hadn't made a move to come across the room for my business card, and I didn't stand and extend it toward him. I decided that the time had come for me to play my trump card.

"One more thing; I almost forgot. This next part may seem odd.

One of the reasons that this particular man is so memorable to all of us who were involved with him back then is that he kept going on and on about D. B. Cooper. You know, the hijacker? Kept telling everyone that he knew who D. B. Cooper was. Does that ring any bells?"

Loomis slid his lower jawbone to the left a good inch, giving his face a cockeyed slant. Then he shifted it the same distance to the right for about ten seconds before centering it. "Oh," he chuckled, and shook his head in a disbelieving gesture. "There's a memory, isn't it? I hadn't thought about that in years, but I'm not totally surprised to hear you say it. There was plenty of talk around the plant about all that D. B. Cooper stuff. Had been for years, actually, since a few years after the hijacking at least. Rumor was that Cooper, or whoever had pretended to be Cooper, actually worked at the Flats. It was all legend. Abominable snowman stuff, as far as I'm concerned. I'm not aware of anyone ever taking it seriously."

He narrowed his eyes and asked, "You didn't? Did you?" He employed a gotcha voice.

I shook my head. "No, I just thought it was curious. Thought it might help you pin down this guy's identity for me. You know, maybe there was one particular employee who just couldn't let the whole D. B. Cooper thing go."

"Bet he even offered to expose him? The real D. B. Cooper?"

"Why would you say that?"

"Happened all the time. Someone would have a beef about somebody and suddenly everybody wanted to know if so-and-so was working or off that Thanksgiving weekend."

"How did it get started? The legend?"

"Don't rightly remember."

"But no one employee stands out?"

He appeared thoughtful for a moment. "Sorry. Maybe the personnel office at the plant can help you with those initials you have. Narrow down your search. I'm sure they still have the records. Maybe even photographs. Maybe they'll let you thumb through the photos."

"That won't work, I'm afraid. We asked around. Personnel records are confidential."

Reggie said, "Ah," and nodded in a way that told me he already knew that. "So, um, why do you need to find, um . . . this particular man?" Something about the exaggerated casualness of his question made me think that he was trying to appear uninterested.

I found that interesting.

"Some people have been hurt. Others are in some danger. We thought he could help us sort some things out." I didn't know what else I could say.

Reggie again said, "Ah."

# TWENTY-ONE

I left Reggie Loomis's ersatz catering business just in time to get to my office to see my next patient, a woman named Victoria Pearsall. By necessity, I fought to set aside my frustration about accomplishing so little during the meeting with Loomis so I could focus on the business at hand. With Victoria, that meant attending to her continuing complaints about the harassment she allegedly suffered at the hands of her boss at Ball Aerospace. I'd listened to these litanies from Victoria on and off—mostly on—for months now and I'd decided that her boss was not only not the ogre she made him out to be but was a man with angelic patience who was a viable candidate for canonization. Despite persistent and, I thought, stellar efforts on my part at reflection, confrontation, and interpretation, Victoria and I concluded the session, as we had each and every previous one, with the great majority of Victoria's plated armor intact. As I said, "See you next week," I knew that this thirty-seven-year-old woman and I still had a long, long way to go to get to the root of her problem.

Which, of course, was her.

I barely had time to pee before my next patient arrived. His name was Riley Grant. Riley had been a patient of mine for almost three years, and the difficult days of his treatment were behind him. Originally, he'd been sent to me by a Boulder County judge who offered him a choice between psychotherapy and thirty days in a concrete room with steel bars in a dull neighborhood by the Boulder airport.

It says volumes about Riley that he asked the judge if he could think about his options overnight.

His crime? After the car he was driving was cut off by a bicyclist who was crossing Broadway on a red light at the Downtown Boulder Mall, Riley sped up in order to cut off the offending bicyclist at

Canyon Boulevard. Riley then climbed out of his car, a big black Lexus, and proceeded to turn the offending bicycle into a piece of modern art that closely resembled a bird's nest constructed by a condor.

When provoked, Riley used to have quite a temper. When not provoked, Riley used to be merely a bully. But that was almost three years ago.

Now he was a reminder to me of the wonder of this work I did. Riley's progress gave me hope for Victoria. And I was confident someday she would give me hope for another patient whose intractable problems vexed me no end.

I worked well into the evening. My last two patients were both men in their late twenties with relationship issues. One was a gay computer cartographer named John Fry and the other one was a straight fireman named Tom Jenkins. Neither of them had been in treatment long. And neither was doing much work in therapy. That day I found myself pressing each one of them harder than I usually did. I wasn't sure why I felt so aggressive, but it didn't seem to make much difference in either treatment. I blamed it on Victoria and reminded myself that to tear down a wall, it was necessary to remove a lot of bricks.

John asked for an extra session the following week. Tom warned me that a change in his work schedule might force him to cancel his next appointment. He said he'd call. I felt a certain symmetry at work.

The night was moonless and dark by the time I locked up the building. Diane was long gone. She'd told me earlier in the day that she was going out house hunting with a real estate agent friend of hers.

One of the casualties of being on the hit list of a mass murderer was the loss of my routine. I felt as though I'd relinquished the capacity to accomplish the mundane or the habitual. Now, every act I performed required that I contemplate the possibility of danger. It was as though I were living in a haunted house that had been set up to spook me at any turn.

Did Diane usually leave the back door to her office unlocked? No, she didn't. Since this time she had, I was forced to retrace my steps and search the entire building where we had our offices to make sure no intruders had entered through her carelessly unlocked back door.

Only a week before, turning the deadbolt would have sufficed.

Outside, I walked once around my car before I got in, immediately locking the doors after me. I winced as I turned the key to the ignition, as though wincing would offer some protection against a car bomb. Twice, in the first couple of days after Arnie's funeral, I'd actually gotten down on my knees and examined the undercarriage of the Land Cruiser, looking for explosives. I stopped the ritual of genuflecting beside my car only after I admitted to myself that unless the mad bomber had conveniently marked his package "Dynamite" or "C-4," I probably wouldn't have been able to tell an explosive device from my catalytic converter.

Lauren was at some lawyers' function that she didn't want to attend, Sam was at an early season Avalanche game with his brother-in-law and niece, and since I'd already checked on Dresden's progress with the renovation and addition over my lunch hour, I had the evening to myself. Usually, I would have enjoyed the opportunity to have a few hours alone. Now, being alone let my paranoia run unchecked. Given the current circumstances, this was not a good thing.

Conjuring up an image of Sam's kidney stone—the fantasy closely resembled Gibraltar passing through a straw—I bypassed Nick-n-Willy's and instead stopped by Sushi Zanmai to pick up some sushi for dinner. I was tempted to sit at the sushi bar and eat, but guilt about my dog motivated me to take the food home. I stuck the styrofoam box in the refrigerator while I took Emily out for an evening stroll. She was still fascinated by the novel urban odors of her temporary home, and our walk through the western edge of the Hill was anything but brisk. She demonstrated not only a need to pee on an astonishing number of mysterious odors, but also a bladder capacity that defied logic. We concluded the stroll with a shortcut home that took us through the old Columbia Cemetery on Ninth Street. Although the walk hadn't been strenuous enough to get my heart rate up, walking through a century-old graveyard on a moonless night with a price on my head sure was.

The sushi was good. I poured a beer and tried to interest myself in the fall television season. It didn't work. The fall season, I mean. I watched a little of the hockey game that Sam was attending, but the Avs were up five-zip in the second period and I quickly lost interest in that, too.

My pager went off and I picked up a message off voice mail. It was Tom Jenkins, my patient from that afternoon, letting me know he was going to have to cover an extra shift the following week and needed to either cancel or reschedule. I made a note to call him at work the next day to try to find a new time.

After considering it for a few minutes, I asked Emily if I should phone Sawyer and tell her about meeting with Reggie Loomis. I interpreted her silence to mean "Sure, why not?"

I phoned Sawyer. The line was busy.

I read the note I'd written myself about Riley Grant. Immediately, I thought about Reggie Loomis. The juxtaposition allowed me to see something that had been hovering just outside the reach of my awareness all evening long.

The two men had a lot in common.

Reggie had told me that he used to be a hothead when he was young, that he had made himself miserable. That fact alone made Reggie a lot like Riley before he and I had started to work some of it out together in therapy. I pondered the question of how Reggie had managed to quiet his own fires, and transform himself from a hothead security specialist into a culinary philanthropist with a La Cornue.

The second time I called Santa Barbara, Sawyer answered, breathless, after the third ring.

"I had a feeling it was you. It's the only reason I picked up. I'm on the treadmill; I usually don't answer when I'm working out."

She was panting. I said, "I'll call back."

"No, no. Only eighty-three more seconds. I hate the damn grades more than the speed. How are you? Take your time answering. It's easier for me to listen than it is to talk."

I spent those eighty-three seconds relaying the gist of my visit with Reggie Loomis and the urban legends about D. B. Cooper.

"I'm done," she said. "Speaking of urban legends, do you get this whole endorphin thing? I've never felt high after exercising. Not once. I only feel sweaty and out of breath and tired."

"I, uh, I like to work out. But I'm not much of a runner."

"Figures. But basically no luck with your interview?"

"Basically. I may go back and see him again. Maybe he'll be more reflective after he gets time to think about it all. What about you? Wait, maybe we shouldn't be having this conversation on our home phones."

"It's okay. I had my house swept."

"What?"

"I have a lot of contacts in law enforcement. I had somebody check my house for the presence of bugs. I'm clean. I assume you are, too. Anyway, regarding Chester? I did good. Real good. I know who Chester is. I know where Chester lives. And I know what Chester does for a living."

I was impressed. "That's great. How did you do it?"

Her breathing was beginning to slow, her words no longer punctuated by sharp gasps for oxygen. "USCF. United States Chess Federation. Given what we remembered about him, I assumed he'd be a member. It wasn't that hard to find out the information. A lawyer friend of mine is a chess player, too. He made the call to the organization for me, pretended he was a tournament director and that they owed this guy prize money. Anyway, Chester's name is Victor Garritson. He's an independent software consultant. And he lives in the desert just outside Cave Creek, Arizona."

"That's near Phoenix, isn't it?"

"Good. Yes."

"What's next for us?"

"Shouldn't we pay him a visit? I think we should pay him a visit unannounced. See the look on his face when he lays eyes on us. You said you take Fridays off, right? So what are you doing this Friday?"

"I guess," I said, "I'm flying to Phoenix."

"Me too," Sawyer allowed. "What a coincidence."

Lauren looked like she had the stamina of steam-table vegetables when she got home from her legal affair. I lit two candles, drew her a bath, and set up a nice plate of maguro, unagi, and shinko maki for her to enjoy in the living room after her bath.

She was pink and grateful and smelled of vanilla and jasmine. All of it made me happy. While she began to eat, I shared the details of my conversation with Sawyer, especially her discoveries about Chester—leaving out his real name—and asked her if she would come with me to Arizona.

"I have a trial on Friday, hon. I can't go with you to Phoenix."

"Any chance of a plea bargain?"

"Fifty-fifty. But you know how that goes. We may not settle until ten minutes before trial."

"Damn," I said.

"You'll do fine," she assured me.

I wasn't sure exactly what she meant by that. Was she offering some confidence about the task at hand, interviewing Chester? Or was she making a more profound comment about my capacity to deal with the jumble of feelings I had about Sawyer?

Before I could inquire, she said, "How was your little meeting to-day? With that patient's boss you were going to talk with?"

"More interesting than enlightening." I told her about Reggie Loomis and the La Cornue, about his charity work, and his lack of specific memory of employees at Rocky Flats. I also explained that he felt the D. B. Cooper thing was a dead end. That the whole theory of Cooper working at the Flats had been tossed around at the plant for years after the hijacking. "He made it sound like it had become an institutional parlor game."

Her eyes smiled softly. She was more interested in Reggie Loomis's kitchen. "I'm envious. A six-burner La Cornue? But no griddle? I'd get a griddle on mine. I'm too addicted to pancakes."

"I didn't see a griddle."

"What color?"

"Blue."

"I think I'd get green. The blue's a little bold, don't you think?"

I teased, "Apparently I haven't given it as much thought as you have."

"Maybe you should. Your Mr. Loomis sounds nice enough. And what he does with the food deliveries to the needy is truly generous."

"I think he considers it kind of selfish. The cooking. He feels he gets more out of it than he gives."

We'd begun playing footsies. "When I got home," she said, "I was so tired that all I wanted to do was sleep. Now, after all this talk about giving and getting, I'm not so sure."

"Really?" I asked. "What did you have in mind?"

"How about Scrabble?"

I leaned forward and slid my hands up her legs. "Scrabble sounds good."

# TWENTY-TWO

On the way out of town to the airport on Friday, I stopped in Spanish Hills to see how Dresden's work on the house was progressing. The hat he was wearing that day came from a remote spot on the northeast coast of Australia called Hook Island. We'd discussed this particular hat before. He'd dived that area of the Great Barrier Reef once already and had told me at least three times that it was his destination again the week after our job was finished.

"We're cooking," he explained, as he showed me the footers and foundation walls for the main-floor addition as well as the foundation for the new garage that was going up on the north side of our house. "As soon as the cement is cured, we'll have these two framed and trussed in no time."

The inside of the house had already gone from the demo stage to the reframing stage, and the outlines of the newly designed rooms were taking shape in an array of studs and electrical and plumbing rough-ins. The tradespeople hired by Dresden were typical Boulder subs. The electrician on the project was a huge man with dreadlocks and a Ph.D. in art history, the plumber was a retooled engineer who liked working for himself but dressed as though he were still employed by IBM.

As I did each time we met I inquired of Dresden about any new evidence of our previous intruder.

As he did each time we met he assured me that I had nothing to worry about.

Reassuring clients was one of Dresden's many innate skills. I'd already decided that he would have made a great nanny.

\* \* \*

The plan I'd worked out with Sawyer had me flying into Sky Harbor Airport in Phoenix, renting a car, and meeting her at a general aviation field in Scottsdale. She said she didn't like flying into big fields, and that it would be easier for me to rent a car at Sky Harbor than it would for her to rent one at the smaller airport.

I kissed Lauren good-bye, wished her luck with her trial, and gathered a few things together for my short trip to Arizona. Just as I was leaving the house she called me back into the kitchen and said, "Look."

She was directing me to the television. A brush and forest fire was out of control near Kittredge. "That's where Gary Hart lives, isn't it?" she asked.

"Is it?" I didn't know where Gary Hart lived, but I knew that Kittredge was twenty miles north along the foothills of the Front Range, in the sharp canyons west of Red Rocks amphitheater. Which meant we were in no danger in our temporary housing on the Hill in Boulder. I was too distracted by my need to get to Denver to pay much attention to the news. "I hope they get it under control. Did you see anything about airport traffic? I need to run."

I arrived at DIA in plenty of time to answer the page that Lauren directed toward my beeper during my drive. She hadn't used our agreed-upon emergency code, so I managed to keep my pulse in double digits as I punched in our home number and said, "Hi. It's me. What's up? Miss me too much already?"

"Hardly. Didn't you tell me that that doctor lives near Kittredge? The one who saw those patients in the emergency room? You know, the one you talked to over the weekend."

"Sheldon? He lives outside of Morrison."

"Kittredge is outside of Morrison, isn't it?"

Oh no. Oh shit. "You don't think—?"

"I don't—"

"Jesus. I hope this is a coincidence. Find out what you can. I'll call you from Phoenix, okay? Wait, let me give you his phone number. Maybe you can reach him." I dug around in my DayTimer and found the number. "His name is Sheldon Salgado. Got it?"

"Yes," she said, her voice tight. I dictated the number.

My United shuttle departed Denver on time and arrived in Phoenix early. I tried to reach Lauren as soon as I got off the plane. The home line was busy. I wasted a few minutes in an airport bar hoping to see the news of the Colorado forest fire on CNN. Instead I raised my blood pressure fifteen points watching three representatives and two senators argue that there was really no need for campaign finance reform.

*Excuse me?*

After trying to call home again—no answer this time; she must have been on her way to work—I took the little yellow Hertz bus to pick up my car. They had my nondescript Ford waiting in my preassigned spot. I surprised myself by not getting lost on the way to the Scottsdale airport. I arrived at eleven-thirty, fifteen minutes before Sawyer had estimated that she would be touching down.

Forest fires, even distant ones, are not uncontaminated emotional events in my life. One of my dear friends had watched people die in a voracious fire in Wyoming, and the scars from that event affected his life every day. I'd heard his brother tell the story of the ferocity of the Wyoming fire and had even flown over the skeletal remains of the forest that had been the fuel. I'd been up between Kittredge and Morrison many times and had no trouble imagining the terrain, the dry lodgepole, and the golden brush. I could see the dream homes and the don't-bother-me cabins that dotted the dirt roads. And I had no trouble conjuring the devastation that fierce wind and abundant fuel could cause to that mountain enclave after a solitary spark.

Inside the spacious waiting area of Blue Skies Aviation, I approached the counter and asked if a plane piloted by Sawyer Faire had landed yet. The man at the counter was in his early twenties but had already lost much of his hair. The embroidery on his polo shirt told me that his name was Guy. His eyes were a distracting pale chocolate in color. After greeting me with a big smile he said they'd had no incoming this morning except for regulars. He offered to check with someone in back to be certain and disappeared into an adjacent office. A moment later he returned and told me that Gloria didn't think that my friend had been in yet. I thanked him, turned, found a pay phone and once more tried to reach Lauren, this time at work.

"Lauren Crowder," she answered, in her professional voice. I knew the voice well. She used it with me when it was time to take out the garbage or when it was my turn to perform the Tootsie Roll patrol duties around our house. Sometimes she used it during the almost-there moments of hurried sex.

"It's me."

"No good news, I'm afraid. The fire is definitely in the vicinity of his house. There's no answer when I call. Television reports said the fire started around three in the morning. So, he and his family—you said he had a family, right?"

"Yes."

"They must have been home when it started. I mean, at that hour? Unless they're out of town somewhere, they had to be home."

"I'd imagine. Any houses destroyed yet?"

"New reports are unclear. One said two 'structures' were engulfed, whatever that means. And I haven't been able to watch the news at all since I got to work. I'm real busy here—I'm sorry. You know, the trial this afternoon? There's a plea-bargain prayer blowing in the door. We're scrambling to agree on a response."

"It's okay. I'll try to find out what I can from this end. Maybe he's at work or maybe his secretary at the hospital knows something. Listen, sweets, um, do you have your gun with you?"

She hesitated and lowered her voice before she responded. "Are we going to fight about it if I do?"

"No, we're not."

"Then, yes, I do."

"Good," I said. Instantly, I couldn't believe that I'd said it.

While I waited for Sawyer's plane to arrive, I tried Sheldon Salgado's office but got a recording. I didn't leave a message. Then I phoned Sam. He was home. I filled him in on my concerns about Salgado and his home in the canyons outside of Kittredge and asked if he could learn anything through cop channels about the progress of the fire.

"Hell, yes. Give me something useful to do. I'm going nuts here. Where can I call you?"

"You can't. I'll get back to you. Say, half an hour?"

"I'll have something by then. Lauren's safe?"

"Just spoke to her at work. She has the Glock with her."

"Good. Still waiting for you to take those lessons."

"I'm thinking about it, Sam. Believe me."

"Call me back."

As I placed the receiver back on the hook, I turned and found myself looking down on the receding crown of Guy's head. I realized the floor behind the counter must be higher than the waiting area and that Guy was a good six inches smaller than I had given him credit for.

He looked up and into my eyes, quite comfortable with his height. "You know what kind of plane your friend flies, by any chance?"

"Yes, it's a Beechcraft, a Bonanza, I think she said. Is she here?"

"There's some tower talk you might be interested in. Come on over—we'll let you listen in."

I followed him to the office in back, where a woman no older than Guy was sitting behind a steel desk examining invoices. She had curly blond hair that tumbled past her shoulders. The phone she was holding had disappeared into the thicket of locks in the general vicinity of her ear. She smiled a toothy smile at me and pointed to a chair with the sharp end of a pencil. Guy remained standing.

Without another word she hung up and said, "Hi, I'm Gloria." She adjusted the volume on a radio tuned to the tower frequency. "I just got off the phone with the tower. They have a Beechcraft Bonanza B-36, call five-six Foxtrot. Ring a bell? It's having a problem with its front gear and they have it circling the field. Does that sound like it could be your friend?"

"What kind of problem?" I hoped it didn't mean what I thought it meant.

Guy explained, "Front landing gear won't come down."

"Oh, my God."

"She has plenty of fuel, apparently. She's going to try a few things to bring the gear down."

"And if she can't?"

Guy's full lips disappeared into a tight pink line. He said, "She's going to have to scratch her belly, I'm afraid."

For some reason I couldn't understand, I knew exactly what he meant.

"What are they saying now?" I couldn't make sense of the voices coming over the tinny speaker.

Gloria listened for a moment. "They're talking to a Learjet that's on final. That's not your friend."

"That's Bert's plane. He's one of our regulars," added Guy.

"Aren't they going to foam the runway or something? Get ready for her? Has somebody called an ambulance?"

"Would you like some coffee?" asked Gloria in a sweet voice. She was trying not to be patronizing. "This is going to take a while to settle out. She'll probably get it to come down."

I thought of Sam and Sheldon Salgado. I said, "No, I think I need to make another phone call. Come get me if anything changes, okay?"

"Of course," said Gloria. "You won't have that coffee? I made it myself and I'm good."

At that, Guy blushed. I said, "Sure. I will, thanks."

Sam answered even before I heard the phone ring. "Alan?"

"Yes. You have something?"

"Talked to a JeffCo deputy, a friend of mine. They have two houses burned, six more are in danger. The fire is on both sides of a county road just outside of Kittredge. They're thinking arson."

"Jesus. Any casualties?"

"None confirmed. It's a big fire, though. He says it's just chaos up there, trying to get crews in and residents out."

"I don't know if it's related to the fire, Sam, but my friend Sawyer's in trouble in her plane. She's circling the airport right now. Apparently her landing gear won't come down."

"You shittin' me?"

"No."

In a voice that let me know he wasn't expecting an argument from me, he said, "If you don't have any objections, I think I'm going to go check on Lauren. I got nothing better to do today."

If this guy was trying to make me feel totally out of control, he was succeeding. A forest fire was threatening a colleague six hundred miles away and a faulty airplane was endangering an ex-lover a few thousand feet above my head. A basic tenet of psychotherapy says that if you want to know what a person is trying to communicate to you, take a look at how his behavior makes you feel.

This time it was easy. This guy wanted me to know how it felt to be absolutely out of control when everything is on the line.

He wanted me to feel vulnerable.

He wanted me to feel helpless.

He wanted me to know how it felt to know that he could rip anything he wanted from my life.

The main question in my mind right then was, did he want me to feel grief? Did he plan for Sawyer and Sheldon to die today?

I prayed not. Because if his goal was to kill them, I felt that Sawyer had no chance at all to fix her recalcitrant landing gear. And if he intended that Sheldon was to die, then Sheldon's corpse was probably already charred and curled into a fetal position in the ruins of his home.

I realized that in my mind I was granting this adversary power that seemed almost superhuman. I was feeling his presence as I might that of a malevolent god, or of some satanic force. I was feeling that he was invincible.

Outside Blue Skies I stood on the tarmac and stared into the brightness. Guy pointed out which dot traversing the airspace above the field was Sawyer's plane. He reassured me that she had plenty of fuel.

I felt like saying, "So what?" It was like telling me that somebody who was having a heart attack had a good appetite.

Gloria was inside, her focus divided between the tower traffic and, at my request, CNN. I had asked her to keep an eye out for news of a forest fire in Colorado. She was so sweet she didn't even ask why.

My pager vibrated on my hip. I'd forgotten that the pager company had told me that with my new state-of-the-art pager, I could roam. Which, the salesman explained, meant I could be reached anywhere. At the time I wondered whether or not that was a good thing.

The phone number on the screen was the DA's office in Boulder. Lauren was calling.

I raced back to the pay phone and called her.

"Sam just told me about Sawyer, Alan. Is she okay?"

"She's still up there. I can see her circling when I go outside."

"Can they do anything?"

"There is apparently a manual backup system, a crank of some kind, something that allows her an alternative way to lower the gear. She's trying it now."

"Then who's flying the plane?"

I hadn't thought about that. "Autopilot, I guess. Anything new about the fire? About Sheldon?"

"No. Sam has calls out. He's out talking to my secretary. He's waiting for his cell phone to ring." She lowered her voice. "Alan, I'm worried about his health. Should he be doing this? Isn't this too stressful for him?"

"I don't know. But my guess is that trying to get him to leave would be more stressful on both of you than allowing him to stay and—"

"Hold on a second. I hear Sam's phone ringing. I think his call just came in."

For a long minute all I could hear was background music. Then Sam speaking, and Lauren responding. Sam again.

To me, she said, "They think his house is one of the ones that burned. Sheldon's house is one of the first two that went up."

My heart felt swollen with responsibility. Had I led this animal to Sheldon Salgado's door? I'd been so careful.

"Casualties?"

I heard her say, "Sam, did they find any bodies?"

To me, she said, "He doesn't know. Just shrugged his shoulders."

# TWENTY-THREE

As I hung up the phone, my mind wandered back a few mornings and I could almost feel the sensation of watching that ceiling joist descend directly toward my head in the rubble of our renovation. I tried to shake off the image as I walked outside to the tarmac and approached Guy. He was facing away from me, toward the north. I asked him to point out Sawyer's plane again. He directed me to the far side of the field, toward a speck that was on the underside of a sheer stream of clouds just above the ridgeline of some beautiful mountains. I had trouble picking it up.

He pointed again and I tried to sight down his arm.

In the distance, I heard one siren, then, I thought, two. I wondered if the emergency vehicles were coming to the airport to prepare for Sawyer's attempt to land. As I finally identified the speck in the distance that was her plane, I said a silent prayer that this whole refrain of terror was merely her ceiling joist falling; that she would duck this bullet as I had ducked that one.

Guy said, "While you were on the phone, um, before? Your friend told the tower that, uh, it wouldn't go. She said she couldn't lower the front gear with the crank. The fix wasn't working."

My knees felt weak. "So is she on her way down?" I wanted to put that off as long as possible.

"Not yet. They have a call out to the FBO at Sky Harbor and to the manufacturer. To see if the maintenance people at Beech have other suggestions."

I was about to ask what an FBO was when I heard Gloria's voice call my name. I turned to see her holding open the door that led from the tarmac to the waiting room. This was my first opportunity to see her out from behind the desk. She was wearing an incredibly short pleated yellow skirt and had the most attractive legs I had ever seen in my life. She held her hair with one hand as the wind gusted and called out, "It's the tower. The controller says she wants to talk to you. Your friend in the plane? She's going to switch frequencies. You'll be able to talk with her on our handheld radio."

Guy and I ran inside.

Gloria resumed her spot behind her desk. I tried to make sense of my temporary fixation on her splendid legs as she sat and those legs disappeared behind the black metal skirt of the desk. Couldn't. I watched her adjust the frequency on the handheld radio to 122.75 and grabbed it as soon as she offered it to me.

"The connection may not be great," she warned me. "Just push that button to talk."

It wasn't.

"Sawyer, is that you?"

"Alan? God. It's good to hear your voice. If my dad was here, he'd say I'm in a fine pickle."

The sound was scratchy. I spent an extra second processing her words. "The gear just won't come down?"

"Not yet. I think if he did me, he did me good."

"Don't say that. This is only intended to frighten you."

"It's working."

"Sorry. Didn't get that."

"I said it's working. I'm scared."

"How much fuel do you have left?"

"Twenty minutes, half an hour."

"You can bring it down, you know. You can. You'll just scratch the belly a little bit."

"It's not the belly I'm worried about. It's burying the propeller. That's when things will get dicey."

"You can do it." I didn't have a clue what it would require of Sawyer to avoid burying the propeller. I was afraid I was doing nothing more than an adequate impression of a shrink standing on the sidelines leading cheers for some psychological athletic competition.

"You know what? Time is passing pretty slowly up here and this is all reminding me of that time on the unit. That patient of Arnie's who had the knife. Do you remember?"

My reaction, which I kept to myself, was that Travis, Arnie's patient with the Swiss Army knife, was a rank amateur compared to whoever it was who had screwed with Sawyer's landing gear. I said,

"Of course I remember. But I don't think I'm going to be of much help this time. You'll do fine on your own."

"Thanks for your vote of confidence." Her tone was sardonic.

I thought she was going to say something else. She didn't. The silence between us grew into seconds and felt awkward. I could think of nothing to say that didn't sound banal. She cracked it. "I'm afraid that I need to go. See if the folks at the Beechcraft factory in Wichita have checked in with any advice. I wish I knew why the manual assist isn't working. But, hey, I'll see you one way or another in about half an hour, right?"

"I'm counting on it," I said. I was aware that the circumstances were beseeching something emotional from me and I consciously fought an impulse to tell her that I loved her.

I assumed it was ancient. The impulse.

"Bye," she said.

Guy walked with me as I returned to the tarmac. We waited, staring at the sky, watching the gray dot that was Sawyer grow in size as the plane approached us then receded into the distant sky and she flew away. Once or twice I lost sight of the plane altogether. I wondered if it had exploded or disintegrated but kept the thought private, holding my breath until the sunlight again glinted off metal or glass and I could discern it in the distance.

Gloria joined us after a few minutes. I smelled her perfume before I heard her approach. She stood between Guy and me, slightly behind us. "The tower was thinking of moving her over to Sky Harbor or Williams, but she's going to have to come down here. There's a UPS plane with a blown tire blocking a runway intersection at Sky Harbor anyway. They're mobilizing the emergency equipment to get in place here."

Could anything else go wrong? "What will it be like?" I asked. "When she comes down."

Gloria touched my wrist as she answered, "Most situations like this end up okay. A lot depends on these winds we're having. They've been gusting like this all morning. In calm air— How experienced is she, anyway?"

"I'm not sure. She flies all the time. It's her own plane."

"That's good. Assuming she's experienced, in calm air she should be able to get it down okay. She's going to have to make sure she keeps that nose up, though, to—"

"Keep the propeller off the runway."

"Yeah."

"She told me about that while we were on the radio," I explained. "But if the wind gusts?"

A tiny plane with two seats and its wing mounted above the cabin began to taxi past us, the sharp drone of its engine stopping our dialogue. Guy yelled in my ear, "That's a Cessna. A one-fifty. It's not like your friend's. Hers is much bigger than that one and has the wing below."

Gloria waited until the small plane had taxied away to answer my earlier question about the wind. "Everything about landing is harder in crosswinds like this. Without the gear down, her margin for error is seriously reduced because the propeller blades are so much closer to the ground when she actually touches down. Does that make sense?"

I nodded.

"The good news is that she'll be running almost dry. The risk of fire if anything, you know, goes wrong will be reduced. The controllers have called a couple of senior instructors into the tower to coach her down. She'll cut all her power at the end."

Guy asked, "Is Tom up there? In the tower?"

Gloria nodded, then explained to me, "Tom's our lead instructor. He taught both of us to fly. He's good."

Guy seconded the opinion about their instructor and then asked Gloria something about another employee who was late showing up for work. As she answered, my mind drifted to Sawyer. Although I'd never seen her plane, I'd been in small aircraft before. I could see her in the little cockpit with the high dash, the propeller blades cutting a neat, perfectly rounded arc in front of her. She hadn't sounded that frightened on the phone. I wondered if she was terrified.

Gloria turned to leave. "Oh, by the way, nothing on TV about that fire in Colorado. Sorry." She reached back and touched me on my shoulder.

"Thanks for checking."

Guy nodded at the sky and asked, "Is she, like, your girlfriend? The woman in the plane?"

I shook my head. "No," I said, "just an old friend." To make conversation, I added, "What about Gloria? Are you and she . . . ?"

He laughed.

We stared at the sky some more.

\*     \*     \*

A minute later, no more, Gloria came running back outside through the glass doors, her pleated skirt and blond waves bouncing in unison. She cried, "She's out of fuel. She's coming in without power."

*What?*

"She's out of fuel? I thought she said she had plenty of fuel? What the hell happened?"

"I don't know. I was inside listening to the tower traffic, and in a calm voice she suddenly reports she's losing power. Tom called over. He thinks the fuel gauges must be inaccurate."

"What now?"

Gloria said, "It means it's an engine-out landing."

"Which means what?"

"Which means that for right now she's flying a glider."

"Her plane will glide all right?"

"Yes. She's done it before; she's practiced engine-out landings. We all have. It's part of the training."

"But not without landing gear?"

"No. She doesn't have any practice doing engine-outs without landing gear. That part's brand-new for her. But at least she won't have to worry about the propeller problem anymore."

"Why not?"

"It won't be spinning. Before, with power, she would have had to cut the engine just as she flared for touchdown in order to still the propeller blades. Now she doesn't have to worry about it. What she does have to do is pray that none of the blades stopped in the six o'clock position."

"Because then she'll bury it?"

Gloria said, "Yes. Then she'll bury it. It'll protrude below the fuselage for sure."

My heart was forcing blood into my arteries ferociously. I could hear it roar in my ears. I could feel the pressure building in my vessels. My muscles were taut and ready for my adversary. I felt absolutely ready to take on a thousand monsters.

But there was nothing I could do.

I asked, "Where will she come down?"

"Over there." Guy pointed. "On twenty-one."

"How soon?"

"Any minute."

# TWENTY-FOUR

I'd like to go over there. To the runway, where we can see her come in. Can we drive over there?"

"Not to the runway," Gloria said. "But we can drive over to Desert Aviation. They're right on the other side of the taxiway. They're in a better position to see her approach."

Guy said, "Good idea. I'll get the truck."

We squeezed into the cab of a little Nissan pickup with the Blue Skies Aviation logo on the doors and followed some indecipherable path on the tarmac to the offices and hangars of Desert Aviation. I assumed that Desert was Blue Skies' main competitor at the airport. Guy parked the truck in a lot that was out of sight of the runway. The three of us hopped out of the cab and ran around the corner of the building. Half a dozen employees were already outside, strung out like pearls on a string, watching the denouement of the events that they, too, had been following on the tower radio.

A couple of the men found Gloria's approach much more interesting than they found Sawyer's. One of them smiled at her. She seemed not to notice. He turned to her and said, "Is that one of yours up there?"

Without looking at him, she said, "No. We're just going to service it. The pilot's his girlfriend." She pointed at me, granting me the smile the other man coveted.

I didn't correct her about the girlfriend part.

Car crashes feel like they happen in slow motion. Plane wrecks, it turns out, actually do. I remembered the video of the DC-10 somersaulting into the cornfield in Sioux City, and the fascinating tape of the 747 almost managing to belly-land just off the beach on that island off the coast of Africa.

The Desert Aviation mechanic, whose interest in Gloria hadn't waned, moved close to us. He had some binoculars around his neck. To impress Gloria, he took on the responsibility of providing a play-by-play on Sawyer's approach. His buddy fell into line doing the color.

The mechanic raised the binoculars. "Okay, she's just turning into final. I'd say she's a mile out."

"No, not that far. Is she low?"

"She's not low."

"If she's low she's screwed."

"She's not low."

"Still no gear?"

"Still no gear."

Gloria leaned over and whispered into my ear, "I think she is a little low. Not awful, but a little. I'd want to be up another hundred feet."

"What does that mean? Being a little low?"

"If she had power, it wouldn't mean anything. She'd just goose the throttle and get the altitude back. But remember she's gliding. If I'm right, she's gonna need some help from the winds to reach the runway."

I didn't like the sound of what I was hearing. "And if she doesn't get them? The winds?"

"She'll hit short. In the sagebrush. And she doesn't want to do that. There're no obstacles out there, but it's not level. And she needs level ground for this kind of landing." She squinted toward the sky. "But first, right now, she needs to fight a temptation to pull the nose up, because that will only drop her faster."

I assumed there wasn't time to remedy my ignorance about the laws that govern flight. Why, I wanted to know, would pointing the plane's nose up bring it down? I didn't ask.

"Glide path looks good," said one mechanic.

"Wrong again. I say she's low," offered his pessimistic friend.

"She's not low."

"You watch," he challenged.

In my periphery, I saw a fire truck pull into position on a taxiway almost directly in front of the tower. A hundred yards beyond it, parked in the shadows, was an ambulance with its engine running. Two paramedics stood in front of their vehicle, their hands cupping their eyes, trying to enhance their view.

Gloria touched my forearm gently, and her kindness shocked me back to attending to the sky above runway twenty-one.

The mechanic said, "She's over the highway. She's coming down short. Glide path *is* a little low. You were right, you little shit."

The little shit gleefully punched his buddy on the biceps. If any money changed hands I was going to kill one of them.

To me, Gloria whispered, "She's not doing too badly. She may still be able to catch the end of the pavement. Come on, Lord. Give her a lift, just a little updraft from the heat. Come on. Come on."

I could see the small plane clearly now. The first thing I checked was the position of the propeller blades. None of the three blades was near six o'clock. Not exactly four and eight, though—maybe three-thirty and seven-thirty. How far out was she? I couldn't tell. But I could tell that Sawyer's plane was no more than seventy-five feet from the ground and that she was descending fast. The wings were rocking up and down and the tail seemed to be scooting off to one side.

"Is she doing that? Why is she doing that to the tail?"

Gloria said, "She's crabbing. Those crosswinds I told you about? She's trying to stay aligned with the runway."

"How's her altitude?"

She squeezed my hand and said, "I sure wish she was up a little higher." Her tone was as light as helium. Almost like a prayer.

The plane was twenty feet from the ground yet seemed to be over a hundred yards from the beginning of the macadam. Sawyer wasn't going to make it.

As though she was reading my thoughts, Gloria said, "Sometimes here, in the desert, you feel it just before you touch down. A little bounce from the heat radiating off the ground. That's all she needs here. Just a little bounce from the sun gods. Just a solar push."

I reminded myself to breathe.

Guy said, "There! Look! She's up a little, isn't she?"

To my amazement, I could see it. I could see the results of an invisible hand that gently lifted the plane five feet higher, maybe ten. And it was apparent that Sawyer was fighting the controls. She brought the nose down once, then again. She jammed the tail over to the left.

"One more," Gloria implored. "We need one more bounce."

And there it was.

A bigger bounce this time. No mistaking it. A certain ten feet. Suddenly, the nose of Sawyer's plane was above the parallel stripes at the end of the runway. Everyone cheered.

Except for me. I waited for the sparks and the screech and prayed I wouldn't see the propeller blades dig into the asphalt.

And then, all at once, it seemed it was over. The emergency trucks started rushing toward the plane. The crowd was cheering. Gloria was embracing me and telling me that God was so good, so good.

I noticed that my beeper was vibrating on my hip, and I wondered if Sheldon Salgado would agree with Gloria about God's good graces.

The Bonanza had scratched to a stop and sat forlornly in the middle of the runway, just left of the center. The door on the pilot's side opened and Sawyer climbed out and stood on the wing. She waved.

Right at me.

I started to walk toward her. No one stopped me, so I started to run. The paramedics got to her first, the firefighters only seconds behind. I weaved through the crowd that quickly gathered around the plane, found her just as she found me, and hugged her tightly.

"Great job," I said. "Incredible landing."

Into my ear, she said, "I don't know about that. But I'm glad you're here. I think I need a doctor."

Behind me someone was saying it was remarkable, that there wasn't much damage.

I thought, maybe not to the plane.

My beeper vibrated again.

Twenty minutes later, Sawyer was huddled beside her plane with Guy and the chief mechanic for Blue Skies Aviation. I went back to the waiting area to find out what my two pages were about.

The number on my pager was that of Sam's cell phone.

"Alan? Where the hell have you been? You didn't get my pages?"

"No, I got them. It's been nuts here, Sam. Real touch and go, but Sawyer got down okay. I'm sure the plane was sabotaged. A real sweet job. Our guy's fingerprints are all over everything."

"Not literally, right? Can't tie him to it?"

"No, I'm babbling. Not literally."

"Well, the news isn't so good here. There are three bodies in that doctor's house. But they're too scorched to ID."

"Oh, God."

"Yeah. I'm sorry."

My reaction to Sheldon's death was going to take some time to sort out. The most pressing feelings were responsibility and anger. Fear was in there, too. I asked Sam, "You feeling okay?"

"Me? I'm fine. But nobody's trying to kill me. It's the rest of you that I'm worried about."

"Is Lauren doing all right?"

"She's upset. But she's strong, you know that. She's in a conference right now, bargaining away one of my collars, probably. A whole gaggle of suits in there with her. I think I'm going to stick around for a while, maybe see her home, you know. Make sure that it's safe."

"Thanks, Sam."

"Listen, you're going to be home tonight, right? We're still on for walking tomorrow?"

"Yeah. I'm looking forward to it. How's the diet?"

"Don't ask."


Sawyer insisted that, despite the mishap with her plane, we keep our plans to drive to Cave Creek to confront Victor Garritson, aka Chester. Even as I drove off the airport property, I was still arguing that we accept the cards that fate had been dealing us and just fly—commercially—back to our respective homes.

"You won't get far using gambling metaphors with me, Alan. It's my territory, remember. And I don't like being intimidated."

"That wasn't intimidation up there. That was attempted murder."

"I'm not convinced."

"Wait a second. You accept that Chester or D.B. or whoever it is sabotaged your plane?"

"We looked. That mechanic and me—he's good, by the way. We couldn't find anything. No evidence of sabotage at all."

"You're saying this was a coincidence? That your landing gear wouldn't come down *and* your fuel gauge misrepresented your fuel reserves? I'm sorry, but I'm afraid your denial is out of control, Sawyer."

She folded the map she was holding with great care and said, "One of the first rules of medicine, and you know this, Alan, is that rare things happen rarely. I treat this as a mechanical problem until we see the evidence otherwise." She poked at the map with her index finger. "Next left. We're going northeast."

I pulled into the left lane.

She asked me, "Ever seen a card shark in action, a really good one? Someone who can deal off the top of the deck, or the bottom of the deck, or out of the middle of the deck, and you're watching for it and you can't see him do it and you can't figure any of it out?"

"Yes. I saw one on HBO." I didn't know where we were going with this conversation.

"What did you think?"

"I was impressed. He announced what he was going to do before he did it and I still couldn't see him do it. Your point?"

"Don't you see? Chester or D.B. or whoever it is that's after us is that clever. We know he's cheating, but he's so good we can't even catch him cheating. What's the lesson. The lesson is we can't play cards with him. Because he'll always, always end up with the aces. And we won't know how he did it."

"You're making my argument for me, Sawyer. That's all the more reason to head home. Now."

"Without seeing this Victor Garritson? No way. Alan, together we have, what, thirty-some-odd years of clinical experience? I spend half my waking hours with sociopaths, either inmates or their lawyers. We'll be able to tell. We'll know if he's the one, Alan. It takes something special, some advanced arrogance, some ultimate confidence, to do this. To cheat while the world is watching and know that they can't catch you. I want to look in Garritson's eyes and see if he has it. That arrogance."

"That's all you want to do?"

"You don't believe me?"

I didn't answer. After completing the turn I guided the Taurus into the right lane and pulled into the driveway of the first restaurant I spotted. "I'm hungry," I explained.

"Uh-oh," she responded.

Our waitress could have been Gloria-from-the-airport's little sister. Blond wavy hair and legs up to who knows where. Sawyer ordered a Coke and toast and jam. I ordered a breakfast that Sam would kill for.

Sawyer noticed our waitress's resemblance to Gloria, too. "Our waitress's twin? That girl at the airport? She's sweet on you."

"Sweet on me? What are you talking about?"

"The one with the pleats and the legs."

"Gloria."

"Yes, Gloria. I think she was yours for the asking."

"You think you know about these things?"

"Yeah. That first day I met you, when I saw you walk into Mona's party, I felt the same thing. I was yours for the asking."

"You sure didn't act like it."

" 'Act' is the operative word. You didn't do any asking."

"I was kind of shy."

"You got over it quickly enough."

I was afraid I was blushing. I said, "I'm happily married to a great woman. I'm not shopping around."

She smiled coyly, shrugged and raised her eyebrows.

I wanted to know where she was heading but not as much as I wanted to change the subject. "Before, back on the highway, when I said I was hungry, why did you say, 'Uh-oh'?"

"Because way back when, whenever you wanted to talk, you know, seriously, you always tried to do it over a meal. You did it again last week when we were in Vegas. I wanted to gamble, you wanted to nosh."

I nodded. It was an interesting observation. At first blush, I had to admit it had the ring of truth.

"This time you're right, I guess."

"I'm usually right about the little things."

"Just the little things?"

"Unfortunately." She sipped at her Coke.

I said, "I do have something serious to talk about. That call I made while you were in the hangar? It looks like Sheldon Salgado is dead, Sawyer. He died this morning sometime."

I waited for her to react.

Her eyelids drifted down and her eyes closed. A tear formed in the outer corner of each eye and her shoulders inched up. I reached over and unwrapped her hand from her red plastic glass of Coke and entwined my fingers with hers. The tears dropped one at a time. The left one migrated down her cheek in an uneven path. The right one fell to her lap.

"What happened?" she said.

Not "What did he do to him?"

I told her about the area where Sheldon lived in the foothills. About the fire overnight. About Sam's call that came with the news that three bodies had been found just as Sawyer was scraping her plane's belly along the runway.

"Three?"

"That's what my friend said."

Sawyer wanted to talk about the third of the three bodies. "You ever meet his baby? Sheldon's baby? She was born during the first week of the second year of the residency. Sheldon and Susie called her Olivia."

"No, I never met her. I wasn't that close to Sheldon. She would be, what, almost sixteen now?"

"Something like that. If she's still alive."

She stared out the window and watched as the driver of an eighteen-wheeler tried to maneuver his rig into a no-prayer space in the small parking lot. Her voice devoid of affect, she said, "She was a gorgeous baby. She didn't deserve to die. Olivia."

I said, "I know." What gorgeous baby deserves to die?

Sawyer shook her head and started to cry. I thought she might weep for a moment as the shock of Sheldon's death seeped into her. But her composure evaporated and she dissolved into grief. She lowered her face into her hands and didn't seem to be able to stop crying.

The rest of the patrons in the restaurant stared at me with rancorous glares. The waitress who resembled Gloria looked as though she would gladly stab my eye out with her pencil.

I realized they all figured I had just dumped Sawyer. I could see the irony distorted in the distance, as if through a thick fog.

# TWENTY-FIVE

Sawyer wouldn't be dissuaded from continuing out to Cave Creek to lay eyes on Victor Garritson. She was actually confident that she could pick a killer in disguise out of the crush of humanity at a cocktail party. "I talk to murderers every day. I'll know him after a few minutes. Next left, we're almost there."

I turned left.

Her anguish over the death of Sheldon Salgado and his family had subsided as abruptly as it had flared. The demeanor she adopted after our brief meal reminded me of the one she had worn to keep me at bay emotionally during our training. She wasn't exactly aloof, not exactly cold. But there was no invitation in her tone, no welcome in her smile. She wasn't telling me to go away. She was telling me to stay exactly where I was.

To watch my step.

"You know, he's changing in front of our eyes, Sawyer. This man, this murderer we're after."

"What do you mean? Like a chameleon?"

"No. I'm thinking maybe deterioration, not camouflage. He's losing patience. The, um, rapidity is troubling. He used to take two years or more to plan one of these murders. Now he hits Sheldon and you in the same night. That's a radical change. He's under pressure of some kind, he must be. Why the rush? I think there's little doubt that he's starting to get sloppy. We need to take advantage of his change in mental state."

"All the more reason to confront Garritson now. We can examine that mental state face to face."

"What are you suggesting? I thought we were going to Cave Creek to 'eyeball' Garritson. What's this about confronting him?"

"Semantics," she argued, shaking the map. "Next right. That's his street."

Victor Garritson lived in a trailer park, the Red Sky Mobile Home Village. The park and its trailers had been well maintained, but were certainly a decade or more past their prime. Red Sky wasn't some contemporary community of "manufactured homes"; this was a trailer park that provided marginal housing to working people living on the margins. No double-wides here, no shiny Ford Expeditions parked beside the front doors. Red Sky consisted of a few dozen trailers, a lot of dust and sand, some mature oleanders, and a few trees that would rather be living elsewhere.

Victor lived in 103. Sawyer barked out directions to his pad as though she'd reconnoitered the place the night before. I stopped the Taurus two trailers away and examined Victor's abode from a distance.

The trailer had been in this location for a while. It was a single-wide that had once been blue and white before the desert sun bleached the aluminum shell from Caribbean Azure to the pale hue of fire-sale toilet tissue. Oleanders obscured one end of the trailer completely. A big brown Ford Econoline blocked the other end, the rust on the vehicle announcing that it had spent most of its earlier years in a locale other than Arizona, one that actually had humidity. Instead of a few steps leading up to the front door of the trailer, a switchback ramp of sun-bleached cedar led from the sandy ground to the entryway.

An air-conditioner compressor hummed loudly.

Sawyer said, "He's home."

No lights were visible. "The AC?"

"That's right."

"If he was in Santa Barbara yesterday screwing around with your plane—and if he was in Kittredge at three o'clock this morning setting fire to the forest around Sheldon's house—he made pretty good time getting back here."

"I haven't flown for two days, so who knows when, or if, somebody touched my plane. And you made it here easily enough from Colorado. He could, too. Anyway, maybe he has his own plane, like me."

"And maybe he's not our guy."

"Let's go find out."

I killed the engine and eased out of the car. The desert heat hit me in the face like a physical blow from an open hand. Sawyer didn't seem to notice.

She mounted the worn wooden ramp with determination and no apparent fear. I had barely reached the switchback when she started pounding on the door of Garritson's trailer.

After ten or fifteen seconds, I heard a reply that was almost a growl. "I'm resting. Go. Whatever it is you're selling, I don't want any. Whatever it is you want, I don't have any."

Sawyer pounded some more.

"Leave me alone, damn it."

She pounded some more.

"What the—? Shit, gimme a goddamn minute."

It was about this time that I wished that Sawyer and I had a plan. Pounding on a homicidal maniac's door unannounced didn't seem like the most prudent thing for us to be doing. At that moment, I had the sinking realization that I was along for the ride with Sawyer on this one. My memories of cocktails in the thunderstorm surfaced and I felt an uneasy feeling with my current role.

She was calling the shots again. How could I slip into such a passive place with her so easily? "Sawyer," I said, in a meek effort to raise a protest. "Doing this, you know? I'm not sure that this is such a great idea."

"He won't recognize us. Don't worry."

"What are you planning on—"

"Shhh."

I half expected a volley of semiautomatic weapon fire to pierce the aluminum skin of the trailer and slice Sawyer and me in two as though we were constructed of nothing more than perforated paper. After she quieted me, I thought I heard a groan from inside the trailer, followed by some labored breathing.

After another minute or so the doorknob turned and the door swung outward violently, almost knocking Sawyer backward off the ramp. I caught her arm and steadied her.

The inside of the trailer was unlit; the curtains had all been shut against the heat. Peering into the darkness was like looking into a cave. I couldn't see who was there waiting for us.

A voice said, "Down here, you idiot."

I looked down and saw the silhouette of a man in a wheelchair. One shoulder drooped a good six inches, and the rest of his body listed in that direction. He wore a filthy sleeveless T-shirt and had a baseball cap on his head. It was hard to be certain in the shadows, but I thought the cap was adorned with the logo of the Arizona Diamondbacks.

Sawyer was apparently as taken aback as I was by the man who was greeting us. Her tone lacked any confidence as she said, "Hello. We're looking for Victor Garritson. Are you Victor Garritson?"

He said, "Actually, I'm Christopher Reeve, doing research on a movie on what it's like to be a crip in a trailer park. Who the hell are you?"

"I'm Anton Faire," she said, without a pause. I remembered instantly that Anton was Sawyer's middle name, her mother's maiden name.

"And you want what, Anton Faire? Bill collector? You can collect all of them that you would like. Don't worry, I have plenty to spare. Child support? Perhaps you can perceive the truth, which is that I can't even support myself. Let me see, what else could you be after? I *know*. Bless you, maybe you're here to give me my daily massage. I sure as hell hope you're as flexible as you are pretty. Are you?" His mouth hung open, waiting for a reply. The man needed some serious dental work. "Come on, come on. So, what I want to know is, do you do hand jobs? I'm the odd one who prefers them to blow jobs. Some give them, some don't. I don't want any moralizing, mind you, just a woman's touch." He paused again, shrugging that one shoulder, his attention fixed on Sawyer. He was ignoring me totally. "No? Well then, I give up. What the hell do you want? Please don't tell me you want to talk to me about Jesus. Whenever I start talking about Jesus . . . no, that hasn't proven to be a good thing. No." He lowered one hand to the wheel of his chair and seemed to get lost in thinking about Jesus. Finally, he said, without conviction, "Do I know you?"

Sawyer was flustered and confused. She said, "I didn't know you were in a wheelchair."

His reply was bitter and cruel. He made a rapid clicking sound with his tongue. "Sometimes I forget, too. Just find myself walking around the house, getting on the treadmill, doing jumping jacks, taking care of business. And then I say, oops, forgot again, better get back in that chair. Can't start pretending you're not a crip, Vic. Get it? Vic for Victor, Vic for victim. Pick one, pick one."

Sawyer looked at me, then back into the tepid darkness of the trailer. "Mr. Garritson, we may have made a mistake. Coming here, I mean. I'm very sorry to disturb you."

"Does this mean no hand job? I get myself all the way to the damn door and I don't even get a little touch? Just a little woman's touch. That's all. I'm quick; it won't take long." He started fumbling at his belt with one hand. The other arm seemed beached in place by his side.

"Good day, sir," said Sawyer. "I'm sorry we disturbed you."

"Now I'm a sir. That's no good. You never get off when they call you sir."

I heard him laughing as we walked away. He cackled, "Oh, you'll be back. You've been here before."

Two or three miles later, she said, "I guess it's not him."

"No," I said, touching her hand where it rested on the edge of the seat. "I guess not."

She wasn't eager to focus on the failure, though. She wanted to strategize. "We need to find D.B. and at the same time we need to start brainstorming about other candidates."

I was less reluctant to focus on our failures. Personally, as a detective, I was feeling like a rank amateur. "I think we're way out of our league. I think we should put all of our energy into getting the FBI more interested than they've been."

"They'll want names, Alan. Everyone who was on the unit."

"Maybe our only choice is to stay alive and be unethical. The alternative is to die ethical and proud."

"Don't forget Eleanor Ward."

"That's the second time you've brought her up. Why is she so important, Sawyer?"

She looked away from me, out the side window. "Because she's an example of what will happen if we give out names." Her lips tightened and her eyes narrowed. "And because she taught me so much. That's why."

"What does that mean?"

"No," she said. "I shouldn't have said that. I'm sorry."

"Please."

She shook her head.

Her reluctance didn't feel provocative, but my patience had deteriorated a lot during those few moments on Victor Garritson's wheelchair ramp. "That's no good, Sawyer. My life depends on you right now, and yours depends on me. Don't keep things from me that may be important."

"You're doing it, too."

I made the mistake of inviting her to continue. "What does that mean?"

"You have feelings too. You're not saying anything about them. You've hardly spoken about your wife."

"My wife? What does Lauren have to do with this maniac?"

"You say you're happily married . . . but my instincts say . . . I don't know, that that's not the whole truth."

I did not want to be having this conversation. "What on earth are you talking about?"

"I think you still have feelings for me."

What she was saying was disconcerting. It may even have been true. "Don't kid yourself. Any tension you feel from me is about this situation. It isn't about us. I admit I've been waiting fifteen years to find out what happened between us. And I still want to know why you left the way you did. You took a big piece of me with you. Maybe I want it back."

"What? Me? Or your dignity?"

"I want to know why you disappeared."

She shook her head. "I can't."

"Can't what?"

In a firm voice she said, "Stop the car. Please. Stop it." She barked the last two words.

I pulled over to the shoulder of the two-lane road. Sawyer immediately popped out of the car and marched back in the direction we had just come.

I followed her. So what else was new?

"What are you doing?" I asked.

"I don't know. I'm walking."

A tractor-trailer whizzed by. I called after Sawyer, almost yelling to be heard above the droning diesel, "Bullshit. I think you always know what you're doing."

She whirled around and faced me. "Finally, the anger."

"Is that what you want? You want me mad? Okay. You hurt me. I trusted you and you trashed me. Sure I was angry."

"Was?" she asked as she walked backward, away from me. "Did I ever . . . did I ever encourage you? Did I? Did I seem to want you to need me?" Her voice seemed foreign, contemptuous. "No. That wasn't me. I liked your company. That's all."

"That's bull. You like that I was a pushover for you. You like that I'd put up with you."

She scoffed, "Don't blame me for your weakness. Despite every warning sign I put up, you leaned on me until you fell and I wasn't around to pick you up. That's not my fault. Don't blame me."

"I don't. I blame me. That doesn't excuse what you did, Sawyer. You ran. You knew that I loved you. And you ran."

"I didn't ask to be responsible for you. And you know nothing about my leaving. Nothing."

"No. You didn't ask to hold my heart. But they break when they're dropped. You dropped mine."

She turned away from the paved shoulder and pounded her feet as she headed off into the desert. She was at least a hundred feet in front of me when she yelled over her shoulder, "You don't know."

I yelled back, "Of course I don't know. You never told me anything. You never even told me you were married."

"Don't judge me. I didn't make any promises to you."

"Is that the rule? If you make no promises, you make no invitations, then nobody can be disappointed? Well, I don't like those rules. I don't remember ever agreeing to play by them."

She faced me with her hands on her hips. The sunlight sparkled in her hair. She had left her sunglasses in the car and the sun was in her eyes, but she wasn't squinting at all. I closed to within thirty feet of her before she spoke again. The words that came from her mouth were as soft as the haze on the horizon. "I wanted to believe that I could be loved without being needed. You were my guinea pig."

I stopped and said, "I guess I failed that test back then. And I'd fail again today."

"Yes," she said. "You failed." Her words weren't especially critical. Merely sad.

"Is that still what you want? You're looking for someone who'll love you without wanting anything from you?"

In a whisper, she said, "Not wanting. Needing."

"I don't get it."

She dropped her head so that I couldn't see her face. "I just want to stop being so scared."

Gracefully, she lowered herself to a sitting position in the dust, and I moved forward and held her while she cried. I cried some, too. Some old tears, some new ones. Some for Sheldon, some for Sawyer, some for me. I realized I didn't know what Sawyer had meant. Was her wish not to be so scared related to the current threats or to ancient ones?

I didn't ask. It felt good to be sitting in the sand and dust, holding her. Comforting her.

Eventually we moved back to the car, mostly just to escape the heat. I stood and looked around before lowering myself onto my seat. I wanted to be sure no other cars had stopped along with us in the middle of nowhere.

I was now officially paranoid.

I ran the air conditioner for a few moments before I started to drive away. My pager vibrated against my hip ten seconds after I pulled back onto the road. I checked the screen. Sam's cell phone number again. "It's my friend. The detective in Boulder? I need to find a phone."

She dug one out of her purse. "Here."

"Would you dial for me, please?" I handed her my pager so she could see the number. "The area code is 303."

She punched the numbers and handed me back the phone.

"Where are you?" Sam asked. "Connection sucks."

"On our way back to Phoenix."

"Any luck?"

"You told me once that you considered eliminating suspects in an investigation to be progress. If that's really true, we made progress. Chester's a definite no go."

"Sorry, I guess."

"Anything new there?"

"Not with your friend or the fire. Identification of the bodies is a day away, at least. But Lauren's fine. I'm going to see her home as soon as she's done here. I called to tell you that Custer and Simes are on their way back to Boulder. They say they'll be flying into DIA today, want to meet as soon as possible. And they want to know if you know where to find Sawyer."

"Did you—"

"I played stupid. You are coming home tonight?"

"That's still the plan, yes. Have to get back to Phoenix and see what shuttle flight I can make."

"Call me when you know. I'll pass word along to Custer and Simes."

"You don't know what they want?"

"I talked to Dr. Simes, not to Custer. If I was planning a picnic I don't think she'd tell me the weather. See you."

I punched the button to terminate the call and handed the phone back to Sawyer. "Custer and Simes want to meet with us. In Boulder, tonight."

"Do they know I'm with you?"

"Sam didn't tell them. Doesn't mean that they don't know." I looked over at her. Her eyes were closed and her head was back against the headrest. "How do you feel about coming back to Colorado?"

"I'm not sure. I haven't been back, you know? Since . . ."

Since what, I wanted to know. I didn't press her hard. "I didn't know you hadn't been back. Bad memories?"

"No, my bad memories aren't in Denver. I didn't go back because of you. I didn't want to face you. I didn't want to see the hurt I'd caused. I didn't want to have to go through what I just went through. I didn't want to have to apologize."

Lightly, I said, "You haven't apologized."

I glanced over and saw the indentation of a dimple. "I haven't been back to Colorado yet."

"Does that mean you're coming?"

"I don't know how I feel about meeting your wife."

"That's fair. I don't know how she feels about meeting you."

"How would you feel about it?"

"Let me see. Meeting with two ex–FBI agents about some asshole who wants to kill me. Arranging a little get-together between my wife and an ex-lover. Sounds like a nice, non-stressful day to me."

She smiled. A bit too sweetly, I thought.

I drove another mile or two before I realized she had never answered my question about Eleanor Ward.

# TWENTY-SIX

United didn't have two seats together on the 6:45 shuttle back to Denver. I took an aisle seat in the last row. Sawyer was in the middle in the exit row on the other side of the airplane. The separate seating arrangement was fine with me. I needed some time to think.

It surprised me that what I thought about was Eleanor Ward.

She had been a kid when she was admitted to Eight East in late November of 1982. The official records would dispute my contention that she was a kid; her chart would indicate that she was actually a nineteen-year-old freshman at the University of Denver with a history of acute weight loss and withdrawal. But she didn't look her age. Chronologically, Eleanor was too old for the adolescent unit. Emotionally, though, she was way too young to be with the adults.

Eleanor—Elly—had long sandy hair that she parted slightly off-center and let fall in waves past her shoulders. She touched her hair constantly, holding it or sifting it between her narrow fingers with the same desperate affection that an infant clutches a blanket or doll. Her skin was as pale as paint and her ghostly complexion made her blue eyes stand out starkly in her gaunt face.

She was five-five or five-six and weighed, I recalled, eighty-one pounds when I met her for the first time in Community Meeting. She was wearing a dress that reached her ankles and that might actually have fit her once. That day, though, it might as well have been a tent. She curled upon herself in the chair, and her hair fell forward so that it came together in the front of her chest to frame her face like a shawl. Her makeup was precise and abundant. She had painted the illusion of cheeks onto places on the sides of her face where I was sure she once hadn't needed to. Her lips were so full that they seemed to mock the rest of her body; they hadn't lost any of their roundness or allure.

At rounds that day, the training staff brainstormed about Eleanor. We, the trainees, discounted her obvious depression and insisted on focusing on her apparent anorexia nervosa. We discussed the state of the art for treatment of eating disorders and asked the nursing staff to assist in coming up with a plan to manage her behavior around food.

Susan Oliphant, the ward chief, let us go with our faux wisdom for a good twenty minutes before she reminded us that our colleague Sheldon Salgado had sent Eleanor Ward up from the ER for admission not only because of her acute weight loss, but also because of her depression and social withdrawal. Susan smiled at Sawyer in an affectionate way and told her that she had confidence that she would soon know what it was all about. She cautioned, "Don't get lost in the eating disorder, Sawyer. It's a fascinating piece. But it's only a piece."

Three days later, Sawyer asked me if I would do psychological testing on her young patient. Psychotherapy, she told me with significant frustration, was going absolutely nowhere and she wondered what was interfering with the establishment of an alliance. Specifically, she was concerned that her young patient had either an underlying organicity or thought disorder. And to complicate matters, Elly was refusing to allow the hospital to contact her family in New Haven to notify them of the hospitalization and to inquire about history.

My schedule had no openings for days, but Sawyer was imploring me for test results as soon as possible. I scheduled Elly for a two-hour appointment that evening at eight-thirty and another the next night at the same time. They were the only times I had free all week.

I gave up my late evenings because Sawyer asked me to, and I was an easy mark for her. But I also did it because Elly was alluring. Not sexually. Her sexuality had evaporated along with her fat stores. But psychologically, being in Eleanor Ward's presence was charged and very fleshy, full of poignancy and promise. That first night, for the first hour, all she and I did was talk, mostly, it seemed, about not talking. She told me that her doctor frightened her. She said she found Dr. Sackett to be intense and impatient and intrusive.

Sawyer, it seemed, reminded her of her mother. When I suggested the connection to Elly, she seemed shocked. That the phenomenon of transference—experiencing or treating someone in one relationship as though that person shared the traits of someone in another—was so apparent to an outsider didn't mean for a second that it was at all visible to the perpetrator.

Elly told me that in contrast to Sawyer, I was gentle. At the end of the first hour, she wondered if I could be her doctor.

During the second hour we completed the first step of the psychological testing process, the WAIS.

The next day, I told Sawyer that Elly's IQ was 127 and that the pattern of subtest scores was not consistent with any underlying organic problem. I explained that I'd know more after the projective battery, but didn't consider it likely that I was going to find evidence of a thought disorder. I recounted the results of the interview that preceded the intelligence test and suggested that there might be a transference problem in the therapy.

And maybe, I added gently, there was a countertransference problem, as well.

Sawyer opened her mouth to defend herself, but didn't. I wasn't sure why, but psychotherapists often have a reflexive need to deny that any of their own issues might be interfering with the progress of a specific psychotherapeutic relationship. I was as guilty as anyone of defending against that aspect of my humanity.

I asked Sawyer, colleague to colleague, what might be going on in the therapy with Elly. She said she didn't know, but that whatever it was didn't feel right to her, either. She danced a little bit but ultimately acknowledged that she thought I might be right about the countertransference. She said she would talk with Susan Oliphant, her supervisor, about it.

The following night at eight-thirty, as I finished arranging the materials I would need to administer a projective battery to her, Elly asked me what I had done to Dr. Sackett.

I said I hadn't done anything other than tell her about our discussion the previous evening.

Things were different with her doctor, she said. Totally different. She told me that she had finally been able to reveal to Sawyer what had happened back in New Haven. She said she had told her everything.

And I ate dinner tonight, she said. Not all the food. But almost half. Okay, maybe a third. But much more than I've eaten in weeks.

Do you want to tell me about it? About New Haven? I asked.

No, she smiled. She didn't. Not yet. One doctor at a time.

We finished the projectives in ninety minutes and I went home and scored the Rorschach before I crawled into bed. The deep depression I expected to find in Eleanor's test responses was absent. I saw footprints of despair, deep marks where despondency had managed to leave indelible evidence. But Elly Ward had somehow escaped the darkest shadows of depression and her reactions to the inkblots showed me that she was beating a remarkable retreat from defeat.

The flight attendant asked me if I wanted more peanuts.

I didn't remember eating two bags already, but the evidence, in the form of rubbish and peanut crumbs, sat on the tray table in front of me. I smiled at her kindness, but declined. In front of me, Sawyer was walking down the narrow aisle toward the back of the plane, making her way to the lavatory. The light in the cabin, from the brilliant sun setting to the west, brightened the left side of her face, glinted off her lips, and highlighted the tan skin on her long neck. Her breasts swayed below her cotton top.

I was not unmoved.

As she passed by me she acted as though she didn't even know I was there, but her fingers grazed my scalp when she reached down to touch the top of my chair.

I heard the lavatory door open and close a few feet behind me. Then I popped the telephone from the back of the middle seat, swiped a credit card down the crevice, and punched in my home number.

Lauren wasn't surprised to hear that Sawyer was coming back to Boulder with me. Sam had told her what had been going on. She saved me a question by letting me know that Sawyer had a room reserved at the Boulderado Hotel. That's where Simes and Custer were staying.

Sawyer exited the lavatory silently. Again, I felt her fingers touch my hair and I admired her ass, mindlessly, as she returned to her seat.

The next day at rounds, Sawyer reported the breakthrough with Eleanor Ward. The precipitant for her patient's depression, Sawyer told us, had to do with the death of her baby daughter almost a year before.

Sawyer reminded us that Eleanor was a nineteen-year-old freshman at the University of Denver. Elly had spent the year between the end of high school and the beginning of college recovering from the traumatic death of her daughter in a traffic accident while she was visiting the parents of the baby's father.

After she discovered she was pregnant early in her senior year, Elly had withstood pressure from her mother to have an abortion and had decided to finish high school, and to postpone college, in order to raise the baby herself. Although the baby's father was out of Elly's life, romantically at least, by the time the little girl was born, his parents turned out to be much more supportive of Elly than her own mother was.

The day that her baby died, Elly was on a picnic with a boy she'd met from Yale, her first date in fifteen months. The baby was enjoying an afternoon with her paternal grandparents.

Tragically, the baby's grandfather died in the same crash that killed Elly's daughter. The Honda Accord they were riding in was unrecognizable after being broadsided by a police car that was chasing a suspected car thief.

Sawyer looked directly at Susan Oliphant as she offered her opinion that Elly's inpatient stay would not be brief, that the eating disorder would have to be well controlled before discharge, and that she would require ongoing psychotherapy for quite a while. Arnie Dresser argued for a while about the indications for drug therapy to treat her obvious depression. The other psychology intern, Alix, felt that Sawyer was dismissing the eating disorder in a manner that seemed cavalier.

Sawyer deflected the criticisms adroitly, looking as clinically assured as I had ever seen her.

No one even asked for the results of my psychological testing.

As the plane dropped low enough so I could see the Rocky Mountains out the left window and the flight attendants began to stow their gear in the galley behind me, I wasted a few minutes trying to figure out what time we'd actually land in Colorado. Arizona didn't subscribe to daylight savings time and it always dumbfounded me to try to figure out what time it would be when I landed there or what time it would be when I landed someplace else after leaving there. I guessed we would land in Denver at seven-ten, eight-ten, or nine-ten.

Which meant I required a three-hour window to account for a ninety-minute flight.

Sometimes I was able to recognize the irony in the fact that I had been charged with the responsibility of assessing other people's intelligence.

Sawyer waited for me to exit the plane. I was the last person off, right behind a woman who had stowed her carry-on bags in various overhead compartments spaning the entire length of the 737. Apparently she thought the maximum number of carry-on bags permitted was two per brain cell. As she exited the cabin, she was juggling six.

In the concourse Sawyer was acting like a tourist, examining the spacious contours of Denver's airport. "I could actually land my plane in here with room to spare," she said. "Do they have indoor runways?"

I almost reminded her that she was temporarily plane-less. But I didn't.

As we stepped onto one of the moving walkways that would take us in the general direction of the train that would carry us to the main terminal, she said, "It's odd, really odd, to be back in Denver. Especially with you. I never, ever thought this day would happen."

"This is DIA, this isn't Denver. Geographically, you're closer to Kansas than to Boulder." In my retort, I studiously ignored the especially-with-me part. "I phoned Lauren from the plane. Simes and Custer are staying at a hotel downtown called the Boulderado. She got you a room there."

"That was kind of her."

"You could stay with us, of course, but we're in the middle of the remodeling I told you about, and—"

"This is a better plan."

"The train's this way," I said. "What do you think they want this time? Simes and Custer?"

"I'm trying not to think about it. Bad news rarely warrants anticipation." She paused and turned her head toward me with a wisp of a smile on her face. "I wonder if they're sharing a room."

"Who? Simes and Custer? You must be kidding."

"No, I'm not kidding. I only saw them briefly, remember. In California. But he's not even trying to fight it. His attraction to her, I mean. She's more reluctant. But she feels the heat, too. You didn't pick it up? When he's with her, he acts like he's at his first cotillion. But Simes isn't sure he's good enough for her."

I thought about Sawyer's assessment. Maybe. I said, "Lauren thinks Simes has multiple sclerosis."

The train arrived. I led Sawyer inside. "Really?" she said. "That's interesting. What makes her think so?"

"She's good at recognizing it. Lauren's had it for years, too. MS. As long as I've known her."

Sawyer looked at me once and touched her tongue to her teeth. "Oh," she exclaimed, in a tone that said, "That explains it."

The train rumbled on, stopping once at the A Concourse and then emptying at the terminal station. I led her upstairs and across the huge tented terminal toward the parking garage and my car.

As we trudged to my car, she asked, "Should I say I'm sorry? About your wife having multiple sclerosis?"

"Sorry for me?" I asked, surprised.

"I guess."

"No. I don't feel burdened by her. Blessed, most of the time."

"How ill is she?"

"Right now she's pretty stable. The past year has been difficult at times. We're almost there."

She didn't miss a beat. "What kind does she have?"

I reminded myself that I was talking to a physician. "Relapsing-remitting. She's on Avonex, interferon. It seems to be helping, she's been more stable lately. No new exacerbations. This is my car."

"A Land Cruiser. How very Colorado of you." I unlocked the doors and she climbed in. "You need to be a little more honest with yourself, Alan. It's not easy having an ill spouse."

"You know that from experience, Sawyer?" I didn't expect her to answer.

"Boy. Do I," she said.

It was dark by the time we cleared the lines at the tollbooth plaza. Sawyer was already asleep beside me.

I gazed over at her every chance I had. I'd slept with this woman many times. But I'd never watched her sleep before. The intimacy of that moment unnerved me.

# TWENTY-SEVEN

**S**awyer and I arrived at the entrance of the Boulderado Hotel a few minutes after nine.

I found it odd that the green leather bag she carried over her shoulder included a stash of toiletries and a change of clothes. I had considered the Arizona jaunt to be only a day trip.

We said good-bye at the elevators and I returned to the lobby and hunted down a house phone. I hesitated. Whether I wanted to or not, I had to call either Simes or Custer to find out what the plans were for getting together. Ultimately, I chose to ring Custer's room instead of Simes's. Milt was easier for me to talk to, and I was curious about what he had learned in New Zealand.

Simes answered the phone in Milt's room.

"Hello, A.J.?" I said. "It's Alan Gregory. I'm back in town. Actually, I'm downstairs. I just dropped Sawyer off at the elevator."

"You're here already? Super. Come on up. What room is Sawyer in? We need her, too."

"She's in 311. Where are you?"

"We have a suite, 416. This is parents' weekend or something at the college. We had to beg for a room. All they had was this suite. But it's a great place to meet. So come on up."

I wanted to ask, "Is it a two-bedroom suite, or one?" I didn't. Instead, I said, "Why don't you call Sawyer yourself? I'll be up in a few minutes. I need to let Lauren know what's going on first."

I moved from the house phone to a pay phone and hesitated again. I decided I needed to reassess my strategy and convinced myself that a little alcohol would enhance the decision-making process.

I climbed the stairs to the second floor and grabbed a small table along the rail of the Mezzanine Lounge. As I often did when I visited the Mezzanine, I wished it had reclining chairs so that I could sit back and gaze in wonder at the stained-glass ceiling fifty feet above my head.

The Boulderado had been built shortly after the turn of the century as one of Colorado's frontier jewel hotels, along with the Jerome Hotel in Aspen and the Hotel Colorado in Glenwood Springs. The most distinctive feature of the Boulderado was the stunning stained-glass ceiling that rose high above the central vault of the lobby. The original ceiling had been destroyed by fire, but an exact replica had been reconstructed during renovations in the 1980s. The ceiling was an architectural extravagance that I welcomed every time I gazed at it.

A waitress came over to my table and smiled. She didn't say a word, but instead raised her bushy blond eyebrows, widened her eyes, and smiled a mannequin smile.

I smiled back. It took more effort than it should have.

With empty hands she pantomimed writing on a pad, pouring something from a bottle, and then raising a glass to her burgundy-painted lips. She swallowed with great drama.

I ordered vodka rocks, squeeze, and used words to do it.

She spun on her heels and departed. I felt as though I were being waited on by Marcel Marceau's granddaughter. But it had been that kind of day, so I wasn't too surprised.

I rested my head on the back of the settee and stared at the glass panels on the ceiling until the mime arrived with my drink. She made a scribble motion and a checkmark in the clear air with the end of her index finger. She then tried to catch the checkmark because it had, apparently, started to float away.

I paid cash. Just dollar bills. I didn't want to see what she might do with a handful of coins.

My options? Meet with Sawyer and Simes and Custer on my own and immediately relay everything they reported back to Sam and Lauren for analysis. Or invite Sam and Lauren to the rendezvous and gain the benefit of their wisdom and experience directly.

The second option was tactically superior except for one flaw. Inviting Lauren to the hotel would force the first face-to-face meeting between Sawyer and Lauren. Was I up for that?

No. I wasn't.

I downed the vodka in less than five minutes and dropped money on the table to cover the tip. I puzzled momentarily over a larger issue: whether by tipping my server generously I was violating my personal policy never to do anything to encourage a mime. I couldn't figure out that dilemma, either. I returned to the lobby, picked up the phone and invited Lauren, then Sam, to the rendezvous in suite 416.

Machiavellian concerns convinced me that I didn't want to be the first to arrive at Simes and Custer's party. I retired to the men's room and peed and washed my hands and face before phoning Sawyer's room to be certain she had already answered a summons that I assumed was as cursory as the one I had received.

She didn't answer. I made my way over the alley bridge to the modern wing of the hotel and took the elevator to the fourth floor.

Simes answered the door in a lime-colored outfit that vaguely resembled a sweat suit. I thought it looked like something an upscale Dallas housewife would have chosen from the Neiman-Marcus catalog in order to appear casual when friends dropped over for canapés. The pair of pine green cowboy boots embroidered in sequins on her chest was a dead giveaway that sweat was never intended to soil this leisure suit.

Milt was across the room in a big chair, talking on the phone. He was dressed in khakis and a white polo shirt and black socks. He waved as though he was glad I was there.

A.J. offered me a drink. I declined and took a seat across from Milt, wondering where the hell Sawyer was.

A.J. lowered herself to a settee and said, "So, you've had a busy day?"

I raised my eyebrows and nodded before recalling my run-in with Ms. Marceau. I quickly added, "So you've heard?"

"Not everything," she said obliquely.

"Ahh," I said, still wondering where the hell Sawyer was. "So what brings you two back to Boulder?"

"We thought we'd learned enough that it was time to put our heads together again."

"What did you learn?" I was trying to eavesdrop on Milt's telephone conversation at the same time I was trying to hold one myself with Simes. It was not one of my better-developed skills.

"That can wait. We ordered a few snacks from room service. Please help yourself."

"I'm fine, thanks." Milt was silent on his end of the phone call. I examined the suite, tried to decide if the design allowed for two bed-rooms. I concluded that it did. Offhandedly, I asked, "Is Sawyer here yet?"

One of the doors I'd been examining opened, and Sawyer walked out of a bathroom. She said, "Yes, Sawyer's here. Where have you been?" She was wearing the same cotton top she'd had on all day, but had replaced her jeans with a black rayon wraparound skirt that did nice things for her legs.

I said, "Freshening up." It was apparent to me that she had done the same. Her hair seemed slightly damp. I figured that I looked like shit.

Milt placed the phone back on the cradle and greeted me.

"A lot's been developed. A lot," he said. Whatever the news he'd just heard was, it wasn't causing him any joy. "A.J.?" He gestured toward one of the bedroom doors. She followed him. I detected a slight imbalance in her gait and considered whether it was from ver-tigo or a foot-drop.

Sawyer said, "I spoke to the mechanic in Arizona who is going over my plane. He can't find a reason that the gear wouldn't come down. Nothing. Weird, huh? He said the fuel gauge has a minor calibration problem, but there's no evidence anybody tampered with it."

"You believe him?"

"Beechcraft is flying someone out from Wichita to take a look at the gear. We should know more tomorrow or the next day."

"What's this all about?" I opened my arms to take in suite 416.

"From what I could gather, it's because of new information of some kind. I also think they missed each other."

Two loud raps echoed from the door. Since Custer and Simes hadn't reappeared, I answered. Sam walked in, nodded a greeting to me, another to Sawyer. To her, he said, "Sam Purdy. You must be Sawyer. Heard a lot about you."

"Likewise," she said.

He began examining the tray of snacks that room service had de-livered. "There's not a damn thing here I can eat. You know, I'm be-ginning to think this diet isn't really necessary." He popped open a Coors from the minibar and sat down in the chair where Milt had been sitting. "Glad you two made it home. Sounds like a hairy day."

Sawyer shrugged and gave him an abridged version of the landing excitement. I followed with the tale of our embarrassment at Victor Garritson's trailer.

"Any chance he was scamming you? Knew you were coming and put together a little charade for you? With the wheelchair and everything?"

Sawyer glanced at me and shook her head. "Anything's possible with a con. But I don't think so."

"Alan?"

"I agree. It didn't seem like an act to me."

A trill of three quick taps came from the door. Sam looked at me. "You expecting someone else?"

"It's probably Lauren."

I noticed that, with my pronouncement, Sawyer improved her already perfect posture and pushed her hair back from her face with her left hand.

Sam got the door. Lauren entered and pecked him on the cheek. I stood and embraced her, and kissed her hello. I wanted to kiss her again. Not a hello kiss. I didn't. She smelled like flowers on the beach.

She let go of my hand and took two long strides across the room to Sawyer. She said, "I'm Lauren, you must be Sawyer. It's nice to meet you." Sawyer stood. They shook hands. I noticed they were the same height.

Lauren looked even more lovely than usual. I couldn't decide whether I was just that happy to see her or whether she had spent an extra few minutes choosing her clothes and touching up her hair and makeup.

Sawyer said, "The pleasure's mine," and sat back down.

Lauren said, "I'm so sorry about what happened today. You certainly handled yourself well."

"Thank you."

Simes and Custer rescued us from small talk by returning to the sitting area. Sam, Lauren, Sawyer and I filled the upholstered pieces, so Milt carried a couple of straight chairs over from a dining table.

Milt offered no preamble. "Lorna's brother tentatively ID'd her remains; dental records confirmed. She died with her husband in New Zealand. The local authorities can narrow down the day the deaths occurred from examining records from the lodge where they were staying." He looked my way before he continued, "Manner? I bet you're wondering about manner. Manner of death on this one is homicide. A rope bridge over a gorge was tampered with. Guy tried to cover his work with fire. Didn't play it very well. No ashes were found below the bodies in the bottom of the gorge. But there were plenty of ashes on top of them. And the fire didn't destroy enough of the rope fiber to disguise the cut marks."

"Fire? Really? You know about last night, don't you?" I asked. "Sheldon Salgado, the forest fire?"

They both nodded. Milt said, "Yes, more fire. It's the closest thing we have to an MO on this guy."

Simes started speaking. "There's more. The cruise ship doctor? Wendy Asimoto? We know more about her death than we did before. The cruise line doesn't think she went overboard. They have a witness who saw her going from the seventh-deck promenade into the main lobby area. That means she was seen going from outside to inside. A few minutes later another witness saw her near the ship's hospital. She wasn't seen after that. That was at one-thirty in the morning."

Sam asked, "Then what do they think happened to her body?"

"That's what I wondered. So I went down to Fort Lauderdale, where a sister ship of the one Dr. Asimoto was on is docked. I asked the captain point-blank if there was a way to dispose of a body at sea without going up to one of the decks and pushing it overboard. He immediately said yes, and walked me to the galley.

"The galley was this stainless-steel wonder—equipment, walls, ceilings, everything. Seems these modern cruise ships have advanced, environmentally sound methods of waste disposal. Much of the waste is incinerated in these incredibly hot ovens. The organic waste, though, is ground through this big industrial food processor and allowed to pass into the ocean as fish food."

"You think she became chum?" Sam asked incredulously.

"Actually, no. The head chef disagreed with the captain on the disposal method. He told me that a body would have to have been cut into pieces no larger than eight inches in diameter to be forced into the processor. Would have been messy and would have taken someone without, um, experience a long time. He said if he was doing it, he would have just used the waste incinerator. A small woman could be placed in there whole."

"Wendy was a small woman," I conceded.

Sawyer nodded agreement.

No one said anything, so Simes continued. "I checked back with the headquarters of the cruise line. They've been cooperative. Their records don't show any inspection of the ship's incinerator after her disappearance. Their next port was Stockholm. I have a call in to the authorities there, as well, to see if they looked. But I don't imagine they did. Why would they?"

Sam asked, "How many people would have had access to the incinerator area?"

Milt smiled wryly at Sam's inquiry. "Eight total. On that particular shift, overnight, only three."

"You have their names? And, I assume, photographs from cruise line personnel records?"

"Names, yes. They've been more reluctant about releasing photos. We're increasing pressure on them through channels."

Simes said, "But for the time being we have nationalities. One was a Greek national, one a Belgian. The third was an American. But—"

Sam cut in. "You should be able to get immigration records on him. Find out when he went abroad. Address, photos, everything."

"Detective," Simes replied, "please remember we are dealing with a sophisticate. The crew member in question may well have used false documents to apply for his job. The name on his cruise ship personnel records was Trevor Elias Cash. A few phone calls revealed that the original Trevor Elias Cash died in Billings, Montana, at the age of three in a farm machinery accident."

"Dead end?" I asked.

"Hardly," Lauren said, touching my knee. She faced Milt. "You'll be able to get immigration records for passengers departing on the same day or shortly after Lorna and her husband departed for New Zealand, right? The murderer couldn't leave for New Zealand before they did in case they changed their travel plans. He couldn't leave long after they did in case he couldn't find them in New Zealand. After he killed them, he probably began his return home quickly, say within thirty-six hours. Perhaps he traveled through a third country as a diversion."

Milt said, "Very good. And the answer is yes. We are in the process of looking for an age and description match for the man we know only as Trevor Elias Cash from among the finite number of U.S. citizens who made their way to and from New Zealand in that time period."

Sawyer said, "This isn't right. He's leaving a trail for us. Why?"

Simes said, "Most sophisticated criminals want to challenge the authorities in some way. They feel we can't keep up with them. He's underestimating us—didn't imagine any of the deaths would ever be determined to be homicides. It's not atypical."

I said, "Sawyer's right. Something's amiss. It's not only the sloppiness. He used to go years between killings, but in the last twenty-four hours it looks like he's made two attacks. Milt's story says that he was sloppy in New Zealand after killing Lorna and her husband. I think he's deteriorating, psychologically I mean. He's not approaching his task the same way that he was at the beginning."

Simes ignored me. "The good news for now is that after our discoveries in New Zealand, the Bureau is interested—finally. If we can tie any of these two murders, or the recent attempted murders, together with evidence, circumstantial or not, the Bureau will come on board. Milt and I feel that the deaths of Wendy Asimoto on the cruise ship and Lorna Pope and her husband in New Zealand hold the best promise for assembling documentary evidence to support a link. We should be able to use immigration and passport data to show the same person was in both locations. I've completed a thorough review of all the earlier records and simply cannot identify any solitary piece of evidence we can use to tie any of them together."

"Other than the victims," Lauren said.

"Yes, other than the victims," Milt said.

"He's on our trail, you know," offered Sawyer. "He could be here tonight, at this hotel."

Milt said, "You'll be fine, miss. I'm sleeping in your room. You'll bunk here with Dr. Simes."

I thought I saw a look of fleeting disappointment on A.J.'s face. But two seconds later she was acting as though the move was her idea.

# TWENTY-EIGHT

The next morning was Saturday. I drove Lauren to her office so that she could catch up on some paperwork and then made my way over to Sam's house so we could walk together. Lauren didn't have much to say about meeting Sawyer. Sam had a lot to say about my procrastinating about learning to use a handgun.

I didn't tell either of them that I was planning to go to Reggie Loomis's house again.

Reggie had told me that he delivered breakfast to his shut-ins on Monday, Wednesday, and Friday, supper on Thursday and Sunday. Since this was Saturday morning, I hoped to find him at home on his day off.

I pulled up to his deceptively modest house a little after nine. A late summer—or early autumn—monsoon had drifted up from Mexico, and cold drizzle blanketed the Front Range. The hogbacks were almost invisible in the low clouds.

I knocked and waited long enough to get pocked with rain. After a minute or so the front door opened. Reggie Loomis was dressed in worn corduroys and a flannel shirt. He wore no shoes on his stockinged feet.

He said, "I figured you'd be back."

"May I come in?"

"You alone?"

My heart pounded in my chest. I actually looked over my own shoulder to see if I'd been followed. I said, "Yes."

"Come in then."

We settled in at the same two stools at the kitchen counter. I smelled cinnamon and my mouth watered. But Reggie didn't offer me any refreshments. He may have expected my visit, but he wasn't happy to see me.

"Three more people have died," I said.

He nodded. "The fire in Kittredge?"

"Yes. The fire." I wondered how he knew. "You've been thinking about this some more, haven't you?"

"Yes."

"There was an attempt made on someone else's life, as well."

"But it failed?"

I thought his voice was registering surprise. "Yes. It failed."

He looked at me across his body, suddenly curious. "Tell me about it. The failure."

I relayed the details of Sawyer's near miss. Reggie asked me to clarify a couple of points. Finally, appearing relieved at my story, he offered me coffee and an apple cinnamon muffin.

"That would be wonderful," I said. "You even bake on your days off?"

"If you love what you do, you don't have days off." He busied himself with his espresso machine.

I watched his practiced movements for a minute, then asked, "How did you know? About the fire?" I was trying hard not to sound accusatory.

"I have a lot of free time. I read all the papers. You said three more people had died. That was the only recent incident I've read about where three people died. Simple deduction."

"You weren't surprised at all when I said three more people had died."

He shrugged and moved his gaze toward the greenbelt. His back was still to me when I asked, "You know who it is I'm looking for, don't you?"

He placed the two demitasse cups on saucers and turned and walked in my direction. "I have an idea. A good idea."

I waited, hoping he would be forthcoming. Instead he asked me for more information. "You think he's killing people? This person you're looking for. This old employee of mine."

"Yes."

"How many, so far?"

"Maybe as many as eight or nine before the fire."

"Why aren't the police interested?"

"Who says they're not?"

"If they were, you wouldn't be here. They would."

Reggie was no dummy. "Until recently, the killing has been accomplished by an almost invisible hand. The crimes have been flawless. No one has even suspected that the deaths were homicide."

"But recently?"

"He's grown impatient. And sloppy."

Reggie stood back up from the counter. He'd forgotten the muffins. He shuffled across the room and placed one on a dessert plate for me. "I don't think you'll need butter," he said as he served me. I didn't doubt him. The muffin before me was the size of a softball and smelled like it came from heaven's bakery.

I waited again. My silence was lost on Reggie Loomis. It seemed to provide no impetus for him to disclose anything. The muffin was delicious. I told him so.

He smiled self-consciously and said, "Thank you."

"You seemed to react before when I said that this man I'm looking for has grown impatient and sloppy."

"Yes. Perhaps I did." He finished his coffee. "The man I've been thinking about would never—never—exhibit sloppiness. And there is not an untidy cell in his entire body. We must be talking about different people."

"People change."

"Do they? Honestly? You're a psychologist, right?"

I nodded.

His tone became challenging and slightly sarcastic. "So how malleable is character, dear Doctor? How often do you effect lasting changes on the architecture of the personality of your patients? I'm not talking behavior, mind you, I'm asking you to reflect on alterations in the underlying structure."

I considered the question while I chewed. "Some would argue that character can be altered. There is certainly evidence to support that point of view. But I admit that there's controversy."

"Example. Can an obsessive-compulsive character ever be free of the desire for perfection? Really, truly? I'm not talking about merely lassoing impulses here. I'm wondering about effecting basic changes in human temperament."

"This man, the one you've been thinking about, he was obsessive-compulsive?"

"No, no, no. My point is that he *is* obsessive." He hesitated. "He was then . . . he is now." Reggie gestured in front of me. "Your coffee cup isn't centered in your saucer. He couldn't tolerate that asymmetry. You've dropped muffin crumbs onto my counter. It would leave him apoplectic."

I brushed at the crumbs and said, "I'm sorry."

Reggie said, "You're a supplicant. You'll always apologize for your messes. Rand . . . ? No."

Rand? That name resonated in my memory. Was that his name? Was D.B. really Rand? And what the hell did he mean by calling me a "supplicant"?

I said, "Rand. That's his name?"

"Yes. Corey Rand. Ring a bell?"

"Oh yes," I said. "It does."


It surprised me that hearing his name unlocked so much of what I'd forgotten or buried about Corey Rand.

After causing a disturbance at work, Rand had been brought by ambulance to the psych ER, where Sheldon Salgado saw him briefly. Arnie Dresser was on call that Sunday, and Sheldon paged him and asked him to the ER to evaluate a possible admission. That piece of administrative trivia was the red light Corey ran that caused his collision with Arnie Dresser.

Arnie was the second person to hear Corey Rand's proposal about D. B. Cooper. Arnie decided that the offer was compelling evidence of delusional thinking. He admitted Rand to the adult inpatient unit and took out a seventy-two-hour hold-and-treat after a frustrating attempt to assess Rand's suicide potential.

Sawyer and I had stolen that Saturday night to get away to a Grand Lake cabin that was owned by Mona Terwilliger's family. We both worked most of Saturday and drove up to the mountains and across the Divide in the dark. We got lost trying to find the cabin, and ended up staying up so late talking and screwing that I remembered watching the sky brighten in the east before I drifted off to sleep on the sofa in the living room. I woke up in time for a late lunch or early supper. Sawyer was in the shower. I joined her there. We ate, we packed up, and then we drove back down to Denver in time to squeeze in a little more sleep prior to Monday.

For a medical school trainee, this interlude constituted a vacation.

Arnie Dresser was not a good therapeutic match for Corey Rand. Arnie was an aggressive diagnostician. He probed. He palpated. He theorized. He confronted resistance wherever he spotted it, intent on stamping it out like nasty vermin in the kitchen. His style could not have been much more different from the one I was working hard to adopt, one I watched Susan Oliphant model almost daily on the unit. Her wonderfully effective style seemed to be based on patience, and listening.

But fate dictated that Arnie Dresser was Corey Rand's doctor, and by the time Sawyer and I heard about Rand at rounds on Monday morning, Corey was being portrayed by his doctor as a severely obsessive man with a teeming reservoir of anger and an underlying thought disorder. After a few questions from Susan, Arnie's supervisor, it became clear to me that most of the venom that Corey Rand was demonstrating was directed toward his doctor. Arnie would call this transference.

A more objective observer might call it something else.

Community Meeting was an interesting affair that morning, too. Census was low for the holiday weekend. The patients who could be trusted outside the unit were all out on pass. As the meeting was coming together, Corey Rand loitered by the heavily screened windows until everyone else was seated, ultimately choosing a location far from any of the other patients and far from Arnie Dresser.

As soon as Susan Oliphant started the meeting, Corey asked to address the group. I remember that his clothing seemed to have been pressed, an unusual sight on a psychiatric unit. I wondered how he had managed it. His hair was combed neatly and his face freshly shaven. His posture would have delighted an orthopedic surgeon.

She asked him to wait.

When his time came, he said that his admission had been an unfortunate combination of misunderstandings and that he would like to be released immediately. He stressed the word "immediately."

Arnie responded that they could discuss that issue in their individual session late that afternoon. I thought Arnie's tone was condescending. From the look on Corey's face, I thought it was pretty clear that he considered his doctor's tone to be contemptuous.

Corey said something like "You can't hold me here and you know it. I'm no danger to anyone. I'm not gravely disabled. My lawyer will have me out of here before I have to spend another hour with this cretin." He raised his chin at Dr. Dresser. "Save yourselves some trouble and some embarrassment. I have some information that the legal authorities want. Allow me off this unit in time to make my next shift at work, and I will divulge that information."

Arnie looked at Susan and rolled his eyes in a "Here it comes, what did I tell you?" look.

Corey continued, "I will trade the identity of the hijacker, D. B. Cooper, for my immediate release."

Susan suggested we move on to other business.

As promised, an attorney retained by Corey challenged the hold-and-treat that afternoon. At Susan's advice—and over Arnie Dresser's objection—the university attorney chose not to contest the challenge. I wasn't around when Corey Rand left the unit that day. And I don't recall ever seeing the man again.

"What happened at work? What was the disturbance that day that got Mr. Rand hospitalized?"

"More coffee? I'm going to have another cup."

"Sure," I said.

He busied himself. "Remember, we were security analysts at a nuclear weapons facility. We were protecting national defense secrets. And we were protecting plutonium. I was senior to Corey. This was, what, 1982? Those days the facility was under constant assault by protesters, and there was a persistent fear of terrorist intrusion. We took our jobs seriously. We had to."

Reggie turned his head to face me as he said, "Corey was good at what he did. So was I. We anticipated potential weaknesses in security. We developed scenarios that outsiders might use against us.

"Corey wasn't well liked. He had a holier-than-thou attitude and thought nothing of reporting other employees for security lapses. Some major, most minor. He caused a lot of people a lot of trouble, made himself a lot of enemies. Although I couldn't prove it at the time, I think most of those guys set him up that day. They laid out a trail of cookie crumbs for him, let him think he'd discovered that a plot was afoot to infiltrate one of the labs that handled plutonium.

"He reported it to me, in great detail. I followed up immediately, of course. The plan seemed quite plausible. When I did begin to investigate what had happened, all the evidence was gone. Vaporized. The whole setup made Corey look like a fool. He lost it, accused everybody in the division of being involved in the conspiracy. Our boss. His coworkers. Everybody. The plant medical officer took one look at him, heard his story about all this imaginary evidence he'd discovered—at the time, I admit, I thought it sounded crazy, too— and had him transported to Denver."

He brought me my coffee and sat back down.

I said, "That's it?"

"Yes, that's it. Except for the sequelae."

"The sequelae?"

"The fallout. His security clearance was suspended pending re-view of his mental condition. He was transferred to a nonsensitive position. He couldn't tolerate the demotion. He quit."

"Then what happened?"

"I don't know. I never heard from him again. When I was pro-moted, I learned that he'd sued the Energy Department for damages. But that was as quixotic a quest as there ever was. He was suing a top-secret branch of the U.S. government. The damn case never went anywhere."

"What year would that have been?"

"Let me see. I imagine it would have been around 1988."

"I don't know if it means anything, but the first of the murders took place the next year. 1989."

"Was it planned carefully?"

"Meticulously. You think it might be him?"

"Who am I to say?"

Reggie stood up and walked to the back windows of his house. He stared out toward the hogback and said, "I think it's clearing a little."

"I hope so," I said.

"You have a name now—you should be able to find your man. We'll chat some more after you do."

"Why after?"

"We will. That's all."

I stood to leave. He didn't turn to see me out.

"Do you think he really knew?" I asked.

"Knew what?"

"Who D. B. Cooper was? I mean, if he was such an obsessive guy, why would he make that claim if he couldn't substantiate it?"

Reggie shrugged and faced me. "Do you think anybody would really care anymore?"

# TWENTY-NINE

Lauren and I were supposed to rendezvous downtown for lunch and then drive over to Spanish Hills to see how Dresden was doing with the renovation. I wanted to talk with Sawyer about what I learned during my meeting with Reggie and see if she had any ideas on how to locate Corey Rand.

But I had at least two complications to overcome.

My first problem was that Sawyer was not only temporarily rooming with A.J. but was also being baby-sat by Custer. I couldn't figure out a ploy that would let me separate her from that formidable herd.

My second problem was that the only two people I knew who had access to public records that might actually help me track down Corey Rand were my wife, an assistant district attorney, and Sam Purdy, a cop. But I couldn't reveal Corey's name to either of them because it would violate the confidentiality of his hospital admission. I reminded myself that Sawyer and I had been totally off base in our suspicions about Chester and that prudence dictated avoiding overconfidence regarding Corey Rand.

Baffled, I stopped by my office on Walnut and checked the Boulder phone book, hoping to get lucky. There were three Rands in the local directory, but no Coreys or names with the first initial C. I tried the Denver metro book. At least two dozen Rands, easy. Again, no Coreys or initial C's.

I picked up the phone and called Reggie Loomis. "It's Alan Gregory. Sorry to bother you again. But he was married, right? I need to know his wife's name. Corey Rand's."

I heard Reggie exhale, the sound almost a whistle. "She was a beauty. A little feather of a thing. Her name was Valerie."

I dragged my finger over the column of Rands in the phone book and spotted a listing in Wheat Ridge for a Valerie Rand. I said, "Thanks. That helps."

Reggie didn't say good-bye. He just hung up.

I punched in the number and heard a gravelly "Hello," followed by a hacking cough.

I asked for Valerie Rand.

"Speaking," she said, coughing once more, a bark as sharp as a knife.

"I'm not sure I have the right Valerie Rand. I'm actually trying to reach a man named Corey Rand, who used to work near Boulder. Could you be of any help in finding him?"

She cleared her throat in a most unattractive manner and said, "You're asking after my husband. But I'm afraid Corey is dead."

"He's dead? When did he die?"

"Labor Day 1995."

"Would you mind if I . . . ? Could I ask, please, how did it happen?"

She was silent for a moment, then broke into a series of deep hacks that must have caused her significant discomfort. "He, um, had a blood clot and a, what do you call it, a hemorrhage in his brain. It happened while he was driving. He drove into a parked bulldozer."

"I'm sorry."

"Were you a friend?" she asked through another deep cough. She placed the emphasis in such a way that I thought she would have been surprised if I was.

"No," I said. "I wasn't his friend. Good-bye. Thank you."

Lauren and I had lunch at Lick Skillet before driving east to see what was going on with our house. I wanted to talk to her about Corey Rand but couldn't think of much more to say than to tell her that I'd gone back to talk with Reggie Loomis that morning hoping he could tell me more about his ex-employee.

She wanted to know if he could. I explained that the lead on the patient we'd called D.B. hadn't exactly panned out.

She wasn't surprised by the news. She'd been assuming all along that the killer would be someone who Sawyer and I never really suspected could be responsible for all the deaths and assaults.

Our friend and neighbor Adrienne—Sam's doctor—had left word for Lauren and me that she and her son were going to be out of town at a urologists' meeting in Florida, so we expected the lane to our house to be quiet, and it was.

The overflowing dumpster had been emptied and parked back in place and was already half full of debris again. I frowned as I looked at it; to all appearances we were throwing away much of our house.

Work had not progressed much inside the structure since my visit the previous morning. The foundation walls for the addition and the new garage were still curing, so the framing hadn't started. Our walk-through took only minutes. We were both careful about where we stepped and we both kept looking up at the joists, but neither of us said anything.

Lauren's shoulders dropped as we stepped outside. She turned back around so she was gazing toward the front door. She said, "It's going to be nice, isn't it?"

I thought, *Uh-oh.*

She continued, "Don't you think we really should have some sort of protection over the front door? It's so exposed. Look."

I didn't need to look. "I thought we'd decided not to." My protest was meek. I was playing purely for appearances.

"We're going this far . . ." She allowed her words to hang. "Anyway, the drawings are already done."

I sighed. "You liked the design with the two pillars, didn't you?"

She smiled and touched me lightly on the back of my neck, letting her fingers drift up into my hair. She said, "Yes."

"I'll call Dresden with the change order," I said, wondering what a covered entryway would cost us.

My guess was twenty-five hundred. Dresden seemed to have an affinity for that number.

On our way back to the Hill, I told Lauren I needed to let Sawyer know what I'd learned about D.B. and asked if she wanted to come to the Boulderado with me. She declined but handed me her portable phone in case she wanted to reach me.

"What about the Glock?"

"It's handy."

"You'll keep Emily with you?"

"She won't leave my side."

I dropped her off at the house and watched her walk inside and close the door before I drove away. Her gait seemed strong. That was good.

＊   ＊   ＊

A.J. told me on the house phone at the hotel that Sawyer was out shopping, walking the Mall. Milt had gone out looking for her.

The Boulderado is only a block north of the Downtown Boulder Mall, the center of culture and commerce downtown. The Mall is a four-block-long segment of Pearl Street that was bricked over and closed to traffic back in the seventies. It quickly became the anchor of a revitalized downtown business and retail district.

I guessed Sawyer would be looking for clothes. Given what I'd seen of her wardrobe to date, and knowing what I knew about women's retail on the Mall from traipsing after Lauren, I guessed that Sawyer would gravitate to either Solo or Jila. I tried Solo first. She wasn't browsing the racks in there.

But she was in Jila.

As soon as the door closed behind me I heard Sawyer's voice from the dressing room. She and a salesclerk were arguing the relative merits of traveling with rayon. I lowered myself to an upholstered bench near the front door and waited for Sawyer to emerge. A minute or so later she paraded out wearing a long brown skirt and a short-sleeved cardigan that was the color of old blood. I watched her examine the outfit in the three-way mirror for about ten seconds before I said, "It's a keeper."

She didn't turn to face me. She said, "I knew you were there."

"No, you didn't."

"You really like it?"

"Yes, I do. The color is great."

She spun and looked over her shoulder at her butt. "I've missed this," she said. "You know how long it's been since I've shopped with a man? Heard a male opinion about stuff like this? Buying clothes together is such an intimate act, don't you think? I think it is."

I hoped the question was rhetorical. I gave both of us some room with my nonresponse. She twirled once more. To the salesclerk she said, "This skirt's wonderful. But I'll take the other sweater." She threw a coquettish smile at me over her shoulder to let me know what she thought of my taste.

"Where can we get some tea?" she asked as we stepped outside onto Broadway.

"Around the corner," I said, and led her to Bookends, a café adjacent to the Boulder Bookstore on the Mall. I asked her to hold the only outdoor table that was available in the busy café and stepped inside to the counter, where I ordered her some tea and poured myself a glass of water.

I carried a small tray to the table and sat down across from her. She proceeded to prepare her tea with an elaborate sense of ritual that sang a melody of solitude and privacy. I watched the practiced steps, feeling a little like a voyeur, and said, "Milt Custer has been looking for you since you left the hotel. And Simes isn't at all happy you insisted on coming over here while Milt was in the shower."

Finally, she sipped some tea from the cup. "Maybe she's stewing because she didn't get to share that wonderful suite with Milt last night. Anyway, think. Would you go shopping for clothes with Milt Custer?"

"I don't imagine he was exactly offering his services as a personal shopper. I think bodyguard is more what he had in mind."

"Nobody's going to gun me down in someplace this public. It's not our guy's style."

I leaned forward and lowered my voice. "I have some news. The murderer isn't our D. B. Cooper fink from the unit, Sawyer. I went back this morning and saw his old boss. He finally told me what I think he knew all along. D.B.'s real name is Corey Rand. Ring a bell?"

Her eyes flattened, but she nodded. "Yes. Yes, it does. I remember now."

"Do you remember how angry he was at Arnie? Remember that Community Meeting?"

She was silent a moment before replying, "Yes . . . yes. But then Arnie had that effect on more than a few of his patients." Her voice sparked suddenly. "Arnie was absolutely livid at Susan for telling the university attorney not to contest the challenge that—what's his name, Rand?"

I nodded.

"—that Rand made to the seventy-two-hour hold."

"I'm not surprised it pissed Arnie off. But the truth is he probably shouldn't have been on the hold in the first place. Anyway, it's too bad. I thought he was a good match for us. This Corey Rand. The characterological structure that he brings to the table fits the profile we put together real well."

"But?"

"But Corey Rand died in 1995. I tracked down his widow, spoke with her on the phone." Anticipating Sawyer's next question, I added,

"Sounds like he had a cerebral aneurysm while he was driving a car. Died."

She leaned back on her chair, holding the teacup in both hands. She was gazing up the Mall to the west, where the foothills framed the entrance to Boulder Canyon. The sky above was a dazzling blue. "Boulder certainly is pretty. How's the shrink situation here?"

I was taken aback by the non sequitur, but followed the best I could. "Congested. Like the traffic. The managed-care fungus has taken its toll."

"Too bad. Any prisons close by?"

"Just the county jail. State and federal prisons are a few hours south of here, clustered around Canon City and Florence. Supermax is there, too."

"That's what airplanes are for," she said. "Boulder does have an airport, doesn't it?"

"A little one. There's a bigger one about ten miles east of here in Jefferson County."

"Ten miles? That would work fine."

"You would actually be able to climb back into your airplane and fly again, without any real trepidation, wouldn't you? Even after what happened yesterday in Arizona?"

"I have a propensity for denial. Haven't you noticed?"

I hadn't, but didn't want to rush into that admission without some additional thought.

"So are you thinking of moving? Leaving California?" I asked, trying to be nonchalant, not even wanting to consider how Sawyer's presence in Boulder would complicate my life.

She shrugged. She wasn't looking at me. She was watching the pedestrians pass by in a steady stream on the Mall. She shook her head, a tiny smile gracing her lips. "Is there a local ordinance against unattractive people living here? But to answer your question, nothing is tying me to California. And it's peaceful here. Reminds me a little bit of Santa Barbara. I like the feel of the place."

"It is a nice town," I said, suddenly a reluctant booster for the Chamber of Commerce.

"Where do you and Lauren live?"

"The house we're renovating is on the east side of the valley. About five miles across town. Place called Spanish Hills."

Over the rim of her teacup she asked, "Why is it called that?"

"I don't have a clue."

"I think I'd like it better close to this." She waved her hand at the Mall. "In town, here. There's a lot going on."

I considered the likelihood that she was pulling my chain. Just hoping to watch me squirm.

I tried not to squirm. "I guess we're back to square one," I said.

"You and me?" she said, still not making eye contact. The sun fell behind some wind-driven clouds and a shadow swept over us with the alacrity of an omen.

I didn't know what she meant by her question. She probably knew that.

"No, I meant, you know, in regard to suspects," I clarified.

"Ah," she allowed. "There's that, too."

I didn't want to talk about Sawyer and me, whatever that meant, in a crowded public café on the Downtown Boulder Mall. I did want to know what had caused her to leave her residency, and me, without warning just before Christmas in 1982. I also wanted to know why she was so averse to a man needing her. But now wasn't the time.

I was surprised when she rescued me from my reverie by saying, "Why do you think he wouldn't tell you D.B.'s name the first time? The boss man from Rocky Flats. Why did you have to go back?"

I leaned across the table again. "This Corey Rand wasn't a flake. He sounds like he was overbearing and obsessive at work, but he wasn't delusional. Careful, precise, by-the-book. That's how he's described."

Sawyer placed her teacup on its saucer and her elbows on the edge of the table. She moved her face to within inches of mine. When I inhaled, I tasted her perfume. Sawyer saw Milt Custer strolling down the Mall from the west. He was taking a detour around a street magician who had drawn quite a crowd. She called out to him, and he returned a wave before he wandered through the bookstore and joined us on the patio. He didn't seem at all distressed that he hadn't found Sawyer before that moment. He held up a heavy bag. "You ever been to that bookstore in the next block up there?"

"You mean Stage House? Used books?"

"No, no. Mysteries. They have everything. Everything."

Sawyer was intrigued by the prospect, I could tell. I said, "The Rue Morgue. I'll show you where it is after we're done."

She said, "Milt, Alan found out that the other suspect we had is dead. Has been for a while. We can't offer you any leads."

I was hoping she wouldn't make any D. B. Cooper jokes. She didn't.

Milt was looking around as though wondering why no waitress

had shown up at our table. I said, "It's counter service, Milt. What are you hungry for? I'll go get it for you."

He held up a finger to slow me down and turned his attention back to Sawyer. "If you two would just put together a patient roster for me, I wouldn't need any leads. I could merely start comparing names with the immigration records."

"You know we can't do that."

"I'm an ex-fed, young lady. I know all about rules and regulations. My feeling is that basically you gotta know when to keep them and when to bleep them. If you know what I mean."

I said, "Sam would agree with you on that."

Sawyer touched Milt on the arm and changed the timbre of her voice to something conspiratorial. "Milt, are your colleagues in the FBI still looking for D. B. Cooper?"

I'm sure I paled.

Milt laughed. "You bet. To some of the older guys, like me, he's still the biggest fish in the whole damn sea. Why?"

"No reason," she said. "Just a personal interest of mine."

"In hijackers?"

Sawyer shrugged and brushed her hair back from her face, hooking it momentarily behind her ears. She said, "Milton Custer, I want you to tell me. Now honestly, mind you. Are you sweet on A. J. Simes?"

Milt's face blushed to the color of a Winesap.

He turned to me and said, "Just coffee for me, thanks."

# THIRTY

I was returning to the table with Milt's coffee when Lauren's cell phone rang in my pocket. I wasn't anywhere close to coordinated enough to answer the phone while walking with a hot cup of coffee, so I tried to act nonchalant as I strolled through the crowded dining room and then outside to the patio, the stupid phone chirping rhythmically in my pocket with every other step.

As I set the mug down in front of Milt, Sawyer raised an eyebrow and asked, "Is that your phone?"

"Yeah," I said, expecting to hear from one of Lauren's colleagues or friends as I pulled it from my pocket. I punched "talk" and said, "Hello."

All I heard in return was a loud *clunk*. The person on the other end had dropped the phone. I repeated my "hello" and waited for whoever it was to recover the receiver from the floor. I listened some more. In the receiver, in the background, I could hear a piercing *wheeep, wheeep, wheeep*. I wondered what the noise was.

Sawyer and Milt looked at me expectantly. Mostly for their benefit, I again said, "Hello?"

With astonishing rapidity my neurons started to fire.

Who knew I had this phone with me? Lauren.

What was the *wheeep, wheeep, wheeep* I was hearing in the distance? The smoke alarm.

Why had she dropped the phone?

Because she had passed out.

*Oh shit.* I stood up and said, "Lauren's in trouble. I think the house may be on fire. That's his thing, right? Fire. I have to go."

Sawyer said, "Wait, Alan. Call 911 first. Where's your car?"

"Around the corner, on Eleventh."

Milt threw money on the table as though we still had a bill to pay and told me to hand him the phone. I did, and one after another we jumped the wrought-iron railing and starting running down the herringboned bricks of the Mall toward the corner.

I fumbled open the doors to the Land Cruiser and jumped in. Somewhere in my consciousness I could hear Milt's voice, precise and authoritative, giving instructions to the dispatch operator at 911. Finally he asked me for the address of the house. I was pulling a hard right onto Pearl Street as I told him.

"Tell them we want an ambulance, too," I yelled at Milt. In the rearview mirror I watched him nod.

I ran a red light to turn onto Ninth, cutting off a family on bicycles. The mother yelled something at me and flipped me off. I deserved it and I didn't care. The intersection at Canyon was a much dicier proposition than the one at Ninth. Running a red blind at Canyon Boulevard was out of the question. Fortunately, the light turned green just as I decided to chance it. The light at Arapahoe was green too, and I knew I was home free. Eight more blocks, no more lights.

Sawyer opened her window, and in the distance I could hear sirens, lots of them, and hoped they were heading to the house. I checked the sky to the west for smoke, but couldn't see anything.

Sawyer asked, "What did she say? Your wife?"

"She just dropped the phone. Didn't say anything. But I could hear the smoke alarm in the background. It's only a few more blocks."

Just before I turned off of Ninth, I saw an ambulance in my rearview mirror three blocks back, lights flashing. To no one in particular I said, "The ambulance is right behind us."

Milt asked, "What's your friend's number? Sam Purdy's?"

I told him.

He was talking to Sam as I pulled in front of the house. A big green pumper was coming down the street in the opposite direction. I couldn't see any smoke coming from the house, and my hopes rose.

I ran to the door, Milt right behind me. The *wheeep, wheeep, wheeep* pierced the quiet neighborhood.

Of course, the door was locked. And of course, it was deadbolted. After fumbling with the unfamiliar keys I got both locks open and rushed inside. Behind me I could hear firefighters yelling at me to stay where I was.

*Right.* That was gonna happen.

Inside, I smelled no smoke. Nothing. I yelled, "Lauren!" But she didn't answer me.

With a fresh bolus of adrenaline, I realized that Emily wasn't greeting me at the door, nor was she trying to eat Milt Custer's leg. I said to Milt, "The dog's not here. Something's seriously wrong. She's always at the door."

I ran to the kitchen. No Lauren. Living room. No.

"Lauren!"

Bedroom?

Before I reached the door to the bedroom, I smelled vomit.

She wasn't on the bed, wasn't in the adjacent bathroom. I finally spotted her lying on the floor in front of the closet, one leg folded below her, one arm across her chest. Her eyes were closed and she wasn't moving.

Milt yelled to the firefighters, "In here. She's in here, the bedroom. Get the paramedics."

I lowered myself to her. Her heart was beating as though it were powered by hummingbird wings. Her respiration was weak. "Lauren," I said. "Wake up. Please wake up."

Behind me, I heard the clomping of at least two people's feet. To one of them, Milt said, "I think she's cyanotic."

From somewhere deep in the house, maybe the basement, I heard a baritone voice yell, "CO is over two-thirty down here. Evacuate. Get everybody out of the house, now. We need to ventilate this place. Get the fan set up out front."

The paramedics pushed me out of the way, and Milt grabbed me by the arm with a hold that had the strength of a Doberman's jaws. In seconds they had Lauren loaded into a stretcher and were taking her outside.

The moment that the paramedic cleared the front door with the leading edge of the stretcher, she screamed, "CO poisoning. I need one hundred percent oh-two, fifteen liters. Get it ready. Set up for an IV and call for the chopper. We need to get her to Denver."

The words I'd heard from the basement finally registered. "CO" meant carbon monoxide. Lauren had been poisoned.

I heard someone say, "She must have been breathing it for a while to totally pass out." Someone else asked about brain damage.

My mind was spinning. Milt finally let go of my arm just as Sam

Purdy drove up and leaped from his car. He ignored me at first, con-
ferring with a firefighter to get the facts. Then he ran over to me and
placed a hand on each of my biceps. At the exact same moment that
he said, "Where's—?"

I yelled, "Emily!"

We bolted back inside past a stunned firefighter who was setting
up a device that looked like a portable airplane propeller on wheels.
He yelled. "No! You can't go in there!"

Sam said, "Don't worry about it, Alan. A few minutes' exposure
doesn't hurt you."

I said, "I don't really care."

This house was as new to Emily as it was to me, and she didn't
have favorite places picked out yet. I didn't know where to look for
her. Sam and I ran from room to room calling her name. He would
yell, "Not in the living room." I would yell, "Not in the kitchen."

When I ran past the door at the top of the basement stairs I smelled
the pungent stink of vomit again and called, "Basement, Sam."

I barely touched the steps as I flew down. The *wheeep, wheeep,
wheeep* was sharp and piercing. Apparently the carbon monoxide
detector that was causing such a racket was down there somewhere.

After two false starts—one in the laundry room, one in a roughed-
in bathroom—I found Emily unconscious in the furnace room, her
heart beating with the same furious rhythm I'd felt in Lauren's chest.
I said, "She's alive," and lifted her eighty-pound body into my arms
as though she weighed no more than a pile of clean laundry. Behind
me, I heard Sam's footsteps. My heart breaking, I said, "We'll need
oxygen for her, Sam. Right away."

"Don't worry," he reassured me, and preceded me up the stairs.

I carried my dog to the ambulance at the curb. Sam took her body
from me. Calmly, he said, "I'll get her oxygen from the firefighters.
You go find Lauren. She needs you."

Lauren was already inside the ambulance, her face shrouded by
an oxygen mask, an IV running into a vein in her right forearm.
The paramedics were busy drawing tube after tube of blood from
her other arm, and they ignored me as I climbed inside the ambulance and stepped up to the left side of the stretcher. I took Lauren's
left hand and lowered my face to hers and kissed her lightly on her
cool lips. I thought I heard a tiny moan and felt some tension in her
fingers. I told myself that was great news and fingered her short
black hair. I whispered, "I love you."

Behind me, someone poked his head into the ambulance and said, "ETA eight minutes at Columbia Cemetery. Get ready to fly."

"What?" I asked. "Where's she going?"

"Hyperbaric chamber in Denver. PSL. We need to super-oxygenate her right away."

"She has MS. You should know that. They need to know that."

"What?"

"She has multiple sclerosis. Relapsing-remitting. Tell them that, okay? They should know."

"What medicines is she on?"

I told them as best I could, trying to remember the list, stressing that she took interferon injections weekly.

"Any other pertinent history?"

"No."

"Out then, please, sir. We have to go."

Without hesitating, I said, "Take my dog, too. Please."

"What?"

"My dog is unconscious. She was poisoned, too. Take her, please. She'll die if she doesn't get help."

One of the two paramedics said, "I'm sorry, we don't do animals." He looked up at me quickly, then away. "But I know how you feel. I have dogs, too."

The other one, the woman, said, "What's the harm?" She gestured at Lauren. "It may help her recover to have her dog in there with her. The chamber's big as a bus—there's plenty of room in there for a dog, too."

"The chopper's gonna refuse to carry a dog."

"Maybe Christopher's flying today. I can handle Christopher. There's no time to argue. We need to roll, now."

"Can I go with you to the helicopter? Can I go with her to Denver?" My words were a naked plea.

"Follow us to the cemetery. I don't know how much room there is on board the chopper."

I called for Sam to bring Emily to the ambulance and explained that she and Lauren were heading to Denver on Flight for Life.

I jumped in my Land Cruiser and drove the few blocks to the old cemetery. At first it seemed we'd arrived at the wrong location. Within a minute, though, I began to hear the rhythmic thunder of big blades cutting through the air. The orange Flight for Life chopper approached from the southeast and landed smoothly in a dusty clearing on the south side of the cemetery. I watched the paramedics efficiently transfer first my wife and then my dog to the care of the Flight for Life nurses. Within a minute they were transferred into the cabin. Seconds later, the doors were pulled shut and the orange helicopter lifted off. A hundred feet above the ground the tail rose, the nose edged down, and the chopper accelerated back toward the southeast. The flight to Denver wouldn't take long.

The paramedics shook my hand, said they were sorry, packed up their stretcher and their equipment, and drove away. That was that.

I thought I was as alone in that graveyard as I'd ever been in my life. A breeze rustled the leaves of nearby ash trees and carried the aroma of a Saturday afternoon barbecue my way.

A headstone right in front of me was inscribed "Tobias Shunt, 1846–1902. Rancher, Elder, Man of God." Beside him, an identical stone was inscribed simply "Wife."

At that moment, I despised Tobias Shunt and hoped he'd had a painful death.

I felt hands caress my shoulders from behind and smelled Sawyer's perfume.

Milt Custer said, "I'm sorry, Alan."

Sam asked, "They wouldn't let you go with them?"

Without turning around to face them, I said, "There was an extra doc on board the helicopter, some training thing. The pilot told me it was either me or Emily. I told them to take good care of Emily." Finally, I shuffled my feet until I was facing Sawyer. Her face was pale, her lips tight, and her eyes betrayed sadness and some intense fear that I couldn't comprehend.

"What's going to happen to them, Sawyer?" I asked.

"They're doing all the right things. They got her on oxygen right away, drew the right labs. They're taking them to Denver to put them in a hyperbaric chamber that will—"

"I know that part. What's going to happen to them? I mean, what happens to someone after she breathes too much carbon monoxide?"

She moved close to me and held both my hands together in front of my chest. She adopted a cushioned tone, a compassionate doctor's voice, one I've often used myself when giving bad news to family members of my patients. "They've both had serious exposure, Alan.

They could recover. There's a chance of that, depending on the level and duration of poisoning. Pray for that, okay? But . . . there is also a chance that they may both have suffered brain damage from hypoxia. The damage could be permanent. The fact that they vomited, that they were unconscious, it's not a good sign. The carbon monoxide replaces the oxygen in the bloodstream and starves the brain of the oxygen it needs. It all depends on how much carbon monoxide they were exposed to and for how long. The window of tolerable exposure is not long."

I looked down at the scraggly grass and glanced at Tobias Shunt's final resting place. My eyes drifted to endless gravestones around his. I asked, "Could they die?" I didn't feel I could form the words and wasn't sure they sounded right as I managed to get them out of my mouth.

Sawyer burst into tears and covered her face with her hands. "Yes," she said, "they could die."

The moment seemed to be monumental, a freeze-frame in time that would change my world forever.

I fixed my eyes on Mrs. Shunt's gravestone.

*Wife.*

I kicked the dust on her husband's grave and asked Sam to drive me back to the house.

"No," he said. "But I'll drive you to Denver to see Lauren. Milt will take care of your house. Milt?"

"Of course."

"I appreciate it, Sam, but I want you here to make sure that they find out how this happened. How he did it. Don't let them miss it."

"Lucy's on her way over. She's on it, and she won't let it slip, Alan. She'll goose the fire department investigators until they have it figured out." Lucy was Sam's partner.

Sawyer had moved to the front end of my car and was sitting on the bumper. She was still crying, hugging herself across her chest.

# THIRTY-ONE

The rest of the day passed.

I decided to drive myself to Presbyterian/St. Luke's Hospital in Denver. Sam followed right behind. For the first couple of hours I waited fitfully outside the white hyperbaric facility, an L-shaped chamber about eight feet in diameter. With its portholes and gauges I thought it resembled a deep-sea exploring vessel. Lauren lay inside one of the airlocks. She was covered by a pale blue woven-cotton blanket. Her hair was still matted in places by her own vomit.

The doctor on duty explained that she had regained consciousness briefly in the helicopter. They had put tiny holes in her eardrums so her ears could tolerate the pressure in the chamber and were in the middle of a second "oxygen period" now. The hood around her head was providing pure oxygen, he said. If she didn't begin to look more lucid soon, he'd order a third oxygen period. He explained the rationale to me twice, but I still couldn't concentrate enough to understand what he meant.

He said that Emily had regained consciousness during the flight and had been transferred to a veterinary hospital nearby. "Maybe your wife will do just as well. We have people come in here who look just as bad as her, or worse, and who walk out the next day."

"What about damage?" I asked. "Neurological damage?"

"No way to know yet. She's controlling her airway. Consciousness is returning slowly. We'll assess her as soon as we can."

"Are there long-term effects?"

"Possibly, sure. We may see some damage when she's conscious. And there may be delayed neurological sequelae. We're getting ahead of ourselves, though."

Sam tried to talk with me a few times, but I was too insulated by my grief and wouldn't let him reach out to me. Finally, I asked him to go home. I wanted to be alone. For most of an hour he ignored my pleas. But just before dinnertime he left. I didn't even have the grace to thank him. I spent my long minutes staring at Lauren through a porthole. Twice she stirred, moved her head, and opened her eyes. Each time I waved maniacally.

My shock was finally abating, and anger—no, rage—was erupting within me with the heat and force of a volcano. Occasionally I would stand and peer into the porthole and see my sleeping wife and I would feel some peace for a moment because I was in such proximity to my family. Then the rage would explode inside me again and I would feel awesome strength, as though I were powerful enough to destroy any adversary. Just as quickly that omnipotence would pass, and I would feel totally powerless because I didn't know whom to tear asunder.

The doctors told me little.

These first few hours were crucial, they said, in terms of survival. Then a day at a time, assessing for evidence of damage. I knew they meant brain damage. A young doctor, a woman with bright eyes and brand-new Adidas, went out of her way to warn me that pets and small children seem to have less tolerance for carbon monoxide than adults do. I could tell she was a dog person and didn't want me to harbor great hopes for Emily's full recovery. I could also tell that it hurt her greatly to tell me that.

Between the lines, I could read how bleak it all looked. There wasn't a single doctor who was encouraging me. None of them told me that directly, though. They hinted and obfuscated and told me stories about patients who had done well. I was sure that I looked too fragile, and too explosive, to be told what looked like the truth.

I phoned Lauren's sister, Teresa, and explained the danger her big sister was in. She agreed with me that we shouldn't tell their parents, who were both in ill health, just yet. She would make arrangements to get to Denver the next day.

After the third oxygen period, Lauren was removed from the chamber and moved to the ICU. She had regained consciousness, they said, but was sleeping. A kind nurse suggested I go home and get some rest, too. She said she had a feeling I would need my energy for the next day. I resisted for an hour but finally concurred. I contemplated checking into a hotel in Denver instead but felt a stronger need for the familiar than for the convenient.

The drive into Boulder seemed to snap by in an instant, and before I gave my destination more than half a thought, I found myself edging down the gravel lane to our half-demolished house in Spanish Hills. The cruddy rollaway trash bin was my first clue that my autopilot had failed and I'd driven to the wrong domicile.

I got out of the car anyway, paused, and glanced toward Adrienne's big house. The whole structure was dark; I remembered she and Jonas were at a conference in Florida or somewhere. The sky above was invisible to me, shrouded by a blanket of clouds that insulated the Front Range. The temperature was balmy, more like mid-August than early October. To the west, Boulder's lights danced through a misty haze.

Deep in my bones, even in the nuclei of my individual cells, I could feel how alone I was at that moment in that valley. The emptiness I felt was total. I was a parched canteen in an endless desert.

I pulled a flashlight from my car and unlocked the front door of the house. A buzzer sounded, and for a moment I thought I'd tripped a wire for a bomb. Reality finally set in. I used up almost the entire allotted forty-five seconds trying to remember the code to disarm our new burglar alarm. Finally, I got it right.

The house, of course, didn't look much different from that morning. Darker, sure.

I made my way across what had once been the living room and parked myself on top of a huge stack of Sheetrock that rested in front of one of the picture windows. I cried silently. I cried, first, for Sheldon Salgado and his wife and his daughter. I cried for Eleanor Ward and Lorna Pope. I cried for Sawyer.

Finally I cried for Lauren and Emily.

I tried to imagine my life without them and I couldn't. And so I cried for myself.

When my eyes were dry and sore I pulled a construction tarp over myself and rested my head on a bag of grout. The Sheetrock made a better bed than the grout made a pillow.

I was totally disoriented when I awakened the next morning. I heard heavy clomps, like footsteps, and tried to imagine what they were. But I couldn't even remember where I was. I sat up, startled, and below me saw Boulder beginning to illuminate for the day. Next I noticed the exposed studs of the construction morass all around me. In seconds, I felt the bone-jarring ache of having slept for six hours on Sheetrock and a grout bag.

The clomping stopped. My pulse jumped as I remembered the carbon monoxide poisoning and the maniac who was trying to kill me, and the terror of the footsteps approaching zapped through me like an electrical shock. I spun around, expecting to come face to face with the asshole for the first time.

Across the room, Sam Purdy was sitting on a sawhorse that was standing where our sofa used to be. He was wearing jeans and cowboy boots and a blue work shirt that wasn't tucked in. In a soft voice, he said, "You really should lock your doors, considering what's been going on and all."

My heart slowed enough so that I could think. I said, "Hey Sam."

He held up a brown bag. "I bought coffee and bagels from Moe's. No cream cheese for the bagels, no cream in the coffee. *Su casa es mi casa.* And my new diet is your new diet." He gazed around at the mess. "Where would somebody go to take a leak around here?"

"Chemical toilet. It's on the side of the house."

He didn't stand up to go pee. He said, "Any change last night?"

I shook my head. "Emily's groggy but awake. Lauren was conscious but was sleeping when I left. Just a sec." I punched in the hospital number. Lauren's nurse was too busy to talk, asked me to call back in a few minutes.

He said, "Sherry said to tell you she's praying. She'll get everybody at her Friends meeting on it this morning."

I managed to say, "Thanks." The adrenaline tide from Sam's intrusion was receding, and I was so chilled that I felt my marrow had thickened in my bones. I gestured toward the brown bag. "I'll take that coffee." He stood and handed it to me. For a while I just held it between my hands for warmth. "What day is it?"

"Sunday."

"How did you find me?"

"I'm a detective," he explained. "Figured you wouldn't go back to the other house. So I guessed you'd be here."

I nodded. "You know, if I'd taken those lessons and had Lauren's Glock with me, you would be a dead man right now. I thought you were him—the murderer. And that's why I don't like handguns."

He appeared to find my attitude toward firearms amusing. But he was compassionate enough not to argue with me right then.

"News?" I asked.

"Heat exchanger in your furnace was cracked. Badly. I talked the department into opening a case file. Scott Malloy caught it and agreed to have the whole furnace removed as evidence."

"I thought you said Lucy caught it?"

"I just told you that to make you feel better. Since I know how you feel about Scott."

Scott Malloy had once arrested my wife. I had forgiven him but was having a hard time forgetting.

"Scott's officially curious now. He says he found some scratches in the brass on the deadbolt on the back door. He's wondering whether there was an intruder. He's going to have a professional look for signs that somebody tampered with the furnace. Carbon monoxide detectors are a different story, though. That's troubling."

"Did you say 'detectors'? Plural?"

"Yeah. There were two. One was unplugged, which I find a little suspicious, right? The other one, a battery-operated thing, had fallen behind the furnace. It was the one that was blaring. You know anything about either of them?"

"Nothing. We just moved into the house. It had been a rental. Lauren probably knows something."

Sam didn't comment about Lauren's unavailability to answer questions. "The neighbors, of course, didn't see shit. And we're upping the patrols by the house, for all the good they seem to be doing." He paused. "Milt said your other lead didn't pan out? The other patient you wanted to find?"

"That's right. The guy looked real good on paper. But he died of an aneurysm back in 1995."

"You're sure?"

I thought about it and considered it an odd question. "Not really. But that's what his widow said. Don't know why she'd lie to me."

Sam's face let me know he found my assertion naive. "What makes him look so good on paper?"

"Psychologically, he's a good match. Character is consistent. Has a history of resentment. He's about the right age. He has a background in security analysis, which would give him an experiential base. And he has motive."

"Tell me."

"He thinks we ruined his life."

"Did you?"

"Maybe. If the story his boss tells is true, though, we had a lot of help ruining his life. But by what we did, we certainly may have contributed to the decline. The proverbial straw that broke the camel's back, you know?"

"By doing what?"

"After he was transferred to the hospital from Rocky Flats he was talking kind of crazy about a conspiracy-type thing at work. The docs who saw him put him on a mental health hold and gave him a diagnosis that ended up hanging around his head like a ticking time bomb. Cost him his security clearance at Rocky Flats, which meant it eventually cost him his job. He filed a defamation lawsuit or something like that in the late eighties. Went nowhere. Don't know what happened to him after that."

I paused. He waited. "Truth is, Sam, that in the current mental health environment—today—there's virtually no chance this guy ever would have been admitted to a psychiatric hospital, let alone put on a hold."

"Why?"

"The threshold has changed. Society has changed. Civil liberty thresholds have evolved. As a culture, we tolerate much more psychopathology and are willing to pay for much less psychotherapeutic intervention."

"Did he need help?"

I thought for only a moment before I shook my head and said, "Yes, probably, but not the kind we gave him. He didn't have a problem that would benefit from a vacation in a psychiatric ward."

"But he's dead? Your guy?"

"Yeah, for a while now." I took a long draw on the coffee. "This is good. Thanks."

"Can you tell me his name?"

"No. What's the point, anyway?"

Sam narrowed his gaze and tightened his jaw before he took a bite out of a jalapeño bagel, chewed it to a pulp, and swallowed. I could tell he was thinking about something. I knew he'd tell me what it was if he felt like it. "A.J. heard from her immigration sources last night. They can't find a match between the cruise ship's personnel list and the departures of U.S. citizens to New Zealand in the days right before Lorna Pope's death."

I raised my eyebrows. "Not even tentative? Nobody?"

"That's what they say."

"What does that do to their theory? Simes and Custer's?"

His upper lip puffed out as he expelled some air in a little burst. "Makes it much harder for them to get the Bureau involved. That's for sure. Other than theoretically, they're still unable to tie two of these deaths together."

My mind locked onto an image of Lauren in the hyperbaric chamber. I found myself fighting tears. "Sam," I asked, "when is somebody going to believe this is really happening?"

He drained his coffee and stared for a moment into the bottom of the cardboard cup. "My own theory on that is that they'll believe it once it's too late. And by my reckoning, given what happened yesterday, it's already too late. So I think somebody important will come on board any day now."

"You just being cynical?"

He shrugged. "You decide. Listen, as much as I like hanging out in drafty, dusty construction messes, why don't I take you to our house so you can shower before you go back to Denver? Sherry and Simon are at her meeting. You'll have the place to yourself."

Around us, sunlight was starting to seep into the dusty cavern that once had been my humble home. He gazed around at the mess. "So this is going to be nice when it's done, right?" he asked.

I laughed.

So did he.


Sam went to use the chemical toilet.

I fished the portable phone out of my pocket and phoned the hospital again. Lauren was still sleeping. "That's not necessarily bad," the nurse assured me. "As soon as she's awake, we'll assess her neurological status. If it's still compromised, she'll probably go back into the hyperbaric chamber. Let's hope she looks great, though, okay?" I translated her words to mean that Lauren was now out of the black-and-white dangers that lurked in the first few hours and had moved solidly into the shades-of-gray dangers that lurked in the next few days and weeks. She promised to call as soon as Lauren was awake.


Sam let me into his house in North Boulder, gave me a towel and a disposable razor, and showed me to the bathroom. When I emerged twenty minutes later, he was gone. A note under my windshield informed me that he had "stuff to do," and that he would call me later on Lauren's phone.

I stopped by the house on the Hill to get some fresh clothes. The place hadn't been designed to admit much sunlight, but that morning it felt particularly dark and bleak. The air inside was so crisp that I could watch my breath vaporize as I stood in the living room.

I edged into the bathroom sideways so that I could avoid looking at the spot where I'd found Lauren on the floor, but finally turned and examined it. The vomit was gone. I was grateful for that. But someone, maybe a paramedic, had left a couple of latex gloves on the nightstand. I swallowed, trying hard not to cry, while I stripped off the clothes I had slept in and pulled on clean underwear and socks, some black jeans, and a polo shirt and sweater.

I was locking the house back up when a heating contractor drove up in a big Ford van. He said Milt Custer had sent him over to do an estimate. I listened to the contractor for a few minutes as he argued persuasively against my repairing the old furnace. He was pretty excited about the new technology and focused most of his attention on the energy conservation benefits of upgrading. Given the Boulder market, it was a pretty good marketing pitch.

But I was in no mood for it. Finally I interrupted him and let him know that I wanted a brand spanking new furnace and two new carbon monoxide detectors, one in the basement and one upstairs. He went back to his truck and showed me a couple of brochures that went into a lot more detail than I wanted to know about the inner workings of my new furnace.

I asked him which one he would put in his mother's home.

He said he would choose this one and poked his index finger at a Lennox model with an attractive female model next to it. The model appeared quite proud of her new furnace.

I said it looked fine and gave him the house key. He seemed pleased by my choice and informed me that he thought he could have it in by noon on Tuesday. I replied that that was fine and inquired about the cost.

He said he would write up an estimate for me, but, ballpark, he was guessing around twenty-five hundred dollars.

I smiled at the amount. I was thinking of asking him if he knew Dresden, but I didn't.

*    *    *

On the way into Denver, I checked my office voice mail, praying that my own personal crisis hadn't coincided with any crises for my patients. I didn't have the time or the energy to help anyone else right now.

The only message was from Sawyer.

"Alan, hi. It's, um, me, Sawyer. I'm so sorry about what happened to your . . . to Lauren yesterday. I know a little bit about how you feel right now, and, well, every beat of my heart is creating good energy for you. If being with me will help you, will comfort you in, in any way, I'd love to see you now. I'm going to stay in Boulder for a couple more days at least. I'm still at the hotel. Let me know."

I pushed the button on the phone that would end the call. I toyed with the idea of phoning her and seeking comfort.

I even started to dial the number of the hotel. Just then, though, I passed under the bridge at Wadsworth Boulevard and noticed for the hundredth time the headstone above the grave of the dog that was buried beside the freeway.

I thought of Emily and how much I was going to miss her if she wasn't okay.

# THIRTY-TWO

Lauren's phone jingled in the pocket of my jacket as I drove past Federal Boulevard.

I found the little "talk" button, pushed it, and said, "Hello."

"Dr. Gregory? This is Angie, you know, at Presbyterian? Your wife's nurse? We met briefly yesterday. We talked earlier?"

I read a world of innuendo in her tone, which was as light and rich as perfect chocolate mousse. "Yes?"

"Your wife? She's awake and she's asking for you. She's looking much better. She's oriented."

"She's, uh, okay?"

"She looks . . . much improved. She's oriented. But we don't really know yet, you know? Gross neurological is good, but it will take some time."

I knew. The effects of brain trauma can be as blatant as pornography, or as subtle and difficult to decipher as fine art.

"Can I talk to her?"

"Not right now. They're drawing fresh bloods."

"I'm on my way in—I'm on the turnpike. Tell Lauren I'll be there in fifteen or twenty minutes. This is great. Thanks so much for the news."

I phoned the veterinary hospital. Emily was up and about and acting hungry.

Above me the sun was breaking through the clouds.

Lauren complained that her brain felt as if it had been processed in a Waring blender, but her mental status gave me joy, and momentarily, hope. Over the next few hours, I washed her hair and brushed it out and rubbed her feet and legs with lotion. I helped her eat and held her as she napped. I repeated to her at least three different times that Emily was recovering well and that I loved her.

I couldn't tell if she was having trouble with her memory or just needed reassurance.

We parted with great ambivalence. Neither of us voiced it, but we both knew that the reason I left was that she was much safer if I wasn't around. I promised I would check in with Sam and Simes and Custer as soon as I got to Boulder.

Sam had been busy during the afternoon while I was in Denver quietly celebrating with Lauren. I caught up with him late in the afternoon at the Boulderado, in the fourth-floor suite that had become a command post for Simes and Custer. A.J. was there with Sam, but Sawyer and Custer were elsewhere. I guessed that they weren't out shopping.

The light was fading and the western edge of town was shrouded in dense shadows. From up on the fourth floor the view of the tree-tops was a brilliant salad of autumn hues. Sam handed me a beer and offered me a big bag of Snyder's pretzels. I checked the label. They were fat-free. He was still being good.

A. J. Simes looked uncomfortable. With anyone else I know I would have assumed that the luminous melon-colored sweater she was wearing might have something to do with her discomfort.

Sam said, "It's great news about Lauren."

"Yes, I'm still pinching myself. She said to thank you for the flowers. She loves them." Sam's wife owned a flower shop.

"That's Sherry's doing. And Emily's okay, too?"

"She appears to be. Although I'm not sure I'd recognize brain damage in her very easily."

Simes said, "I'm so relieved for all of you."

"Thank you, A.J."

Sam munched some pretzels and finished off his can of beer. "We made some progress today."

"On what? The furnace?"

He shook his head. "No," he replied and waited until our eyes locked before continuing. "On Corey Rand."

I opened my mouth wide to stretch my jaw muscles and to keep myself from saying something I would regret.

"You didn't tell us his name, Alan," Simes said from across the room, as though that would make me feel better about having un-wittingly violated the man's confidentiality.

I recalled my conversation with Sam that morning. The facts I'd offered about Rand's dismissal from Rocky Flats, and the subsequent lawsuit he filed against the plant. For a detective like Sam Purdy, it was the equivalent of marking Corey Rand with fluorescent paint and putting him under a black light. Immediately, I wondered if it had been my intention all along to give up Rand's identity.

"What kind of progress?"

Sam stood and walked to the window. "You're not planning on protesting at all? I expected a truckload of grief from you." He sounded disappointed.

"What kind of progress?"

Simes said, "It wasn't difficult. Finding him. Rand. Once we knew where to look for him."

"You mean once I led you to his door."

She smiled self-consciously.

I repeated, "What—kind—of—progress?"

Sam said, "I talked to Valerie, his widow. Went and saw her in Wheat Ridge. She have some terrible cough when you talked to her?"

"Yeah, she did. Does she smoke?"

"Like an out-of-tune diesel. Anyway, I seemed to make her uncomfortable."

"Sam, I'm sorry to disappoint you with this news, but you make a lot of people uncomfortable."

"I'll grant you that. But most of them, in my experience, are uncom-fortable because they're hiding something."

"What was Valerie Rand hiding?"

"May I?" interrupted A.J.

Sam wasn't accustomed to being deferential, but he yielded the floor gracefully.

"A little history to start." She screwed the cap off a bottle of local water from Eldorado Springs and sat down on the sofa. "This is all preliminary. We've only been on it since late morning, right?"

I said, "Right. That's to be expected, since I didn't hand Corey to you until early morning."

She didn't bite at my sarcasm. I noticed that she had decided to tell her story without notes. "Once his security clearance was yanked, he left Rocky Flats. He wasn't fired, by the way. He quit after he was demoted to a clerical position that didn't require security clearance. Anyway, he struggled for a while trying to find a new career. He tried to make it in law enforcement. Was a sheriff's deputy up in . . . what's that place called, Sam?"

"Estes Park."

"Yes. Estes Park. But he never made it out of his probation. I got the impression from the sheriff that his, quote, 'style' made him a bad fit for the department. After that, he bounced around in other peripheral security-type jobs. Tried . . . aerospace, uh, Martin Marietta in . . . I'm sorry, Sam?"

"Jefferson County."

"Thank you. I don't know what's going on with me and names today. He was a security officer there. He lasted less than a year. Insubordination was the reason given by the company for denying Rand unemployment benefits."

"I'm getting the picture," I said. "He was a malcontent. It's not surprising, given the profile."

"Yes, a malcontent. After he was canned by Martin Marietta, he and his family left their home in . . . shit."

"Westminster."

"Due to foreclosure. Things got even more rotten then. His wife left him and took their son to live with her family in Wyoming, um, Cheyenne." A.J. seemed pleased that she'd finally remembered the name of a geographic location. I wondered if the concentration and word-finding problems were a routine part of her MS.

"But they didn't divorce?"

"No, as a matter of fact, they reconciled in 1990 or so. Surprisingly, he seemed to have started getting his life back together. He was managing a Radio Shack store in—oh, God damn it."

"Lakewood."

I asked, "Is this history all from Valerie?"

A.J. said, "No."

I turned to Sam for an answer. He wouldn't look at me. The nutritional label on the back of the pretzel bag fascinated him. I half expected him to inform me how much fiber there was in a handful of Snyder's.

"Where then?"

"Sources."

"Alan, it's not important," Sam said, warning me off.

"What is important, then?"

A.J. answered, "Corey Rand was five feet eleven inches tall. He had green eyes and blond hair that some people described as golden. His build could best be described as average to stocky. Records we've obtained show that his weight varied over the years from one-sixty to one-eighty-five."

The description seemed to match the hazy image of Corey Rand that I had in my memory. "Yes? So what?"

A.J. reached onto the desk behind her and picked up a single sheet of paper. She handed it to me.

I'd barely gotten over my distraction at the letterhead on the page— Department of Justice, Federal Bureau of Investigation, Washington, D.C.—when she summed up the contents of the memo for me.

"Corey Rand's characteristics match the age and physical description of the solitary American who had access to the incinerators on board the cruise ship the night that Dr. Asimoto disappeared."

It didn't seem like much to go on. "As do, what? Maybe two million other people in the United States?"

She exhaled and took a tiny sip from her bottle of water. I thought it was her method of biting her tongue.

"We can't rule him out, yet. That's what's important."

"He's dead." I knew I was arguing because a dead suspect did nothing to help me with my yearning for vengeance for the assault on my wife and dog.

"He wasn't dead back then."

I stared at Sam until he blinked, then fixed my gaze on Simes. She didn't blink. I said, "Now you've decided that you're looking for more than one killer? Is that what I'm hearing?"

Sam said, "Got to have an open mind, Alan."

A.J. recapped the bottle. She said, "What if? Stay with me here, okay? What if Matthew Trimble's death, the drive-by in L.A., wasn't part of all this? What if it was what it appeared to be, that is, a random act?"

"I'm listening."

"And what if Amy Masters's tanning-bed death was really accidental? What if the reason that the local authorities found no evidence of tampering with that bed is that there wasn't any?"

"What are you saying?"

"I'm hypothesizing that perhaps we should be investigating fewer deaths than we are. It would leave us with Susan Oliphant's death in the plane crash, Wendy Asimoto's death on the cruise ship, and Arnie

Dresser's death while hiking. And, of course, Lorna Pope's death in New Zealand."

Her argument seemed weak to me. "You're forgetting Sheldon and his family. But that's not the point. I could make an argument to exclude any of them. Why choose Matthew Trimble and Amy Masters?"

"I'm hoping that you can tell us that, Alan. You were on that inpatient unit with Corey Rand. I wasn't."

# THIRTY-THREE

The original litany of murder victims had been so compelling to me that I hadn't considered that any of them should be excluded from the list. But I wanted time to think about it alone.

"Do you know where Sawyer is?" I asked A.J.

"No. But they're due back soon. She and Milt."

"I'm hungry. I'll be downstairs in the restaurant getting something to eat. Tell her that, would you please? Ask her to join me."

Sam asked, "You want some company now?"

"No," I said. "Not especially." He looked more perplexed than injured at my response.

Downstairs in the restaurant I ordered a sandwich and a beer and tried to remember who had been working on the unit during the two days of Corey Rand's admission so many years before.

Sawyer and I had driven to Grand Lake for our one-night holiday and we had almost completely missed Rand's brief admission.

Had Matthew Trimble been on that weekend? I wasn't sure. He wasn't taking new admissions, though; Arnie was. Maybe Matthew was out of town and missed Rand's entire stay on Eight East. It was Thanksgiving weekend. A lot of people were taking time off.

And what about Amy Masters? She was a supervisor—my supervisor—and not a clinician. She didn't have her own patients to follow on the unit, and her involvement during off hours was rarely required. Many weekends went by when she didn't show her face on Eight East at all. I tried to recall whether she typically attended Monday-morning Community Meetings. I thought not, but I wasn't sure.

I decided it was possible that Corey Rand had never met either Matthew Trimble or Amy Masters.

Could I also convince myself that Rand *had* met all the other victims?

Susan Oliphant? Easy enough. I recalled the interaction between her and Corey as she directed that Monday morning Community Meeting. She was definitely there and was definitely involved in the decision to release him from the unit.

What about Wendy Asimoto? Sheldon Salgado had told me that Wendy was originally supposed to be Corey's psychiatrist, so she must have been at the hospital that weekend. It was even possible that Corey and Wendy had met in the ER before Arnie took over Corey's inpatient care.

Lorna Pope? In my mind, there was no doubt that if Lorna wasn't away for the holiday, she would have met Rand. Lorna, the unit social worker, would have been all over Corey and his family first thing Monday morning, assembling family history, arranging family meetings, and preparing initial reports.

Sheldon Salgado? No doubt Corey Rand and he had crossed paths in the psych ER. I'd spoken with Sheldon myself and he had the notes of his contacts with Rand in his consultation log.

Sawyer and I? Yes, we met Corey at Community Meeting.

Perhaps A. J. Simes's new theory had some merit. Maybe Corey Rand, if he was the killer, was a little more selective than we had given him credit for.

The only problem I had with the new hypothesis was that Corey Rand had been dead when Arnie Dresser and Lorna Pope were killed. And Corey Rand had been dead when someone sabotaged Sawyer's plane, killed Sheldon Salgado and his family, and poisoned my wife and dog.

What were we missing?

Sawyer showed up in the restaurant as I was asking the waitress for the check. I stood to greet her and found myself welcoming her embrace more than I should have. She held me for longer than she needed to, rubbing my shoulder blades with her open hands. I was aware of her breasts pressing against my rib cage.

"They're really all right? Lauren and your dog?"

"They seem okay. No one's one hundred percent sure. But it certainly looks better today than it did yesterday. Emily will stay at the vet hospital for a couple of days of observation."

She sat opposite me and leaned back in her chair. "I'm so happy for you. I was so scared yesterday at your house." Her eyes appeared rueful as she continued, "We've sure been dodging a lot of bullets lately, haven't we? You and me?"

I nodded. I couldn't believe how tired I was. I should have had coffee with my sandwich, not beer. "You were just out with Milt? Were you two working on something?"

"Hardly. He wanted to show me that bookstore he found. But mostly he wanted to talk about A.J. We sat on a bench on the Mall. He wanted romantic advice. He thinks A.J. is interested but he can't seem to get her to respond. Milt's wife died in a car accident four months after he retired. Can you believe it?"

Of course I could believe it. "And you provided the advice?"

She raised an eyebrow. "I'm not exactly proud to admit it, but I recognize a kindred spirit in A. J. Simes. She's afraid of Milt and what he has to offer her. Like I was afraid of you."

"You were afraid of me?" I tried not to sound as surprised as I was.

She flagged down the waitress and asked what the soup of the day was. Cream of pumpkin. She ordered tea and soup before she responded, "Yes, I was afraid of you, Alan."

"Why?"

"I was married, remember?"

"You thought I was a threat to your marriage?"

She smiled playfully and said, "Were you always this thick? Did I miss something back then?" She rearranged her silverware into perfect alignment before she said, "No. You weren't a threat to my marriage."

"What then?"

She refolded her napkin on her lap. "I need to tell you what happened . . . to me . . . before . . . I came to Colorado . . . before . . . I met you. With my first husband. You can't understand what I'm talking about unless I do."

"Okay," I said, and settled back on my chair. I hoped I was about to learn what I'd been trying to discover for so many years.

"When I met you that day at the party at Mona's condo, after you left me that note in my *New York Times*, I was a widow."

A widow? I felt stupid. Beyond stupid. "I'm so sorry. I've been— Jesus, I didn't know."

She shook her head forcefully, dismissing my protest. "How could you know? I didn't want you to know about any of that. No one knew at the school but my clinical supervisors and my therapist. I didn't trust anyone with what happened. I thought if the school knew what I was going through, they would judge me to be too fragile for the residency."

"It was recent? His death?"

"Sometimes it still feels recent. The second year of the residency started on July first. He . . . my husband . . . died . . . the previous January."

"God, I'm sorry."

The waitress delivered Sawyer's tea, and she started the elaborate ritual of preparation. She chanced a quick glance my way and read something in my eyes. Through tight lips, she cautioned, "I haven't told you much, yet." She was warning me not to jump to any conclusions. I decided to allow her to proceed without any more of my promptings or inane attempts at comfort.

"It wasn't just that he died. What happened was . . . my husband killed himself." She looked up from her tea again, but away from me, out the window. "I had told him in November, the fifteenth to be precise, I had told him that I wanted a divorce, and . . ."

Her words were halting and seemed to sweat thick beads of anguish. "He didn't take it well. He said he would change however I wanted him to. He, um, he told me he would do anything to keep me. That he couldn't live without me. I didn't take him at his word, though. No. I thought it was just his insecurity talking, and his insecurity was why I had already decided to leave him."

I was confused. How could her friends in Colorado not know about her husband? "Were you already in Denver?"

"No. I did my first year and a half of residency in Chapel Hill. In North Carolina. I thought you knew that. A supervisor there, a friend, arranged for me to repeat the second year in Colorado after . . . after . . ."

"Your husband's suicide?"

She nodded. "And after my baby died."

*Her baby died?* She said the words so quickly I wondered if I had heard her correctly.

Sawyer was staring at the reflections of the light waltzing off the tea in her cup. "Your baby died?" I wondered aloud, my voice as soft as her infant's skin.

She closed her eyes and swallowed. Her shoulders jumped up suddenly and then collapsed. She looked sallow and lifeless. I didn't speak. Neither did she. The sounds of the restaurant seemed to roar in my ears. I reached across the table and took her hand, gently prying it from the handle of her teacup.

She pulled it back.

"I had a baby once, a beautiful baby," she whispered in a tone that told me everything, that said, "I once had a life. A real life."

I guessed that I could jump to the end of the story she was telling, and because I could, my impulse was to close the book and walk away. I was in a mood for nothing but happy endings. But instead I waited.

"My baby was a little round bundle of love." She almost smiled. "He, um, he had her—her name was, um, her name was Simone, and . . . and she was so sweet and she was so pretty . . . and he had her for a couple of days while I was on call. That was what we'd worked out after I moved out, that he would watch her when I was on call. And . . . he, um, he killed her. He killed my little baby at the same time that he killed himself. He killed her so that I couldn't have her. And so that she couldn't have me. He wanted me to know what it was like to have something so essential ripped from his life."

The chair next to her was vacant. I moved across the table and sat on it before I slowly eased her against me. She seemed small in my arms. I waited for convulsions to rack her bones and tears to flow from her eyes, but they never came. I thought of her the day before, after Lauren and Emily were poisoned, when she was sitting against the bumper of my Land Cruiser, in anguish that I couldn't understand.

And now I could.

"When I met you, you terrified me," she said, her words so soft they were almost lost in the din of the restaurant. "You were gallant and handsome and . . . romantic. But you needed me, Alan. I could feel it. I could just . . . feel your insecurity at times. And I couldn't let that happen again. I let him need me—my husband—and look at what happened. He wouldn't let me go. And then he took my baby. He took Simone from me. I couldn't let you need me. I couldn't. It was too dangerous, and too soon."

She sat up straight, releasing herself from my embrace, turning toward me on her chair.

She touched the side of my face with one hand and then reached up with the other. She flattened both palms against my cheeks. "And now? Now I think I may have read you wrong back then. Don't you love irony?"

"What do you mean?"

"I don't know," she said. "It's all come full circle for us. Before, back then, I thought you would drag me under, drown me even. But today? Today we need each other just to stay alive. How is that for the ultimate insecurity? The ultimate dependency."

My instincts told me that something crucial had been omitted from Sawyer's story. My mind flew back to her anguish at the cemetery the day before. "What was his name? Your husband?"

She looked at me oddly and said, "Kenneth Sackett. Kenny. He was a, um, banker. His family has a bank. Had a bank. They sold it to NationsBank a while back. I made a lot of money on the stock he left me. Even more irony, huh?" She nodded to herself as though she was acknowledging that she'd actually answered the question correctly.

"How did he do it? How did he kill himself . . . and your baby?"

Her hand jumped to her mouth as though some invisible string yanked it there. She blurted, "You already know, don't you? How do you know?"

I didn't know how I knew. I shrugged.

The waitress chose that moment to deliver Sawyer's soup. Its color was the hue of a fall sunset. The waitress's name was Kim, and she asked, of course, if everything was all right.

I answered that everything was fine. Sawyer actually giggled at the lunacy of the exchange.

When Kim had retreated out of earshot I said, "Yesterday, Sawyer. It must have . . ."

"Yes," she acknowledged. "Yes. It certainly did."

"I'm sorry."

"Just like with you, yesterday, I found them myself. I came home from work and found them. Kenneth and Simone."

"But the outcome wasn't as happy for you then as it was for me today."

"No. That's been my life. No happy endings."

She spoke with such finality I thought she was done with her story. But instead, she was just steeling herself for what came next.

"I had stopped by the house—his house, the one where we'd lived while we were married—to pick up Simone after I left the hospital at around, I don't know, seven-thirty in the evening. Nobody answered the door, but it was unlocked. I wandered around inside looking for them, cursing him for not being home. I figured he'd gone out somewhere and had dropped Simone off at her grandmother's house. Finally, I checked her room. In her crib, lying across her favorite teddy bear, there was a note that said, 'We're down in the garage.'

"That very second, I knew. I flew down the stairs and through the kitchen and yanked open the door to the garage and I . . ."

Her voice faded and she tempered her breathing. She was trying to find the strength to finish this story.

"Kenny loved his car, just loved it. It was this red Pontiac Firebird he'd had since high school. When I went in the garage, it was there. The engine was off but the whole garage smelled like exhaust. He was in the front seat, on the passenger side, slumped over, vomit all over the place.

"He had put Simone in the backseat. The garden hose from the exhaust came into the car right next to her. She was strapped in her car seat, surrounded by her toys. He'd, um . . . the shithead . . . he'd, um, taped a wedding picture of us on the dashboard in front of the driver's seat, and he'd . . . hung a picture of me over the back of the seat so that when Simone looked up before she died, she would see me. I would be the last image she ever had."

She was silent for a full minute or more, but I was sure she wasn't done. She didn't turn to face me as she resumed her story. "What, um, what galled me the most was that he left her alone to die in the backseat. He couldn't see past himself enough to even comfort her as she lay there dying. I'll never forgive him for that.

"Never."

# THIRTY-FOUR

**S**am Purdy walked into the restaurant, paused, and started to look around. Sawyer waved him over to our table.

She greeted him and invited him to join us as though she was delighted he was there and his presence would interfere with nothing of significance. I couldn't think of a thing to say in protest. They immediately started chatting about a cold front that was approaching Colorado after freezing cats in Montana. To my amazement, Sawyer had moved from revealing the pathos of her daughter's murder to participating in a mundane discussion about the weather with an ease that to me felt pornographic. I was tempted to ask Sam to leave us alone so that she and I could talk some more and come to something that felt like closure. But Sawyer had obviously talked enough. Or at least as much as she intended to.

Sam explained his presence. "We just decided—Milt and I, upstairs—that somebody should be with each of you all the time until this . . . thing is concluded. So I'm here to keep you company." The waitress, Kim, brought him a menu. Before he opened it, he asked me, "Should I bother? Is there anything in this place that your little doctor friend is going to let me eat?"

Sawyer said the soup was great. He looked at it and seemed to draw away physically from the creamy mixture the way a vampire might be repulsed by a bowl of roasted garlic.

I said I thought he could find something that was on his diet. As he lowered his eyes to the pages, I stared at Sawyer, who wouldn't look back at me.

I wanted to know more about Simone.

I wanted to know why she couldn't trust anyone.

I wanted to know why she couldn't trust me.

Sam ordered an egg-white omelet and dry wheat toast. Sawyer asked for a fresh pot of tea.

I thought about things for a moment longer and announced that I was going for a walk, or something.

Sam made a face that communicated precisely how childish he thought my departure was in light of the fact that he had just volunteered to be my bodyguard. But he let me go without verbalizing a protest. I stopped in the lobby and used a pay phone to call Lauren. Her phone rang through to the nursing station, where a nurse informed me that Lauren was resting.

"How is she doing?"

"Well, she's tired. I imagine that's why she's resting."

"How was she doing before she started resting?"

"I think she was tired then, too. That's why she decided to rest."

I gave up and offered my tempered gratitude.

The woman who answered the phone at the veterinary hospital was much more forthcoming about Emily, who she said was doing "Great. She's my favorite. Is she always this much fun?"

I thought, *No, she isn't.* But I didn't say anything to dispel whatever transference was at work.

I stepped outside onto the flagstone steps of the hotel and felt the distinctive chill of autumn. That cold front that had so fascinated Sam and Sawyer was no longer approaching us from Montana; it had definitely arrived. Crisp gusts of wind were cutting through the canyons, whipping leaves from the trees, and knifing through my clothing as though I were dressed in rags. I examined the eastern sky and saw blues and blacks. When I turned to attend to the western sky, I saw strings of clouds the color of Sawyer's pumpkin soup.

Before I checked my watch, I guessed it was almost seven o'clock. But it was only 6:40.

I needed to find a place to sleep for the night. I had a plethora of bad options. One of my two available residences was a major construction zone. The other didn't have an operable furnace. Sam would offer the sofa bed at his place. A hotel probably made the most sense. First, though, I needed some clean clothes.

I found my car on Spruce Street and drove across downtown, over the creek, and up to the Hill. I parked outside for a few moments with the engine running, listening to the last few minutes of *Fresh*

*Air* on NPR. Terry Gross was interviewing Scott Turow. Her inter-viewing style perplexed me, as it always did. If she were heading from L.A. to New York, she'd just as soon detour through São Paulo. But she somehow always got to her destination, and I was usually fascinated and grateful I'd gone along for the ride.

I climbed down from the Land Cruiser and made a quick tour of the exterior of Lauren's house. I unlocked the front door and stepped inside, immediately noting that the air inside was no warmer than the air outside. I prayed that this particular cold front wasn't quite cold enough to freeze plumbing and then decided not to worry about it. If the pipes froze, so be it. It wouldn't kill anyone.

The new furnace I had ordered wasn't downstairs where I expected it to be. It was sitting in a box at the top of the basement stairs. I was no mechanical genius, but I figured that the furnace had a ways to go, geographically speaking, before it was capable of generating any environmentally friendly, fuel-efficient heat for this little house. The contractor had said he'd have it up and running on Tuesday. I was now guessing Wednesday and wouldn't have been surprised by Thursday.

I avoided the bedroom for as long as I could. I swept up the dirt the rescue folks had dragged inside. I walked downstairs to the base-ment and found myself trying to remember what Sam had said about there having been two carbon monoxide detectors in the basement. One was made to operate on house current, but it had been unplugged. The other was operated by batteries, but it had fallen down behind the furnace.

The old furnace had been ripped out and carted away. I stared at the empty space and decided that it made no sense. Why would Lau-ren have installed two CO detectors in her basement? And why would one, the presumably more reliable one, be unplugged?

I climbed the stairs and went into the kitchen, picked up the phone, and called the hospital again. Lauren answered her own phone this time. The sound of her tired voice stirred me.

"Sweets, it's me. How are you doing?"

"Still a little foggy. But okay. Where's Emily? How is she?"

"Great. They love her at the vet hospital. They're threatening not to give her back to us."

She laughed gently. "You're pretty tired still?" I asked.

"Yes. I just woke up and I'm ready to go back to sleep."

"I wanted to remind you that you're due for Avonex tomorrow.

You remember? I'll bring it down when I come to visit so that they can give it to you."

"Thanks," she said. She admitted, "I'd forgotten all about it."

I tried to be reassuring. "It's okay. It'll take a few days for you to sort everything out. Listen, I've been trying to make some sense of all the carbon monoxide detectors you have in the basement of the house on the Hill. There were two of them down there. Why?"

She didn't hesitate before responding. "That all happened about six months ago, I think. My tenant—remember Suzanne?—she asked me to put one in for her. I did. I originally got the battery-operated kind but when I tried to hang it on the wall, I didn't hammer in the nail hard enough and it fell off the wall and dropped and fell behind the furnace. I couldn't get back there to get it out. It was kind of stuck. I didn't know whether it was still working or not and I knew I'd never be able to change the batteries, so I went back to Mc-Guckin and bought another one, one I could plug in. I've been wondering why it didn't warn me earlier, you know? Why it wasn't screaming at me when there was so much poison in the house."

I didn't tell her that it hadn't warned her because someone had unplugged it. I said, "We're all trying to figure that out. Scott Malloy is all over it, has somebody checking the old furnace, and Sam is making sure nobody misses anything important. I have a new furnace going in tomorrow. You get some rest. I'll see you sometime tomorrow. I love you."

I hung up, wondering about the state of Lauren's memory, gratified that she remembered the history of the carbon monoxide detectors, and ambivalent about the fact that she didn't show any indication that she felt that the CO poisoning might have been attempted murder. She actually didn't even seem to recall the whole series of events that had followed Arnie Dresser's funeral.

Briefly, I envied her that.

I finally made my way to the bedroom to pick out some clothes that were not only warm but also appropriate for work the next day. The room was freezing. I toyed with the idea of collecting every blanket, comforter, and sleeping bag I could find in the house and burying myself under them so I could sleep in our bed.

I talked myself out of it. Instead, I packed up some more clothes and grabbed my appointment book and briefcase before I began searching the house for something else. The first place I tried was Lauren's little office. I had no success. I tracked down her briefcase, which was locked. I shook it gingerly and decided that what I was looking for wasn't there. Her purse was hanging on a chair in the kitchen. Nope. Finally, I found it in the little leather ass-pack she carries to the health club when she works out.

The Glock.

Damn, but the thing was heavy.

The first place I tried to stash it was my jacket pocket, but its heft totally distorted the shape of my coat. It felt way too obvious having it there. Next, I gingerly hooked it into the waistband of my trousers but immediately became uncomfortable at the general direction that the barrel was pointing, so I pulled it back out of my pants and stuffed it into the bottom of the little carry-on that I'd packed full of my clothing. After one last look around, I locked up the house and hopped back into my car with the knowledge that I was now officially carrying a concealed weapon. I felt fully the burden of being a felon, my eyes as much on the rearview mirror as they were on the road as I drove the dozen or so blocks to the hotel.

I had to admit, though, that the presence, close by, of that hunk of metal was just the slightest bit comforting. I puzzled over the question of whether that comfort index would increase or decrease once I actually figured out how to use the damn gun.

Parents' weekend at CU was over and the young assistant manager at the desk of the Boulderado seemed delighted to rent me a room for the night. We wasted a little too much energy haggling over price, however. I suggested to him that at the rate he initially quoted me, I'd just as soon stay at the Golden Buff on Canyon Boulevard. We both knew that his occupancy wasn't hovering particularly close to one hundred percent, and he came around to my way of thinking relatively quickly. He even feigned graciousness about offering the lower figure.

I was aware the whole time that I had a loaded 9mm semiautomatic in my luggage and wondered, of course, if it was the Glock, and not I, that had been doing the negotiating.

The thought reminded me of a conversation I'd once had during therapy, when I inquired of one of my patients what heroin was like. He warned me that horse was "so good you should never try it."

I considered the possibility that possessing a handgun was somewhat like tasting heroin. Both were artificial comforts that temporarily and unreasonably increased one's sense of well-being. Was the sense of comfort of possessing a pistol "so good" I should never have tried it?

Time would tell.

I found my hotel room, a nondescript little place on the second floor that had a stunning view of the alley. In a lesser town, that might have meant overlooking filth and mayhem. But downtown Boulder has great alleys. Neat, well lit, and paved with concrete. The choice of rooms was the assistant manager's petty revenge, I decided. I washed my face, brushed my teeth, and decided to leave the Glock in my bag while I made my way up to the Mezzanine Lounge for a drink or two.

The mime was on duty again.

Before sitting down I scouted for a location in the expansive lounge that wasn't her responsibility. But since the Broncos were playing a Sunday night game and this wasn't a sports bar she was the only waiter working the floor.

She remembered me. Instantly, I regretted leaving her such a healthy tip the last time I was in. She waved hello from across the mezzanine with that annoying arm-bent-shoulders-and-head-swaying gesture that only a mime would dare employ. I didn't wave back and actually considered fleeing through an exit before she could get all the way around the balcony railing to me.

Before she made it to the table, I heard Sam's voice in my ear. "Don't you find it goofy that these doctors will let me drink beer every day but don't want me to eat a damn hamburger? I find that goofy."

The word "goofy" was part of the residue of his upbringing on Minnesota's Iron Range. Every time he used it, he made me smile. "Hi, bodyguard," I said. "Can I buy you some carrot sticks?"

He sat on the settee across from me and followed my gaze up to the ceiling. "Nice glass," he offered in understatement as the waitress arrived. Naively, he smiled at her in welcome. She rewarded him by doing her mime thing.

He watched her act to its conclusion before he shifted his eyes to me. He stared at me incredulously, as though he'd just somehow stepped into the bar scene from *Star Wars* and he figured I was the only one who could get him safely back outside. Without changing my expression, I ordered vodka and told her I thought that Sam was doing okay with his beer.

She curtsied.

"Don't ask," I said.

"This damn town, I swear," he muttered, and moved on. "Listen, downstairs? Did I walk in on something hot and heavy with you and Sawyer?"

Sam's perspicacity ambushed me sometimes. "I'd say it was a delicate moment, yeah. But not what you think."

"What do I think?"

"Sam."

"You're not, you know, doing her, are you?"

"Sam." My voice was tired. Tired enough, I hoped, to get him to move in another direction.

"Well, sorry if I intruded. You talk to Lauren tonight?"

"Yeah. She's real tired, which the doctors seem to expect. But she seems okay. Her short-term memory has some black holes you could hide a galaxy in, but her thinking in general seems clear."

"Will she get out of the hospital soon?"

"It's day to day."

"Emily?"

"She's good. Making everybody happy at the vet hospital."

"The firefighters told me she did a smart thing. She found the cold-air feed for the furnace and lay down right under it. So she got some fresh air along with the carbon monoxide."

The story made me happy, and I promised myself I'd lighten up on the jokes I frequently made about the size of her brain. I said, "That reminds me, I asked Lauren about the two detectors." I related the explanation of why there were two carbon monoxide detectors in the basement.

"Wow. So the one with the battery that she couldn't reach is the one that saved her life?" He shook his head and smiled. "The best-laid plans, right? The asshole was good this time, Alan. Lock on the back door *may* have been picked, by the way. Furnace *may* have been tampered with. But you know as well as I do that there's no way in the world we'll get usable prints off of the other carbon monoxide detector, so who can say whether it was unplugged intentionally or not? But the killer didn't know about the other one, the one that fell behind the furnace. Couldn't have. And it's the one that stopped him."

"No leads, though?" I didn't expect any.

"None."

"How are you feeling?" I asked casually.

"Hungry. Other than that, like normal."

"But then normal apparently included a kidney stone the size of Gibraltar, right?"

He took a long swig of beer and then wiped his mustache with a napkin. "Can we talk about something more upbeat than me being in excruciating pain? Like, oh, let's say, the risk of you being murdered?"

"Sure. What do you think about A.J.'s current hypothesis? About there possibly being more than one killer?"

"It's not her hypothesis. It's mine."

"Really? You convinced her of something? She doesn't seem that . . . ?"

"Malleable. No, she doesn't."

With stealthy silence, Ms. Marceau returned with my drink. She delivered it without affectation. Sam stared at her with marked suspicion, as though he had an inkling she might be about to draw a gun, or break unexpectedly into the I'm-locked-in-a-glass-box routine.

Instead she set her cocktail tray on the table, took two baby steps backward, raised her arms, contorted her face, and tried, rather successfully I must admit, to imitate Edvard Munch's *The Scream*.

Sam lunged at her and she ran away with exaggerated cat steps. "Can you make her stop?" he implored me.

I shook my head. "You're the cop. Unfortunately, I tipped her well last time I was here. I'm afraid it encouraged her."

"Like feeding a damn raccoon." He belched politely, if that's possible. "Went like this. If this Corey Rand is so good, why throw him away? That's what I was thinking. You like him. Sawyer likes him. I kind of like him. His only problem as a suspect is that he has a damn good alibi for the killings since 1995."

"Damn good alibi is right. Major problem there, Sam."

"Not if he wasn't in it alone."

"You have an idea about his partner?"

"Not yet. Have you guessed how I got here?"

"Yeah. The change in MO between the early murders and the more recent ones. Sawyer and I have been theorizing a psychological deterioration. You're just seeing another hand at work. But the motivation doesn't work for me. Who else would have the same motive for the same killings?"

"I don't know. I admit I don't know that yet. But you can't get lost in motivation at the beginning. Think. Did someone have a motive to kill JonBenet? I don't think so. Maybe a predilection, perhaps even a need. But a rational motive? You can't start there always. Sometimes motivations are distracting at the front end of an investigation."

"Where to now?"

"I want to meet this boss of Rand's. See if he has a clue about any of this. What's his name?"

"Reggie Loomis."

"I want to meet Reggie Loomis."

"Now?"

"Why not? He's probably home watching the damn football game. I know I wish I was."

"Sam, you don't have to do this. I mean, I'm really grateful, but you should be home with Sherry and Simon, not here with me."

"That's not what I meant."

"Isn't it?"

"So you think Loomis is home."

"I doubt he's watching the football game. More likely he's making stock or preparing the dough for tomorrow's breads."

"What?"

"Never mind, you'll see." I threw six dollars on the table without bothering to ask for my tab.

Sam asked, "She won't chase us, will she? Like mimes do sometimes?"

"If she does, Sam, it's fine with me if you shoot her."

"Cool. Do you mind if Sawyer comes along with us to visit Loomis?"

"I guess not. Why?"

"Because I've already asked her."

# THIRTY-FIVE

I didn't want to be chauffeuring Sawyer and Sam to North Boulder. I wanted to drink another vodka, plot my escape from the mime, retreat to my little hotel room alone, and spend some time pondering Sawyer and what had happened to her daughter, Simone. Sawyer had handed me important pieces to an old, long-incomplete puzzle, and I yearned for an opportunity to spin those pieces around, compare their contours, and see where they might fit on the board.

An unconscious corner of my awareness kept throwing Eleanor Ward's image into the mix. She had been there back then, too. On the unit. At the same time that Corey Rand was a patient.

And Eleanor Ward was the last patient Sawyer discharged before she packed up her things and left Colorado, and me, for good.

In addition, I now knew an additional fact. Eleanor Ward and Sawyer Sackett had both lost infant daughters to traumatic deaths.

Sawyer and Sam were arguing about Sawyer's speculation that a romance was simmering between Milt and A.J.—Sam said no way, Sawyer was totally sure—as I drove the car down North Broadway toward Reggie Loomis's neighborhood. I had enough self-awareness to know that I was confusing my mysteries. Part of me was consumed with understanding what had happened between Sawyer and me way back when. And part of me was consumed with solving the mystery of Corey Rand and his possible participation in these murders.

I reminded myself to try to keep my mysteries straight.

I found it odd, too, that I wished I had Lauren's Glock with me.

Sam took a break from arguing with Sawyer to ask me where Reggie Loomis lived.

"On Fourth, near Juniper."

"Which side?"

"West."

"On the greenbelt?" The edges of the question were gilded with envy.

"Yep."

"Nice neighborhood for a retired government worker."

"It's not one of the scrapes, Sam. It's one of the original houses. Looks like he's lived there forever."

"Still," he said. He was cooking something up, but as the smell drifted back my way, I couldn't tell what it was.

The front of Reggie's house was dark, but I wasn't dissuaded. Reggie Loomis didn't live for appearances.

Sawyer said, "Looks like no one's home."

"He keeps a low profile. Let's knock."

We strolled up the walk in single file and I stepped forward and rapped twice on the door.

I thought I smelled cinnamon wafting in the chill air, along with some other enticing aroma that wasn't quite registering in my memory. "I think he's here. I smell food."

Sam looked at his wristwatch as though it was important to time Reggie's response to my knock. I kept my eye on the peephole in the door, waiting for it to darken. Finally it did. Reggie was checking us out.

Sam tensed. He had noticed the shadow across the peephole, too.

After another ten seconds, Sam said, "So, is he going to open it or not? I'm not exactly warm out here."

"He's considering it."

I waited a full minute. I timed it on Sam's wristwatch, which he held up for inspection about every ten seconds. I knocked again.

Reggie slid the dead bolt about two Sam-sighs later. He ignored my companions and looked directly at me as he said, "Yes."

"I brought some people with me, Reggie."

"I can see that."

"Are you busy? Can you spare a few minutes?" I noted that he was unconcerned with Sawyer, but had begun an examination of Sam.

"I am busy preparing tomorrow's breakfast. Cinnamon rolls? Perhaps you can smell them. Although I find them unsophisticated, I'm afraid I've become known for them. I'll be doing baked eggs in the morning and need to finish the prep work before I head to bed. Perhaps another time?"

"Those rolls sure smell good to me," Sam interjected, his voice padded with false camaraderie.

"And you are . . . ?" asked Reggie. His voice was not padded with false camaraderie.

"Sam Purdy."

"And you are . . . with?"

Sam smiled. "I'm with my friends here. You know Alan, of course. And this here, this here is Sawyer. We'd be grateful for a little bit of your time and I promise we won't stay long."

"This really isn't a convenient time for a visit. I'm sorry. I have work to do. People depend on me. Please call tomorrow, Dr. Gregory. We can find a time."

Sam said, "Lives may be at stake, Mr. Loomis."

Reggie rolled his eyes at the overt manipulation. But he said, "Then come in. If you must."

We followed Reggie into his main room. He immediately stepped over to a CD player and flicked on a clarinet concerto.

Sam's face didn't hide his disappointment at not finding the football game, though he had no discernible reaction to the configuration of Reggie's house or the splendor of the kitchen equipment. But Sawyer did.

"Wow. Nice kitchen," she said.

I explained what Reggie did, how he prepared and delivered food to shut-ins around the county.

"That's very generous of you," Sawyer said.

Sam nodded in the general direction of the La Cornue and said, "Something sure smells good."

I admonished him, "They're not exactly on your diet, Sam."

He inhaled deeply, as though he could be nourished by the aroma alone, and muttered, "Shit."

Reggie hadn't offered any refreshments, and he wasn't prompted to by Sam's infelicitous comment.

Sawyer glided slowly around the kitchen, touching the La Cornue, examining the espresso machine, and grazing her fingertips along the marble and granite countertops. She asked kitchen questions. Reggie answered in a fashion that was more guarded than I would have expected from him.

Finally, she chose a seat next to Sam and me at the counter. Reggie stood by the stove across the room. I felt a bit like a judge at a tribunal.

Sawyer stunned me by asking, "I've always wondered, Mr. Loomis. Why do you think that D. B. Cooper requested four parachutes during the hijacking? I mean, we now know that he was working alone, right? And he had things impeccably planned, so why did he ask for four?"

Sam blinked twice.

Reggie looked at me and, I imagine, saw the incredulity in my expression. "What?" he managed to ask.

Sawyer's voice was all casualness and curiosity. "Why four parachutes? You know the legend, right? After the airplane landed in Seattle, he requested two hundred thousand dollars in twenty-dollar bills, and he asked for four parachutes. Why four? Why not one? Why not two or three?"

Reggie's eyes jumped from Sam to me and then back to Sawyer. "Why . . . why are you asking me that?"

"You were a security analyst. One of your things was anticipating terrorists, right? Figuring out scenarios. Well, D.B. was like our first commercial domestic terrorist. And Alan says the whole D. B. Cooper thing was like a parlor game for the people where you worked. I'm just wondering what you guys came up with for an explanation of all the extra parachutes old D.B. requested."

Reggie backed up against the La Cornue. His voice as defensive as his posture, he demanded, "Why did you come to see me tonight? All of you?"

Sam knew what role to assume when he was in situations like this with his detective partner, Lucy. But Sawyer's line of inquiry about D. B. Cooper had apparently left him speechless.

Sawyer acted as if she expected an answer to her question. I didn't imagine it would be forthcoming.

I said, "Corey Rand is dead."

Two beats passed before Reggie said, "No. I'm so sorry. I'm just, so, so sorry to hear that." His words felt a little rushed.

Sam glanced at me. If he were to score Reggie's lie, I don't think he would have given it more than a six point five. Why was Reggie pretending he didn't know Corey Rand was dead?

I said, "You didn't know?"

He turned and squatted and lowered the oven door. The aroma of cinnamon dough almost bowled me off my stool. He fussed with the pan and finally pulled it from the oven and placed it beside the one that was already baked. "Done," he said.

"Would you like to know the circumstances of his death?"

"My—ouch!" He yanked his hand back from the edge of the pan. "My, yes, of course."

Sam kicked me on the ankle and said, "Car accident. Hit and run. No witnesses. Internal injuries."

Were I a judge of Sam's fabrication, I would have held up a card that read nine point oh.

Reggie walked across the room to the sink and started running cold water over his burned finger.

Was he going to let Sam's lie stand?

He asked, "Was it recent?"

Sawyer and I stayed silent. Sam said, "Last year, around the holidays."

He shut off the faucet before he said, "So Corey Rand isn't responsible for the recent deaths you three are investigating?"

I was about to shake my head but was able to perceive the outlines of the trap Sam was setting in time to say, "Which deaths are those?"

Reggie stared hard at me. His look was disdainful. It said, "Nice try, amateur." He dried his hands and responded, "The fire deaths, of course. In Kittredge. We discussed them, remember? The last time you were here, Doctor."

I nodded.

Reggie made himself busy cleaning the counter. Without facing us again, he said, "I'm afraid I'll need to excuse myself now. I'd like to prepare for bed."

When we were back outside, Sam commended me. "Nice pickup in there. I wasn't even sure you were paying attention to what was going on."

"Thanks. It didn't work, though. He saw it coming."

"That's just it. He did see it coming. And that tells us exactly what we need to know."

"Which is what?"

"That he knows more than he's letting on to us about Corey Rand and about all your dead colleagues." He turned to Sawyer. "And, pray tell, what the hell was all that D. B. Cooper shit about?"

Sawyer was climbing into the backseat. She settled herself and caught my eye in the rearview mirror. I shook my head just a little. She smiled.

"Sorry," she said to Sam. "I can't tell you. Confidentiality. I'm sure you understand."

Sam muttered, "No, I don't understand. And Alan will be happy to tell you I'm not much of a fan of shrinks and confidentiality." He pulled his seat belt around his waist and clicked it into place before he yanked the rearview mirror his way and focused it on Sawyer in the backseat. "And here I've been thinking that you and I were going to get along. Anybody hungry but me?"

No one was hungry but him.

I wanted to know what we were going to do next, and all Sam would tell me was that he wanted to talk to some people he knew from Rocky Flats, see if he could discover a reason for Reggie Loomis to be so slippery with us. I assumed he would learn about the D. B. Cooper rumors as soon as he started sniffing around at the nuclear weapons facility.

"When will you get final word on whether somebody tampered with our furnace?"

"I'll ask Scott. But I'm not holding my breath. If they say it was tampered with, what does that tell us that we don't already know? If they say it wasn't, are either of you suddenly going to feel any safer? I don't think so."

"It will give Simes and Custer something to take back to the FBI, though, right?"

"Wrong. The FBI is looking for something that ties two of these things together. With only one point to work with, you never get to draw a straight line."

On the rest of the short drive back to downtown, Sawyer quizzed me about property values and seemed disappointed that the desirable parts of Boulder were almost as expensive as Santa Barbara. Twice she said about Loomis's shack, "His little house would really cost that much?"

Sam muttered something about trying to live around here on a cop's salary, and Sawyer wisely dropped it.

As I parked near the hotel, Sam asked, "So where are you sleeping tonight? Is your new furnace in yet?"

"It's in the house, but it's not quite in the basement. I have a room here, too. At the Boulderado."

As I looked up, I noticed that Sawyer was staring at me in the mirror in a way that made me uncomfortable. I glanced quickly over at Sam, hoping to stifle an invitation to sleep at his house. "I'll be safe here. He's not going to take out a hotel full of people, is he?"

Sam didn't answer immediately. "Well, is he?" I repeated.

"No, probably not. A wing, a floor, maybe. Not the whole hotel. What room are you in? I'll call early tomorrow."

Before I could recall my room number for Sam, Sawyer said, "Sam, are you with us on some kind of . . . I don't know, official basis? Don't you have other responsibilities?"

He smiled sideways at me before he responded. "I'm terribly sorry. I can't tell you. Confidentiality, you know. Listen, anybody want to do breakfast tomorrow? That egg-white thing I had for dinner wasn't half bad."

I said that I had to be at my office early. Sawyer said she was going to sleep as late as she could.

At Sam's behest, I agreed to accompany Sawyer up to the suite she was sharing with A.J. The elevator ride up was particularly awkward.

"You never told him what room you were in," she commented as the doors swooshed shut.

"No," I said. "I guess I didn't."

"Well, in case I need to reach you, where are you? You know that A.J. and Milt are going to want to know."

I felt in my pocket for the plastic card key. "Two eighteen. It's small, and dark, and not particularly charming. It may have the same address as your suite but it's certainly not in the same neighborhood."

"But then you don't have to share your room with an ex–FBI agent with an attitude who gives you the third degree every time you want to use the toilet."

"That's true. I don't."

We exited the elevator at her floor. I stopped in front of the door to the suite. "Your plane will be ready tomorrow? Is that true? They can fix it that fast?"

"Maybe. There wasn't that much damage. A little sheet metal to replace. Test the damn landing gear."

"Are you ready to go home?"

She shrugged. "Milt says I shouldn't, doesn't think it's wise. If I do go back, he wants to hook me up with a bodyguard, somebody he knows from his days in Chicago. Sounds awful. I don't know what I'll do. Sometimes the night tells me things. So when my head hits the pillow, I'll be listening to the whispers."

She leaned forward slowly with her eyes locked on mine, her lips slightly parted. She moved toward me, at the last moment tilting her head to the side. She kissed me on the cheek.

I said, "Good night."

After waiting for the elevator to arrive for a good three minutes I finally realized I hadn't hit the "down" button.

# THIRTY-SIX

**W**ith the curtains closed in my hotel room I was able to convince myself that I was actually ensconced on the top floor with a stunning view of the Flatirons. I wanted to end the day with another vodka, but the urge was not quite strong enough to motivate me to once again confront the mime lurking in the Mezzanine Lounge. The conundrum, I decided, was that I would only be able to find her act tolerable after I consumed more drinks than I would ever be able to tolerate her serving to me.

I could have walked over to one of the half-dozen bars close by on the Mall. I didn't. The minibar provided a tiny shot of Absolut that I sipped straight from the bottle while I flicked on the TV. I found a movie with Nicolas Cage on HBO, and stared at a nine-dollar jar of pistachios for much longer than I really needed to before I started getting ready for bed.

The bedside clock argued forcefully that it was too late to call Lauren, so I checked my pager to make sure the battery was fresh in case the hospital needed to reach me. Then I sat down next to the clock radio to make certain that the previous guest in this room wasn't a prankster who would get a sadistic chuckle from leaving the alarm set to wake me at some ungodly hour. The alarm was indeed set. The time the little jester had chosen to jolt me out of bed to the not-so-soothing sounds of KYGO was 3:48 A.M. I unset the clock, stripped off my clothes, and walked into the bathroom to take a shower.

There was a part of me that knew she would come. A part of me that welcomed her visit. Avoiding this moment would have been easy. I could have taken a room at the Golden Buff across town.

And there was a part of me that dreaded her visit. The dread wasn't actually about the visit. The dread was about how I would deal with it.

Does falling in love with one woman clean the slate and erase the love that was once so passionate for another woman? Does it?

Because I was living proof it doesn't.

Do I send her away? Tell her that her visit is inappropriate?

Because it is.

Do I tell her I'm not interested? Tell her that was a long time ago and my feelings have changed?

Have they?

Do I act as a friend might act and offer a shoulder so that she can begin to untangle her anger and unburden herself of all the feelings that are surfacing about her daughter's death?

Because a friend would.

As an intellectual exercise, I could enjoy the quandary. In fact, in my office on Walnut Street, with a patient across the room from me, I could have examined the facets of this therapeutic diamond for the full duration of many forty-five-minute hours. But as a married man naked in a hotel room with an ex-lover trilling her fingers across my door, I wasn't much enamored with the puzzle.

I was edging down the dark tunnel toward sleep when the tapping started, and it took me a while to separate the rhythmic sounds I was hearing from the comfortable reverie of pre-dreaming. Finally awake, I said, "Wait, wait. Just a minute," jumped from the bed, and immediately ran into a wall. I made my way to the closet and pulled on the robe that the hotel had provided—according to the card that was attached to the belt—for my "comfort and pleasure." Apparently, hotel management was under the mistaken impression that I would somehow be most comfortable pretending that I was five foot four and, say, one hundred and twenty pounds.

The full-length mirror adjacent to the closet let me know that three-quarter-length sleeves and an above-the-knee hem were never going to be my most alluring look in boudoir attire.

I winked into the peephole.

It was Sawyer. She was smiling, but she didn't look happy.

In my hotel room, there was one chair and there was the bed. In my comfortable hotel robe, I could sit modestly on neither. After inviting Sawyer inside, I excused myself and retreated to the bathroom to pull on jeans and a T-shirt.

She had chosen to park herself on the bed, on the side that was mostly still unruffled. She was wearing red and black animal-print tights and a matching top that accentuated her breasts. Her hair was casual and she hadn't retouched her makeup since we'd said good night earlier. She didn't look a day younger than she was, and I found her incredibly alluring.

For one of the few times in our relationship, she was as uncomfortable as I was. "This isn't, um . . . I need . . . we can go someplace else if you'd . . . I just need to talk, I think. I don't want you to . . . I mean, I hope—"

"It's fine, Sawyer. Can I get you something?" I parked my butt on the chair by the window and waved at the minibar as though it contained a genie ready to meet any of her desires.

"No, thank you. I'm grateful to you just for opening the door to me. It's more than I expected. More than I deserved, for sure."

The tension in the room was so dense that it felt as if it could crush the air from my chest. To lighten the mood, I said, "I need to tell you that I was, I don't know, touched—deeply—by what you decided to share with me earlier. About your marriage and your daughter."

"Simone." She spoke the word with such reverence that if love were helium, it would have been enough to float her baby girl from her grave.

"Yes, Simone. I only wish I had known about her. You know, back then."

She fiddled with the hem of the bedspread. "I wasn't ready to grieve with everyone. With anyone, really. I knew if I told people, everyone would treat me differently. Remember that resident who had the osteosarcoma? What was his name? I don't know; it doesn't matter. But everybody had an opinion on what kind of cases he should be allowed to take. I just wasn't ready for that kind of scrutiny. I convinced myself that I needed to work, that . . . that was best for me, working, the harder the better, not thinking about what Kenny did to my baby."

I was suddenly aware of my posture. I asked, "And keeping away from men—that was best for you too?"

"No," she said, her eyes fixed on her hands. "Men were candy for me. I'd pick one and take a tiny bite and throw away any flavors I didn't like. I hurt a lot of men a little during those few months, and that felt . . . I don't like this about me, Alan, but it felt good. I loved attracting men and flirting with them and . . . nibbling at their centers and then . . . moving on. I had planned to do the same with you. And then you came along and you didn't seem to want to just play the game. I didn't feel like I was a conquest to you. You actually wanted me."

"And . . . you felt, needed you."

"Yeah, that was your mistake." She smiled to herself, not to me. "Needing me. When I felt you begin to need me, it scared me. I started seeing Kenny in your eyes and . . ."

"You left Denver because of me? I'd always assumed that your leaving Denver showed how little you cared about me."

She shook her head. "See, that's your insecurity." She shivered as though recalling an unpleasant memory. "But that wasn't it. You're forgetting about Elly." She stood up, took two baby steps, and faced the window. She parted the curtains, using both her hands. Her perfume sifted through the still air in the room and reached me, settling around me as though I were holding a bouquet of fragrant flowers. "Nice view," she said.

"Thanks. They charge extra for it, but I'm into the urban alley experience, so I figured what the hell." I stood then, too, and immediately wondered why. I figured I would regret getting up, but sitting right back down didn't feel right either. "Elly lost a daughter, too."

"Yes. Elly lost a daughter, too. She was another gorgeous baby. I doubt if you remember—why would you?—but her daughter's name was Priscilla. During those weeks between Thanksgiving and Christmas, I somehow taught Elly how to begin to grieve her loss, how to let go and move on. And, somehow, she . . . returned the favor and showed me it was okay for me to begin to grieve, too. But she was way ahead of me. After those weeks with her, I couldn't keep it in any longer—the pain, the anger. I talked to Susan about it for a long time. And my therapist, too, of course. We all agreed it would be best if I left the residency and went back to Raleigh and dealt with . . . my feelings about Simone. Maybe I'd come back and finish up in Colorado later, maybe I wouldn't."

"You didn't say goodbye to me. You never explained why you were leaving." My tone surprised me. These words weren't an accusation on my part. They were a plea for her to help me understand.

"I convinced myself that since I hadn't let anyone in the door, I didn't owe anyone the courtesy of a good-bye. That was my rationalization, anyway. The truth is sadder. The truth is that I didn't want to see how much I had hurt you. Because I knew you cared, and I feared you cared too much. And I knew I was going to hurt you, deeply. By leaving, by my dishonesty, by everything I'd done. I didn't want to witness it. Part of it was cowardice. And part of it, the bigger part, was that . . . I was too afraid of what men could do when they're hurt."

"I would never have harmed you, Sawyer."

She shook her head viciously, her blond hair flying off her shoulders. "I once believed that about Kenny, Alan. That he could never harm me. When I was having so much trouble establishing an alliance with Elly, you taught me an important lesson about transference, remember? Don't forget the lesson you taught me. God knows that I never have."

I stepped toward and embraced her from behind, my hands folded over her abdomen, my face buried in her hair. She crossed her arms over her chest and grabbed one of my arms with each hand. I felt her ass against my groin.

The room lights flickered, and I wondered how to move away, feeling desperately how much I didn't want to.

The lights darkened once again, staying off for two or three seconds before returning.

I inhaled the smell of her and filtered through a thousand memories before I thought of Lauren, and the room went dark again.

This time it stayed dark.

"Power failure," Sawyer said. "Ooooh. Where were you when the lights went out?"

I reached past her and parted the curtains. The alley lights were dark, and the traffic signals at the corner were black dots. Through the walls of the adjacent room I heard an anxious voice saying, "What? What is it?"

"It's not just the hotel," I said, pointing at the street. "It looks like this whole part of the city is dark."

She turned and faced me, our bodies now in full contact, our lips inches apart. I could taste her breath and feel the air stir as it caressed my skin. I wondered which one of us would look away first.

She tensed and looked to one side and then the other. She furrowed her forehead and said, "Oh, shit, Alan. Do you think?"

Immediately, I knew what she was talking about. I yanked her backward away from the window, and she tumbled on top of me onto the bed. Her weight on me was a comfort, and I felt the contours of her body as familiar and precious, like the memory residue of a special old aroma.

Our chests were heaving from the combination of emotions. Each inhale heightened my arousal. I stammered, "We should phone Milt."

She didn't move. She admitted, "Probably. But he'll tell us to stay where we are, don't you think?"

"Probably." I didn't know what to do with my hands. "I'm not sure this is a good idea," I said.

"Staying here?" Her voice was a murmur. She was gazing at me through bedroom eyes.

"No. Staying in this position."

She didn't move right away. She asked, "You're sure?" I felt her hips rotate and I knew I was getting hard.

"Sawyer, at this moment, I'm not even sure of my name."

She started to smile. Outside, a car braked hard, tires squealed, and time stood still as the protracted screech ended in a vicious crash. Seconds later, someone yelled, "Anybody have a phone? Somebody call 911. On no! We need an ambulance!"

I started to get up, and Sawyer rolled off of me onto her back, onto the bed. Her top had ridden up, and I could see the swell of the bottom of her breasts. She didn't try to cover herself. I turned my attention to the window, pulling back the draperies an inch or two.

"I can't see anything, the accident," I said, turning back to her.

She put her hands behind her head and her top rode up even higher. At that moment, I recalled every contour of her nipples. They were small, with aureoles no larger than nickels. They would grow hard with the slightest touch.

I exhaled, and my voice came out too loud. "I'll call Milt," I said, moving to the other side of the bed. I grabbed the phone and punched in the number for Milt's room. He picked up on the first ring, obviously groggy.

"Milt? It's Alan. The power's out in the hotel, in this whole part of town, actually. I doubt if it means anything, but I'm feeling a little paranoid."

He was quiet for a few seconds, maybe ten. I said, "Hello? Milt?"

His tone was crisp, authoritative. He said, "It's probably nothing. But get away from the window and stay where you are. I'll be down in a minute. Three knocks. Check me through the peephole."

"Okay. Um, Sawyer's here, too."

"I know," he said, his tone packed with disapproval.

Before the receiver was back on its cradle, Sawyer asked, "What did he say?"

"He said to stay put. He's coming down."

"I told you so." With her right hand she pulled her top down and covered her breasts.

For some reason I'm not sure I want to understand, at that moment I remembered I had the Glock.

# THIRTY-SEVEN

**M**ilt's nostrils kept flaring as though he were sniffing for the odors of sex.

His manner was disapproving. My guilt said it was about Sawyer and me being alone in my hotel room, but his gruffness could have been typical of him after he had been waked up to baby-sit relative strangers. He said hello to each of us without making eye contact with either of us, told us where to sit—Sawyer on one side of the bed, me on the other—and got on his cell phone, surprisingly, to Sam Purdy. He explained to Sam what was going on and asked if Sam could make a call or two to try to figure it out.

We sat in silence for two or three minutes waiting for the phone to ring again. When it did, Milt listened uninterrupted to Sam for most of a minute, before he said, "Thanks. Yeah, tomorrow."

He pinned me with his eyes. "There's a short in a transformer in a substation. Sam said something about a fried raccoon." He made a face that I interpreted as "That kind of shit doesn't happen in Evanston." He continued, "Are you two in any immediate danger? I think not. If our guy wanted you to leave the room, to leave the hotel, he would have set a fire or set off the fire alarm and waited to ambush you as you evacuated. And ambushing people in public isn't his style. I don't see how this helps him, blacking out part of the town. Do either of you see a margin in this?"

I shook my head politely, feeling as though I had been summoned to the principal's office. Sawyer was examining her nails. She said, "No. It doesn't make sense. We overreacted."

"Then let's call it a coincidence and say we all try to get some sleep."

No one moved. Milt offered his hand to Sawyer. "Come on, Doctor. I'll see you back upstairs."

She said, "That's really not necessary."

He said, "But it will be my pleasure. Don't want to take any foolish risks, right?" I thought I saw the shadow of a smirk on his face as he turned to me. "Double-lock this door. Put out your 'Do not disturb.' Don't order room service. Keep those curtains closed."

"You mean you want me to forsake this view?" I said.

After they left I lay in the dark for half an hour, not even thinking about sleeping. The power grid came back on line in a startling flash of light, and I wasted another half hour or so flipping through the channels on the TV, trying to understand why infomercials were proliferating.

I think I managed to spend some of the remainder of the night sleeping, the rest of it wondering whether I actually would have had sex with her.

The bedside phone rang at 5:17. As I was trying to make sense of my surroundings, my dreams, my erection, and the insanely loud noise blaring beside my head, my pulse raced to a level that evolution intended only as response to the assault of a wild animal.

By the third or fourth ring, I had puzzled out that I was in a hotel room and that the phone required attention. In rapid sequence, I thought: *Hospital. Oh shit. Lauren,* and scrambled after the receiver. I mumbled a "Hello" that caught in my throat. It felt as though I would choke on the word.

"Dr. Gregory?"

Did I recognize that voice? I said, "Yes."

"Reggie here. Reggie Loomis. Hope I didn't wake you."

Thank God it wasn't the hospital.

I glanced at the clock. "It's barely five o'clock in the morning, Reggie. Of course you woke me."

He said, "Sorry," but he didn't sound it. "I have a one-time offer for you and your lady friend. But it doesn't include the cop."

How did he figure Sam for a cop? I rubbed my eyes as though greater visual clarity would help me at the moment. "I'm waiting."

"Here's the situation. My ride—the church lady with the big Chevy?—she can't help me deliver the breakfast meals this morning. Her son is home sick from school. Fever. Rash. I know you have a big car. Here's the deal. You give me a ride around to drop off food at the shut-ins, and while we're driving around, I'll tell you and your lady friend what I know about all this D. B. Cooper propaganda that you both seem so goldarned interested in."

The offer was curious. Why was Reggie suddenly so willing to spill the beans about D. B. Cooper? During my previous visits, he'd been evasive about the legend, and he certainly hadn't been responsive to Sawyer's frontal assault the night before. This was a contingency specialist; I felt confident that he must have alternative backup transportation to deliver his meals. Why did he want us? And why did he want to talk about D. B. Cooper?

I tried to remember my work schedule. My morning was free, I thought, until about ten forty-five, and then I had patients stacked like a wedding cake until dinnertime. "I need to check my calendar and find Sawyer and see if she's interested. I'll get back to you."

"No can do," he insisted. "We need to leave here by six-thirty at the latest. Yes or no?"

I exhaled and pulled the covers around me with my free hand. Did I fear Reggie Loomis? Did I even consider it a possibility that he was involved in this conspiracy that had consumed my life since Arnie Dresser's funeral?

No, I didn't.

Did I care enough about this D. B. Cooper thing to take his offer? Not really. But something was telling me that there was more to be learned from this errand than this old man's musings on the legend of an ancient hijacker. Maybe something about Corey Rand. *That* interested me.

And, I reminded myself, I'd get to do some good. Help some people who needed help.

I said, "Okay. We'll be there at six-fifteen."

"I'll have plenty of coffee, and don't worry about eating first. This shift includes breakfast, of course."

I remembered the aromas of the previous evening. "Cinnamon rolls and baked eggs."

"Not to mention fresh fruit cups with mint. I found some killer pomegranates at Alfalfa's. Pomegranate juice does things for the rest of the fruit that you just won't believe."

Sawyer climbed into my car right on schedule at 6:10.

I greeted her warmly but was careful not to touch her, keeping both my hands on the wheel. I felt awkward. She seemed serene. "How did you get away?" I asked. "Wasn't A.J. suspicious?"

She nodded, blowing warm air onto her fingers. "Does this thing have heated seats?"

"No."

"Too bad. I just told her that you and I were going to have breakfast together before you went to work. She didn't seem to be worried about it."

"If Milt had been there, he wouldn't have let you go."

She cupped her hands around her mouth again. I heard her blow through her fingers. "Milt was there, I think. A.J. closed her door behind her when she came out to ask me about the phone call. I think he was in there with her."

"Huh," I managed, momentarily trying to picture the parameters of that tryst before allowing my mind to wander elsewhere.

Sawyer asked, "So Reggie's offered to tell us what he knows about D. B. Cooper? That's why we're doing this?"

"That's the offer. I'm actually hoping to learn more about Corey Rand than about D. B. Cooper. Rand is the one who was so consumed with him—Cooper. Maybe we can get Reggie talking about Rand's fixation."

"What about Sam?"

"Reggie said the cop wasn't welcome."

"He made Sam for a cop?"

"Apparently."

She lowered her hands to her legs and slid them beneath her thighs. "Reggie could have some guilty knowledge. You thought about that?"

"Yes, I have."

"And we're delivering food?"

"To shut-ins. We're going to be do-gooders this morning, Sawyer." She shivered. "I have two questions."

"Yes?"

"First, why on earth do shut-ins want to eat breakfast so early? Why don't they sleep in?"

"Sorry, I can't help you with that one. Second?"

"Do you want to talk about last night?"

I flicked on my headlights, checked my mirrors, pulled away from the curb, and said, "No, I don't think so."

\* \* \*

As I drove west on Kalmia on the way to Reggie's house I glanced in my rearview mirror and saw the first glow of light in the eastern sky. The moment I turned left onto Fourth, I noticed that Reggie was standing on the four-by-four slab of concrete that sufficed as his front porch.

Sawyer and I strolled up the walk. Reggie didn't say good morning. He said, "You're late."

I pulled my left hand out of my pocket and checked my watch. The time was precisely 6:17. "Two minutes?" I said.

"Excuse me? If your patients are two minutes late for therapy, do you let them get away with it?"

The truth was that usually I did. But I admitted his argument by saying, "No. I guess not." Left unsaid was that I didn't schedule appointments with my patients on one hour's notice at six-fifteen in the morning.

Reggie huffed, "Well, we'll just have to make up the lost time along the way. Let's get these meals loaded into the car. I'm afraid that your coffee and rolls will have to wait."

Sawyer didn't make the slightest move toward the front door. In an even voice, she said, "Don't be petty, Reggie. We get our coffee now or we don't work. It's that simple."

I smiled. This was the woman I remembered.

Reggie's catering service was, no surprise, organized with the precision of an operating room or an airplane galley. Separate storage units kept the hot food hot, the cold food cold, and the room-temperature supplies, room-temperature. Moments after closing the doors, the interior of the car smelled like a Paris café, but without the permeation of Gauloises.

"Where to?" I asked.

Reggie was riding shotgun. "We'll head south and work our way back to this end of town. We have some canyon stops to make, too."

"Broadway?"

"Yes. First home on the list is right below N-CAR."

"Is that tarragon I smell?"

"Yes. It is."

His directions were flawless. As we arrived at a nondescript split-level with a million-dollar view, he gave us the drill. "My guests are not accustomed to their homes being invaded by strangers. Mrs. Savage, my usual driver, accompanies me inside to help set up the meal and to collect the dishes from our previous visit. I would like one of you to do the same at each house. You may alternate. You should each get a feel for this work that I do."

I'd finished my coffee. Sawyer's hands were firmly wrapped around her mug. I said, "I'll do the first one."

I popped the rear hatch of the Land Cruiser and stepped around to open it. Reggie prepared the first tray, choosing a large cup of fresh fruit, a ramekin of baked eggs, and a cinnamon roll the size of his fist. He drew coffee from a big urn into an insulated pitcher and added small cartons of skim milk and orange juice to the tray. "I used to do fresh-squeezed. But I'm afraid it wasn't totally appreciated," he explained, apologizing for the carton of Tropicana.

"This is a young widow, Mrs. Levitt. Her husband was killed in a traffic accident that caused her severe injuries. She has been one of my guests for almost six months. By the way, I will not be introducing you to her as 'Doctor.' I'm not intending to diminish your stature, but for most of my guests, presenting you as 'Doctor' would be intrusive and confusing. I'm confident that you understand." He looked at his watch before lifting the tray. "We continue to run a few minutes behind schedule. I allow seven minutes inside each house, except for the last one. I alternate which guest comes last for each meal, and I linger there with that guest, visiting. I've explained this to you already."

I nodded.

Reggie opened the front door with a key. Inside, he pointed me toward the kitchen and explained I would find the previous meal's dishes in a brown paper bag on the sink. I was to retrieve them and wait by the door.

I heard the sounds of the *Today* show, Katie teasing Matt about something, and Mrs. Levitt's high-pitched, excited voice greeting Reggie. She started cooing over the breakfast tray, and Reggie began asking about her children. About a minute later, I heard, "Mr. Gregory?"

I followed the sounds of the TV and found Reggie sitting beside Mrs. Levitt on an awful chartreuse sofa in the living room. Mrs. Levitt was indeed young; I guessed late twenties. She was painfully thin and pale and was covered to her waist by a chenille blanket. A thin scar extended upward from her right ear, across her temple, and disappeared into her hairline. One arm hung useless by her side. She raised the other one to shake my hand. I stepped forward and touched it gently. "This is so kind of you," she said. "Helping like this."

"It's my pleasure to help." At that moment, it was.

"My balance isn't very good anymore. And with only one arm . . . well, you know. Mr. Loomis is a lifesaver."

We visited for maybe two more minutes, until Reggie began a gracious transition to the door. I followed his cue. Moments later we were back in the Land Cruiser on our way to a house just south of the Bureau of Standards. I poured myself more coffee while Reggie and Sawyer delivered breakfast to an elderly male inhabitant of a brick ranch that was dwarfed by junipers.

Our next two stops were tract homes in Martin Acres, followed by a cluttered one-bedroom apartment near Baseline and the Boulder Turnpike. Thus far, I realized, the stops had been no more than three or four minutes apart.

I was well aware that I had nothing in my stomach but a couple of mugs of coffee.

I was also well aware that thus far no one had mentioned D. B. Cooper.

# THIRTY-EIGHT

I waited patiently, I thought, through one more breakfast stop, this one at an apartment building behind the old CU Credit Union building on Baseline. While Sawyer and Reggie delivered the breakfast tray, I went around to the back of the car and poured myself another mug of coffee. They returned right on schedule, and as soon as they were buckled back into their seat belts, I asked, "Well, Reggie, what about D. B. Cooper? You said you would fill us in."

He was gazing out the windshield to the northwest. He said, "Our next guest lives in married student housing in that complex off Arapahoe behind Naropa. You know where that is?"

"Yes, I do." I didn't start the engine.

"Well, then, scoot, scoot." He tapped his watch. "We've almost made up our lost time. If we make the lights, we'll be back on track."

I still didn't start the engine.

He glared at his watch as though it were lying to him.

Reggie sighed and said, "Okay. Okay. Drive. I'll talk."

I decided to take Twenty-eighth Street over to Arapahoe, which probably was a mistake even this early in rush hour. I missed the first traffic light and listened to Reggie punctuate my braking with a sigh.

He started by saying, "I don't know how much you recall about the Cooper legend. But it was a big deal back in 1971. Captivated the country. Divided the country, really. Seemed at the time that half of us wanted him caught and the other half were rooting for him to continue to elude the FBI and make them look like fools. You have to remember those days in the early seventies. This was right after the bombing in Cambodia, during the height of Vietnam. There was a lot of anti-government sentiment going around."

The light changed, and I inched forward, pulling up the on-ramp onto Twenty-eighth Street. We were soon stacked up behind a UPS truck halfway back from the light at College.

In a voice his ex-wife had probably detested, Reggie said, "You should have taken Thirtieth."

"Probably," I acknowledged.

He was energized as he returned his attention to the Cooper saga. "The crime itself was something special. It was innovative. No one had ever hijacked a commercial jet for ransom in this country before. It was planned meticulously. The man was so ordinary that hardly anyone remembered him well enough to describe him. He left no fingerprints on his ticket or near his seat. His escape was brazen and a work of pure genius. He actually parachuted out the rear stairs of a 727 into the mountain drainage above the Columbia River and disappeared into thick cloud cover.

"Despite the fact that the government combed his drop zone for months they never found a thing. No dead hijacker, no parachute, no ransom, no candy wrapper they could tie to him. Nothing. He disappeared into thin air."

From the backseat, Sawyer asked, "I think Alan and I know all that. But what was so captivating about him for your colleagues at Rocky Flats? Why did all of you get so enthralled?"

"We didn't. Not then, anyway. Back in '71, when it happened, I don't think we paid any more attention to the hijacking than the rest of the country did. Maybe less. The security department was busy then. I mean, we were consumed with our responsibilities. The plant was in constant danger of terrorist intrusion by outsiders. Antiwar people, anti-nuclear people, environmental people. We had to keep an eye on all of them and anticipate their incursions. We had a hell of a lot of plutonium to protect. And a ton of secrets to secure. We even had one demonstration where there was a Save the Whales banner." He laughed at the memory.

I cleared the light at College and made it halfway to Arapahoe before traffic again crept to a stop.

"In 1976, the media made a big deal of the five-year anniversary of the hijacking. You know how they do it, the TV people, on anniversaries. Overkill. They replayed all the old film, they reinterviewed the pilots and the stewardesses—they weren't flight attendants back then—and they did long pieces about all the work the FBI had done. They took crews back to the Columbia drainage and searched for evidence all over again. At the plant, we all got talking about it too, and one day someone in the department suggested that it couldn't have been just any Joe who could do it. It would have to have been someone like one of us to pull off a caper like that.

"The crime was so sophisticated, so clean, so meticulously prepared and researched. It would have taken a cop, or a fed, or a security specialist trained in counterintelligence. Well, the idea kind of snowballed and people began to talk and rumors began to spread and . . . you know how it goes."

I asked, "Was Corey Rand the one spreading the rumors?"

"Corey wasn't even there in '71 at the time of the hijacking. But he was on board five years later. He didn't start the whole thing, the Cooper finger-pointing. He never even participated in any of the coffee-machine talk—remember, he was an outsider. Nobody liked him much, even then. But he sure ran with it. He made a personal decision that he was going to figure out the whole damn crime and see what kinds of special skills and special knowledge it would've taken for Cooper to pull it off. He used to say that if you could identify what you had to know to do it, pretty soon you would know who could do it. From the list of who could, you could find who did. It became a, I don't know, an obsession with him."

The light cycled once, but we moved forward only a couple of hundred yards. Taxiing behind the UPS truck was like driving behind a brown brick wall.

Sawyer wondered, "Did he? Did Rand ever figure it all out?"

Reggie hesitated and said, "He thought he did." He grew silent.

I urged him to continue. "Go on, Reggie."

"I had become Corey's only friend in the security department. I say 'friend,' but Corey couldn't really be anybody's friend. He didn't know how. He was a difficult man to get along with, had this set of rules that he lived by that—I don't know—it put people off. He couldn't really relax and be part of the group. After not too long on the job the other guys started calling him 'Adolf,' and . . . well, things got worse and worse for him over the years. He was passed over for promotions and he grew more vindictive and things just kept snowballing. At the end he was totally isolated except for me.

"I tried to protect him for a while. Put him under my wing, so to speak. Tried to get him to recognize the difference between a rule being broken and a rule being bent, but he was more rigid than a concrete slab, and hell, to tell you the awful truth, he was just about as cold."

We finally cleared the light and turned west on Arapahoe. We were getting close to the married student housing complex.

"Then the guys set up that final sting for him. I wasn't in on it; they knew I would've put the kibosh on it if I'd known what was going on. Years later, one of them admitted to me how he and two of his buddies had set Corey up." He shook his head at the memory. "It was a good dupe they did, worthy of a bunch of security analysts, I'll tell you that. They laid the tracks just right to lure him in, and they cleaned up the tracks just right so you couldn't tell they'd ever been there. By the time I looked around, I couldn't find a trace of their scam. But I remain surprised to this day that Corey fell for it. He was a bright man, certainly brighter than they were."

The light at Folsom was green. Reggie said, "Next left. So, anyway, their plan worked. It turned out that they got rid of Corey just like they had hoped."

Sawyer asked the question that was on the tip of my tongue. "This man who admitted to you what they'd done to get Corey out of the way? What became of him?"

I glanced over and saw Reggie's eye twitch. "Funny you should ask. He died in a hunting accident in 1987."

"Let me guess," I interjected. "The shooter was never identified and the killing was ruled accidental."

Reggie started breathing through his mouth. It was the only change I could see in his demeanor. He pointed out the windshield. "This is the parking lot, Alan. And it's your turn to help," he said.

I caught Sawyer's stern face and wide eyes in the rearview mirror before I got out of the car to assist Reggie with the next shut-in. Sawyer tightened her jaw and nodded her head, once up, once down. She raised three fingers and smiled that rueful smile that left her cheeks dimpled.

Reggie refused to elaborate on either D. B. Cooper or Corey Rand during the short drive to our next destination, a tiny frame cottage near Boulder High School. While Sawyer and he were inside, I called the hospital to check on Lauren's progress. According to the nurse, she was asleep and seemed clear cognitively, with the exception of short-term recall for the time before the poisoning. There was some minor concern about changes in her liver function. She said the doctor would tell me more later in the day after the new labs came back.

She didn't sound too worried about the new liver concerns, so I decided that I wouldn't be, either.

We moved from one of Boulder's most modest neighborhoods to one of its grandest, from the simple frame house near the high school to a mansion on Mapleton Hill. I drove north across town on side streets, well aware that I would miss plenty of lights along the way. I'd already decided to allow Sawyer room to press Reggie for more information.

She picked up the ball deftly. "The 'two buddies' you talked about, Reggie. Whatever happened to them?"

"I know what you're thinking. And I don't . . . I just don't think it's . . . it wouldn't be . . ."

"The two buddies? What happened to them?"

He looked away from us, out the side window, before he spoke again. "One of them was a NASCAR fanatic named Ricky Turner. I know what you're thinking, and you're right. He died in a one-car accident in Boulder Canyon after he got blitzed at the Pioneer Inn up in Nederland. Police determined that he was doing over sixty when his car left the pavement. It actually landed on the *other* side of Boulder Creek from the road."

"Year?"

His tone irritated, he said, "I told you I was willing to talk about Cooper, not about old feuds. Anyway, it was an accident. He was drunk as a skunk." Sawyer and I waited Reggie out. "What year? Hell, I was still at the Flats when Turner died. Must have been 1988, '89, maybe '90."

"You seem to remember all that pretty clearly, Reggie."

"I was his boss. I went to the funeral."

"I think maybe I see a pattern here," I said, as I turned on Pine, which would take Sawyer and me right past our hotel.

Sawyer pressed an obviously reluctant Reggie Loomis. "The other buddy? What about him?"

"I don't think he's in town anymore. I lost track of him before Ricky killed himself in that wreck."

"His name?"

"Don't. You should just let this rest. It's not what you think."

"Come on, Reggie."

"We called him Jacko. His name was Jack O'Connell. I think he moved back to where he grew up. Some place on Long Island. Worked in security at one of the nuclear power plants there."

"Was he at Ricky's funeral?"

"You know, come to think of it, I don't remember seeing him."

No one spoke again until I pulled up in front of the stately mansion on Mapleton Hill. Reggie said, "My next guest is Sylvia Henning. Miss Sylvia. She lives alone here, if you can believe it. Has for over thirty years. She's been one of my guests from the very start."

"I guess it's my turn to help," I said.

"Miss Sylvia doesn't like strangers. Help me get the tray together. But I'll take care of her all by myself. And I'll be a few extra minutes with her. Why don't you put together some food for yourselves and eat while I'm inside?"

Sawyer and I prepared trays and carried them over to the elegantly landscaped island that separated the westbound lane of Mapleton from the eastbound lane. She examined the palatial homes and asked, "Old money up here?"

I said, "You bet." I settled onto the smooth face of a decorative granite boulder. "Sawyer, do you think?"

She was sitting across from me. "Yes, I think," she said and dug into her ramekin of eggs. I smelled a fresh burst of tarragon.

"It doesn't make sense. We're chasing a ghost, you know?"

"You mean Rand?"

"His wife told me he was dead. Why would she lie to me?"

"People lie all the time. Some of them don't even need reasons. I spend most of my professional time with people who lie with every third breath just so they can stay in practice."

"I don't know. I'm troubled by it. If Rand's dead, this is all for nothing. We can't finger a dead man for killing our colleagues."

"What else do we have?" she asked.

I ate most of my fruit salad before pausing to use the cell phone to call Sam at home. I asked him to check on the whereabouts and well-being of a Jack O'Connell, ex-Boulder, ex–Rocky Flats security, currently doing security work at a nuclear energy facility on Long Island. He didn't ask why I wanted to know, which meant he figured he already knew why I wanted to know. Sam liked people to think he was ahead of them even when he wasn't.

He said he'd get right on it.

Sawyer said, "Bet he's already dead. This Jacko guy. Want to do a wager on how Corey Rand got to him?"

"Not especially, no."

"There's good news here, too, Alan."

"What's that?"

"It's taken our minds off what happened last night."

She made me laugh. "I called the hospital while you were inside the last house with Reggie. The nurse said there's something screwy with Lauren's liver functions. Is that common after carbon monoxide poisoning?"

She swallowed and tried not to look concerned. "How screwy?"

"Doctor is going to fill me in later."

She said, "Well, I wouldn't get alarmed," which, for some reason, is one of the most alarming things that physicians can ever say to me. "But there are rare—let me emphasize, rare—cases of elevated liver enzymes after CO poisoning. I'm not sure anyone really understands the pathogenesis. It sounds to me like her doctors are just being prudent."

"Now I'm getting alarmed."

She reached out to touch me before pulling back. She looked down. "The eggs are great. Go ahead, you'll need the protein."

# THIRTY-NINE

Once he was back in the car, Reggie wouldn't answer any more questions about Corey Rand. "Corey wasn't part of the deal I made with you two. You want to talk Cooper, we can talk Cooper. If not, we can listen to music. You have any Vivaldi?" he asked before offering directions to an apartment house near Community Hospital.

"No Vivaldi. Did he ever tell you?" I asked, careful not to actually mention Rand's name. "You know, did he ever tell you who it was he suspected of committing the hijacking?"

"He never told me the name, no. But he came to me once and laid out the case in some detail."

"Well, you seem like a good student of these things," Sawyer prompted. "Were you convinced?"

"The presentation," he said, "was compelling."

"But were you convinced?"

"He had identified . . . a guy. A guy at the plant, in our department. The guy made sense for a number of reasons. Crucial, of course, he was off-duty over Thanksgiving weekend that year. But that didn't tell me much. My thinking was, so what? All nonessential personnel at the plant were off over Thanksgiving weekend. Then Corey pointed out that this particular guy came back to work a day later than expected, on the Tuesday after the holiday instead of the Monday. Rand said that gave him an extra day to make his way back from the Pacific Northwest, a day Corey said he needed because of some unexpected problem.

"What problem? Well, what first focused Corey's attention on this man, apparently, is that the guy came back to work with a broken ankle. His story at the time was that he was doing some early season cross-country skiing up above Rollinsville and hit a rock on a down-hill and broke his ski and his ankle."

Sawyer said, "And Rand thought that was bullshit, that the ankle break was actually evidence of trouble on the parachute drop?"

"Right. But Corey didn't stop there. Once he had this guy in mind, he locked on him like a heat-seeking missile. He went back and looked at the man's military records and found that when he was in the Marines, the man graduated from parachute school. That's important not just for technique reasons, but also because it meant that Cooper knew the safe parameters for a parachute drop from that plane. Cooper gave specific orders to the pilots. He told them to fly the plane unpressurized at ten thousand feet. That was so he could safely lower the airstairs in flight. He specified that the gear be down, that the flaps be set at fifteen percent, and that the airspeed should at no point exceed one hundred and fifty knots."

I said, "He knew what he was doing."

"Cooper didn't miss a detail. The crime was a thing of beauty. When he jumped, he waited until the plane was in the clouds so the military jets that were tracking them couldn't see him leave the plane."

I pulled up in front of the apartment house that was our next humanitarian stop, hopped out of the car, and prepared a tray. I was getting efficient at it. Reggie and I were in and out of the apartment and back in the car within the allotted seven minutes. Sawyer picked up the story as though she'd frozen the conversation in time.

"Doesn't sound like Rand had much to go on. Circumstantial, every bit of it."

"Oh, he had more. Corey kept looking at the guy. He found out where he worked before he came to Rocky Flats. Turns out that two jobs back he was employed in security at a company in Reno that did contract maintenance for American Airlines, among others. Corey checked further. One of the planes that the company serviced for American was Boeing 727s."

"Which means he could have had knowledge about the rear airstairs, and how they operated?" I asked.

"Exactly."

I was thinking about old conversations with my wife the assistant district attorney about the components that prosecutors use to assess suspects. Means, opportunity, and motive. M-O-M. "Rand's hypothesis covers means and opportunity, Reggie. What did Rand come up with about motive?"

"I'm not done. This guy that Corey Rand was so sure about. Turns out he grew up in a suburb of Portland, not even seventy-five miles from the drop zone identified by the FBI."

"Still, as Sawyer pointed out, it's all circumstantial," I said, trying to imagine the words Lauren would use to assess the story. "Where am I heading next? What's our next stop?"

Reggie shrugged. "Rand was convinced. That's what was important to him. The last two stops are up Sunshine Canyon."

I headed west on Mapleton into the canyon. "Back to motive for a minute. How did Rand figure motive?"

"Two motives. One, of course, was money. Remember, Cooper got away clean with two hundred thousand dollars. And the second motive was retribution. Vengeance, if you will."

"Retribution?" I wondered. "Against whom? Northwest Airlines?"

"No, the FBI. Rand figured this guy wanted to show up the FBI, to . . . I don't know exactly. Maybe prove that he was better than them? Repay an old slight? Something like that."

Suddenly Reggie sounded tired. I was confused by his supposition of Cooper's motive and said, "That doesn't make sense. Why would he hijack an airplane to get back at the FBI?"

Reggie touched his fingertips together, one at a time, until all ten digits were touching. The gesture appeared childish, yet composed. At a subdued volume, he said, "Corey had a theory. I don't recall that I know what it was, exactly."

From the backseat, Sawyer apparently had missed the burp that I had seen in Reggie's demeanor. She asked, "What about the money those two kids found? When they were digging along the banks of the Columbia River years ago? When was that? Nineteen . . ."

"1980," he said, without a smidgen of delay. "The kids found fifty-eight hundred dollars in twenties while they were playing along the shore of the Columbia in 1980. The serial numbers proved that the money came from the hijacking."

"But doesn't that show that Cooper didn't make it down safely? That he crashed during the parachute drop and the money ended up in the river?"

"Nope. It doesn't prove that at all. Corey figured the missing money was all part of Cooper's planning genius. Corey's theory is that Cooper dumped some of the ransom on the banks of the river, hoping that people would come to the conclusion that he'd drowned in the river during his parachute drop and then washed out to sea with all the rest of the evidence. Ergo, everyone would stop looking for him on land. What was six thousand dollars to Cooper? Three percent of the ransom? Pretty cheap for an insurance policy that might get the search called off."

I backtracked toward Mapleton on Ninth and cut west into Sunshine Canyon. The sun was high enough in the eastern sky behind us to begin to brighten some of the curves and hollows of the twisty road. "How far up the canyon are we going, Reggie? I have to be back at your house by ten."

"Quite a ways up, I'm afraid. A neat little log cabin. I'll tell you when we're getting close. I only visit this particular guest in good weather. Almost got stuck up there once last winter. But don't worry, we'll be back on time."

The log cabin enjoyed a sunlit eastern exposure, and its ridge-top position provided an incredible view down the Front Range. The house itself was a simple rectangle constructed of stacked ten-inch logs topped with a red metal roof. Every window was covered by iron grating. The storm doors on the front were constructed of heavy black steel.

Reggie explained. "Theodora, Theo, has grown a little paranoid since her stroke. She's remarkable, though. You'll like her."

I parked in a narrow clearing between a gleaming white propane tank and the house. Theo met us at the door. She was no older than Sawyer and me. Her stroke had severely impaired her speech, and she used a four-legged cane to get around the house. Reggie was right; I did like her. Her courageous adjustment to her stroke reminded me of Lauren's adaptation to multiple sclerosis. "You never know how brave you can be until it's your turn to be brave," Lauren had told me once.

Theo had had her turn.

Our visit lasted the prescribed seven minutes.

I waited in the car at the last stop in the canyon, a shack of a place on an old horse ranch on the canyon floor only half a mile or so out of Boulder. This was the culmination of our morning, and Reggie used his entire allotment of time for this final visit. Twenty minutes.

We were back at his place on Fourth Street, as promised, by ten. With a grin on his face, he said, "See you in two days."

"What?"

"I need your help one more time. Please. Mrs. Savage, you know, the big Chevy lady? She canceled until Friday. I'll make it worth your while, I promise. I'll tell you more about Corey. Okay? And you have to admit the food alone is worth the trip."

I said I would go. Sawyer said she thought she would have returned to California by then.

I stayed anxious all day long. Lauren's doctor finally paged me around three o'clock with good news about her liver function. It appeared the earlier tests might have been anomalous. He planned to repeat them one more time before he discharged her, hopefully the next day. Only some short-term memory problems clouded her mental functioning.

The vet hospital in Denver told me that Emily was ready to come home but they would be happy to board her until I made it back to Denver.

Sam paged me at half past four. Again at four forty-five. Once more as I was escorting my four-fifteen patient out the door.

I called him at home.

"Hi. Sorry it took me so long to return your page. I was with a patient." To Sam, I knew that would sound like an excuse, not an explanation.

"Whatever. To answer your earlier question about the employee from Rocky Flats? Well, Jack O'Connell died in 1992 in New York. He was electrocuted in his own home. The local cops thought it was suspicious, looked at it real carefully. Felt his wiring might have been tampered with. Case is still open, and manner is still pending. Now tell me how he fits."

I explained that O'Connell had been a coworker at Rocky Flats of this man who was admitted to the psychiatric unit back in 1982.

Sam interrupted. "Corey Rand?"

"Yes. O'Connell—they called him Jacko—he was one of three guys who arranged the setup that got this man Rand in trouble at work and then admitted to the hospital, and finally cost him his security clearance and his job."

"I take it the other two are dead now, too? The other guys who helped O'Connell."

"Yes. One died in a hunting accident on the western slope. No shooter was ever identified. The other one died in a one-car accident in Boulder Canyon after a night drinking at the Pioneer Inn up in Nederland. DUI."

"Get a name and year on that one? The DUI?"

"Just a second." I'd scribbled the facts in a notebook. "Ricky Turner. Late eighties. 1988, '89, maybe '90."

"Now tell me how you learned all this."

"Sawyer and I spent some more time with Reggie Loomis, Rand's old boss at Rocky Flats."

"Was Milt with you?"

"No."

"I thought we had an agreement about protection for you and Sawyer."

"Loomis said we couldn't bring you or any other cops or he wouldn't talk about . . . you know, Rand."

"Now I wonder why the hell he said that. I'm still thinking maybe that man has something to hide."

"My interest is Rand. Not Reggie Loomis's petty crimes."

He chewed on my words for about ten seconds. "You ever go out and meet Corey Rand's widow?"

"No, I just talked with her on the phone. Why?"

"I went over to her place again today." He hung his words like a night crawler on the end of a line.

"And?"

"Hell of a cough that woman has. Hell of a cough. You think maybe she has TB or something? I feel like I should wear a mask."

"Sam, please. I have another patient in a few minutes."

"Mrs. Rand lives on a nice little three-acre horse ranch in Wheat Ridge. They have a couple of real pretty Appaloosas. Summers we used to go to this place when I was a kid that had Appaloosas. I like 'em. Anyway, Mrs. Rand takes in a few boarders, I mean horses, that kind of boarder, though none of them are as nice as those Appaloosas. But a very, very nice place. I began to wonder how the widow of a ne'er-do-well Radio Shack manager might be able to live in a place like that. So I checked the records of her husband's estate. She inherited zilch, basically. But it turns out that she was sole beneficiary of the half-million-dollar life insurance policy that Mr. Rand had been paying on since 1991. When he crashed his pickup and bought the ranch, she cleaned up, and she bought the ranch, too. So to speak."

"Yeah?" I knew he wasn't done.

"Then"—he tried to sound bored as he continued—"I didn't have anything better to do, so I had the local coroner's office pull up Mr. Corey Rand's death records for me. Accident he died in was bad, included a vehicle fire. Took place on private land out at one of those gravel mines on '93, near Golden. Body was badly disfigured at the time of the autopsy. Rand's pickup truck ran smack into a big Caterpillar front loader. The bucket almost tore the damn truck in half. Coroner eventually decided that Rand had an aneurysm that caused him to lose control of his truck. ID was made by his wife and son. I was not surprised to learn that his body was cremated the same day it was released by the coroner."

*Son.* I hadn't given a moment's thought to Corey Rand's son.

"How old is the son?"

I could almost hear Sam smile over the phone line. "He is almost twenty-nine years old."

I rearranged the cards that Sam was dealing. "You think the three of them faked his death?"

"Why not? If they pull it off, it gives Rand a get-out-of-jail-free card in case anybody like us ever gets a clue about all these murders. And it gives his wife and kid a bonus of a half a million bucks to refresh their not too happy lives. Not to mention that it fits right in with Rand's whole fuck-the-system-that-fucked-me attitude."

"You know anything about the son? What's his name?"

"Patrick Rand."

"What do you know about him?"

"He's a firefighter in Lakewood."

Lakewood is one of Denver's western suburbs. "That's interesting."

"Given all the fires and the poisonings we've been dealing with, yes, I'd say it's interesting. Something else, too."

"Yes?"

"One of his coworkers thinks he was off-duty when that lady and her husband were killed in New Zealand."

"A lot of people were off-duty then, Sam."

He let my skepticism drop with a thud. "Another thing about firefighters is they work long shifts and then they have long periods of time off."

"Which means what?"

"They have plenty of time to indulge in hobbies."

"Like killing people."

"Keeps them off the streets."

I continued, "So if you're right about this conspiracy, where's Corey Rand? Where's Patrick's dad?"

"Around here somewhere, buddy. Around here somewhere."

# FORTY

**M**y sister-in-law, Teresa, arrived in Denver the next morning, only an hour before Lauren was discharged from the hospital. I didn't want the two of them anywhere near Boulder, so I rescheduled my morning patients, drove to Denver, and moved Lauren and her sister into a downtown hotel. Lauren reluctantly acknowledged that they would be safer if I spent the night in Boulder, thirty miles away.

Before I kissed her good-bye I handed Lauren the Glock. I could tell from her eyes that she thought it would be prudent for me to keep it. But her rueful smile told me that she had no faith I could actually use it.

Without a word, she accepted the gun and made it disappear into her big purse.

I was feeling some apprehension that she would ask me where I'd be sleeping that night and how close by Sawyer would be sleeping. She didn't ask. In her silence, I sensed trust, and I felt strength and love that I wondered if I deserved.

Lauren trusted me more than I did.

Back in the car, I phoned the vet hospital and put off retrieving Emily for another day, then rushed back down the turnpike and fit seven forty-five-minute therapy sessions into what was left of the afternoon. At the end of the day I was surprised to find that Sawyer was still registered at the Boulderado. At the front desk she'd left me a handwritten message that the folks in Phoenix were still waiting on a part for her airplane and that it wouldn't be ready until the next day at the earliest. If it was still possible she wanted to join Reggie and me the next morning on his rounds.

I called the suite she was sharing with A.J. to let her know what time I'd be leaving for Reggie's house in the morning. No one answered. Not knowing how things stood between Sawyer and A.J., I didn't leave a message.

Like a dutiful subject, I phoned Milt and told him I was safely ensconced in my room. He answered as though my call were an intrusion. He said he already knew I was back. I asked him if he knew where Sawyer was.

"She's with Dr. Simes. Dr. Simes needed some medical attention and Sawyer was kind enough to go with her."

"What kind of medical attention?" I expected him to say something about multiple sclerosis.

"Dr. Simes is quite private about her health. I hope you will respect that." Milt's words said "hope," but his tone said "expect."

"I know quite a few people here, Milt, in the medical community. I may be able to be of some help."

"Thanks for offering. I'll pass it along." He paused and transformed his voice into something even more parental and bilious than the one he had been using. "What you did yesterday was . . . bullshit. You know that, don't you? You put yourself and Dr. Faire at risk."

I tried to respond rationally. "We learned some things. It was worth the risk, I think."

"Your friend Sam doesn't trust that man. Mr. Loomis."

"Sam was happy for the information. And you don't know Sam very well, Milt. He doesn't trust too many people."

"In our line of work, that point of view often has merit."

"Milt, Reggie Loomis is responsible for us knowing about Corey Rand. Without him we wouldn't have a clue about a possible subject. And I think he has even more that he can tell us."

"I've been busy all day on that. We're trying to access Rand's records. Especially travel. He's most vulnerable on travel. We should know more by tomorrow."

"Don't worry, Sawyer and I are being careful."

He said, "We're getting close to him, you know. Once we get the travel records sketched out we can compare his whereabouts with all the other crimes. This Mr. Rand. And I'm sure he knows we're on to him. Don't underestimate a cornered animal."

I wanted to ask which Mr. Rand, father or son, they were closing in on. But I said, "I understand the situation. I'm not planning on being a cowboy."

"No, Dr. Gregory, I don't think you do understand. Rand's teeth are bared now. He never expected to be identified. All along, he's been thinking he's been committing the perfect crimes. He expected to be another D. B. Cooper. A legend in his own mind. But now we're on his tail. He's not going to act according to form. Lock yourself in for the night. Page me if you go anywhere. I'll be out checking on some things."

Milt's warning caused me to feel the absence of the Glock. I found myself surprised at how peculiar and intimate the loss felt. It was as though I'd gone to rub my eye or pick my nose and discovered that I'd misplaced one of my fingers.

As I double-locked the door I began to wonder about the D. B. Cooper allusion Milt had used. Was he on to something about Reggie, or was that an inadvertent caution? I wasn't sure.

I tried watching the local news and got bored. I stared out the window at the alley and wished I'd paid for a better view. I contemplated confronting Ms. Marceau in the Mezzanine and getting a little drunk. I thought about going for a walk on the Mall. Ultimately, I decided to stop acting so damn paranoid and opted to go see what progress Dresden and his gang had made on our renovation in Spanish Hills.

Before I left, I called Sam at home to see if he wanted to come along. His machine picked up and I got the pleasure of listening to some cute instructions from Simon, Sam's son, about what to do after the beep. I declined. I paged Milt and left him a message where I'd be, what I'd be doing. The last call I made before I left the room was to Adrienne, my neighbor, to see if she was back home from her travels. I got her machine. I had second thoughts about heading out alone and shushed them.

I was anxious driving across town, literally trying to talk myself into believing that this silent enemy wouldn't go after me twice in the same location. Mostly, I convinced myself that although what I was doing was foolhardy, it probably wasn't any crazier than flying down Left Hand Canyon at fifty miles an hour on my road bike or skiing down Pallavicini at A-Basin on days when the moguls were bigger than Volkswagen Bugs.

\*    \*    \*

I couldn't help but smile as I drove down the lane. My old house looked like a new house. Dresden and his carpenters had been busy. The main-floor addition and the freestanding garage were not only framed but also sheathed with insulating sheets, and the roofs had already been decked and tar-papered. For a few minutes I stood outside on the lane and admired the profile. Dresden had roughed out the new front porch, too, and I felt an odd sense that for the first time in my adult life I'd be living in a house that looked like it might actually be inhabited by a grown-up.

Although Lauren and I had mentioned it cautiously and only in passing, standing there with my hands in my pockets and my feet on the gravel, I felt a crystal-clear awareness that this new structure was large enough for a family. It was actually meant for a family.

I unlocked the front door and extinguished the alarm before I flicked on a light switch and was astonished to see the new recessed cans in the ceiling beam brilliantly down on me.

*Houston, we have power.*

A short hallway that led to the new main-floor bedroom was framed and Sheetrocked, effectively separating the front of the house from the back for the first time ever. The new bedroom felt huge, and the tall corner windows framed the Flatirons just as our architect had promised they would. The master bathroom seemed to have enough plumbing rough-ins for a family of eight to use individual fixtures simultaneously.

I meandered back toward the original structure into the space where the old kitchen had gone through a strange mitosis. Doubling once and then, somehow, once again, the new space had been mysteriously reclaimed from someplace in the house where I wasn't going to miss it. I stared at the spot where the new range would be installed and promised myself I'd pick up some extra court-ordered evals for a year or so and see about the La Cornue that Lauren coveted.

I sighed and felt a shiver up my spine. Looking around this space, I felt my future with Lauren as precious and real, as though I already held our first baby in my hands. Conceptions would happen here. First steps. Many tears. All the joy that life promised and all the sorrow that life delivered would happen within these new walls.

Without hesitation, I was eager to get started with her.

But first, I reminded myself, I had to stay alive for a few days while Sam and Milt found the Rands.

I was impatient to settle back into the house. My eyes flew around the shadowy space. The Sheetrock needed tape and mud. The whole place needed trim. There wasn't a fixture to be found in the bathroom or kitchen. A lot of tile was yet to be laid. And the painters would be here for weeks. Weeks.

But I felt my future in this place. It felt satisfying, a fullness I associated with sitting back after a fine meal. I wanted to digest it awhile.

Like for a lifetime.

I stopped for dinner at Tom's and sat alone in a booth. I ate a complete meal of foods that were discouraged on Sam's diet. I considered taking in a movie, but decided not to. I actually convinced myself that Milt and Sam and A.J. were hot on the Rands' heels and that the bad guys were on the run.

The dark sky was spotted by flurries the next morning as Sawyer and I made our way to the car. On the late news the night before, the weather folks had promised that this little disturbance approaching from the west was nothing to worry about. They promised we would get a "light dusting," unless, of course, that nasty little upper-level low over New Mexico slid a tad farther north than anyone expected it to. If that happened, well, then we'd be talking upslope conditions, and all bets would be off.

Stay tuned.

As Sawyer snapped her seat belt she smiled at the storm and said, "I miss the snow. This is pretty."

I admitted that it was but didn't caution her about the possible consequences of the migrating low-pressure system. Instead I asked, "How's A.J. doing? Milt told me she was ill last night."

Sawyer made an apologetic face. "She asked me not to talk about it, Alan. I'm sorry. We saw a specialist last night. I think she'll be okay."

"Was it, um . . . you know? I mean, because of Lauren, she and I know the best neurologists in town. We'll be happy to make contacts for her."

She touched me on the arm. "Let's just leave it that your wife has good antennae, okay? But we didn't need a neurologist. I think A.J.

will be fine." I saw Sawyer's breath in the cold car. She rubbed her gloved hands together and said, "I wonder what Reggie cooked up for us this morning."

I felt calm beside her. She had no way of knowing about the clarity that I had found while visiting my home the night before. She had no way of knowing that her special place in my heart had altered its orbit a few degrees. She had no way of knowing that our pasts might always touch, but our planets would never collide.

We were silent for the next few minutes until we arrived on Fourth Street. Reggie waited impatiently on his little porch, anxious to get to work. Sawyer ignored his exhortations and made a beeline for the coffee before she lifted the first cooler.

Compared to our earlier effort only two days before, we loaded the car with the breakfast goodies in half the time.

Reggie wasn't chatty. Twice I tried to steer him to resume his tale about D. B. Cooper and Corey Rand. But each time he shook his head a little and closed his eyes, shutting out my questions. I feigned patience, as I would during therapy, reminding myself that we had a lot of time.

We kept our roles from our earlier delivery route. Reggie didn't want his guests to have to deal with any more new faces, so Sawyer and I delivered trays to the same homes that we had two days before.

The breakfast from Chez Reggie was simple but elegant. A fruit salad of late berries and perfect crescents of early Satsuma tangerines. Fresh brioche that had been transformed into tantalizing baked French toast. Coffee and juice. And a puffy croissant. "This is for later," Reggie would tell each guest as he offered the croissant. "Just a little snack to hold you over. I made the preserves myself from last summer's Palisade peaches. I think you'll like them."

We squeezed in a couple of extra stops. One of the new guests had been hospitalized two days earlier, the other had been out of town. Our new efficiency allowed us to absorb the minutes into our schedule with ease.

Sawyer and I once again ate while Reggie alone delivered the tray to Sylvia's mansion on Mapleton Hill. This time, however, we ate in the car. The flurries were beginning to transform from charming into storming, and the car offered protection. The French toast was the best I'd ever tasted. I decided my reward for the morning was going to be the recipe.

Sawyer asked, "I wonder if we'll still go up the canyon. Given the weather."

"The little ranch where we ended up the other day is close to here, only half a mile or so. I don't think that's a problem. But Theo's log cabin is way up there, halfway to Gold Hill. I hope Reggie doesn't want to try to make it."

She nodded at my assessment. She looked away from me briefly before locking her eyes onto mine. Her voice cracked and she said, "So what happened yesterday? You decided you could live without me?"

Her words could have been framed by levity, but they weren't. I sipped some coffee before I replied. "More, I think, Sawyer, I decided I couldn't see my future without her. Without Lauren. I love her." I glanced down only after I was done speaking.

She was facing away from me. "Ironic, don't you think? I mean, look who's insecure now. Look who needs who now. It's no prettier when I see it in the mirror than it was when I saw it in you years ago."

"That's not it, Sawyer. I'm not afraid of you needing me. I made the right choice with Lauren. I feel my future there. You've shaken me up a bit by showing up again. It's left me feeling stronger. More certain about things with her."

"She allowed that, didn't she? She let you see how far you would go?"

"She trusts me, I guess."

Sawyer laughed, the sound gilded with irony. "Oh no. That's not right. You don't quite get it. Lauren crossed her fingers about you. About you loving her enough to come back. The person she's been trusting since I showed up and confused things . . . is herself." She cupped her chin in her gloved palms. "Maybe I can learn something from her, too."

I'd been busy patting myself on my back for how strong I'd been in resisting Sawyer's temptations. It wasn't easy accepting the proposition that the true show of strength had been Lauren's, not mine.

But I knew what Sawyer was saying was true.

Reggie hopped back in the car and said, "Hurry. Let's do the ranch. Theo's our last stop today."

"A lot of snow coming down, Reggie."

"We'll see how the canyon looks after we do the horse ranch. This has four-wheel drive, right?"

"Right," I admitted. I didn't tell Reggie that I didn't consider it license to be reckless.

# FORTY-ONE

The decrepit little horse ranch on the floor of the canyon was Sawyer's stop. I stayed in the Land Cruiser with the engine running, trying to keep warm. By my reckoning, a good half inch of snow fell during the seven minutes that Reggie and Sawyer were inside.

After he climbed back onto the front passenger seat, Reggie seemed to hesitate about proceeding farther up Sunshine. He fidgeted with his gloves and raised and lowered the zipper on his jacket. Finally, he said, "Let's give Theo's place a try. She really doesn't get too many visitors. This may be my last chance to visit with her for a while."

Through the windshield I watched the profile of a pickup truck as it slithered up the canyon road. The snow continued to fall in curtains, and the flapping windshield wipers made rhythmic traverses across the glass. I said, "If that's what you want to do, Reggie, I'll head up the canyon. But if it gets bad, we'll turn around."

"Deal," he said.

He was silent for the first mile or so up the canyon. My focus was locked on the slick surface in front of me and on my fervent desire to stay halfway between the often difficult to distinguish shoulders. Once I edged over to the right to permit a Mazda Miata to float by on its way to town. Seconds later I was distracted by the high beams of a truck that was parked up a driveway perpendicular to the canyon road. The truck's engine was running, steam rising to envelop the cab in fog. Reggie stared at the parked truck, too. Then, without preamble, he rotated on his seat and faced Sawyer in back. He said, "There were two reasons Cooper took four parachutes."

When she didn't reply immediately, he continued, "You were wondering about that, remember? D. B. Cooper's rationale for demanding four parachutes."

"Yes. Yes, I was." I chanced a glance in the mirror. Sawyer's eyes met mine. Hers were narrowed and cautious. Behind her in the distance I thought I spotted headlights on the road. Just as quickly, the orbs of light were gone.

"Well. The first reason Cooper insisted on four parachutes was because he didn't want the authorities to know whether or not he was acting alone or whether he had unknown accomplices on the plane. Obviously, if the FBI was forced to consider the possibility that he had accomplices, then their contingency responses became more limited. By requesting more than one parachute, he forced his adversaries to consider the possibility that he was not acting alone. Make sense?"

Sawyer nodded. I checked the mirror again for headlights.

Nothing back there. I slowed.

"Second reason. Cooper obviously suspected that the authorities might try to booby-trap the parachute they were providing for him. Had he asked for only one, I'm sure that they would have given serious consideration to doing just that. But by asking for four, and by keeping two stewardesses in reserve as hostages, he left open the possibility that he not only had accomplices, but that he might force one or both of the stewardesses to jump from the airplane with him. With that risk in place, the authorities, of course, couldn't take the chance of sabotaging one of the parachutes. The possibility existed that it would end up being worn by a hostage."

I asked, "Did Corey Rand figure all that out?"

Reggie replied, "It wasn't hard to figure. It doesn't take a genius to figure out why somebody did something after the fact. That's just hindsight. The genius is in the anticipation. Remember, we were contingency planners. Our job was to avoid getting caught in traps like the one that Cooper set."

For a pleasant moment I realized that Reggie had described the challenge of psychotherapy with an elegant precision. Any average therapist could help any average patient understand why the patient had done something maladaptive. The genius came when therapist and patient could anticipate the next trap, so the patient could avoid getting caught by the same circumstances again.

Sawyer said, "I hadn't thought of that, Reggie. That's an interesting theory."

"It's not a theory," he said, his voice hollow. "It's the way it was."

I smiled at the assurance I was hearing but quickly moved my attention back to the narrow, glassy road. The shoulders had disappeared beneath the shroud of fresh powder and I was thinking hard about turning back.

"Do either of you see anyone behind us? I thought I saw some lights a way back."

They both turned and gazed out the almost opaque rear window. Sawyer said, "So? Maybe we're not the only ones crazy enough to come up here in this weather."

Reggie said he didn't see anything, but his tone told me that my concerns were resonating with him. "One passed us earlier. A pickup truck," he added.

Sawyer and Reggie didn't resume their conversation about D. B. Cooper.

The storm paused, and for a few moments I was driving uphill toward a thin ribbon of blue sky that was barely visible through a break in the clouds. Again I checked for lights in my mirrors. Nothing. I figured we would be at Theo's cabin in less than five minutes. I considered dropping the four-wheel drive into low but decided that the Land Cruiser was doing okay, considering.

I asked, "So where's the parachute?"

Reggie pulled his gloves from his hands and took out a little tub of lip gloss. He smoothed the wax over his lips. "Buried," he said.

"Isn't that risky? Why not carry it out?"

"Too bulky. He buried it in a hole he pre-dug before the crime. He had stashed a motorcycle for his getaway close by. Easier to hide from a search helicopter in a motorcycle than in a car. He wouldn't have had room to take the parachute with him."

"The jump was that accurate? That he could hike to his motorcycle? Even with a broken ankle?"

"The jump was that accurate."


A thin plume of smoke snaked from the tin chimney of Theo's cabin. The scene was a postcard, the cleared ground around the cabin carpeted by five inches of white powder, the roof frosted, the windowsills dusted. The joints between the big logs were etched with white. I parked the Land Cruiser halfway between the big propane tank and the front door.

Reggie said, "This is why she won't move to town. I've offered to help her out, help her find a place. But she loves it up here. The serenity, she says. She can't leave the serenity."

"That's not much of a fire she has going, considering how cold it is," Sawyer observed.

"Theo burns coal, not wood, to save money on propane. There's usually not too much smoke from the chimney. I'll stoke it when I get inside. This is the last stop, Alan. Help me with her tray, and then give me my time with her, please."

I checked the fuel gauge to make sure I had enough gasoline and told Sawyer to leave the engine running for heat. Reggie and I pulled the tray of food together, covered it, and trudged the twenty feet or so to Theo's door. Behind us, a pickup truck sliced through the snow on the road. Reggie paused, too, and watched it pass. I thought it was the same truck that had driven past us when we were parked at the horse ranch at the bottom of the canyon. How had it gotten behind us?

Reggie's eyes followed the truck until it disappeared toward the west. He turned and rapped twice on Theo's door with his gloved hand. The dull sound was swallowed by the insulation of the storm. He removed a glove and tried the knob on the security door. It turned in his hand.

"That's funny," he said. "Theo's usually pretty security-conscious. Mmm." He yanked the door open and tried the latch on the plank door behind it. That lock was unlocked, too.

"I hope she's okay," he said as much to himself as to me. "Maybe she left it open for me. Theo? Theo?" he called. "It's Reggie Loomis."

I held the security door with one hand, the tray in the other. Reggie kicked the snow off his boots and padded inside. The interior of the cabin was freezing, barely warmer than the air outside. I followed him in, closing the two doors behind me to try to ward off the chill.

"Theo? Theo?" Reggie whispered, almost apologizing for the intrusion. He immediately took long strides toward the back of the cabin, where a door was propped open. He barely avoided tripping over a bucketful of coal that was spilled just this side of the threshold. He slammed the door shut and again called Theo's name. His voice caught as he exclaimed, "Oh, my God," and broke into a run toward the far side of the main room.

I looked over Reggie's shoulder and saw streaks of bright red in a shadowed corner and lowered the tray of food to a nearby table. The red was so plentiful that at first I imagined that I was looking at a plaid blanket that had been carelessly tossed out of the way.

In seconds, Reggie was on his knees at Theo's side. He was remarkably composed. In a steady voice, he said, "I think she's still breathing. Cover her, okay? I need to get Sawyer. Sawyer's a physician, right? We need to get Theo down to town fast." He stood and ran from the cabin as I pulled a crocheted throw from a dusty old velvet sofa. I lowered it over her.

The left side of Theo's head was sliced down the side in three or four parallel tracks, and her neck was splayed open so widely I could see tendons and tissue and blood vessels. A huge chunk of flesh was missing from the biceps of her arm. Fresh blood pumped weakly from the exposed vessels. Her beautiful blond hair was matted flat by her own blood.

Sawyer rushed inside and looked past me at Theo. "Oh, no. Oh my God. Who did this to her? Oh, Jesus." She made fists with both her hands. "I don't even know what to do. I'm a damn psychiatrist. She needs a trauma surgeon."

Behind me, I heard a creaking sound. Without bothering to turn, I said, "Reggie, call for more help. If she doesn't have a phone here, there's one in the car." I wondered whether Flight for Life would fly a chopper in this weather. Probably not. I felt so helpless. I wanted to patch Theo up as I would repair a disintegrating snowman or a broken doll. But she seemed to be missing so many pieces.

The next noise I heard wasn't Reggie seeking help on the telephone. It was another creak accompanied by a low bass rhythmic rumble—a primal warning—that caused me to freeze.

The sound I heard was a growl.

Sawyer whispered, "What was that? Does she have a dog in here?"

I turned slowly, raising myself to my feet. "I don't know," I said.

The cabin was small. I saw no dog.

Sawyer said, "I don't see a dog."

My eyes climbed a wooden pole ladder to a loft that Theo had probably used as a bedroom in the days before her stroke. At the top of the ladder, in the darkness near the rafters, I saw two orange circles the size of dimes. "Look up in the loft," I whispered to Sawyer.

"What is it?" Sawyer asked.

"It's a cat," I said.

"A cat?"

"Yes. A big cat." My voice was as soft as the snow outside. "I think it's a mountain lion."

# FORTY-TWO

Sawyer asked, "What on earth is it doing in here?"

My first thought was that it was dining. But after that momentary irreverence passed, my mind trailed quickly to the pickup truck on the canyon road. Could the Rands have something to do with this? I said, "It looks like it came in when she was outside getting coal for the stove. She had the door propped open."

The cat was perched above us as still as a painting. Although those luminescent orange disks were, I was certain, taking in every move Sawyer and I made, I couldn't discern even the slightest flicker of life in the cat's eyes. Yet I knew that with a quick tensing of some powerful muscles that cat could be flying through the air toward either Sawyer or me in less time than it took me to blink.

I forced my mind to recall every news story I'd ever heard about human–mountain lion confrontations along the Front Range. Confrontations were rare. Dead humans were even rarer. But they happened. A young boy had been killed recently in Rocky Mountain National Park.

This cat, I had to assume, was hungry. And by the looks of the wounds on Theo, we had interrupted it quite early in its meal. Sawyer and I were now, unfortunately, standing like sentries between the cat and its kill. Probably not the safest place in the world to be.

*Where's Reggie?*

The news stories always gave the same advice on how to survive a confrontation with a mountain lion: Stay together in a group. Act big. Make noise. Don't approach the animal in a threatening way.

"We need to move a little so we're not between the cat and Theo.

Don't look it in the eye. Don't be threatening. But we need to act big."

"I don't know what you mean. How do you act big?"

"First, step sideways a little, right after me. Stay close so we look bigger together." We moved in lock step until we were three or four feet away from Theo. The act felt cowardly. I wasn't ready to sacrifice Theo to the cat, although I didn't see how she could possibly survive her injuries. But I knew I had to convince this mountain lion that it didn't have to protect its kill by coming through us.

"Now slowly unzip your parka," I said to Sawyer. She did. So did I. "Good. Now raise your arms above your head. Do it *slowly*. Stand as tall as you can." Sawyer raised herself up on her tiptoes.

Beside me was an aluminum and canvas camp chair, the collapsible kind that people take car camping. I reached down and lifted it up and handed it to her. "Here. It will make you look bigger," I said.

She grasped it as though she had fallen overboard and I was offering her a lifeline. Quickly, she suspended it between her two raised hands.

*Where's Reggie?*

My eyes were adjusting to the darkness near the rafters. In my peripheral vision I watched the predator watch us. The cat was as beautiful as a creature could be. Its coat was full and plush for winter. Its profile was all strength and grace. And it still hadn't moved a muscle from its crouch. From it, though, I felt as much potential danger as I might if I were traversing an avalanche field in a snowmobile.

I wanted a weapon in my hands and longed for Lauren's Glock. My hands felt behind me on the wall for an elk rack that Theo had mounted for decoration. I lifted the rack into my hands and immediately wondered whether I had just succeeded in masquerading as this cat's favorite food. I held onto the sharp antlers anyway.

*Where's Reggie?*

Sawyer whispered, "Will it let us out the door?"

The door was in the general direction of the cat. I didn't have a clue how the cat would interpret us approaching the door. "We'd have to get two of them open," I said.

"Do we have a choice?"

"Where's Reggie?" I finally said out loud.

"What could he do?"

"Open the doors for us, if nothing else," I said.

"Could we run for it?"

"We can't outrun that cat if it decides to chase us. I was actually hoping it might choose to leave if the doors were open."

She made a noise that was appropriately skeptical. "How do you know so much about mountain lions?" she asked.

"I don't," I said.

# FORTY-THREE

**W**ith my admission of ignorance about its habits, the cat finally moved. It was as though it suddenly understood how defenseless we were.

The first movements were a raised paw and, on the opposite side, a simultaneously cocked ear. Sawyer sucked in air and I held my breath before finally hissing, "Act big. Don't look at it." She raised the camp chair above her head and I shook the rack of antlers above mine. Our unzipped coats widened at our trunks. The cat moved another paw and raised its body an inch or two from the floor of the loft.

I felt the strange awe I'd had once when I chanced upon some barracuda while snorkeling in the Mexican Caribbean. The combination of beauty and danger was almost paralyzing.

The paw closest to the pole ladder reached down and felt gingerly for the first rung. "It's coming down," Sawyer said. "It's coming down."

The cat rose on its haunches and raised its head in our direction, temporarily unconcerned with its bloody kill in the corner. The other front paw felt for the upper rung on the ladder. My eyes scanned frantically for another weapon. Theo was security-conscious enough to have bars on her windows and doors—she must have a weapon handy to protect herself. The cat lowered a paw another rung. The back legs felt for purchase at the edge of the loft.

Sawyer said, "Oh my God."

I saw it, finally. Theo's gun. Her final protection was a shotgun. I counted two barrels, side by side. The huge gun was resting lazily on the sill of the window between us and the door, mostly hidden by some gingham curtains. Unfortunately, the barrel end, not the trigger end, was closest to me.

"Have you ever fired a shotgun, Sawyer?"

"Why? Do you see one?"

"Yes, on the windowsill right by me."

"My dad had one."

The cat felt for another rung.

Sawyer's father had taught her how to fly; I sure hoped he had taught her how to shoot. "Give me a quick lesson."

"I guess we need to assume it's loaded, huh?"

"Yes."

"Theo lives alone. Pray that it's ready to go. There's probably a safety you need to release. After that, just point in the general direction of the cat and fire. You don't have to aim very well."

"I can do that," I said, unconvincingly. "Walk with me toward the window so I can reach it."

We shuffled sideways.

The cat growled and bared its fangs.

"Jesus. Oh God." I think the prayer I heard was Sawyer's. Though it might have been mine.

Holding the elk antlers in one hand, I reached out with the other and grabbed the barrel of the shotgun. The steel I touched was as cold as a snake's heart.

*Where's Reggie?*

The cat leaped down to the foot of the ladder and landed with a muffled thud that mimicked the sound of the blood pumping through my ears. The lion was now closer to Theo than we were. But it was closer to us than it was to Theo. I wasn't breathing and didn't think Sawyer was either.

Outside, I heard a car. The cat did, too. Its ears twitched. Seconds later, voices. Outside. Male voices. I thought, *Reggie got us some help.*

The cat's eyes widened; its jowls moved.

I maneuvered the shotgun so the barrels were no longer pointing right at me and felt along the side of the weapon for the safety. My fingers found a steel lever and I pushed on it until it stopped moving. I felt for the trigger guard, slowly inserting my index finger and caressing the curved steel of the first of two triggers. I felt a chilling awareness that if this damn gun wasn't loaded and cocked, either Sawyer or I, and perhaps both of us, were going to be mauled by this cat.

The cat was again absolutely still, staring right at Sawyer. I slid closer to her. The arm above my head supporting the antlers was almost numb. I needed to put them down to fire the gun.

The voices outside grew more distinct. The handle turned on the security door.

The cat leaped at Sawyer.

With a rush, she lowered the camp chair to protect herself and I raked the space in front of her with the antlers, trying to keep hold of the shotgun at the same time. We struck the lion together and managed to deflect it to the side, where it landed on its flank between Sawyer and Theo.

I couldn't shoot it there. I might hit Sawyer. And I'd definitely kill Theo if she wasn't already dead. Blood trickled from the lion's ear. It shook its head and righted itself.

The latch clicked on the inner door, the plank door, and a huge man in a black parka and a fur hat filled the entryway to Theo's cabin.

I said, "Careful. There's a mountain lion in here."

"What?" he said, his voice disbelieving.

The cat hissed.

The big man said, "Oh, shit." Pause. "I've seen that cat around here. Did it kill Theo?"

"It attacked her. Do you know her well?"

"Yes. I'm her neighbor."

"Is the gun I'm holding ready to fire?"

"Definitely."

"Then I think we need to get the cat away from Theo so I can use it."

# FORTY-FOUR

**S**omebody was outside with you?" Sawyer asked the big man.

"He's still out at the road, waiting to direct the ambulance. Said something about a pickup truck, said you'd know what he was talking about."

The man surveyed our dilemma and said, "Let's all slide away from him, toward the loft. You'll have a clear shot."

We started to slide, trying to be the biggest animals in the world. The cat seemed focused solely on the smallest prey in the room, Sawyer. As she slid away, it actually feinted toward her.

Across the room, beneath the loft, I heard a mechanical clicking. So did the cat. The lights on a VCR flickered and the TV came on. The opening credits for *Guiding Light*. Theo had timers set to turn on the TV and to videotape a soap.

The noise from the TV seemed cacophonous, and the cat edged cautiously toward the sound. I tracked its every deliberate step with the barrel of the shotgun. The moment it was clear of Theo, I fired.

The TV imploded.

I was unprepared for the recoil, which almost blew me over. For many minutes afterward it seemed as though everyone around me was whispering.

An ambulance arrived soon after the cat died, and the attendants found Sawyer kneeling over Theo, crying quietly, pronouncing her dead.

I used Lauren's cell phone to call Sam Purdy and told him what the sheriff was going to find in this quaint log home up Sunshine Canyon, and asked him to run interference.

Sawyer and I left our business cards with Theo's neighbor at the cabin. We assumed that the sheriff's investigators would want to talk with us at some point. We concluded that we could leave before the authorities arrived because Theo's cabin wasn't actually a crime scene. After all, could a mountain lion be charged with B&E or homicide? Neither of us had any faith that the investigators would ever find any evidence that the Rands had managed to lure the lion inside the cabin.

Both Sawyer and I were skeptical anyway. They were too savvy to rely on a predator to do their work.

Reggie was cocooned in a shell of grief as we drove back down the mountain. Despite compassionate prompts from both Sawyer and me, he didn't say a word the whole way back, though he did make a point of constantly checking the passenger-side mirror.

I never spotted the pickup truck again.

Sawyer was rattled too. She wanted to get back to the Boulderado and make final plans to return to Phoenix to get her plane. She planned to take Milt up on his offer to find someone to provide her some protection. She agreed to page me if she was leaving before tomorrow. For now, I had to get back to work. I had patients scheduled and I wanted to see them, maybe even needed to see them.

Sam and the two ex–FBI agents were going to stay busy looking for the Rands.

Back at my office, I checked in with Lauren and her sister. Teresa answered the phone, said Lauren was sleeping and seemed well. I didn't tell her about Theo's cabin and the cat, didn't see what good it would do.

My day at the office started as had a thousand before it. I reveled in the routine of seeing familiar patients at familiar times and listening to their familiar dilemmas. I was surprisingly serene with Victoria Pearsall as she ruminated about her shitty boss. I stayed a step behind Riley Grant as he further consolidated his gains. Each forty-five-minute session was a comforting bracket that seemed to insulate me further from the morning's terror. I did six sessions in six and a half hours. Diane was kind enough to bring me a couple of empanadas and some lemonade for lunch. I wolfed the food down but didn't taste a bite.

Midday, I got a page from a sheriff's investigator who wanted to talk about the mountain lion and Theo.

I didn't call back. I didn't want to think about anything other than my patients' problems, which felt much more mundane than my own.

As four-thirty rolled around, the end was in sight. I had two more sessions to go—my two resistant young men in their twenties—before I would drop by the Boulderado to say good-bye to Sawyer and drive to Denver to be with Lauren for the night. She and I would have to talk about getting bodyguards.

Diane and I worked our office suite without a receptionist. When a patient arrived, he or she flicked a switch marked with either Diane's name or mine in the waiting room. The switches lit a red indicator light in the corresponding office. My red light flicked on right on schedule at 4:28. I expected to see my regular four-thirty appointment, Tom Jenkins, the man in his late twenties whom I'd been treating for a few months for relationship issues and anxiety. Usually I found his stories tedious, his resistance to my intervention fatiguing. But I had to concentrate when I was with him, so he would most definitely be distracting.

Before going out to retrieve him from the waiting room I went to the bathroom and peed, then to the little kitchen, where I poured myself a fresh mug of coffee, which I carried back to my office and placed next to my chair. I made the short walk toward the front of the house and opened the waiting-room door.

The waiting room is roughly square, with seating on only two of the four walls. From the doorway, I can see only one of those walls, which is furnished with a burgundy sofa that Diane picked out during a recent Crate and Barrel phase. Sawyer was sitting on the sofa, looking nervous.

I was surprised to see her. "Hi. Are you on your way home already? I wish you had paged me; I have two more patients to go."

She didn't speak, but I watched her eyes flit briefly toward the wall I couldn't see from where I was standing. I took one step into the room, turned, and recognized my four-thirty, Tom Jenkins, sitting in one of the three upholstered chairs lining the wall. I said, "Hello, Tom. I'll be with you in just a minute. Come on back, Sawyer."

Tom stood but didn't face me. His voice was apologetic as he said, "I'm afraid she's with me, today." He showed me a handgun. He didn't point it at me, just pulled it from his jacket pocket and held it out in front of him. I thought it resembled Lauren's Glock. Not identical, but equally menacing.

I said, "Oh, damn."

Sawyer nodded twice, slowly, and arched her eyebrows in an "I'm sorry. What could I do?" exclamation.

Months earlier, Thomas Jenkins had been referred to me by his internist, a man I'd never heard of. Maybe that should have made me suspicious. It hadn't. I didn't pretend to know every internist in the metro area. Tom had come in to see me for the first time maybe three months before Arnie Dresser ever went for his final hike in the Maroon Bells. Long before A.J. and Milt intruded on Lauren and me during our lunch in Silver Plume.

Tom wasn't an atypical patient. He was an isolated man who called his loneliness "solitude." He described a history of jealousy and possessiveness in a long series of brief, immature romantic relationships. He described symptoms of anxiety that temporarily had me ruling out panic attacks. The only odd part of his presentation was that he was a self-pay patient in the brave new world of managed-care headaches.

But, of course, that made him more attractive to me, not less.

Oh yes. He had told me he was a firefighter in Longmont, fifteen minutes down the Diagonal from Boulder.

A firefighter. Just like Patrick Rand. Though Patrick worked in Lakewood, twenty miles away.

I shouldn't have been ambushed by him like this. But I was.

I said, "Your name isn't Tom, is it?"

"Why don't we go back to your office?" he suggested. "All of us." He turned to Sawyer and said, "Doctor? After you."

She stood and walked past me into the hallway that led toward my office. He moved across the room and turned the dead bolt on the entry door of the house. "You next, Doctor," he said to me. I wondered if Diane was still in her office, and that thought precipitated chilling snapshot memories of the last time I'd seen a gun in these offices.

God, there had been a lot of carnage that day. I lost a moment trying to date the memories.

As though he were reading my mind, my patient said, "Your partner is gone for the day. Lucky for her."

We marched down the hallway to my office. Inside, he closed the door and moved toward the chair where I always sat. He said, "Coffee smells good. I always wondered why you never offered me any."

Sawyer and I sat side by side on the gold and gray couch that was directly across from him. I said, "Should I call you Patrick? Or Mr. Rand?"

He didn't react. "I wouldn't be here like this if I didn't know that the game had gotten risky, Doctor." He rested the pistol on his lap and rubbed his eyes with his hands. "But I have to tell you—that mountain lion today? Can you believe it? That cat saved some lives, I'll tell you what." He half smiled and shook his head.

"I don't think I know what that means," I said. The words, I recognized, were therapist's words.

"It means today wasn't the first time I followed the three of you to that cabin."

"That was you in the pickup?" It was hardly a question.

He raised one eyebrow in surprise and admiration. I decided to point out his failure and try to milk it. "You were sloppy. Your father would never—never—have allowed us to spot him."

The words caught him mid-blink and he held his eyes shut for three or four seconds. My gaze wandered to his pistol.

He nodded and opened his eyes, catching me staring at the gun. "You're right. He was much better at this than I am. I'm afraid I almost blew it for him, all that he had worked for. But my plan at the cabin was good, considering the circumstances. I was going to blow the propane tank. Either the explosion or the fire should have engulfed your car and the cabin, gotten the two of you no matter where you were. But the cat, hell, now there's a wild card for you. Damn cat shows up and pretty soon half the emergency equipment in the county is on its way up there. Even though it didn't work, you have to admit my plan was sound. I did that whole thing—reconnaissance, planning, execution—in one and a half days. My father couldn't have done that, what I did. No. No way." He grew silent, reflecting on something. "I've mentioned him some to you, haven't I? He was such a weird character. He'd plan his meals a week in advance, right down to how many slices of bread he'd eat on Friday night along with his three fish sticks and whether or not he'd use jelly on the bread. A day and a half to get that whole plan in place? Not a chance. Sometimes I think it took him a day and a half just to decide to move his bowels."

Sawyer asked, "How were you going to set the propane off?"

He smiled and blinked, didn't answer. He was a magician protecting the secret of his best trick. "Did the lady die? The one who lived there? Did the cat get her?"

"Yes," I said, waiting for him to react to the news. He didn't seem to care. Theo's death wasn't particularly consequential to him.

"You tell me, then, so how did those two get on to me? The FBI types? Why did they suddenly show up to help you out?"

"Dr. Dresser had noticed that a lot of his old friends were dying. He was a journal writer and E-mail nut. He kept his mother apprised of his concerns. When he died too, she got suspicious. Involving the FBI was her idea. And her money."

"How did they find me?"

"They didn't. We did." I looked at Sawyer. "We tracked down your father through our memories of old patients. Had some false starts. But we put it together from there."

"Did Loomis help?"

I lied. I said, "Not really."

He fingered the gun as though it were a hypodermic full of truth serum he could employ anytime he chose.

"Well. He helped me. But then I had a little leverage with him. Ironic, though, about Dr. Dresser's writing tripping me up. It was my father's notebooks that got me going in the first place."

Tom, or Patrick, seemed to want to talk. I was surprised how much this felt like his usual therapy session. Except for the gun, of course. And Sawyer. Through my anxiety I was trying to decide how much of what I knew about this young man was psychologically accurate and how much of it had been act. I quickly decided that he wasn't sophisticated enough to fool me about his character and I could expect those traits to endure through this encounter.

I could have reflected back to him the juxtaposition of his mention of Reggie Loomis and his father's notebooks in the same breath. I didn't.

Sawyer did. "You're talking about your father's speculation about D. B. Cooper, aren't you?"

"Speculation? You know, I don't think so. You should see the case on paper in black and white. Dad had Loomis down cold for that hijacking. But he liked Loomis. Respected him. Emulated him, even. Dad wouldn't ever have turned Reggie Loomis in to the feds for that hijacking. Reggie doesn't know it, of course, but I wouldn't have turned him in either. The threat was good leverage, though." He shook his head. "Damn cat got in the way, that's all." He smiled. "My father used to hold up his index finger sometimes and make these important pronouncements. He called them 'life lessons.' Well, here's a life lesson for you." He held up an index finger. "You can't plan for everything. No matter how hard you try, you can't plan for everything."

In my therapy voice, I said, "I don't understand something. Why did you decide to take up your father's work? Why not just leave it alone?"

He scrunched his face up in a consternated way I'd seen in his previous visits to my office. As he relaxed the muscles, he said, "Couple of reasons. From the time I was little, I learned to share his hate for all of you for what you did to our family. That was one. Second, I wanted to prove something to him, I guess."

With obvious disbelief, Sawyer asked, "So your father isn't dead?"

Patrick widened his eyes and smiled at the question in a manner that increased my already swollen discomfort. But he didn't answer. "Did I blow it in New Zealand? I shouldn't have done that, should I? Gone overseas?"

I answered, "The FBI agents are confident that they can use immigration and airline records to identify you. Eventually, anyway."

"You know, I knew that. I *knew* that. But I did it anyway. Jeez. Stupid. Sorry, Dad."

"Your father went overseas once, too. The cruise ship killing. It appears that he had a false passport, though. You didn't?"

He shook his head. "That was my favorite. Of all the notebooks of the killings, that was my favorite. He planned it forever. Do you know how he did it? How he made her disappear?"

"Yes," I said. I knew he was talking about Wendy Asimoto's gruesome end, and he seemed oblivious to the fact that he was sitting with two people who might have cared about her. He only wanted to talk about the ingenious way his father had disposed of her body. "Your father incinerated her body on board the ship."

He clapped. "Bravo, bravo. You figured that out? Perhaps I underestimated all of you."

"Did your father do the drive-by in L.A.?"

He looked embarrassed. "He wasn't proud of that one. He called it a 'duck shoot' in his journal. Vowed not to use guns again. No matter how well planned."

I stared at the pistol. "But he broke his vow with the hunting accident?"

Patrick raised his eyebrows. "You have the order wrong. The hunting accident came first."

Sawyer said, "You didn't sabotage my plane, did you?"

He shook his head. "Your plane? No. What happened to your plane?"

She told him.

"No, I wouldn't have done that. Sabotaging landing gear isn't lethal enough. Any good pilot could do what you did. That would be an even more lame attempt than what I did with Dr. Gregory's furnace. And anyway, that would have been copying. I didn't want to copy him. I wanted each of mine to be original. Each one of his killings was original. I wanted mine to be, too. Life lesson," he said in an odd baritone voice as he raised the index finger of his right hand. "Always avoid a recognizable MO."

He stared at me. His eyes were warm. "You're a better therapist than Dr. Dresser. I actually think you helped me a little. Do you know he wanted me to take Zoloft? I pretended I was. It made him feel better. The right medicine always makes the doctor feel better." He smiled bashfully. "Thought you might want to know."

"You were Dr. Dresser's patient, too?"

"Yes. Getting to know each of you first was particularly cool. Dad couldn't have done that part, of course, but he would have appreciated it. The panache."

"Was I going to be your next victim? Or was Sawyer?"

"If the feds hadn't shown up, you mean? You were next. Then I was going to go to California, live there a while, get to know Dr. Faire a little, and take care of her and that other lady."

*What?* "Other lady? What other lady?"

He widened his eyes. "I'm sorry, but I'm bad with names. She's older, I guess, uh—"

"Dr. Masters? Amy Masters?"

"Right, that's it. Don't tell me she's already dead?" He made a tsking sound with his tongue and the roof of his mouth.

Sawyer nodded.

"I guess I can cross her off my list, then."

"You didn't kill her?" I asked, feeling relief she hadn't been murdered.

"I would have. But, no, I didn't."

"How were you going to kill me?"

"You mean if things hadn't gotten so rushed?" He waited for my nod. "Your bike. It would have been a piece of cake. You know that route you do in Left Hand Canyon? Where it's real steep on the downhill?"

"Yes." I did that ride a couple of times a month when the weather allowed. When the conditions were perfect, I could fly.

"You seem to do it pretty regularly. I figured I'd precipitate a little rockslide when you were going about fifty. There's one curve where I figured you would lose control for sure and go over the edge. It's two hundred feet down, maybe more."

"You know, I guessed you would use my bike. The other stuff you did, the beam falling on my head? The carbon monoxide? Those were impulsive? You were improvising when you did those things?"

"Yeah. The beam especially. But you have to admit, despite my lack of planning, you were pretty damn lucky. One of the guys at the station said he heard from a friend in Boulder that you guys had two CO detectors instead of one. Who has two CO detectors? What are the odds of being tripped up by that, huh? Dad would have forgiven me that one, I think. No amount of planning can overcome something like that. And that beam in your house? That was my fault. It was supposed to be the whole damn roof that came down. My engineering skills are rusty."

"What about me?" Sawyer asked.

"Sorry. So sorry. Hadn't got there yet. Life lesson: One at a time. One at a time. Don't try to plan two murders at once. Each one requires tremendous creativity. Actually, when you think about it, it's an art. Murdering people and not arousing any suspicion. None. Imagine? It's an art."

He looked at her. Then at me.

"Really," he insisted. "It is."

# FORTY-FIVE

**H**e lifted the gun with both hands and hefted it as though he wanted to assess its weight. "Since I know they're watching me, I have to be careful what I do next. It's why I bailed out with the propane. Too many possible witnesses. This next one has to be pretty believable if I want to get away with it. Dad always said life's performances are hardest when you have an audience."

"Who is watching you?" Sawyer asked.

"You don't know?" He examined her eyes, then mine. "Really? The FBI guy and that Boulder cop—the one who seems to be your friend, Dr. Gregory. They have my townhouse staked out right now. Which tells me they don't have a warrant, not that they'd find anything even if they did. But that means that they really don't have any evidence tying me to anything. Not yet, not enough to take to a judge. Despite their suspicions, I could still walk. My first goal, of course, was never to be identified as a killer. My secondary goal was never to be convicted. That one's still within reach, I think." He threaded his finger through the trigger guard. "As long as you two don't survive."

Sawyer and I both reacted physically, the g-forces of fear forcing us back against our chairs.

"Don't worry. I'm not going to shoot you unless you get stupid. Dr. Gregory, would you please get Dr. Faire a piece of paper? A blank one."

I did.

"I need a prescription from you," he said to Sawyer. "Make it for . . . Xanax. Good. Put my name on it, my real name. Good. Sign it. Date it. Good. Oh, almost forgot, your DEA number, too. Yes. See, now you're one of my doctors, too. I like it like that. Things feel complete. Hand it over to me, please."

He folded the paper carefully into quarters and tucked it in his shirt pocket. "Now we go." He stood and swept my keys off my desk. He waved the gun as though he were a theater usher directing us to our seats with a flashlight. "Out the back way, I think. We'll be taking your car, Dr. Gregory. I'm afraid you two are about to have an unfortunate accident. But I really do have a nice place picked out for you to die."

A door leads from my office to the backyard of the old house. My car was parked on the adjacent driveway. The snow that had been so persistent up at Theo's cabin that morning had never really amounted to anything down here. The ground was dotted with leaves from a nearby ash and debris from our neighbor's linden, but there was no snow remaining on anything.

I had already decided that I might as well do something desperate here in town. Lauren had taught me once that no matter what immediate jeopardy it caused, you should never let a kidnapper take you someplace where his control over you increased. My best location for a last-ditch effort was here in town, on my own property.

I caught Sawyer's eye and hoped she could see my determination. Patrick Rand apparently did. He kept the pocketed handgun focused on her, not on me, underlining what the consequences would be if I tried anything. "Don't be foolish," he warned. "I want you to drive, Dr. Faire. Dr. Gregory, you ride up front. I'll be in back. We'll go straight up into Boulder Canyon."

Lamely, I said, "Your father did Boulder Canyon for a car crash. One of his coworkers from the plant. You don't want to repeat that, do you?"

"Nice try. You *have* pieced a lot of this together, though. You're both quite resourceful. I respect that and I'll keep it in mind. But we're not going to have a crash in Boulder Canyon. Actually, we're going to turn up Magnolia. There's a lovely place up there that I want to show you."

He never took his eyes off me or his gun off the middle of Sawyer's back as he spoke. His calm demeanor chilled me. I was absolutely certain he would shoot Sawyer if I tried to escape.

"Take those damn catering things out of the back of the car, please. Stack them over there. We'll need a lot of room. If I see you open a single case to search for something to use as a weapon, she's dead."

I followed his instructions to the letter.

In a minute we were on our way.

The road up Magnolia cuts off Boulder Canyon not too far from town. But the foothills of the Rocky Mountains rise precipitously west of Boulder. By the time we got to Magnolia, the cliffs were already steep, the road was already treacherous, and the possible isolation was almost total. On these winding roads I couldn't figure out how Rand was going to get us to crash at a high enough speed to kill us and still manage to ensure his own escape.

I couldn't piece it together. Was he going to jump from the car?

Dusk was blacker in the canyon than it was up Magnolia, where the light of a moon that was only two days past full shimmered off the fresh snow and the golden grasses of the high meadows. Sawyer actually commented on how pretty it was.

He directed her to take a turn off Magnolia down one dirt road and then down another. The congested housing that was clustered on both sides of the main road was quickly behind us. The road we were on was narrow, twisty, and in ill repair. There was no way he was going to engineer a crash up here that would guarantee two fatalities and one survivor. I began to question his judgment.

He ordered another turn, and then another. The last one took us from the road up a steep driveway marked by a sign from Mock Realty. The sign informed us that we were driving onto 6.3 acres with a great building site and a well. The long driveway had been badly rutted by runoff, and the big Land Cruiser listed hard to the left as we climbed.

"Keep going," he said. "Careful, now. Don't want any accidents, do we?"

At the top of the driveway, which probably extended almost a quarter of a mile, we reached a relatively flat clearing. The day's light was almost gone, but it was apparent that this building site commanded stunning views to the south and east. Far in the distance, the sky above Denver glowed as though irradiated.

I grew even more nervous as he said, "Pull straight ahead. Go on."

Sawyer urged the big car forward across the clearing and slowly approached the edge of a cliff. The cavern below us was dark. I couldn't tell how steep the incline was. I couldn't tell how deep the fall would be.

I figured plenty steep and plenty deep.

Five feet from the edge, he said, "Stop."

She did. He said, "No, a couple more feet." I heard her sigh as she gingerly edged forward. I wondered if she had worked out in her mind what was about to happen.

"Kill the lights. Turn off the engine for now. Good." He opened the door to the backseat. Chill air filled the car. "Don't move."

I didn't need to look; I could hear what he was doing behind us. He was lowering the sections of the backseat so they would be flat with the cargo area.

"Okay," he ordered, his voice crisper now. "Now undress. Both of you."

We stared at each other. I saw sorrow, not fear, flood Sawyer's face and imagined she was thinking about two other deaths staged in another car. He said, "Come on, everything. Take everything off."

Sawyer didn't look surprised at Rand's order. Maybe she had discerned what was coming. I tugged off my sweater in a swift motion. She was wearing a suede coat. She struggled out of it. I helped her get it off her arms.

"Come on. Don't procrastinate. Dad hated procrastination."

As we unbuttoned our shirts, I pondered whether I wanted to take my chance going over the cliff in the car, or if I preferred to risk death at the hands of this man and his semiautomatic handgun.

Methodically, in the least erotic manner I could ever have imagined, we removed the rest of our clothing. It took a couple of minutes and then I was naked beside Sawyer and, except for her socks, she was naked beside me.

"Start the car now, Dr. Faire. It's way too cold for two old lovers to do it up here without heat, right?"

"No," she said, without conviction. I glanced over at her. She was covered in gooseflesh. Her tiny nipples were as hard as the steel in our murderer's hands.

"Do it," he said. "And the second you do, I want to see your hands on your heads. Both of you."

She hesitated for a good twenty seconds, then reached out and turned the key. The car obeyed the command; the engine rumbled to life. We raised our hands as instructed.

"Now," he said. "Climb into the back. Don't get out. Climb right over the console. One at a time."

While Sawyer moved gracelessly to the back of the car, I watched Rand, hoping for an opening. The barrel of his gun never left her. I could throw open my door and run into the night. I might actually make it. No way Sawyer would.

Defeated, I followed Sawyer to the back of the vehicle.

"Now, start. Go ahead. You know you want to do it. I might even let you finish before I . . . well . . . whatever. You won't know when the end is near. I'll be quiet. Enjoy. Go on. Go on." His voice was encouraging, generous.

Obscene. He was managing to rape both of us at the same time.

The whole thing could not have been more incongruous. Sawyer sat next to me, naked. I could smell her. Almost taste her. The view was heavenly. The setting serene. And all I wanted to do was run.

Suddenly, she reached up and hooked my neck with her elbow, pulling me down to her.

"No," I said, resisting. "No." She clutched me tighter to her.

My face was buried in her hair. "Somebody's here," she whispered. "Get ready to open the back." With that she kissed me, pulling me sideways, upright, then over, so that our heads now faced the back of the car and not the front. I could feel the fabric of her socks against the top of my feet and the weight of her breast against my arm. With my left hand, I groped randomly for the latch on the back hatch door.

I whispered, "Got it." *Please. Whoever is out there. Say something. Do something.*

*Stop this.*

The sounds almost overlapped as Rand simultaneously closed the rear passenger door and opened the driver's door. I raised my head to see what he was doing.

"Uh-uh," he warned. "Ignore me. Focus, now. Enjoy. She's very pretty. It's a good way to go."

All he had to do now was reach into the car with one leg and one hand. Put his foot on the brake, slide the gearshift into drive, and release his foot from the brake. Those simple movements were all that was left between life and death for Sawyer and me.

# FORTY-SIX

Rand was watching us. I could feel his eyes.

His father, I was certain, would not approve of his taking a respite from the task at hand to quench his voyeuristic thirst.

I pushed Sawyer's shoulder back away from me, exposing her chest to his view. Instantly, she seemed to understand what I was doing, and she raised her leg onto my hip, angling her crotch for his appraisal.

*Time,* I thought. *We need time.*

"Go on. Go on," he urged.

I touched her neck and she slid her hand to my side and let it migrate down between my legs. She touched me almost chastely.

*Go ahead, keep watching, asshole. Keep watching.*

He did, for a good minute. I stayed limp in Sawyer's hand.

Suddenly, the weight of the car shifted, and I knew the time had come. He was moving toward the gearshift and the brake. I threaded my fingers under the latch of the door and pulled it hard. The noise was distinctive as the mechanism released and the hatch door popped open two inches, then stopped.

He barked, "No!"

A gunshot, crisp and frank, pierced the air. Sawyer and I ducked. I held my breath as though my inflated lungs could deflect a slug.

The balance of the car shifted again and Rand yelped. He seemed to be trying to swallow the sound of his own scream. The car lurched forward a few inches and tugged, like a big dog straining against its leash. The engine raced again as Rand hit the gas pedal with his foot while he was searching for the brake. Another gunshot rang out, accompanied by a loud thud.

I pushed the hatch door up with my forearm. Sawyer and I were fighting to untangle from each other so we could scramble out the back of the car before Rand sent it over the cliff. I heard a familiar sound—*clunk*—as he dropped the gearshift from park into drive.

Finally the heavy car began to ease forward as Rand's foot came off the brake. Gunshots filled the air, ringing out in rapid order. At least two guns, maybe three. I couldn't tell. With all my strength I pushed Sawyer toward the open hatch, my efforts throwing me back farther into the car.

I felt the incline change, gravity's new tug pulling all the blood from my heart. The clearing we'd been on was rapidly becoming cliff. I pawed at the carpet, climbing the cargo bed as though it were a ladder, desperately clawing to get to the still-open hatch door.

My mind jumped to thoughts about Lauren and the baby we'd barely talked about having.

With a sudden shudder the car angled down farther. I figured the incline was now close to forty-five degrees. I managed to hook my fingers on the frame of the back door but I couldn't get enough purchase with my bare feet to propel myself out against the steep incline. Hands suddenly clamped onto my wrists. One, then another.

A woman, not Sawyer, ordered, "Let go, Alan."

I did, feeling that with the release of my curled fingers, I was giving up any hope of escaping the car. I was dying. But the hands on my wrists held firm and, as though in slow motion, I felt the car drive out from under me. My chest cleared the bumper first, and a split second later so did my legs. I fell in a heap into dust and rock.

Below me I heard a crash like a minor traffic accident, and then two seconds later, a horrific crunching sound echoed through the canyons around Magnolia as my Land Cruiser found the bottom of the cliff.


A. J. Simes and Reggie Loomis had arrived up Magnolia in a yellow cab, which was still waiting at the bottom of the long driveway. Sawyer and I made the driver's day by climbing into the backseat of his cab nearly naked.

He didn't even try to pretend he wasn't staring at Sawyer. He asked, "Were those gunshots I heard?"

I said, "I didn't hear anything." Sawyer was wearing A.J.'s coat, this one a shade of teal that would probably be dangerous around people with seizure disorders. It barely reached her thighs. She was shivering. I was wearing Reggie's blue denim workshirt. I was shivering, too. "Could we have some more heat, please?" I pleaded.

"Sure," he said. Feigning nonchalance, he added, "Where to?"

"The Boulderado," I said.

"They must have relaxed their dress code."

I wasn't in any mood for his comedy. "On second thought, just run the meter. I have a feeling we should stick around for a few minutes."

A few minutes became ninety. Although they were treating us like victims, not offenders, the sheriff's investigators proffered plenty of questions neither Sawyer nor I wished to answer. The cops also had blankets, though, and that was good.

The gunshots that had felled Rand had come from A. J. Simes's weapon. That fact made her the center of attention. Sawyer and I waved to her as she was moved into a sheriff's car to be transported somewhere for questioning.

Reggie Loomis was nowhere to be found. Disappearing was apparently one of his best things.

A deputy sent the cab on its way and drove us down to town and the Boulderado. Getting from the hotel entrance to our rooms was awkward. Wrapped in borrowed blankets, we sneaked in a side entrance and used the house phone on the second floor to ask that room keys be brought our way. The explanation that the bellman extracted from us for why we didn't currently have clothing or identification was long and mostly fictional. Fortunately, he recognized Sawyer, and we got the keys. Once inside my room, which momentarily felt like a palace, I phoned Lauren and reassured her that our biggest problem appeared to be over but I wouldn't make it to Denver tonight. She said she'd been worried and asked why I wasn't coming down. I told her that I'd had some trouble with my car and I'd explain more tomorrow.

I paged Sam and waited a few minutes for him to return the call. He didn't.

I showered until the chill left my skin.

Sawyer and I rendezvoused, as planned, under the stained-glass roof in the Mezzanine Lounge forty-five minutes later. The mime wasn't on duty. I figured it was an omen, a good omen. Sawyer had arrived before me, her hair still wet. I noted that her clothing could not have been more demure. She'd already ordered a bottle of champagne and some diet cola.

The wooden staircase from the lobby to the mezzanine of the Boulderado is grand in design and permits a grand entrance. The one we witnessed next was special.

I heard Milt's voice before I saw any of them, but as their heads cleared the tread of the top step, I could see all three. Milt and Sam were cradling A.J. between them, as though she were a queen on a portable throne. In my mind, I was assuming that she was being carried up the stairs because climbing that long rutted driveway to save our lives had cost her whatever precious energy she had left in her legs.

Sawyer and I jumped up and ran to meet them.

"These two sprung me," she said, her voice girlish. Milt said he hadn't done anything. Sam shrugged.

Sam said, "He's dead. Rand. They're getting a warrant now for his truck and his townhouse. The truck was parked about a quarter of a mile from where he tried to kill you two. Let's hope he's left some evidence behind that will tie him to all of this."

A.J. said, "Turns out I only clipped him. Twice. Leg and shoulder. He got his foot caught in the car, though, and he went over the cliff with it. Rolled on top of him a couple of times. He died in the crash." She sounded disappointed that her shots had only wounded him.

"You saved our lives," Sawyer and I said, virtually simultaneously.

"I'll be happy to take some credit for that," she said, beaming. "But I have to share it with your friend Mr. Loomis. He tracked me down this afternoon at the hotel and dragged me over to your office to warn you about young Mr. Rand. Loomis doesn't have a car. And I don't . . . drive anymore. When we pulled up to your office in a taxi, we saw you and Sawyer coming down the driveway with someone in the backseat of your car. We figured that we were already a little late with our warning. So we improvised and followed you into the mountains in the cab." She shook her head and laughed at the memory.

"Where did Reggie go afterward, A.J.? After the shooting?"

"Told me that there were some good reasons for him not to be associated with any of this. Before the sheriff showed up, he was gone."

"And where were you two?" I asked Milt and Sam.

Milt answered, "Rand tricked us. Left word at work he was on his way home from a hiking trip to Rocky Mountain National Park.

One of his colleagues at the fire station was helping us out, and he let us know Rand's plans. We spent all day staking out his town-house, waiting for him to get home." He faced A.J. and said, "Sorry. Got duped."

She touched him affectionately on his wrist and allowed her fingers to linger. "It all turned out fine," she said.

The waitress delivered three more champagne glasses. Sam eyed her suspiciously until she actually spoke. Sawyer raised her Pepsi, and she and I toasted the cops. All three of them.

Sam went along politely with the toast. Then he ordered a Budweiser.

# FORTY-SEVEN

Our celebration ended near midnight.

Sawyer was leaving for Phoenix on the first shuttle the next morning, and, with an audience of law enforcement officers, she and I said our final good-byes. I think she preferred that our parting be public and not sentimental. I whispered in her ear that I'd never forget her. She whispered back that she'd always remember me. We never spoke a word about our last evening naked together.

Before meandering back to my little alley-view room, I thanked the three cops who had helped save my life.

In the alcove beside my hotel room door, a man sat on the floor, his knees up, his head resting on his folded arms.

Reggie.

"Hello," I said. "I wondered when I'd see you again. I think I owe you some serious gratitude."

He raised his head and said, "Least I could do after leading you into that ambush up at Theo's house."

I shook my head to indicate I didn't get what he was talking about.

"That truck? Up the canyon? The one you were worried about? I spotted it again when I ran out of the cabin to get help for Theo. The pickup?"

"It was Rand. He was going to blow up the propane tank. That's what he told me."

"I wondered about that, thought he might be up to something. That's why I stayed outside and sent Theo's neighbor in. I was afraid it was Rand and thought I should keep an eye out for him. Anyway, when I got back down to town, I had an old colleague of mine run the license plates on the pickup for me. Sure enough, it was registered to Corey's widow."

"What convinced you it was Patrick and not his father?"

He shrugged. "Corey was a perfectionist. The truth is that if he was after you, you'd be dead. Anyway, Corey's kid called me to tell me he'd found some of his father's things. Just before he asked me if I needed help with my food deliveries."

I nodded.

"I said I didn't. He asked if the same folks who helped me yesterday were going to help again the next time."

"And you said yes."

This time he nodded. "I wasn't thinking," he said. Reggie had a padded envelope in his hand, a large one, big enough for a book. He noticed me looking at it. "Got this in the mail today." He nodded toward my door. "Do you mind if we go into your room?"

I used the card to let us in. He took the chair. I sat on the bed and offered him the splendor of my minibar. He declined.

From the envelope he slid a marbled black and white notebook, the kind that school kids have toted for a hundred years. "Rand sent this to me today. The kid, Patrick. But the notebook was put together by his father, Corey."

I didn't reach out for it. "Is that the D. B. Cooper notebook?"

His eyes asked, "How did you know?" He picked the book up and smacked it on his thigh. "It's actually the Dan Cooper notebook. A reporter copied the name incorrectly off a manifest early in the investigation. The hijacker originally checked in calling himself 'Dan,' never 'D.B.' Corey knew that, of course."

He lifted it toward me. "You want to see it? A lot of interesting stuff in here."

I lowered my eyes to the notebook before raising them back toward Reggie. I shook my head. "No, not really. I don't think so."

He nodded. "Think Sawyer does?"

"I doubt it. She's leaving town tomorrow. My guess is that she has better things to do."

He exhaled through pursed lips. "Want to know where I grew up?"

"No."

"If I was in the service?"

"Not especially."

"If I had parachute training?"

"Not curious. Sorry, Reggie. Listen," I said, "you and I both have lives to get back to, people who count on us. Let's say we do it."

"Just like that?"

I sensed a shiver shimmying up my spine. I said, "Doesn't feel like 'just like that' to me."

# FORTY-EIGHT

Dresden finished our renovation right on time and took off for his scuba trip to Australia. Lauren and Emily and I moved back into the Spanish Hills house over a long weekend at the beginning of December.

Despite a paucity of furniture our home was lovely. We enjoyed a late Thanksgiving dinner feast and promptly decorated for Christmas.

Lauren and Emily seemed to have recovered completely from the carbon monoxide poisoning.

No one was trying to kill any of us.

And Lauren and I were busy trying to make a baby.

Adrienne had removed the stent from Sam's plumbing, and, as expected, he gradually repressed the pain and dread that had erupted from his brush with kidney stones. His new diet resolution became a curious memory long before the New Year.

Sawyer called frequently. She'd speak, happily, to whichever of us answered the phone. Lauren commented after one conversation that Sawyer was busy finding new reasons to have a life instead of gilding old reasons not to. I found the words sage.

I left Patrick Rand's four-thirty psychotherapy appointment open for a while. I did it on purpose. Each week I used the time to drive up Magnolia in my new car and ponder all that had happened and the vagaries of the cards that fate had dealt.

The line between lucky and unlucky in life is so thin, I knew, that it is often carved with a laser.

# ACKNOWLEDGMENTS

As always, I asked for and received plenty of instruction, guidance, and assistance on the way to completion of this novel.

Over the years Tom Faure of the Boulder County Coroner's Office has been an ever patient teacher. Hopefully, I've finally learned my lesson, and I will never again need to beseech him to explain the difference between "cause of death" and "manner of death." Stan Galansky, M.D., and Terry Lapid, M.D., offered medical support and, more significantly, friendship. Cathy Schieve, M.D., provided a curbside consultation, literally. Earl Emerson assisted me with my research by doing what he does so well: he told me a great story. Bob Holman answered a battery of questions while he showed me around in his Beechcraft Bonanza, even generously permitting this retired pilot to take the controls for a while.

There are always family ties. I'm grateful to Colin and Amy Purrington for being romantics and to Sara Dominguez for being so darn sweet. My mother, Sara Kellas, sells so many books she should be on commission. Rose and Xan, you've been there every day. What else can I say?

Elyse Morgan, Mark Graham, Harry MacLean, Tom Schantz, Karyn Schiele, Alison Galansky, and Rose Kauffman read the manuscript during its development, and the final version benefited greatly from their observations. Patricia and Jeff Limerick have provided support over many years in many ways. In New York, Al Silverman, Lori Lipsky, Michaela Hamilton, Elaine Koster, Phyllis Grann, and Lynn Nesbit each left their professional mark on this book. I couldn't have been in better hands.

I'd like to acknowledge an old debt, too. Years ago Dr. Bernard Bloom was my dissertation chair at the University of Colorado. He taught me many enduring lessons, most of them by example. Virtually every day he demonstrated that the most essential thing a writer does each day is put his butt in the chair. Bernie, thanks for that and for all your graciousness and wisdom.